MW00987130

A Success That Hasn't Happened Yet

The adventures of an ensemble of characters in a college town provide a sharp and funny commentary on modern life.

a *SUCCESS*
that hasn't happened yet

G. McKinley Scott

Published in the United States by Mind Lunch, LLC
We provide good food for your mind.
Reno, Nevada

Do you have comments or questions about this book? Do you want to know how to order it?
We would love to hear from you.
Contact us at publisher@worldsgreatestnovel.com
(We're not modest.)

ISBN: 978-1-7376866-0-6

Dust jacket illustration and design by Alison Kolesar
Hardcover design by Alison Kolesar
Interior design and typesetting by Lindsay Lake
Printed and bound by Lakeside Book Company
First edition
Second printing

Contents

A Success That
Hasn't Happened Yet

Chapter One

When I was in medical school, several of my professors said that right now is an excellent time to do research. When they said that, they got me interested in a career in academic medicine. What they didn't say, but should have said, is that right now is an excellent time to do research *if you have research money.*

My education about the real world started when I met Joan. I met Joan at a medical conference when I was completing my residency and she was a rising star in the academic world.

Joan gave a talk about sex research. I had never thought sex was something that could be studied scientifically and should be studied scientifically. But I listened to Joan, and she changed my mind. She said there had been advances in technology which created new opportunities in sex research. Joan spoke passionately about how it might be possible now to discover what was going on in each area of the brain during every form of sexual interaction. She said it might now be possible to learn things that would help a lot of people.

Joan was undeniably charismatic. She had a gift for impressing people, charming them, making people want to be with her, making people believe she could do great things.

She was not only charismatic, Joan also had a great academic record. She was near the top of her class in medical school. As a resident, and later when she did a fellowship, all the teaching physicians raved about her. She went out into the world of academia as a young researcher and was an assistant on some research teams at some really good places. Her groups published some papers that got a lot of people's attention.

When I met Joan at the conference, I told her I wanted to have a career in academic medicine and I asked her if there was any way I could work with her. She listened to my appeal and liked my enthusiasm. She offered to meet after the conference and really explore a collaboration.

We met after the conference and talked about our hopes and dreams. Joan wanted to be the leader of a research group. She had been a member of groups, but she had never been the leader. She told me she wanted to look around and find a place where she could set up her own lab. She said if she had her own lab she could be one of the world leaders in sex research. I wanted to be part of that. She invited me to be her research assistant, which I thought was a great opportunity.

Joan liked cute little college towns. She found an adorable college town with a really good medical school. She persuaded the medical school administration that they needed a sex research program and she was the person to lead it. They hired her, and they also hired me to be her assistant. I thought we couldn't possibly fail to grasp our research dreams.

Joan was still young but she had a big reputation and so she had no trouble getting research money. She didn't have any trouble at all. Every grant administrator wanted to give her money. So she set up a well-funded research program at this medical school in this darling little college town.

It was May. The weather was nice and all the lawns were green. The campus was pretty and the air was clean and invigorating. I felt lucky to have this unique opportunity to be Joan's research assistant in this enchanting college town.

I thought everything was going to be wonderful, so it came as a surprise to me when Joan was accused of embezzlement and she fled to the Maldives to avoid prosecution. I know I have character flaws myself. I know that. You don't have to tell me that. But at least I have never been accused of embezzlement. At least I have never had to flee to the Maldives to avoid prosecution. At least you can say *that*.

Well, what would you expect? Naturally all the grant administrators tried to take back all the grant money immediately. Of course Joan took most of it to the Maldives with her, but the grant administrators took back the money that they could find. And of course the medical school took away my job. I was completely innocent, but they took away my job. They didn't need me, because I was hired to be an assistant doing sex research in Joan's lab, and now they didn't have Joan or grant money or a sex research lab.

So I was left with nothing. I didn't have a place to live because all this happened the first week I was in town and I hadn't found a place to live before it happened. And of course after this happened I couldn't find a place to live because I didn't have a job. Landlords don't want to rent to jobless people. But I didn't want to leave the area because I had already fallen in love with this charming little college town. I know you want me to tell you the name of the town, but I don't want to do that. The people of the town don't want their university to be famous for scandals, and I respect their wishes.

The medical school's experience with Joan didn't end their interest in sex research. Joan had convinced them it was an area where a research program could make important discoveries and could make the school famous. After Joan fled to the Maldives, the school was even more interested in sex research, because the school wanted to prove that Joan was an outlier and everyone else at the school was fine and the school really could run a legitimate honest research program in sex research.

I asked the school whether they would let me do sex research without Joan. The school told me I could set up my own sex research lab at the school, which was a wonderful opportunity, but I would have to find the money for it. I said I would do that.

Alyssa Lincoln was the university's general counsel and vice president for community affairs. The medical school told me to talk to her about my various problems and maybe she could help me. I went to see her and she offered to let me sleep on a cot in a storage closet in her house. I was very happy to have an offer of a place to live and I accepted immediately. I had rented rooms from women landlords when I lived in other towns, during my education and training, so it was sort of business as usual for me, although I had never lived in a storage closet.

It was also business as usual for Alyssa. She liked to rent out rooms in her house to people affiliated with the university who needed a place to stay. She was renting a bedroom to two scientists, Irina and Dimitri, who were visiting the university for a year as research faculty in the chemistry department. Irina and Dimitri were a young married couple originally from Saint Petersburg, in Russia. They had left Saint Petersburg and gone to graduate school at Oxford University in England. After graduate school they had taken jobs as postdocs at Oxford. Now they had moved from Oxford to our cute little American college town for a year.

Irina and Dimitri were apparently very much in love. Whenever I saw them they were affectionate with each other, and at times seemed more like kids in high school than like serious chemistry researchers. I wanted to know them better but I didn't see them very much, because they worked long hours.

Alyssa asked the medical school to give me some kind of a job, so I would have at least a little income. The university gave me a low level assistant job at the medical school, helping recruit patients for other research that people were doing at the school. The job gave me an office, and it was an opportunity to get experience in the research process and to meet people, and I could take time off to look for money for my own research, and that was good, but the job paid almost nothing. I started sending out applications for grant money but nobody wanted to give me any.

When Alyssa first showed me her house, she said it was her humble cottage. Alyssa was unpretentious. But the house was very nice, not what I think of as a humble cottage. Alyssa had a beautiful old two story house in a good neighborhood about three blocks west of the university. The exterior was all brick. Inside she had beautiful hardwood floors, and walls painted in cheerful pale pastel colors, and nice high ceilings throughout the house. Her house was on a double lot and was the largest house in the neighborhood. All the rooms in her house were big. Downstairs she had a living room, a dining room, a kitchen, a pantry, a recreation room, and two half bathrooms. Upstairs there were three large bedrooms, one of which she used as her office, and there were three large full bathrooms.

Alyssa was divorced and her son was grown and out of the house, so she could rent a bedroom to people and still have enough space for herself. She told me her son was a lawyer, as she was. She said her son was working for the attorney general in an office in the state capital, which was a small town in an adjacent county. I wondered whether there's a gene that makes people want to become lawyers.

My storage closet was up on the second floor. It was a nice big storage closet. It didn't have any windows, so it was not like a bedroom, but I liked living in her house.

I asked Alyssa how she cleaned her beautiful floors. I know from experience that if you have hardwood floors the best way to get the dust off them is to push a Swiffer over them. Alyssa said she ran a vacuum cleaner over her floors occasionally. I told her I would be happy to run my Swiffer over her floors. That would be easy and would work better than vacuuming them. She said that was a good idea. I'm not a fanatic about cleaning. My desire to do housework is not greater than my desire to eat pizza when I'm hungry, or to rest when I'm tired. But beautiful old hardwood floors are a treasure, and treasures need love.

One of the good things about living in Alyssa's house was her dog. Alyssa had a dog named Abraham. Abraham was a handsome golden retriever. He had wonderful control over the muscles of his face, so he could raise one eyebrow without raising the other, and he could crinkle his nose on one side and then shift and crinkle it on the other side.

The house had a fenced backyard, which Abraham liked. Sometimes he would sit out there and monitor the yard. Other times he would sit inside the house in the living room and look out the front window. He learned my schedule, and he would sit in the living room and wait for me in the evening and greet me when I came home after work. He wasn't a jumper. He never jumped on people. He was more of a tail wagger. He would wag his tail, and if he was standing close to the door his tail would bang against the door. Abraham liked all the people in the house. He didn't care whether you had money for your research or didn't have money for your research. I was happy he was part of the household.

Chapter Two

When I first moved in to Alyssa's house, the light in my storage closet wasn't working. To get some light I left my door open and the light from the hall came in to the closet.

Alyssa said the light had been a problem for several weeks. She had tried putting in a new light bulb, but that hadn't made any difference. Another light on that side of the house also wasn't working, and some electrical sockets on that side weren't working, so it was some kind of a circuit problem. Alyssa went outside to the back of the house and opened the electrical panel and looked at the fuses but she didn't see anything wrong.

Fixing it hadn't been a top priority for Alyssa until I moved in there. When I moved in she called an electrician but they were busy and couldn't come right away.

Chapter Three

Alyssa asked me whether I wanted to meet Lexi, who lived down the street. Lexi was a professor of physics, and was looking for research money like I was. Alyssa pointed out Lexi's house, which was across the street and two houses down the street from Alyssa's house. We could see it clearly from Alyssa's house.

I was curious, so I said yes. So Alyssa called Lexi and asked her if she wanted to meet me, and Lexi agreed to come over for a few minutes in the morning before work.

The next morning Alyssa and Abraham and I greeted Lexi at the door.

Alyssa smiled. "Good to see you again," she said to Lexi.

Lexi smiled. "I want to meet your new tenant."

"Come in," Alyssa said.

Lexi came in. She was carrying a small paper bag with something in it She looked at me. "And here he is."

"My new tenant. Doctor Jackson Rose," Alyssa said.

Too formal, I thought. "Jack," I said to Lexi. I smiled.

Alyssa looked at me. "My neighbor, Professor Alexandria Lieblich."

She pronounced it LEEB-lick.

Lexi smiled. "Lexi," she said.

I extended my right hand to shake hands with Lexi. "Hello. It's good to meet you."

Lexi grasped my extended hand with both of hers. "Welcome to the university. I hope you like our little corner of the world of academia."

"I do," I said.

Lexi released her grip. "Let me know if I can help you."

"Thank you," I said.

Lexi was not pretty, but she was cute. She had blonde hair and a cute face and a nice smile. She wasn't very big. She was a contrast to Alyssa, who was taller and had dark brown hair and broad shoulders and was stocky.

Lexi was wearing a grey skirt and a white blouse and a grey jacket. Her shoes were some kind of athletic shoes with soft soles. My clothes were nothing special. I regretted not being better dressed.

"Let's go in the living room," Alyssa said, and she led us there.

Abraham accompanied us into the living room. "How do you like Abraham?" Lexi said.

I looked at Abraham. He was looking at Lexi. "He's great," I said.

Lexi went over to Abraham and kneeled down. Abraham wagged his tail. Lexi rubbed his chest with her left hand and talked to him as if she were talking to a child.

"How have you been, Abraham? How do you like your new housemate?" Abraham continued to wag his tail.

"He likes you," I said.

Lexi stood up again.

"He's a sweetheart," she said.

There was a cushion on the floor which was Abraham's dog bed. Abraham stretched out on his cushion.

"Jack, do you like bagels?" Lexi said. "I brought some cilantro bagels. Would you like to try one?"

I like bagels but I had never tried cilantro bagels. I hesitated. "Cilantro bagels?" I said.

Lexi smiled. "You need to try one. If you don't try one of these, you'll regret it. Maybe not today. Maybe not tomorrow. But soon, and for the rest of your life."

I laughed.

Alyssa smiled, but she didn't laugh.

"I borrowed that line from a movie," Lexi said.

"Yes, I remember that movie," I said.

"I remember that movie too," Alyssa said.

"It wasn't a movie about bagels. I repurposed it," Lexi said.

"You're an innovator," I said.

Lexi smiled. "Have a bagel."

I extended a hand toward her bag of bagels. "Yes, I want one of your bagels."

She gave me her paper bag.

"Thank you," I said, and I took a bagel and gave the bag back to her. I started eating the bagel. It was good.

"Alyssa?" Lexi said, and offered her bag of bagels to Alyssa.

"Thanks," Alyssa said, and took one out of the bag.

"My research partner made these," Lexi said.

"Veronica made these?" Alyssa said.

Lexi nodded. "She likes to make things."

Alyssa nibbled on the bagel. "It's different."

"Are you eating one yourself?" I said.

"I've been eating bagels all week. I've eaten too many already," Lexi said.

Lexi had a nice voice. It was clear, pleasant, easy to listen to, like the voice of a singer. It was a little deeper than most women's voices. I'm not a voice expert, but she could have been a mezzo soprano. Maybe even a contralto.

But she was more like a dancer than a singer. Everything she did was graceful, like a ballet dancer. If her name had been Russian I would have thought she was related to dancers from the Bolshoi. But her name wasn't Russian. I wondered about her background.

"Sit down and make yourselves comfortable," Alyssa said.

"I can't stay. I have to go to work in a minute," Lexi said to Alyssa. Lexi remained standing, and so did Alyssa and I. Lexi looked around at Alyssa's living room. "Do you like living here, in Alyssa's house?"

"It's not bad. I'm in a storage closet, but that's better than being out on the street."

Lexi looked surprised. "You're in storage?"

I smiled. "It's not bad. It's a nice house."

"Do people ask you when are you going to come out of the closet?"

I laughed. "That's something that depends on the context, isn't it?"

Lexi looked at Alyssa. "You put him in a storage closet?"

"That's all I can offer. Irina and Dimitri are renting the guest bedroom."

Lexi looked at me. "I'm sorry I can't offer you part of my house. I don't think it would work. I have a daughter in college here. She lives with other students on campus but she comes home frequently. Her father remarried and took a job in another town, so I'm the main family connection for her."

"I understand. Living in a storage closet is all right. Except the light doesn't work."

Lexi frowned. "The light doesn't work?"

"Alyssa tried changing the light bulb, but that doesn't help. It's some kind of a circuit problem. But the fuses look all right. She called an electrician."

"You're living in a storage closet and the light doesn't work? That's no way to live. We need to fix this." Lexi looked at Alyssa. "Where's your electrical panel?"

"It's outside, in the back," Alyssa said.

"Let's look at it." Lexi started towards the door, and Alyssa and Abraham and I followed her. We all went outside to the back of the house, and found the electrical panel on the back wall. Lexi reached out to the panel and opened it up and looked at it.

"Your house is like mine. You've got these old fuses. Newer houses don't have fuses. They have circuit breakers," Lexi said to Alyssa. "Your fuses look all right."

Lexi reached in to the electrical panel with her right hand and touched one of the fuses.

"Sometimes the fuses can come loose a little bit. Sometimes they're not tight in the sockets. These old fuses need to be tight to make a good connection."

Lexi gripped a fuse and tried to turn it clockwise as hard as she could, and then gripped another and did the same thing, and did this to all the fuses in the panel.

"Sometimes vibration can cause the fuses to become loose," Lexi said. "So if someone was using a power tool doing some work with your panel, that can cause the fuses to become loose, even if the workers never touch the fuses."

"I upgraded my heat pump earlier this spring. They were working on the panel when they did that," Alyssa said.

"That could have loosened your fuses," Lexi said, and closed the panel.

"Thanks for your help," Alyssa said.

"Yes, thanks," I said.

"I need to go to work," Lexi said. "When you have time, look at your light upstairs and see if we fixed the problem."

I said, "I'm going to do that right now."

Lexi looked at me and smiled. "I enjoyed meeting you."

We shook hands.

I smiled. "And I enjoyed meeting you."

She left us. We watched her walk away.

"What do you think of my neighbor?" Alyssa said.

"She's nice," I said.

Alyssa and I went inside and went up to my storage closet. Now the light was working. I got ready for work and I walked over to the medical school.

Chapter Four

This chapter is an optional chapter. You can read it if you want to read it or you can skip it if you want to skip it. The reason I'm making it an optional chapter is because it talks about endometriosis and medical research, and I know some people don't want to read about that. I'm a physician, so to me that's just a part of life. It's part of a day at the office for me. But I know other people don't always feel that way. So if you don't want to read it, you can skip to chapter five now.

If you're still reading this, I'll tell you that I started out helping with recruiting for some people who were doing endometriosis research. The endo research group was at The Women's Health Center, which was a treatment and research center that had offices scattered around the medical school. They published the typical recruiting ad, saying they were doing studies and if someone had certain symptoms the person might be eligible to be in a study. The ads always have a name of someone to contact for more information. I was that person.

I got a call from someone who said her name was Morgan Young and she saw the ad and she wasn't sure but she thought she might want to be in a study and could she come over to my office at the medical school. I said certainly and we set up an appointment and we met. She came to my office and we shook hands and we sat down and talked.

Morgan looked like she was about twenty years old. She was medium height, had long straight dark brown hair and blue eyes, had large breasts and a thin waist and looked athletic. She looked like she had enough muscle to play sports, and no fat anywhere.

She was dressed conservatively. People who are young and fit and who have endo symptoms and nothing else are perfect candidates for an endo study.

We talked about the research process, and we talked about her symptoms and her medical history to see if she was eligible for one of the studies. The main symptom of endometriosis is painful menstruation, so we talked about her periods.

"The research teams here at the medical school do what we call clinical studies, or clinical trials. Studies and trials mean the same thing," I said.

She nodded her head. "I understand."

"I'm not one of the researchers doing the studies. I'm just assisting with recruiting people who are eligible for the studies."

"I understand."

"As you saw in the ad, the research group is looking for people who have certain symptoms."

"Yes."

"Tell me about your symptoms."

Morgan winced. "My periods are agony."

"Do your symptoms affect your activities of daily living?"

She frowned. "On bad days I can't go to work. I've used up all my sick leave, so I have to take unpaid days off. And I'm on a volleyball team, in a recreational league, but I can't play when I have symptoms."

"What do you take for your symptoms?"

"Pain pills."

"Does that help?"

"A little bit."

"Do you have any other symptoms?"

She stopped frowning and seemed to relax a little bit. "No."

"Do you take any other medications?"

"Birth control pills."

"What does your doctor think is causing your symptoms?"

"You should say 'what do my doctors think.'"

"You have more than one?"

"My primary sent me to some referrals."

"What do they think?"

"They're not sure."

"Did anyone say you have endometriosis?"

"They said it's possible but they don't know."

"Do you have any other medical problems?"

"No."

"Are you willing to sign a release so the research group can look at your medical records?"

"Yes."

Her answers reaffirmed my belief that she was a great candidate for a study. "With your history I think we can offer you something."

She smiled. "Good."

"But I want to caution you that we cannot promise you that this study or any other study will help you. Clinical trials only study things that are uncertain. That's the nature of experimental medicine. If something is certain, it doesn't need to be studied in an experiment."

Her smile faded. She nodded her head. "I understand," she said softly.

"There's a group of endometriosis researchers at The Women's Health Center here at the university. They're running a diagnostic study that's looking for people exactly like you. And one of the advantages for you is if you enroll in it there's a chance the study could produce some results quickly, and when you have the results you could sign up for a treatment study."

"Maybe I should do that."

"Before you sign up for any study you need to understand what it will be doing and you need to think carefully about whether it's right for you. So let's talk about the diagnostic study."

Morgan frowned again. Sometimes that can be a sign of disapproval, but not always. Sometimes it's just a sign of being undecided and thinking carefully. I wanted Morgan to be in the study, but it had to be her decision and not mine.

"How does it work?" she said.

"The diagnostic study is looking at genetic testing of tissue. The diagnostic study is looking at whether genetic testing can replace the standard method of making the diagnosis. The standard method is doing a laparoscopy. That's a surgical procedure. Did your doctors ever talk to you about a laparoscopy?"

"They mentioned it. I'm not eager to have anybody cut me open, so I never pushed anybody to do one."

"If you enroll in the diagnostic study, you won't have a laparoscopy. You'll have an experimental nonsurgical procedure instead."

"What will they do?"

"One of the doctors doing the study will do a pelvic exam, and during the exam they will insert a thin little experimental plastic device inside your cervical canal, and use that to take some cells from the wall of your cervix, and then remove the plastic device. Then later they will do genetic analysis of the cells."

"Genetic analysis? Why are they doing that?"

"Some previous researchers have found some preliminary evidence that patients with endometriosis have abnormal genetic changes in cervical cells. We want to look at that in more detail. Genetic analysis has the potential to greatly increase our ability to understand this disease."

Morgan stopped frowning. "That sounds encouraging."

"The study also has what is known as a control group. A lot of studies have control groups. A control group is a group used for comparison. In this study, the control group does not have symptoms of endometriosis. They get the same exam procedure. Their cells get the same genetic analysis. Having a control group helps make it a good study."

"I understand."

"Then someone on the research team looks at the genetic analysis of every person in the study, including all the people with symptoms and all the people in the control group. The researcher says whether each genetic analysis shows abnormal genetic changes or not. The researcher looks at each genetic analysis without looking at whether it comes from someone with symptoms or someone with no symptoms. That makes it what we call a blinded study. Do you see why we do it that way?"

"I think so. It's more objective that way. If the observer doesn't know which group it comes from, then she's not going to be influenced by her expectations about each group."

"That's right."

Morgan was bright. Explaining things to her was easy.

I continued my explanation. "And then someone else on the research team reveals which genetic analyses are from people with symptoms and which are from people in the control group," I said.

"So you can see whether the genetic changes go with the symptoms."

"Yes."

The more I talked with her, the more I wanted her to sign up for the study. But I wasn't going to tell her what to do. She needed to decide for herself.

"The researchers have printed some information that you should read while you're deciding what you want to do," I said. "The information will help you think about what you want to do."

I had a desk drawer with lots of printed material. I looked in the drawer for some booklets. I found what I needed and offered some printed material to Morgan. She stood up and took a step toward me and reached out and I gave her the information.

"This booklet will tell you more about the diagnostic study."

"Thank you."

"And here's something else for you to read. This will tell you about the research process."

"Thank you."

She went back to her chair and sat down again.

"The printed information is very important. Before you enroll, you need to read and understand the material about the research process and the possible risks and benefits of everything that will be done in the study. Enrolling in a research study is a serious decision and you should only do it if you understand what's involved and you've thought carefully about your decision."

"I feel like I'm studying for a class in school."

"Yes, it's a little bit like that."

She looked at the covers of the booklets. "I hope I can understand all of this. Does it have a lot of medical jargon in it?"

"No. The writers don't use medical jargon."

She looked inside the booklets. "They don't? I thought using jargon was a requirement in research."

"The people who write research documents at our medical school don't use it. The writers want people to understand all the risks."

"They're not tempted to hide the risks a little bit?" she said, still looking in the booklets.

"They think people will sign up for a study even if people understand the risks."

She looked at me. "I can understand why people might do that. I'll read these carefully."

"Good."

"You said there's a chance the study could produce some results quickly."

"That's true, because the study has almost finished enrolling people. If you sign up for it in the near future, I think you'll be one of the last ones in. And if you wait a while, some other people will probably be the last ones in, and the study will go on without you. After the study finishes enrolling people, the researchers are going to run the genetic analysis quickly, because they want to find people who can be in a treatment study. Clinical studies are not usually this fast. Some studies can take many years."

She didn't say anything. She wasn't frowning, but she wasn't happy. She glanced at the research documents I had given her. She looked at me again.

"I don't know," she said. "I can see how this might help me. And after this, the treatment studies might help me."

She paused.

"But it might *not* help me. And it's more doctor visits and testing," she said.

"That's true."

"What do you think I should do? Do you think I should sign up for the study?"

"I think you should carefully consider it and decide whether it's right for you. It's your decision."

"I don't expect a medical miracle. I just want to reduce the pain. I just want to be normal. I want my periods to be just messy and uncomfortable like they are for many women."

"Yes. I understand. I'm an optimist, so I think eventually medical science can make progress. I can't promise this study will do anything. But eventually medical science can find a way to make you uncomfortable."

Morgan looked a little bit happier.

"Do you really think so?" she said. "I've been to lots of doctors already. They've all failed to help me."

"Failure is a success that hasn't happened yet."

"I've heard that before. My mother liked to say that. But I don't think she was the original person who said that. I don't know where she heard it originally."

"I think Benjamin Franklin said it originally."

Morgan smiled a little half smile. "My mother wasn't old enough to know Benjamin Franklin."

I didn't say anything. Morgan looked serious again.

"This has been such a struggle for me," she said.

"Medical science is getting better."

"I want to believe you. I just don't know. As you said, success is a failure that hasn't happened yet."

"Something like that."

Morgan shifted her body in her chair. She looked down at the floor and then at me.

"I feel so weary. I'm so tired of going to doctors. It's such an endless struggle. I don't know whether I want to go through all this process."

"You should talk to Donna."

"Donna?"

"She's our dean for research. And she's the head of our Institutional Review Board. No research can happen without approval from the Institutional Review Board. So Donna knows all about research. And she's very empathetic. She understands what patients go through. She won't push you to do anything. She'll listen to you and she'll help you understand what it's like to be in a research study. She's much better than I am."

"You're not bad. I do feel better talking to you." She smiled for a few seconds. "You create the impression that you know what you're doing."

"I've had a little training."

"Acting training?"

"Medical training."

"I won't hold that against you."

"Thank you."

"How can I talk to this Donna person?"

"I'll call Donna and tell her you want to see her. Then you can make an appointment for yourself. And then after you talk to Donna, if you decide you want to be in the study, then you need to look at the contact information I gave you and make a follow up appointment over at the office of the endo group. From what we've talked about so far I think you qualify and can enroll if you want to be in it."

"I understand."

Chapter Five

If you skipped the last chapter, I'll summarize it for you. A woman named Morgan Young came to the research office and started talking to me about signing up to be in a research study on endometriosis. That's your summary. Now we'll start where the last chapter ended.

"Do you have any questions for me?" I said to Morgan.

"How much will it cost me if I enroll in the study?" she said.

"That's an excellent question. In general, there's no cost to you to be in any research study. All the doctor visits, all the diagnostic and treatment procedures, all the medications are free to you. The researchers have a grant that pays for those things. However, if you have other medical problems during the study and you're treated for those problems by someone outside the study, you're responsible for those expenses."

"Thanks. I'll read the information and talk to Donna and decide what I want to do."

"Good."

"You said you're not one of the investigators doing the study. You're just assisting with recruiting people into the study."

"Yes."

"Do you have a research specialty of your own?"

"I hope to set up a lab to do sex research."

She laughed. "Really?"

"Yes. It's a legitimate academic field of research. A lot of people have problems related to sex."

She looked serious. "Do you think so?"

"Yes I do. So I think sex research has value."

"Sometimes I think problems related to sex are really problems related to love."

I wasn't sure what she meant. I didn't say anything.

"What about people who have problems with love, but not with sex itself. Can research do anything to help those people?" she said.

"Did you have anything specific in mind?"

"For example, people who love someone but they can't quite have what they want."

"I don't know. That would be hard to study."

"I think it's like drug addiction sometimes. Researchers study drug addiction. So maybe researchers can study things that are like that."

I wondered whether she was talking about her own problems. "That would be a good research topic. I'm just not sure how it could be studied," I said.

"Keep it in mind."

"I can't study anything unless I can get some research money. It's hard to get money for sex research."

"It's hard to get money for any research. I know all about the struggle to get research money."

"Do you do research?"

"No, but I work for people who do research."

"Where do you work?"

"I work over in the Shaeffer Building here on campus. I'm the secretary to Chairman Richardson in the physics department."

"I know someone in the physics department."

"Who do you know?"

"I know Professor Lieblich."

Morgan smiled a big smile. "You know Lexi? I work with her all the time. Come on over and visit us sometime. Do you know Professor Chebychev?"

"No, sorry. Are they in the physics department?"

"Yes. They're doing research with Lexi."

"I'd like to meet them."

"And we have a student assistant who helps the department. Come on over and meet everybody."

"I want to do that."

"We have a good group of people."

"I want to meet all of them."

"You'd like them."

Morgan paused. She looked down a little bit, at what I was wearing. She stopped smiling.

"Can I give you some advice?" she said.

"Sure."

"This might be a little bit critical."

"That's fine."

"You should iron your clothes," she said softly.

I glanced down at my shirt and pants. "Are my clothes wrinkled today?"

She frowned. "Yes, they look a little bit wrinkled."

"Sorry. Sometimes I try to iron things but not all the time. Even when I iron things, sometimes they still look wrinkled. My ironing is a failure."

"Your ironing is a success that hasn't happened yet. Do more of it. You'll get better. Make it a habit. Do it while you're watching your favorite medical videos. Exploratory laparotomies made simple. Something like that."

"I'll try that."

"Of course, I don't judge you by your clothes. But other people might do that."

"Thanks. That's good advice."

"I need to go back to the department," she said briskly.

"Thanks for coming in."

"I'll talk with Donna."

"She can help you."

"That would be nice if I could make some progress with my symptoms."

"Yes."

"I didn't go to college. With my symptoms it seemed like too much of a struggle. But if I could make some progress I would like to go."

"I hope you can make some progress."

"Thanks for all your information."

"Thanks for talking with me."

Morgan and I got up and walked to the door.

"Do you ever get tired of what you're doing?" she said.

"No. I like research."

"I mean, do you get tired of talking with women about their cycles?"

"No. It's part of research. Do you get tired of talking about your cycle?"

"Yes."

"You'd like to talk about something else?"

"I'd like to talk about *your* cycle. But you don't have a cycle."

"Everybody has cycles of one kind or another. My cortisol level cycles every day. Yours does too. Cycles are part of life."

"Cortisol?"

"Yes."

Morgan smiled. "Next time I see you I'll ask you about your cortisol cycle."

I smiled. "Yes. Ask me."

We shook hands.

"Come see us sometime, over at the physics office," she said.

"I will."

Morgan left my office.

I appreciated her comments about ironing. I wondered how much ironing skill I could develop. I wondered whether there really were any videos on exploratory laparotomies made simple.

Chapter Six

Lexi called me on a Wednesday and invited me to have lunch at her house on Saturday. She said she was sorry our meeting at Alyssa's house had been so brief, and we should meet when we had more time. She said her daughter would probably join us. I said that would be good.

I asked her if she wanted to see a copy of a research proposal Joan had written. I thought it might interest Lexi. She said she would like to look at it.

On Saturday I crossed the street and walked past two houses and came to her house. It was an old two story red brick house on a narrow lot, like almost all of the houses on the street. It looked well maintained. It had a driveway on the side that went back to a garage. There was a big garden in front of the house, with a thicket of long slim green leaves but no flowers. And there was some kind of fruit tree next to the garden.

I went up to the front door and rang the bell. Lexi opened the door. She was wearing a dark blue summer dress with a shirt-waist, and sandals and thin white stockings. She looked good. My clothes were as casual as hers.

She smiled a big smile. "Welcome," she said. "Come in."

I smiled at her. "Hello, Lexi."

I went in and we stood and talked near the door. Her smile faded but she still looked happy.

I gave her the copy of Joan's research proposal. Lexi thanked me.

"I like your house," I said.

"It's my humble cottage," Lexi said.

"Alyssa says *her* house is *her* humble cottage."

"My house is humbler than hers. It's my humbler cottage."

"Your garden looks good."

"I have a larger garden in back."

"What's the plant with all the long green leaves?"

"Those are my day lilies. They're just leaves right now. In a few weeks they'll have flowers."

"I like your day lilies."

"With your name you should like roses," Lexi said.

"Roses are good also," I said.

"I've never tried to grow any roses. I don't know whether I would be good at it."

"I'm sure you would be."

Lexi took a step away from the door.

"My daughter, Hadley, isn't here but she's going to join us for lunch. Do you like linguini?"

"I love linguini."

"You can help cook it. Let's go in the kitchen."

"All right."

I followed her as she went to the kitchen.

"First we need to heat the water," she said. She looked quite serious. Cooking linguini was apparently a serious business. I hoped I didn't disappoint her with my general lack of cooking ability.

She got a large pot and gave it to me. "Can you put some cold water in this, please? Fill it about three quarters full."

I went to the sink and put water in the pot.

"Put it on the front burner and we'll turn on the burner," she said. "Medium heat is good. We just want it to simmer."

I put the pot on the burner and she turned the burner to medium heat.

"Let's wait for Hadley before we do anything more," she said. "Would you like to sit in the living room?"

"All right."

We went in the living room.

"Would you like something to drink while we're waiting?" Lexi said.

"Not for me, thanks."

"Make yourself comfortable."

We sat in some of her chairs. Mine was quite comfortable.

"I'm sorry I'm not good at these conversations where people get to know each other," she said.

"I'm not either," I said.

"When I was in college I took conversational French, and I got a good grade in it. But that only helps me when I'm talking to a French person."

"I'm sorry I don't speak French."

"I should have taken conversational English."

"When I meet someone I try to find things we have in common."

"Yes, that's a good idea, but it's hard to do," she said. "A lot of those things that people like to say about themselves don't apply to me, or I don't know enough about them. I don't even know my astrological sign."

"I don't know mine either. So that's one thing we have in common."

"And I can't tell you about my tragic childhood and how my parents didn't love me, because I didn't have a tragic childhood and my parents did love me."

"That's something else we have in common."

"Maybe this will be easier than I thought," she said.

"Yes, I think so," I said.

"Is there anything you'd like to talk about?"

"Whatever you want."

"Sometimes people are interested in my name."

"Yes, tell me about your name."

"It's German. Liebe means love, and lich is like. Lieblich means different things, depending on the context. The dictionary says it can mean sweet or sometimes it can be translated as lovely. Or sometimes it can mean kind. Or sometimes it can mean pleasant."

I wondered whether it could be translated as cute. But I didn't say that.

"That's a lot to live up to," I said.

She smiled. "Of course, the people who wrote the dictionary never met me. If they met me they might give Lieblich a different definition."

"What would they say if they met you?"

"I have no idea what they would say."

She paused. She looked serious. "After you get to know me better, I'm sure you'll have a translation of your own," she said. "When you make your own translation, tell me what it is. I'd like to know."

"All right."

"Your name Rose makes me think of Shakespeare. A rose by any other name would smell as sweet."

"Yes. My name is just a name. If I had a different name I would still be the same person."

"Yes, that's true, but a name isn't nothing. It's a connection to other people, an important connection. You're connected to your Rose relatives."

"Yes, that's true."

"Sometimes people do things just because of a name, and its connections," Lexi said.

I wasn't sure what she had in mind.

"I suppose that's possible," I said.

"My mother's family name is Maranville. Does that name mean anything to you?"

"No. Sorry."

"Maranville is the name of a famous baseball player from the early days of professional baseball. Rabbit Maranville."

"Rabbit?"

"Yes. Rabbit. Players had colorful names back in that era."

"So is your mother related to Rabbit? Rabbit Maranville?"

"She always claims she's related. But Rabbit is not a close relative. Rabbit is not my grandfather or anything like that."

"That's a great name," I said.

"I think the Maranville name was one of the reasons my father married my mother," Lexi said.

"Really?"

"My father is crazy about baseball. He would never admit he married my mother because of her name, but I'm sure the name intrigued him. Falling in love with someone is an irrational process. A name can be important."

She was giving me an introduction to the power of names. Or maybe it was the power of baseball. I hadn't thought about that before.

"Did your parents give *you* the name of Maranville? As your middle name?" I said.

"No. My parents didn't want me to be called Rabbit. They thought of something they liked better for me."

"What's that?"

"My middle name is Cartwright. Do you know that name?"

"I think Alexander Cartwright invented baseball. Is that right?"

"You know some baseball history."

"Not very much of it."

"For many years Alexander Cartwright was considered to be the man who created the rules of baseball."

"He's not still considered that?"

"The most recent research suggests other people were also important, but Alexander Cartwright is still a famous baseball name. I almost have his first name, and my middle name is his last name."

"I'm pleased to know you, Alexandria Cartwright Lieblich."

"And I am pleased to know you, Jack Rose."

"I'm sorry I'm not related to or named after any famous baseball players. Or anyone famous in any other field of human endeavor."

"You're mentioned in a famous quotation from a famous play by Shakespeare. That's better than being related to any number of silly sports heroes."

"That's kind of you to say that."

She smiled briefly. "That's what my name says I should do."

I didn't try to respond to that. I wanted to know about her work at the university.

"You're in the physics department?" I said.

"Yes. I'm in experimental physics."

"You teach that or do you only do research?"

"I do both."

"What are your students like? Do they have to be mathematical geniuses to understand what you're saying?"

"No, it's not like that at all. It's concepts that anybody can understand if they're interested in learning about it and they have a good teacher."

"I think it would be a challenge."

Lexi smiled. "I like teaching," she said. Her smile grew bigger. "I like introducing students to something new and showing them it's not mysterious. I like helping people pick up new skills." Now she had the biggest smile I had seen from her. "It makes me happy."

"And you also do research?"

"When I can find some money."

"Do you like research?"

"When I can find some money." Her smile faded away. For a few seconds she looked grim. "When I don't have money, it's a struggle."

"What are you studying?"

"I study neutrinos."

She pronounced it new-TREE-knows.

"I don't know anything about neutrinos," I said.

"Neutrinos are tiny particles," she said. The expression on her face brightened a little bit and she spoke with casual confidence, as if she felt she could explain anything to anybody. I imagined her standing in front of a classroom full of diverse students.

"How tiny are they?"

"They're teeny tiny. Think of the smallest thing you can think of."

"A grain of sand."

"They're much, much smaller than that."

"A molecule of water."

"They're tinier than that."

"That's pretty small."

"They're considered to be elementary particles. One of the building blocks of the universe."

"What do you do with them?"

"I detect them. My research group detects them. My research group built the world's greatest portable neutrino detector. I have great people on my team. And if we can get some more money, we can demonstrate it to people around the world who might be interested in using it, and we can do great things."

"Is there any particular reason why people want to detect these little particles?"

"I believe our detector can be used to verify compliance with international arms control treaties."

I didn't know anything about neutrino detectors but I was pretty sure if she could do that, it would be a really good achievement.

"You're doing some serious stuff, then," I said.

"I think it's serious. But it's hard to get people to take me seriously."

"I hope your team is getting some recognition for your team's achievement."

"We published a paper. Some people said they liked it."

"And money? Are you getting money?"

She shook her head.

"That's the sad thing. We're not getting any more money for it. I'm working hard trying to find research money for my team, but I can't find any."

She paused.

"Obviously we got *some* money, to do as much as we've done, but we haven't found any more," she said. "We have a great machine and we're out of business. My search for money is a failure." She looked down at the floor.

"Failure is a success that hasn't happened yet," I said.

Lexi smiled and looked at me. "I like that."

"I'm not sure who said that originally. I think it may have been Benjamin Franklin."

"That's good."

She had already won me over to her side. I thought to myself, "Come on, grant administrators, give her some money."

I said, "Why is your team not getting any more money?"

"There's probably more than one reason. I suspect I know several reasons."

"What are they?"

"One reason is that very few people know anything about neutrinos. So people don't think neutrino research could be important. People in experimental physics are familiar with neutrinos, but outside of my field people don't know anything about them. So what I do isn't popular. It doesn't have broad support."

"Yes, I think that would be a problem."

"When I apply for a grant, the first thing that happens is my application is reviewed by specialists. They understand what I'm doing. And I usually get great evaluations from every specialist who looks at my application. They give me the highest rating."

"That's impressive."

"But usually the specialists are just reviewers. They don't make the final decision. A top level grant administrator or a top level committee makes the final decision. And generally the administrator or the committee who decides which applications get funded is choosing between my proposal and other proposals which also have positive evaluations and are in different fields."

"Yes, it's a competition between different areas of research."

"And the top administrators are not familiar with what I'm doing."

"That's frustrating."

"They don't understand it enough to be interested in it. They don't know about it, so they can't be enthusiastic about it," she said.

She paused. I didn't say anything.

"And that hurts my chances. I know it does," she said.

"Certainly."

"But if that were the only problem, I think I would be successful at least occasionally."

"What else is there?"

"There's also my personal characteristics."

"Your personal characteristics?"

Lexi shifted her body in her chair. She seemed to relax. She began to speak with a softer voice. She was no longer the physics teacher instructing me. Now she was a neighbor, a friend, telling me about her own life.

"When you met me, what was the first thing you noticed about me?" she said.

"I noticed what you're wearing."

"Did you notice anything else?"

"I noticed your appearance generally. I noticed what you look like."

"Did you notice that I have blonde hair?"

"Sure. Immediately."

"Do you think I'm cute? Don't answer that."

I did think she was cute. But I didn't say that.

"When I speak at a conference, if I say something about international arms control treaties, people are thinking, 'Look at her, she's a cute blonde.'"

If I saw her speak at a conference, I probably would think that. But I didn't say that.

"That's the category people put me in. Cute blonde."

She was quite serious but without any rancor. I nodded. I didn't say anything.

"When people put me in the category of cute blonde, they think that's all I am," she said. Now she was irritated. "They don't also put me in the category of someone who understands international treaties."

"Yes, I understand, but when you apply for grant money, that's not the same as speaking at a conference."

"Why not?"

"If you want to hide your personal characteristics when you apply for a grant, a lot of times you have an opportunity to do that. A lot of times the grant process is based on evaluating paper applications without interviews."

"That's true, but people already know who I am. I've been working in this field for a while. I speak at lots of conferences. Lots of people see me. I try to meet as many scientists as I can, in my field and not in my field, just trying to get people interested in my research. And I meet all kinds of science writers and bloggers. I talk to them about what I'm doing. Sometimes they write about me for the general public, not for specialists in my field. Sometimes they add my picture to their articles, because they think that attracts readers. I can get publicity. I just can't get money."

I nodded. "Yes," I said softly.

"I apply for money repeatedly. People might not know anything about neutrinos, but they know my team has a portable neutrino detector. If a grant administrator sees a grant application about a portable neutrino detector, even if it's submitted anonymously, they connect it to me."

I nodded again. "You're right."

"And you know what they say."

"They say, 'That famous baseball player is asking us for money,'" I said.

Lexi laughed, which I thought was endearing. Some people take themselves ultra seriously and wouldn't think something like that was funny.

"No, that's not what they say," she said.

"What do they say?"

She was serious again. "They say, 'That cute blonde has sent us an application for a grant. But she doesn't look like an expert on anything.'"

I wasn't convinced she was right. "You think they always say that?"

"Don't you think they say that?"

"No, I don't," I said. "If your physical features are nice looking, if you have physical features that are valued in our culture, people pay more attention to you. People listen more to what you say. People value your ideas more."

"I don't think my features are valued in the way you say they are."

"Blonde hair is valued."

"People think blondes are dumb."

"Certainly there are jokes about dumb blondes, but the people who tell those jokes are just trying to entertain people. Don't be too sure jokes describe how people feel in real life."

Lexi looked doubtful.

"You're a smart person who has blonde hair. That's my translation of Lieblich," I said.

She smiled. "I wish you were a grant administrator."

"Joan had blonde hair, like you do. Nobody thought she was dumb."

"Did it help her get money?"

"It didn't hurt her. Let's put it that way. People paid attention to her. They listened to what she said. They thought what she said had value."

Again she looked doubtful. "My grant applications are highly rated. Why don't people offer me research money?"

"Maybe they will."

"I think it's because of my personal characteristics."

"I'm skeptical of your theory."

She frowned. "I don't believe I can be successful with blonde hair. I'm considering coloring my hair black. If I had black hair, people would take me seriously."

I winced. I shook my head. "No, don't do that."

"I might need to do it."

"Can I use your borrowed line?"

"Which line is that?"

"If you do that, you'll regret it. Maybe not today. Maybe not tomorrow. But soon, and for the rest of your life."

"Why do you say that?"

"Because you shouldn't change your hair color unless you have a really good reason."

"What's a really good reason?"

"I can't think of one right now."

"How will I recognize a really good reason?"

"When a really good reason comes into your life, you'll know it. Nothing you've said so far is a really good reason."

"I'm not sure I want to wait. The next time you see me, my hair might be black."

I tried to imagine her with black hair.

"I hope I can still recognize you. Alyssa might need to invite you to come over again so she can reintroduce us."

Lexi smiled a little half smile. "You think I'm crazy, don't you," she said.

"No, no. Not at all."

"You think blondie has lost her mind."

"No, I think you're firmly in contact with reality. Except you're wrong about your hair."

"What's *your* explanation for why I can't get money?"

"You want to hear my explanation?"

"Yes."

"I don't want to offend you."

"I won't be offended. What do you think?"

"I don't think your problem is that you're too blonde," I said softly. "I think your problem is something you touched on earlier."

"What's that?"

"Your work doesn't excite people. You're too bland."

"I'm too bland?"

"I think so."

"So my analysis of my problem was off by only a couple of vowels?"

"Yes."

"I was so close."

Lexi turned her head and stared at the floor. She looked sad. I didn't say anything.

She looked at me again. "I can't really change how exciting my work is," she said.

"You need a better name for what you're trying to detect."

"Can you think of one?"

"What if you said you're trying to detect, say, wizard dust?"

She laughed. "Wizard dust?"

"Yes. You could say in a footnote that you define wizard dust to mean neutrinos. Lots of people are interested in wizards. You might attract some money."

She smiled. "I may have to do that."

"It might help."

She became serious. "Thank you for listening to me complain," she said.

"I don't call it complaining."

"What do you call it?"

"I call it insight."

"That's kind of you to say that."

"No, you're the kind person. I'm the flower. We already covered that."

Lexi looked surprised. Then she smiled a little half smile. "That's right. I forgot."

"Try to remember that."

She was serious again. "Thank you for listening to my insight. And thank you for your comments."

"Looking for money is not easy. I don't have all the answers. I'm just some guy with a lot of opinions."

"Your colleague, Joan, was able to get lots of research money. So we know it's possible for women to get research money."

"She got a little too much money, I think. She wasn't able to resist the temptation of taking it for herself."

"You're going to do what Joan was supposed to be doing?"

"That's right. If I can find some research money, I'm going to do sex research."

Lexi smiled. "How does that work? Do you go around having sex with people? For research purposes, of course."

"No, no. It's nothing like that. It's a legitimate field of research."

She looked serious and a little bit worried.

"I hope all the grant administrators think it's real science," she said.

"They do, I think. Joan convinced everybody the field is real science. And unfortunately she also convinced everybody the people in the field are questionable."

"That could be a problem."

"At least I don't have to worry about my personal characteristics."

"What do you mean?"

"My hair is brown and I'm not cute. People aren't going to look at me and say, 'Look at him. He's a cute blonde.'"

Lexi looked doubtful. "They won't say you're blonde. That's true."

"Do you think they'll say I'm cute?" I said.

She smiled. "You can't ask me that. I'm not going to answer that."

"I'm sorry I asked you that."

She was serious again. "I think you're in a good place to do sex research. Two of our local companies are in the sex business, generally speaking."

"Yes, I know. This town has a company that makes condoms and a company that makes sex dolls."

"Maybe they would be willing to give you some research money."

"It's possible."

Lexi looked off to the side a little bit.

She looked at me again. "I'm trying to think of anyone else that might help you," she said.

"I appreciate your interest."

She brought her left hand up to her face. She rubbed her face for a few seconds and then took her hand away.

"You might like the lectures the university gives on how to find research money. Are you familiar with those?"

"I heard there might be some lectures, but I've never been to one. I don't have the schedule."

"I go to them. I think they're interesting. You want to go to the next one with me?"

"Yes, that would be good," I said.

"I'll look at the schedule and I'll call you when I'm over at the physics department."

"Thanks. I'm lucky I met you."

"It's way too early for you to decide you're lucky you met me."

"Why do you say that?"

"We can't predict the future."

"I'm an optimist."

"You've been abandoned by Joan, the only place you can find to live is in a storage closet, and you're an optimist?"

"Temporary setbacks."

Lexi stared at me without saying anything. After a few seconds she spoke to me as if she had made a major discovery. "I think you might be strong enough to survive at our university."

"I like it. It's a good place."

"What's your background?" She was back to a normal conversational tone of voice. "You're a doctor?"

"I'm an MD, yes. You're a doctor too, right? A PhD doctor?"

"Yes. I have a PhD."

"I don't have a PhD."

"Do you feel like you need one?"

"No, I don't feel like I really need one. But still if I had one it would be one more diploma I could put on the wall of my office to impress people. Maybe it would help me get research money."

"You know what you should do? You should become a notary public. I have a cousin who's a notary. When you become a notary you get a beautiful document that looks sort of like a diploma, and it has lots of tiny printed words that nobody can read from a distance. You could frame it and hang it up high on the wall and cover it with tinted glass so nobody can see it too clearly. It would be very impressive."

"Maybe I'll try that."

"So you're on the faculty at the medical school?"

"Yes. I have a special faculty appointment. That means I'm not regular faculty. It also means they pay me almost nothing. If the janitor works overtime, he makes more money than I do. The school expects that when I find some research money, that will include money to pay me a decent salary."

"Who's here with you? Children?"

"No."

"Wives?"

"No."

"Ex-wives?"

"No."

"Girlfriends?"

"No."

"Ex-girlfriends?"

"No."

"Pet llamas?"

"Do people really keep llamas as pets?"

"I think some people do."

"I've never tried that."

"You're all alone?"

"Abraham greets me when I come home from work."

"He's a darling," Lexi said softly.

She shifted her body in her chair.

"Do you want to see my neutrino detector sometime?" she said briskly.

"Sure."

"On the day that we go to the lecture, I can show it to you after the lecture."

"Yes, that would be good."

Lexi's cell phone chimed. She had it in a pocket. She took it out and looked at it.

"Hadley sent me a text message. She's on her way over here." Lexi looked at me. "Would you like a quick tour of the house while we wait for her?"

"Yes, I'd love a quick tour."

We got up out of our chairs and she began the tour. I followed her as she showed me her house. The interior of her house had beautiful hardwood floors and high ceilings, just like Alyssa's house. When I looked at her hardwood floors I wondered how she cleaned them.

"You have nice floors," I said.

I stopped and so she stopped and we looked at her floors together.

"I love the floors. Beautiful hardwood," she said.

"What do you do to get the dust off them?"

"I go over them with a dust mop sometimes."

"You ever use a Swiffer?"

"I'm not familiar with Swiffers. Are they good?"

"They're wonderful. Much better than a dust mop. I'll bring mine over sometime and clean your floors and you can see how it cleans."

"Thank you. I appreciate that."

"Swiffers are not perfect. There's one kind of dust they won't pick up."

"What kind is that?"

"Wizard dust. They can't even detect it."

Lexi smiled but she didn't laugh.

"Let's look at some more of the house," she said.

She started walking again and I followed her around the house.

The floor plan was similar to the floor plan in Alyssa's house, but the rooms in Lexi's house were smaller. The first floor had a living room, a nice modern kitchen, a dining room, a recreation room, and two half bathrooms. Upstairs were three bedrooms and three full bathrooms.

She finished showing me the house and asked me what I thought.

"It's a nice house."

"It's my humbler cottage."

Chapter Seven

Hadley arrived and Lexi introduced us. Hadley had a backpack which she took off and put in a hall closet.

We stood in Lexi's living room and talked with Hadley. Hadley was thin like Lexi, and taller than Lexi. Hadley was cute like her mother, but not pretty.

Hadley had long straight hair that came down below her shoulders. She wore it parted on one side and held by a clip on the other side to keep it off her face. It was a pale lavender color.

Hadley had nice eyes. She was wearing a little bit of eyeliner.

She was wearing a cream colored shirt and light grey pants, with a black belt that was woven out of some kind of yarn. She had soft blue shoes with white soles.

"Do you like my hair?" she said to me.

"It's not bad." The lavender was all right but I wasn't sure it was the best possible color for her. "How did you achieve that color?" I said.

"It's Kool Aid," Hadley said.

"It's Kool Aid?" I said.

"Yes, it's easy to do. It's a fast process. And not expensive. So it opens up lots of possibilities. What do you think about my eye liner?"

"It looks good. Is that Kool Aid also?"

"No, it's squid ink."

"Squid ink?"

"Yes. Some people use it in pasta. But I use it as makeup. It's a great solid black color."

"I never heard of that."

"How do you like it all together?"

"Everything goes well together."

"You won't see it on the cover of a magazine. But I like it."

"Magazine covers are overrated." I looked at Lexi. "What do you think, Lexi?"

"I like the lavender better than some of the other colors she tried."

"I tried green for a while and Mom said that just didn't look good on me at all. And I tried blue and she didn't like that either."

I tried to imagine Hadley with green or blue hair.

"I agree with what you said," Lexi said to me. "The lavender is not bad. I think that's the consensus." Lexi looked at Hadley. "Isn't that what George told you also?"

"He did say that," Hadley said to Lexi.

I tried to imagine Hadley with blonde hair like her mother. She might look better with blonde hair, but I didn't say that.

Hadley looked at me. "George is a friend at school."

"Are you hungry?" Lexi said to Hadley.

"I'm starving."

"Want some lunch? We're having linguini."

Hadley smiled. "Yes, I'd love some linguini."

"Let's go in the kitchen. Everyone can help," Lexi said.

We all went to the kitchen. The pot of water was simmering on the stove.

"The water's ready," Lexi said to me. "You can add the pasta and turn up the heat a little bit and stir."

I added the pasta and turned up the heat and stirred the bubbling mixture.

"We don't put salt in our pasta," Lexi said. "We like other flavors. Do you like mild red pepper?"

"On pasta? I haven't tried that," I said.

"Would you like to try it today?"

"Sure."

"We can add it when the pasta is ready."

"Do you add cilantro?" I said.

"Not when Hadley is with us."

"I don't like cilantro," Hadley said.

"She didn't get my gene for liking cilantro," Lexi said.

Hadley smiled. "Maybe I was switched at birth. Maybe I'm not really her daughter."

Lexi laughed. "We both like a lot of the same foods."

"I like linguini. I like ground turkey," Hadley said.

"You can make the salad," Lexi said to Hadley.

Lexi got some ground turkey out of the refrigerator and put it in a glass container and cooked it in the microwave. Hadley prepared a salad for us and put it in a large bowl.

I stirred the pasta until Lexi said it was ready. She got a colander from a cabinet. I drained the pasta with it and put the pasta in a large bowl. Lexi added the ground turkey to the bowl.

"We like to mix the turkey in with the linguini," Lexi said.

She got two containers out of the refrigerator.

"Some homemade pepper sauce and some diced tomatoes," she said.

She added some of their contents to the pasta.

"We like to eat in the kitchen," she said.

There was a big table next to the wall. Hadley and Lexi put plates and place settings and the food on the table. We served ourselves and sat down and started eating. Everything was delicious. Nobody said anything at first. Then after we had eaten some of the lunch, Hadley asked me about my work.

"Mom says you're looking for money for research," Hadley said.

"Yes, that's right," I said.

"It's hard to find research money," Hadley said.

"Yes, definitely."

"You can have a really good research project and not find any money."

I nodded my head. "That's right."

"I know that from Mom's experience."

"That's right. She was telling me about it."

"What kind of research are you doing?"

"I want to do sex research."

"Did you know Joan? The woman who created the big scandal?"

"I was going to be her assistant. How did you hear about Joan?"

"Everybody at school knows about Joan. There's three things that most people care about on campus. Money, sex, and sports. And Joan was connected to two of them."

"People only care about money, sex, and sports?"

Hadley looked at Lexi. "Some people care about other things," Hadley said softly.

Lexi nodded.

Hadley looked at me. "I care about other things," she said.

"What kinds of things are you interested in?" I said.

"I'm interested in English. I want to teach English someday."

"She didn't inherit my love of cilantro, but she did inherit my love of teaching," Lexi said.

"That's true. Maybe I really am her daughter," Hadley said.

"Are you studying English now?" I said.

Hadley nodded.

"This is summer school now. I'm taking one course," she said. "We're studying some great writers. One of them is Shakespeare. Right now we're reading his sonnets. 'Shall I compare thee to a summer's day?' He's great at describing people in love."

Hadley looked at Lexi. "Mom, did you ever read his sonnets?"

"Yes, a long time ago. I remember he makes the reader feel the passion when he describes people in love," Lexi said.

"He makes you understand the power of it. How people in love are driven by their love. They upend their lives because of this force they can't really control," Hadley said.

"That's true," Lexi said.

"It's kind of scary when you think about it," Hadley said.

"You should never be scared by love," Lexi said.

"Never?" Hadley said.

Lexi didn't answer immediately.

"I guess maybe sometimes it should scare you," Lexi said.

Hadley looked at me. "What do you think?"

"I agree. Shakespeare was a great writer. He understands human passions," I said.

"Yes. He understands what it feels like to love and to want," Lexi said.

"He knows what drives people," I said.

"The need for an intimate connection," Lexi said.

"What people hunger for," I said.

Hadley ate some salad.

"But what happens when you can't have what you want? What do you do then?" Lexi said.

"I don't know," I said.

"Then you go to the grocery store," Hadley said.

"You go to the grocery store?" Lexi said.

"Yes, and get some more linguini," Hadley said.

"Linguini?" Lexi said.

"Yes. But there's still some left. Would you like to help me finish it?" Hadley said to me.

Hadley and I ate the rest of the pasta.

"Are you reading anything else for your class?" I said.

"We're reading something by F. Scott Fitzgerald." Hadley smiled. "I love his work. He's such a great writer."

"Which of his books are you reading?"

"He wrote a famous novel about somebody who's looking for something that's gone and isn't coming back. Did you ever read that?"

"Yes. I love his beautiful phrases," I said.

Hadley looked at Lexi. "Did you ever read that?"

"A long time ago I listened to it as an audio book."

"Did you like it?"

"I don't remember the details very well. But I remember it's beautifully written. It's wonderful to listen to it."

"You want to hear some of it now?" Hadley said.

"Sure," Lexi said. "Are you going to read it to us?"

"Yes, I want to read it to you," Hadley said to Lexi.

Hadley looked at me. "Do you want to hear it?"

"I'd love to hear it," I said.

"If you wait here just a moment, I'll find it and read it to you."

Hadley left the kitchen and came back with a book. She sat at the table and opened her book and found a certain page in it and started reading it to Lexi and me.

"I thought of Gatsby's wonder when he first picked out the green light at the end of Daisy's dock. He had come a long way to this blue lawn and his dream must have seemed so close that he could hardly fail to grasp it. He did not know that it was already behind him, somewhere back in that vast obscurity beyond the city, where the dark fields of the republic rolled on under the night," Hadley said.

"That's great writing," Lexi said.

Hadley continued reading. "Gatsby believed in the green light, the orgastic future that year by year recedes before us. It eluded us then, but that's no matter—tomorrow we will run faster, stretch out our arms farther. . . . And one fine morning—

So we beat on, boats against the current, borne back ceaselessly into the past."

"That's wonderful," I said.

Hadley closed the book and put it on the table. She looked sad.

"The people who are running faster and stretching out their arms farther can never have what they want. It's gone and it's not coming back," Hadley said.

I thought about what Hadley had read to us.

"I should go back to school," Hadley said. "Good luck with your money search."

"Thank you," I said.

"Do you write up research proposals and send them to people who might give you money?" Hadley said to me.

"Yes, that's one way of looking for money. But it's not enough. People who want research money have to be constantly looking for sources any place they can find them."

"That sounds like that takes up a lot of time."

"It does."

"How do you fit that in with your regular responsibilities? Aren't you busy working as a doctor saving lives and everything?"

"Actually, the medical school hasn't given me any important responsibilities. I help out with recruiting patients for some of the research groups, but I'm not busy saving any lives this semester."

"You're not busy saving lives? That's good. I mean as long as they don't need you to save lives it's good that you have some time."

"Yes. Time is good. Money would be nice, but time is good."

Hadley looked at Lexi. "I'm going back to the campus," Hadley said. "I'll call you."

"All right," Lexi said.

Hadley looked at me. "I enjoyed meeting you. I hope to see you again soon."

"And I enjoyed meeting you, and listening to you read from that novel."

She smiled. "I love that."

We walked with Hadley as she went to the hall closet and retrieved her backpack. She put the Fitzgerald book in her backpack and put her arms through the straps of the backpack and pulled it onto her back. We walked with her to the front door and said goodbye, and she left us.

Lexi and I cleaned up the kitchen. When we finished, Lexi said, "Jack, have you ever played Yahtzee?"

"No. What is it?"

"It's a dice game. It's fun. Would you like to learn how to play it? I can show you."

"You might be disappointed. I don't have a lot of talent for dice games."

"It's easy."

"Sure. I'd like to learn how to play it."

"Do you have time now?"

"Yes, I have some time."

"Let's go into the living room."

We went into the living room. Lexi went to a closet and brought out a folding table and a small cardboard box and set up the table. We moved two of her comfortable chairs up to the table and we sat down. She opened up the box. In it were dice and paper and a pencil.

"I have five dice here. You need five dice to play it. You roll the dice and you try to get various combinations. Some combinations are worth more points than others. You write down your points as you play. It's hard to get all the combinations you want. You can roll the dice a certain number of times and then you see what your score is. The person with the highest score wins. I'll show you as we play it."

"All right."

We played some games of Yahtzee and Lexi showed me how the rules worked. I'm not a very good dice game player, but as I played more I started to see the attraction of the game. We played for a while and had a good time.

Lexi got great delight when her roll of the dice got a good combination. When she won she was so happy that it made me happy, although in theory I should be unhappy that I lost. She had that same joy that children have when they play children's games.

"Any time your life is stressful and you don't know what to do, you can play Yahtzee. It makes you feel better," she said.

She was right. I could see that playing this dice game helped her release the pressure that she faced in her career in the very competitive world of top level experimental physics.

Eventually I needed to leave. "I have to leave. I have some work I need to do. This is my last game." We finished the game and I said, "Thanks for entertaining me."

"Thanks for playing Yahtzee with me, Jack." We both got up from the table and walked to the door. "And thanks for bringing me the things from Joan."

"I hope that helps you."

"What do you think made her so successful? How was she able to get so much money?" Lexi said.

"I think there were probably several reasons why she got so much money. She had a really good record in school, and in her years in residency training. And she knew how to ask for money. She had the ability to write great research proposals. That skill is probably more important than the ability to actually do great research. And when people met her, they liked her. Liking someone can be partly for superficial reasons. We already talked about her blonde hair. But she also had a personality that people liked. She could charm people. She could make people fall in love with her. People wanted to help her."

"I wish I could charm people. I wish I could make people fall in love with me," Lexi said wistfully.

She was serious, but I had to smile. "I think you can probably do that."

I walked out her front door and she followed me.

"Wait. Before you go, I want to ask you something," she said.

I stopped. "All right."

"Do you want to work with me? Looking for research money?"

I wasn't sure what Lexi thought we would accomplish by working together. I wasn't convinced we would find more money together than we would find separately. But I wanted to try it. She was bright, and I liked being with her.

"I want to work with you," I said. "But I'm not sure I can help you. I'm like everybody else outside your field. I don't know anything about your particles. Your neutrinos."

She smiled. "Not neutrinos. Wizard dust."

"I think *you* can probably help *me*," I said. "I think you're good at the money chase, even though you're not always successful. I think you have moxie."

"I remember that. That's from a children's book. A story about bunny rabbits. Flopsy, Moxie, and Cottontail."

I laughed.

"No, wait," she said. "It was Mopsy."

"How do *you* feel about working together?"

"I'm not sure I can help you. I don't know anything about medical research. But I think we would be good together. Your naive optimism would keep us going even through our darkest days."

She was probably right about that.

"You're a good judge of people," I said softly.

"Working with you would be an experiment," she said. "It would be an experiment to see what happens when people in different fields look for money together. I'm an experimental scientist, so I like doing experiments. I think we should do it."

"Medical research is very similar to your research. You study particles, I study people. Same first letter."

"Oh, yes. I see. That is similar."

"Yes, let's work together." I extended my right hand. We shook hands.

"Goodbye, Jack."

I turned away from her and took a step towards the street.

I noticed the tree that was next to her garden of day lilies. I stopped and turned back towards Lexi. "What variety of tree is that?"

Lexi looked at the tree. "That's my apple tree. In a good year, it produces lots of nice big apples."

"How do they taste?"

"They're tart. They're not sweet. They're good for making apple butter."

"Will this be a good year?"

She looked serious. "It depends on the context." Mentally I was one step behind her when she said that, and I didn't see where she was going. Then she smiled a big smile. "I think we'll have a very good year. I don't know whether we'll see any apples." I thought that was a charming thing to say.

I smiled. "Goodbye, Lexi." I turned and walked towards the street.

"See you soon."

I looked back at her. "Thanks for everything."

I walked over to the medical school to do some work. I wondered whether I possessed any useful skills that would help Lexi. Probably not. Maybe she could teach me some.

On the next Saturday, I brought over my Swiffer and ran it over Lexi's floors and she liked the results, so I started doing that every Saturday morning. She saw how easy it was and she started helping me. After we did the floors, we always played Yahtzee. Hadley studied at school then or went places with her friends, so we had the house to ourselves.

If I had been successful finding money to do research, I might have been spending Saturday mornings working on research projects. Playing Yahtzee with Lexi on Saturday morning was more fun than working on research projects. I'm not an advocate for failure, but sometimes it has some advantages.

I thought maybe I would fall in love with Lexi in those first weeks after I met her. But it didn't happen. That was a time when we were friends and nothing more than that. When I realized I wasn't falling for her, I started to think that I was immune to her, that nothing would ever happen between us.

Maybe someday I'll make a list of all the things I've been wrong about. It will be a long list, of course. It will take a lot of time to write everything down. When I make my list, I won't write things down in a random order. I'll put my biggest errors at the top, and smallest errors at the bottom. At the top of my list will be my predictions about me and Lexi.

Chapter Eight

A few days later, Morgan called me. "Doctor Rose, I'm going to be in the study."

I was delighted. "I hope it discovers something that will help you."

"I read all the information you gave me."

"Good."

"And I talked with Donna."

"What did you think of Donna?"

"She's nice. I felt better after talking with her."

"Good."

"And then I went over to the endo research office and signed up."

"I'm glad you're in the study, Morgan."

"Donna told me there's another Morgan that researchers at the medical school are studying."

"Another Morgan?"

"Yes. But this Morgan's not in the endometriosis study. And she's not on campus. Do you want to know where she is?"

"Where is she?"

"The zoo."

"The zoo? Really? Researchers here are studying a Morgan who works at the zoo?"

"She doesn't *work* at the zoo. She's *in* the zoo."

"She's in the zoo?"

"That's right, Doctor Rose. She's a gorilla. She's in a study about heart disease in gorillas. Donna says this is the first time anyone at the medical school has studied a gorilla. The whole Institutional

Review Board went out to the zoo to study all the details of the research proposal before they approved it."

"How did the gorilla get your name?"

"From a contest. Donna says the zoo is part of an international gorilla conservation of the species program. The zoo had a contest to see who could write the best essay about gorilla conservation. They said the winner could name a gorilla at the zoo. The winner was a high school student named Morgan. She wanted to name the gorilla after herself, so the zoo named the gorilla Morgan."

"I'm glad Morgan and her relatives are being conserved."

"Donna told me her gorilla jokes. You want to hear Donna's gorilla jokes?"

"Sure."

"How do you stop a silverback gorilla from charging?"

"How?"

"Take away his credit card. What's the difference between a gorilla and an insurance company?"

"I don't know."

"A gorilla has a heart. What's the difference between a gorilla and someone who believes in conspiracy theories?"

"I don't know."

"A gorilla has a brain. What song does a gorilla sing in December?"

"I don't know."

"Jungle Bells. What weighs twice as much as a gorilla and eats twice as much food as a gorilla?"

"I don't know."

"Two gorillas. What weighs twice as much as a gorilla and eats one and a half times as much as a gorilla?"

"I don't know."

"Two gorillas trying to lose weight. What weighs twice as much as a gorilla and looks like an elephant?"

"I don't know."

"Two gorillas in an elephant costume."

Morgan paused.

"Those are all I can remember," she said.

"Why is the medical school doing gorilla research?" I said.

"Donna says gorillas can have heart problems. Nobody knows exactly how gorillas develop heart problems. The medical school is studying Morgan the gorilla to try to learn more. Some people in cardiology are using ultrasound to look at the heart of the gorilla Morgan."

"How does that work?" I said.

"Donna says the zoo has one place at the gorilla enclosure where there's a fence and not the usual moat to keep the gorillas in the gorilla area. The zoo workers trained Morgan the gorilla to stand at the fence inside the gorilla enclosure. The zoo workers stand on the other side of the fence, outside the gorilla enclosure, and feed gorilla food to Morgan the gorilla when she stands there. And then while Morgan stands there, the doctors join the zoo workers and use ultrasound to look at the gorilla's heart," Morgan said.

"Why doesn't a veterinarian do that?"

"Because the people docs are using ultrasound just like they do with people. The vets don't have that kind of experience."

"I hope they can learn something that will help gorillas."

"I hope the university learns lots of things that help all kinds of Morgans."

"Yes, the university will become a center for Morgan research."

"This university is a great place to be, Doctor Rose. Lots of things happening here."

"I'm sure of that, Morgan."

Chapter Nine

Lexi called me and told me the schedule for the series of lectures about finding research money. The next lecture was coming up soon. We agreed to go to it together.

The next lecture was scheduled to be given in a classroom in the Knowledge Center. The Knowledge Center is the name the university gives to a building that contains the main library on campus plus some classrooms.

I don't know why the university says the Knowledge Center is just that one building. Isn't pretty much every building that has teachers and students a knowledge center? I would say the whole campus is the knowledge center. On Friday night, I think the bars across the street from the campus are the knowledge center.

On the day of the lecture I met Lexi outside the Knowledge Center and we went in together. I wore a light grey business suit with a white shirt and a red tie and dark shoes. Lexi was wearing something more casual, cream colored pants and a shirt with a colorful red print pattern and soft blue shoes with soft white soles.

"You look nice," Lexi said.

"I'm trying to look respectable."

She smiled. "You're trying to fool people?"

I laughed.

"You're doing a good job," she said.

"You look nice also," I said.

She was serious again. "I wore my comfortable clothes today."

"I like your comfortable clothes."

"What do you think of my shoes? These are my comfortable shoes."

"I like your comfortable shoes."

"These are great for walking." She smiled. "And running up the stairs."

"Running up the stairs?"

"It's great exercise. And it relieves stress. Have you ever done it?"

"No."

"You should try it sometime."

"I'm not a great runner."

"You don't have to be a great runner. Anybody can do it."

"Do you always run up the stairs?"

"No, not always. Sometimes I'm thinking about other things. Sometimes I'm thinking about things other than exercise." She looked at my shoes. "Are those shoes comfortable?"

"Very comfortable."

Lexi and I arrived at the classroom early. It was a large room with a big video monitor next to the front wall, with a little camera. The front of the room had a table and a lectern next to the table. The rest of the classroom was filled with padded chairs facing the front of the room.

We went to some seats in the front and we sat down.

"How often does the university give these lectures?" I said.

"The university offers something several times a year. They have different people give it each time," Lexi said.

"And you've been to previous lectures in this series?"

"Yes. Several of them."

"They must be good if you've come back to hear another one."

"They're not bad. I try to get as many ideas as I can get for finding research money."

"If we go to these lectures, do we learn how we can be showered with more money than we can possibly spend?"

Lexi laughed. "Yes, that's exactly right."

"Good. That's the kind of lecture I want to go to."

"Actually, the people who give these lectures always say that research money is hard to find. But it's not impossible. Looking for research money is as difficult as looking for someone who never ends a sentence with a preposition," Lexi said.

"Oh, I just ended a sentence with a preposition. I wasn't speaking grammatically correctly."

"I don't mind. I do the same thing. You can speak any way you want to speak. I'm just saying when you're looking for research money, you're looking for something that you don't find very often."

"Do you know the person who's speaking today?"

"I do know the person speaking to us today."

"Are they good?"

"I haven't heard her speak on this topic before. I hope she's interesting."

"How do you happen to know her?"

"She's the housemate of my most important research partner."

"What's her name?"

"The speaker's name is Elizabeth White. But nobody calls her Elizabeth. If you don't know her very well you call her Professor White. And if you know her well she likes you to call her Snow."

"Snow?"

"She does arctic research. Maybe she'll talk about some of it today."

"Are your team members going to be here today?"

"No."

"Why not?"

"There's only one other person currently on campus who's on our team. She's busy today. Her name is Veronica. Veronica made that bagel that I gave you at Alyssa's house."

"That was a good bagel."

"Veronica is my most important research partner."

"Is Elizabeth White, I mean Snow, the housemate of Veronica?"

"Yes. Snow is the housemate of Veronica."

A woman came in the room and walked down to the front of the room. She was carrying a box of something. She spotted Lexi.

"Lexi, welcome to my lecture."

"Hi Snow. Can I help you set up anything?"

"No, I got it, thanks."

Snow put the box on the table in the front of the room and came over to where we were sitting. Lexi and I stood up to greet her.

"Who's your friend, Lexi?" Snow said.

"This is Doctor Jackson Rose. He's looking for some research money, so I brought him with me today."

I shook hands with Snow. "Everybody calls me Jack."

"It's good to meet you, Jack. All my friends call me Snow."

"You certainly have a distinctive name. Does your name help you get people's attention?"

"Yes, I agree Snow is a distinctive name. I don't know whether it helps me get attention. But if my name makes people interested in what I say, that's good."

"Do you ever have any problems because of your name?"

"It doesn't cause me any problems for me. But sometimes people around me don't like it. They're afraid they'll be called one of the seven dwarfs."

"I think the Disney company should give you money, because you're reminding people of Disney characters."

Snow smiled. "You have a great instinct for looking for money from nontraditional sources. I think you're going to be successful."

"I think you're the one with the great instinct, because you've already been successful. I haven't found any money yet. I'm certainly going to listen carefully to your lecture today."

Snow looked at Lexi. "How is the money chase going for you, Lexi?"

"I'm working hard, Snow. I'm applying for grants. And I'm meeting people. I talk to anybody who will listen."

"I think you're already doing what you need to do. But thanks for coming to hear me."

"I'm sure your lecture today will help me," Lexi said.

"I need to get set up for the lecture. Jack, I enjoyed meeting you."

Snow went to the table in the front of the room, and Lexi and I sat down. Snow adjusted some equipment and turned on the video monitor. The screen showed what was on the table. She went to the lectern.

"Let's get started," Snow said. "Hello, everyone. Welcome to our class on finding research money. My name is Elizabeth White. My friends call me Snow. I see some of my friends here today."

She looked around the room and smiled at some people.

"For those of you who don't know me," she said, "I'm the executive director of the American Society for Arctic Research, and I also teach a course here in arctic geochemistry. Now, as you might imagine, people who do arctic research have had lots of experience in writing grant proposals. And not just any kind of grant proposals. We've had lots of experience in writing *successful* grant proposals. Our work would not be possible without successful grant proposals. So I've been asked to come here and talk with you and tell you the secrets of writing successful grant proposals."

Snow went to the table.

"When you write a grant proposal, you need to show how your research will have an impact on your field. If you don't convince people your research will have an impact on your field, you're not going to get any money. It's just that simple. Now, does everyone understand the concept of impact? I need a volunteer to help me here. Who wants to help me demonstrate the concept of impact?"

Snow looked around the room. She looked at Lexi and said, "Lexi, would you like to help me with this?"

"Sure, if you think I can help."

"Come up here to the table."

Lexi went up to the table. Snow reached into the box and took out something.

"This is a cheap ceramic vase," Snow said.

Snow reached into the box again and took out something else.

"This is an ordinary hammer, just like one you have around your house that you might use to hit a nail with."

Snow showed the vase and the hammer to the class.

"Now, hit the vase with the hammer and demonstrate the concept of impact," Snow said to Lexi.

Lexi took the hammer in one hand and the vase in the other hand. She held the hammer close to the vase and hit the vase with the hammer. She hit it hard enough to produce a loud clank, but not hard enough to break the vase.

Snow took the vase and hammer from Lexi. "Thank you. You can go sit down." Lexi returned to her chair.

Snow spoke to the class again. "Now, what you saw a moment ago might meet the dictionary definition of impact, but when you're trying to get grant money, you need more than that. Let me show you what you need when you're writing a grant proposal."

Snow put the vase on the table and held the hammer with both hands and drew it back and then brought it down on the vase as hard as she could. There was a loud crash and the vase shattered and ceramic pieces went across the table and onto the floor.

"When you're writing your grant proposal, you want the reader to feel your research will have that kind of impact. So you need to start with a compelling research proposal, and then you need to express it in a compelling way."

Snow went on to talk for a while about how to write. She didn't break any more vases.

Chapter Ten

After the class Lexi said, "Want to see my neutrino detector now?"

"Yes, I want to see everything you can show me."

We left the Knowledge Center and Lexi guided me over to the west side of campus. She stopped a couple of hundred feet from a large three story red brick building with big windows. I stopped with her and we looked at the building.

"This is where I work. This is the Shaeffer building. The Frederick and Nancy Shaeffer Science and Engineering Research Center," she said.

"Frederick and Nancy?"

"Yes."

"How are they related?"

"They were husband and wife."

"Looks nice."

"The Shaeffers gave the university the money for this."

"I like it."

Lexi looked at me. "If you give enough money to the university, they'll name something for you."

I looked at Lexi and considered my financial situation. "I have about five dollars I can give them. Is that enough?"

"If you give them five dollars, maybe they'll name a trash can for you."

"How did Frederick and Nancy make their money?"

"Are you familiar with the sex doll industry?"

"No. I know there's a sex doll business in this town, but I don't know anything about it. Joan was planning to ask them for money, but her legal problems arose before she had a chance to do that."

Lexi smiled. "I thought maybe you were a customer."

"No. I've led a sheltered life."

"You never played with dolls?"

"When I was growing up, I thought dolls were for girls."

"You *have* led a sheltered life. I can tell you some things you need to know."

"Thanks. I'm lucky I met you."

Lexi frowned. "No. It's still way too early for you to decide you're lucky you met me."

"I'm sorry. What do you want to tell me?"

"Frederick and Nancy Shaeffer started a sex doll business many years ago. The Shaeffer Sex Dolls Company. When they first started, it was tiny. No factory. No employees other than themselves."

"They started a little business making sex dolls in their home?"

"The story I heard was that they started it in their garage."

"Nancy was helping her husband make sex dolls?"

Lexi nodded. "That's right."

"Doesn't seem like something a woman would be interested in."

"Sometimes people can surprise us."

"Why did she want to do it?"

"She wanted to be an entrepreneur, like her husband. And she was good at it. Both of them had a lot of ability. The company they started is still based in our little college town and now it sells products all over the world."

"Why has the company been so successful?"

"Technology. Shaeffer sex dolls are the most technologically advanced sex dolls in the world."

"According to their advertising?"

"It's not just claims in ads. The Shaeffers have been written about in the press. Their work is pretty well known."

"Is that why the Shaeffers gave money for a science and engineering building? Because they liked technology?"

"They wanted the university to be a world leading center of technology, like their company is."

"They were generous."

"Yes, they were."

I looked at the Shaeffer building. In the distance I could see some students entering the building. I looked at Lexi again. "Can students study sex doll engineering here?"

"I'm not aware of a specific course in sex doll engineering. But they can certainly study technology that can be used in sex dolls. And can be used in other industries also."

I wanted to know more about the Shaeffer family. I wondered how much Lexi knew about them. "Is the Shaeffer family still active in the business?"

"Yes, very much so. Frederick and Nancy are no longer living, but their son, Captain Shaeffer, is chairman of the board of the business now."

"Captain Shaeffer? Why is he called a captain?"

"That's just what everyone calls him. I don't know how that got started."

"You know anybody in the Shaeffer family?"

"I know Captain Shaeffer's daughter. Her name is Britta."

"Britta?"

"Yes. Britta Shaeffer Richardson."

"How do you know her?"

"She's married to our department chairman. Chairman Richardson."

"Does Captain Shaeffer give money to your department?"

"When his daughter got married, Captain Shaeffer gave some money to our department, through his company. That was years ago. He hasn't given us any money recently."

I thought about what Lexi was telling me.

"So in a way your department is in bed with sex dolls," I said.

Lexi frowned. "Don't say that to anyone we meet."

"I won't."

Lexi's expression changed. She looked more like a teacher talking to one of her students. "I see what you mean. Our school is in a town that's the home of a company that makes sex dolls. Our department chairman is married to the daughter of the chairman of the board of the sex doll company. Our department has received money from the sex doll company. And our building was paid for by the founders of the sex doll company. Sex dolls made us what we are. We're all here because of sex."

"I think that would be true even if there were no sex dolls."

"I suppose you're right."

"Does Britta work for the sex doll company?"

"No, she's not in the business. She's a high school science teacher. She's nice. You'd like her."

"I'd like to meet her sometime."

"I'll see if I can arrange something."

"Thanks," I said.

I looked at the area around the building. There was a garden area where lots of long thin green leaves were growing in front of the building. I pointed to the garden. "Nice little garden there," I said.

"Does that look familiar? Those are day lilies. They're almost ready to bloom."

"Looks good."

"I planted those."

"You're the gardener?"

"I didn't work on any of the other landscape, but the real gardeners let me put in the day lilies. They know I like day lilies."

I didn't say anything. I stood there and looked at the building and the landscape. It was a nice addition to the campus.

"Let's go in. I'll introduce you to some people," Lexi said.

We walked up to the entrance and through the front door and into the lobby.

"The physics department shares the building with some other departments," Lexi said.

The building had high ceilings, which gave it a bit of grandeur. A large plaque on the wall in the lobby contained a quote that was apparently said by some famous researcher.

"Our mission is to follow the evidence, wherever that takes us," the plaque said. That was a nice sentiment, and I wanted to believe it. But was it always true? Based on my own experience it might be more accurate to say, "Our mission is to look for research money, wherever that takes us."

"We need to talk to Morgan. Let's go this way," Lexi said.

My mission on my visit was to follow Lexi, wherever that would take me. I followed Lexi down a hall to a reception area where Morgan was sitting behind a desk. We stood near her desk. She smiled at Lexi. "Hello, Lexi."

"Hello, Morgan," Lexi said. "I'd like to introduce you to Doctor Rose."

"We've already met," Morgan said.

"Yes. I ran into her recently on campus," I said.

"You should be more careful," Lexi said.

"Doctor Rose, it's good to see you again," Morgan said. "Welcome to the physics department."

Morgan was conservatively dressed for the office. I looked at her hands. She wasn't wearing a wedding ring. I hadn't looked at her hands when she was in the research office. I had just assumed she was married. Maybe I was wrong.

"How's your cortisol level?" she said.

I smiled. "It's healthy at the moment."

"Was the lecture good?"

"It was interesting," I said.

"I hope you find lots of research money."

"Thank you. I'm an optimist, but I haven't found any yet."

"Remember what Ben Franklin told your mother. Failure is a success that hasn't happened yet."

"Yes, that's right."

I looked around the office. I noticed the walls in the reception area were covered with pictures of people playing baseball.

"Would you like to meet our chairman, Chairman Richardson?" Morgan said.

"If he's available," I said, looking at the pictures of the baseball players.

"Let me look at his calendar and see where he is now."

Morgan turned to her computer and typed on the keyboard
and looked at the screen.

"Oh, too bad, he's in a budget meeting with one of the deans. So
you won't be able to meet him today. Maybe some other time."

I looked at Morgan.

"Who are all the baseball players?"

"Those are all people who played baseball for the university."

"Why do you have them on the wall?"

"That's Chairman Richardson's love," Morgan said. "He's a big
sports fan. I sometimes think he loves sports more than physics."

I looked at the pictures. There were probably more than a hundred on the wall. Maybe two hundred.

"Do you want some great tickets?" Morgan said.

I looked at Morgan. "For the games?"

"Yes. The chairman is a good friend of the university director
of athletics. If the chairman likes you he can get you some great
seats."

"Thanks, Morgan, but I'm not a big sports fan."

"You don't want tickets?"

"I'm not going to watch any games."

"You'll be missing something that's pretty important in this
town."

I looked at Lexi. "Does your chairman know you're related to
Rabbit Maranville? And your middle name is Cartwright?"

"Yes, I told him that," Lexi said. "I told him the first time I met
him, before the department hired me. That might be the reason I
got the job."

"Does Chairman Richardson like to talk about baseball with you?"

"He loves to talk about baseball with me. He has department
parties at his house. Most of the department goes. When I'm there,
he loves to spend his time talking to me about baseball."

"Do you ever get tired of talking about baseball?"

"Sure. When he has department parties, his wife Britta helps
with preparing and serving the food. To get away from the chairman, I like to go into the kitchen and help Britta with the food."

I looked again at the wall and the pictures of all the baseball players. Down almost at the bottom of the wall, below all the baseball players, was a picture of a gorilla.

I looked at Morgan. "Why is there a picture of a gorilla on the wall?"

"That's Morgan. Morgan the gorilla, at the zoo."

"Where did you find that picture?" I said.

"I told our student assistant, Tia, that there was a gorilla with my name at the zoo. Tia printed that from the zoo's web site. Tia said if a gorilla is going to be using my name, then people are going to want to see what she looks like."

"She's nice looking, for a gorilla."

"Yes, I think she promotes the name Morgan rather well."

"She looks happy."

"Maybe somebody just told her where she can get some grant money," Lexi said.

"You should meet our student assistant while you're here. Tia has many talents and she likes to help people. She's a good person to know," Morgan said.

"Yes, I'd like to meet her," I said.

"Let's go say hello," Morgan said, and led Lexi and me to a little room down the hall. The door was open. We stood at the doorway and looked into the room. A large poster on the wall said "*Muñecas sexuales de Shaeffer—las mas avanzadas del mundo.*" A young woman was sitting at a desk working with a desktop computer. She had short straight black hair and dark brown eyes and light brown skin. She looked up from her work.

"Tia, I'd like you to meet Doctor Rose. He's a friend of Lexi and me," Morgan said.

Tia smiled at me. "Hola, soy Tia. Mucho gusto," she said rapidly.

"Doctor Rose, this is Tia. She's an excellent student worker in the physics office," Morgan said.

"I don't even pay Morgan to say that," Tia said less rapidly.

Morgan and Lexi listened as I talked with Tia.

"Hello, Tia. It's good to meet you. What are you studying here at the university?"

"I'm a computer science major."

"I like your poster."

"Some friends gave me that."

"Good luck to you in your studies."

"Thank you. Let me know if I can help you, any time."

"Thanks."

"De nada."

Morgan and Lexi and I walked back to Morgan's desk.

"I told Jack I'd show him the neutrino detector. Is it still in double L 100?" Lexi said.

"Yes, it's still there," Morgan said.

"Can I sign out the key?" Lexi said.

"Sure," Morgan said.

Morgan pulled out some papers from a drawer. Lexi looked at them and signed one. Morgan gave her a key.

"If anybody comes looking for me, tell them I'm in a meeting and I'll contact them later when I'm available. But if Chairman Richardson gets back from his meeting and is looking for me, tell him Stockholm called, and I went to Sweden to pick up my Nobel Prize," Lexi said.

Morgan laughed. "Yes, I'll say that."

Lexi and I left Morgan. I followed Lexi down a hall.

"You have to sign out a key? For your own neutrino detector?" I said.

"It's actually property of the university. The grant money that paid for building it was money that was officially granted to the university."

"So that makes it theirs?"

We came to some stairs.

"Yes. Let's go down to the basement. This building has an elevator, but I never use it," she said.

I followed Lexi down some stairs.

"Double L is lower level," she said.

"Why do you never use the elevator?"

"I never use the elevator because I need the exercise of going up and down the stairs. People don't get enough exercise. Do you agree, doctor?"

"You're right. I need more exercise myself."

We reached the basement. I kept following Lexi as she led me down a hall in the basement.

"It's not like the school is doing anything with the neutrino detector. It's just sitting down here in the basement in a storage room. One of my goals is to get it into my name," she said.

"How would that work?"

"I need to get the university to decommission it. They need to declare it has no value and make it deaccessioned property. Then they need to give it to me."

"Can the university do that?"

"Certainly they can do that."

We arrived at room one hundred. Lexi opened the door. All the lights were off. I stared into the darkness as Lexi reached in with her right hand and found the light switch on the wall and turned on the lights. A meagre amount of light half illuminated the room. Helping people see in the storage room was apparently not a priority of the physics department. We walked in. Room 100 was a big storage room with a lot of strange things in it that looked to me like parts that fell off an unidentified flying object.

Lexi led me over to the neutrino detector. We happened to walk through a spider's web and I got spider silk on my hands. The neutrino detector was about the size of a small closet. It had lots of metal boxes of electronics stacked together and some things that looked like tanks for some kind of liquid.

The neutrino detector was held together by stylish metal exterior panels that had an unusual asymmetrical shape which I thought was attractive. The panels had been painted with a pretty design. It looked like the work of a professional artist. I felt sad that this impressive technological and artistic achievement was imprisoned in the basement in this dark dungeon room.

"This is it. This is the world's greatest portable neutrino detector," Lexi said.

"This is the best neutrino detector I've ever seen," I said.

Lexi smiled. "Have you ever seen another neutrino detector?"

"No."

"Then your comment is not just empty rhetoric. It's really true. Thank you for your support and encouragement."

"I like the pretty exterior panels and the painted design."

"I designed the shape of the exterior panels, and we got some machinists to help build it. And I painted it."

"You have artistic ability."

"I want people to like my machine even if they don't fully understand what it does."

"If the university goes through that process you were talking about and gives it to you, who would be the person at the school who would do that?"

"It's the responsibility of the department chairman to manage property of the department, so he could decommission this. He probably would need some administrators outside the department to go along with him. Which they would do if he asked them."

"Have you spoken to the department chairman about this?"

"Many times."

"And what does he say?"

"He says it's against department policy. As if he has no control over it. Which is ridiculous because he can *make* department policy. He just wants to keep the machine."

"What does he want to do with it?"

"He's an empire builder, as are almost all department chairpeople. He wants the university to patent the technology my team invented and he wants to license the patents to make money for the university."

"That's sort of what you want, right? You want money."

"What he wants is pretty much the opposite of what I want. He wants to charge lots of money to use the technology, which will discourage people from using the machine. I want to promote the use of the machine as widely as possible. He wants to use the machine as a source of money, and spend the money on things other than the machine. I want to use sources of money other than the machine, and spend the money on improving the machine and promoting the use of the machine in new applications with people who aren't familiar with it yet."

"You mentioned the Nobel Prize earlier when you were talking to Morgan. Do you think you could win the Nobel Prize in physics for this?"

"The Nobel Prize in physics? Oh no, certainly not."

"Why not?"

"Because the physics prize committee is looking for people the committee thinks are pioneers in physics. The idea of detecting neutrinos is an old idea. The first neutrino detector was detecting neutrinos back in 1956. So the physics prize people think we're not pioneers. Even though our detector is much better than any previous one."

"That's too bad you can't win a prize for your work."

"I actually think it's possible we could win the Nobel *Peace* Prize for this. But for that to happen we would need other people to be using our invention. And right now we can't get anybody interested in it."

"How could you win the Nobel Peace Prize?"

"One of the sources of neutrinos is nuclear reactors. And nuclear reactors can be used to make the nuclear material that goes into nuclear weapons. Our detector can be used to monitor nuclear reactors. If some nations sign some treaties limiting the production of material for weapons, we have the best way to monitor compliance. Our detector can monitor reactors that everyone knows about, and it can also detect hidden reactors that someone is using clandestinely."

"I remember when I first met you, you mentioned your detector could be used to verify compliance with international arms control treaties."

"This is the best way to do that."

"Why is your detector the best?"

"Our detector is portable. You can easily transport it in a small single engine airplane. So it can go anywhere in the world. Our detector is noninvasive. It doesn't have to go inside the reactor. Our detector is directional, so it can tell whether the neutrinos are coming from the direction of the reactor."

"Clever."

"If you want to detect neutrinos from a reactor, you need to screen out other particles from other sources that might look similar to neutrinos in your detector. The best way to do that is to put the detector underground and let the earth block other particles. Our detector is so small that it's easy to dig a hole in the earth and put the neutrino detector underground."

"Also clever."

"Yes, we are all so clever, except we are not clever enough to find any research money. Our technology is perfect except that nobody is using our machine and we have no money for more research. But other than that, everything is wonderful."

"I have confidence that things will get better for you."

"Well, they couldn't get much worse. Have you seen enough?"

"Yes, I think so."

Lexi turned to walk out. "So that's it. That's the detector."

I followed Lexi out of the room, and turned off the lights and closed the door.

"Do you want to meet Veronica?" she said.

"Your most important coworker?"

"Yes. Coworker and bagel maker. Housemate of Snow."

"Yes. Is she working in this building?"

"She's in a lab down here working on a different project for another research group at the moment. Let's see if she has time to talk with us."

I followed Lexi down the hall and around some corners in the basement. We arrived at the lab. Lexi opened the door and we looked in. It was a large well lit room. On one side a woman was working with a lot of electronic equipment.

"Veronica, do you have a minute? I brought over my new friend. He's new here at the university. I'm showing him around."

Veronica came to the door to greet us. She was wearing a white lab jacket over a dark blue shirt and light grey pants and some kind of dark work shoes. She was wearing safety glasses, and she had her long hair held up with clips on top of her head.

"Hi Lexi," she said.

"Jack, this is Professor Veronica Chebychev."

"Hello Professor," I said.

Veronica smiled. "Everybody calls me Veronica. The only people who call me professor are the sales reps from electronics dealers."

Veronica took off her safety glasses and removed the clips from her hair and let her hair down.

"Veronica, this is Doctor Jackson Rose."

"Jack," I said.

We shook hands.

"It's good to meet you, Jack. Are you a physicist?"

"No, I'm a medical doctor."

"Oh, you're that kind of a doctor."

Veronica was amazingly pretty. She had long black hair which was straight except where she had put a wave in it so it curled down over her forehead and then out to the side of her head and then swooped down to her shoulders. She had a narrow face and big brown eyes and a pretty nose and a wide mouth with perfect teeth and a beautiful smile. She was tall and thin and had long legs. I wondered how many hearts she had broken.

"Thank you for the bagel. It was good," I said to Veronica.

"You tried one of the bagels?"

"I gave him one of the cilantro bagels," Lexi said.

"I'm glad you liked it. When I'm cooking just for myself, I don't use cilantro. But Lexi likes cilantro and I made those bagels for her."

"They're delicious," Lexi said.

"Did Lexi show you the neutrino detector?" Veronica said.

"Yes, I think it's a great achievement," I said.

"I wish you were a grant administrator," Veronica said.

"That was my wish also," Lexi said.

I was thinking about Veronica's name. "Chebychev is a famous name in mathematics," I said to Veronica. Lexi listened while Veronica talked with me.

"Indeed it is. How did you know that?" Veronica said.

"I took a few math courses in college. Are you related to the famous mathematician?" I said.

"My father always liked to say he was a descendant of the mathematician, but in the histories that I've read, the mathematician only had a daughter and no sons. So any descendants would not have carried the Chebychev name."

"That's too bad. I sometimes meet people who claim they're a descendant of some famous scholar, and it generally makes a nice impression."

"Yes, it does."

"And from what I know of the academic world, making a good impression seems to be preferred more than revealing the sometimes disappointing reality."

"You're new here at the university?"

"Yes, that's right."

"You're new and yet you're not naive. I think you'll be successful here."

"No. I'm just a beginner. I'm sure I'm still naive about things. I welcome all the help you can give me."

"I'm afraid I'm not much help. I can't even get money for our group."

"We were just at a class on how to get money. Snow was the speaker. Lexi says she's your housemate."

"Yes, Snow is my housemate."

"Maybe you need to break some ceramic vases."

"Break some ceramic vases?"

"In her lecture today, Snow broke a vase, to illustrate her idea about describing the impact of a research proposal."

"I'm sorry I missed that."

"You're a neutrino researcher with Lexi?"

"I am when there's money for neutrino research. But when there's no money I do other things for other people. Here I'm building some of the electronics for a research project that's trying to detect dark matter."

"Dark matter?"

"It doesn't interact with light or much of anything else, so we call it dark matter. It's sort of like neutrinos, but it's harder to detect."

"Can you get research money for that?"

"Yes. It's popular right now."

"Is your degree in physics?"

"No, I have a PhD in electrical engineering."

"You look like you're working hard."

"I don't have anything to show you today. I'm just putting things together. I'm not running anything today. But if you come back another time I can show you something."

"That would be interesting."

We exchanged contact information.

Lexi and I said goodbye to Veronica and walked back to the stairway. Lexi looked at me and smiled. "I'll race you up the stairs."

"All right."

She ran up the stairs, with me close behind. When we got to the top of the stairs I was breathing hard and my heart was pounding. She was laughing.

"I won," she said.

"Yes, you beat me."

"I think exercise is a good stress reliever."

"If that's true I should just spend my day going up and down the stairs."

We walked towards the reception area.

"I don't want to compete with you in anything important," she said. "I want to help you, if I can."

"You're helping me already."

We arrived back at the reception area. Lexi gave the key back to Morgan.

"Thanks, Morgan," Lexi said.

Lexi looked at me. "Is your heart pounding?"

"A little bit. I think my pulse is returning to normal," I said to Lexi.

Morgan looked at me. "What were you doing?"

"We've been relieving stress, according to the professor here," I said.

"Relieving stress?" Morgan said.

"Getting some exercise using the stairs," I said.

"Did you see the neutrino detector? What did you think?" Morgan said.

"It's great," I said.

"Lexi has achieved something really outstanding," Morgan said.

"I think she'll win a prize someday," I said.

"I don't think anyone will give me a prize. I don't even think anyone will name a gorilla after me," Lexi said.

"Maybe you won't have a gorilla named after you, but I'm sure you'll be recognized for your work," Morgan said.

"Maybe somebody will name a trash can for me," Lexi said.

"A trash can?" Morgan said.

"We were talking earlier about the university naming things. I said if he gives the university five dollars they might name a trash can for him," Lexi said.

Morgan laughed a little bit, then she was serious. "I'm going to name a trash can for both of you right now. And you don't have to donate anything."

She opened her desk drawer and took out some paper and scissors. She cut out a small piece of paper. She wrote on it "The Professor Alexandria Lieblich and Doctor Jackson Rose Trash Can." She took a tape dispenser out of her drawer and pulled off a piece of tape and attached it to her piece of paper. She got up and went to a trash can near her and taped the sign on the trash can. "Now you've been recognized for your work."

Lexi smiled. "Thank you. I'm honored."

"It's a dream come true," I said.

"We need to go. Thanks, Morgan."

"Thanks for your hospitality," I said.

"Come see us any time," Morgan said.

Lexi and I left the reception area and walked out of the building. The physics department was an odd combination of cold machinery and warmhearted people.

Chapter Eleven

"I want to talk with you about something. Do you have time now?" Lexi said to me after we left the Shaeffer building.

"I have time. What do you want to say?"

"We need to talk where nobody else will hear us. Can we go to the outdoor running track?"

"I don't know where that is."

"It's in this direction." She guided me towards the track.

"Is that a good place?"

"Yes. It's open to the university faculty at this time of day. And this is usually not a popular time over there. There probably won't be anybody over there now."

"Good plan."

"I want to get your perspective on something."

"I'm not sure my perspective is terribly valuable."

"When I'm worried about something, I don't want it to be just my worry. I want it to be your worry also."

"That's very generous of you."

"I think that might be another meaning of Lieblich. Woman who is generous."

"I learn something new every day."

The weather was warm with a few clouds in the sky and a soft breeze and low humidity. It felt good to be outside. It took a couple of minutes to walk over to the athletic facilities. We arrived at the track and the gate was open and nobody was using it.

"Let's walk around the oval," Lexi said, and so we did, at a relaxed slow pace. "What did you think of Morgan?"

"She's nice. I like her."

Lexi spoke quietly. "I like her too."

"She seems pretty young."

"Yes. She's about my daughter's age."

"I noticed she wasn't wearing a ring. I guess she's not married."

"That's right. She not married."

"She seems like a nice person. That's all I can say."

"I like her too," Lexi said again. She stopped walking. I stopped also. Lexi looked at me. She didn't look happy.

"Pretty day. It feels good to be outside," I said.

"Jack, I'm worried about Morgan."

"Why are you worried about her?"

"I think she's making some poor choices."

"What poor choices is she making?"

"I'm sorry. I said I wanted to walk and then I stopped walking. Do you want to keep walking?"

"If you want to."

"Let's keep walking."

"Sure."

We started walking again.

"Last week was the annual Western Experimental and Theoretical Physics Conference," Lexi said. "Everybody calls it the WET Conference. Chairman Richardson had been saying for months that he was going to go to the WET Conference. I went to one day of the WET Conference because I wanted to meet people and promote my neutrino detector. When I got there I looked for Chairman Richardson, and I discovered he wasn't registered. He didn't go. After saying for months he was going."

"You think he took a vacation?"

"There's more to the story. Morgan, the person we were just talking to, was on vacation at the same time as the WET Conference."

"Might be just a coincidence."

"When I was at the WET Conference, Britta called me. Britta Shaeffer Richardson, chairman Richardson's wife. She said she was trying to find her husband and thought he was at the conference. I told her no, he was not at the conference."

"He was taking a vacation without his wife?"

"That's called adultery, Jack."

"You don't know he was committing adultery. Maybe he just wanted some time alone."

"He wanted some time alone with Morgan," Lexi said.

"Two people taking a vacation at the same time could be just a coincidence," I said.

"It's not a coincidence. It's the classic love triangle. A man, his wife, and the man's mistress."

"That's not the classic love triangle. And I'm not sure we know what's really going on."

"I like Morgan. I wish she would make better choices."

"Yes. If she's doing what you say she's doing she needs to make better choices. But we don't know that she's doing that. We should find out what's really going on instead of speculating."

"How are we going to do that?"

"I don't know. It's a difficult problem."

"As a doctor you must have faced lots of difficult problems."

"Yes."

"What's the first thing you would do as a doctor facing a difficult problem?"

"Increase my fee."

We didn't say anything for a while. We continued walking around the track.

"Maybe she *is* going to bed with him. But maybe we should stay out of it," I said.

"Why should we stay out of it?"

"They're both adults. They're capable of making their own decisions. Why should we get involved?"

"He's exploiting her, Jack. He's just using her. I don't like to see her exploited like this."

"How do we know he's just using her?"

"You've seen Morgan. You know what she looks like."

"Maybe he loves her."

"Do you think that's likely?"

"I don't know."

"Does he love her, or does he just want what's between her legs."

"I'm not sure."

"I know you're not sure, but which do you think is more likely?"

I considered the possibilities.

"He wants what's between her legs," I said.

"Yes, Jack. He's exploiting her."

I didn't respond. We continued walking.

"And what about the chairman's *wife*? What about Britta? He's being unfaithful to her," Lexi said.

"I don't approve of adultery. But I'm not sure we should get involved in this."

"Are you *sure* we should *not* get involved in this?"

"No, Lexi. I'm not sure of that either. I just don't know that we can help anybody. I don't know what would happen if we tried to help anybody."

"Do you wonder what would happen?"

"I do wonder what would happen. Yes."

"Are you a little bit curious?"

"I am a little bit curious."

"Do you think we might make a difference?"

"I don't know what we might accomplish. Maybe nothing. Maybe something."

"Do you want to find out?"

Lexi had talked me into it.

"Yes, I do want to find out. I want to do the experiment."

"We should talk with Morgan," Lexi said.

"Yes. We need to talk with her. Does she like wine?"

"I'm not sure."

"In vino veritas."

"We can talk to her in a relaxed setting," Lexi said.

"And maybe someone else can join us," I said.

"Yes. And serve some wine. In nice friendly atmosphere."

"And just see what happens."

"Yes. See what happens."

We walked a little more around the track.

"I need to get back to the medical school. Any other problems you want to give me before I go?" I said.

"No, that's it. I don't have any more I can give you today. Sorry."

"Then maybe you'll give me more tomorrow."

"Yes, maybe tomorrow."

"I'll head on back."

We stopped walking.

"Thanks for your interest in my work," Lexi said.

"Thanks for showing me around."

We shook hands.

"Good luck to you in all your work. Break some vases," I said, and left Lexi.

Chapter Twelve

I mentioned to Alyssa what Lexi had told me about Morgan. Alyssa was interested in the problem and wanted to help. She said she would be happy to entertain Lexi and me and Morgan at her house on a night when Irina and Dimitri weren't there, and maybe something positive would result from that. We all agreed to meet for a meal.

About a week later, at about five thirty in the evening, I was sitting with Alyssa on a comfortable sofa in her large living room in her nice old house. Alyssa's other tenants, Irina and Dimitri, had gone out for dinner and a movie. Lexi and Morgan were coming over.

Alyssa's living room had a wood burning fireplace which she never used, and it had a large window almost floor to ceiling, looking out on her carefully tended lawn. She had a large video monitor in the room and a laptop computer. The monitor was showing Madame Butterfly by Puccini, with English subtitles. I had seen Madame Butterfly before and was vaguely familiar with it.

Alyssa's dog Abraham was lying on his cushion on the floor. He didn't appear to be very interested in Madame Butterfly. He was calm and welcoming with visitors, so he was a good match for Alyssa's guests.

Lexi gave Morgan a ride to Alyssa's house. They arrived and said hello. They brought in some food which they added to the food already in the kitchen, and then they joined us in the living room and found comfortable places to sit. Alyssa paused the opera so we could talk.

"I made some meat loaf with tomato sauce. I didn't put any salt in it. I put cilantro in it. Morgan tasted it already. She says it's edible," Lexi said.

"It's good. I like it," Morgan said.

"What exactly is cilantro?" I said.

"It's an herb made from the leaves of the coriander plant. Coriander is good for you. But don't tell anybody else that," Lexi said.

"Why not?" I said.

"Some people don't believe something can be good for you and also taste good."

"How is coriander good for you?"

"It helps your body in some way. That was in the news. I don't remember everything the news report said. I just know it helps you."

"Does it help you get research money?"

Lexi smiled. "Maybe that was it. Maybe it helps you get research money."

"Do you put cilantro in everything?" I said.

"Oh no, it doesn't taste good in everything."

"How do you decide what tastes good with cilantro."

"You have to try it. You have to do the experiment."

"Did you say you didn't put any salt in your tomato sauce?" Alyssa said.

"I don't like salt. When you taste the tomato sauce, I think you'll like it, without salt," Lexi said.

"It's probably healthier without salt. But you probably don't want me to tell anybody that," Alyssa said.

"Exactly right. Don't tell anybody that. If you say something is healthy, some people think that means it tastes bad," Lexi said.

Alyssa looked at Morgan. "Morgan, forget I said it was healthy."

Morgan smiled. "I'm not afraid of healthy food."

Lexi looked at Morgan. "You're a brave woman."

"Sometimes," Morgan said.

"I'm sure it will be good," Alyssa said to Lexi. "Before we eat, I thought we might want to listen to some beautiful music." Alyssa looked at Morgan. "Would you like to do that?"

"Yes, we need some beautiful music," Morgan said.

"We're listening to Madame Butterfly. Would you like to listen to Madame Butterfly?" Alyssa said.

"Yes, definitely," Morgan said.

Alyssa unpaused the opera.

"Morgan, would you like a little wine as we listen?"

"Yes, please."

Alyssa went to a table where she had put a wine bottle and some glasses and some other things. She poured a glass of wine for Morgan and gave it to her.

"Who else wants a little wine as we listen?" Alyssa said.

Morgan was the only person who wanted it. Alcohol just makes me sleepy, so I'm not much of a drinker. Lexi was Morgan's driver, so Lexi wanted to stay sober. I don't know why Alyssa wasn't drinking. Maybe she thought she could help Morgan more if she was sober. Alyssa offered grape juice or water to those who didn't want wine. Lexi and I took some of the water. Alyssa took some grape juice for herself.

We all watched and listened to Madame Butterfly together. We watched and listened for a while and Alyssa got up briefly and offered some more wine. Morgan took a little more. Alyssa passed around some snacks. We sampled the snacks and listened to the beautiful music of Giacomo Puccini.

The video came to the end of a scene and Alyssa put it on pause. "I love Puccini," Alyssa said.

"I don't know the story of Madame Butterfly very well," I said.

"It's a sad story. The leading man in the story is pretty slimy. He pursues the leading woman in the story and she falls in love with him and then he breaks her heart," Alyssa said.

"That is a sad story," I said.

"Do you like opera?" Alyssa said to Morgan.

"Yes, I do, but I haven't seen very much of it. I don't know very much about it," Morgan said.

"Some operas can be artificial and contrived, but some can really open up and expose human nature. Some operas can speak the truth in a powerful way through beautiful music and a compelling story," Alyssa said.

"What truth is Puccini trying to speak to us in Madame Butterfly?" Morgan said.

"Maybe he's saying some men in some circumstances will hurt women," Alyssa said softly.

Morgan didn't say anything.

"Madame Butterfly in a way reminds me of my youth and some of the people I knew when I was young. Do you want to hear my own tale of woe, or am I boring you?" Alyssa said.

"No, you're not boring me. I want to hear your tale of woe," Morgan said.

"When I was in college as an undergraduate, I was pretty seriously involved with a guy. At least it was pretty serious on my part. I was in love with him. We were having sex pretty regularly. I was using an IUD so I wouldn't get pregnant. I loved him and I wanted to marry him and have children with him. He kept saying not yet. Finally I learned he had another lover he was seeing also," Alyssa said.

"What did you do?" Morgan said.

"I stopped having sex with him. I went to my doctor. I told her to take out the IUD and put it in a box. Which she did. Then I went to talk to my guy. I showed him the IUD. I said let's become parents together."

"What did he say?" Morgan said.

"He wasn't interested. So we broke up. I don't know what happened to him after that. He was just using me as a container. Just like somebody takes a pitcher of water and pours part of it into a glass. He was emptying something from his body and draining it into my body. That gave him pleasure. That's all he wanted. Nothing more than that."

"You did the right thing," Lexi said.

"What do you think, Jack?" Alyssa said.

"I think you did the right thing."

Alyssa picked up an open bottle of wine. "Morgan, would you like some more?" Alyssa said.

"Yes, please."

Alyssa filled Morgan's glass.

"Do you want to watch some more Puccini?" Alyssa said.

"I would like to see a little more," Morgan said.

Alyssa started the video again. We watched some more Madame Butterfly. Morgan drank her wine. The video came to the end of a scene and Alyssa switched it off again.

"I'm getting hungry. Is everybody ready for some food?" Alyssa said.

Everybody said yes. We all went into the kitchen and got the food and heated up some of it in the microwave. Abraham followed us into the kitchen.

"Are you hungry, Abraham?" Alyssa said to Abraham.

Abraham looked at Alyssa and raised one eyebrow. Alyssa got out some dog food and put it in Abraham's bowl on the floor. Abraham politely waited for Alyssa to finish and then he scarfed his food down.

We brought the human food into the dining room and served ourselves. Alyssa had put out some plates and some place settings. We all sat down. Alyssa was across from Morgan and I was across from Lexi.

Alyssa looked at Morgan. "When I have guests I usually ask one of them whether they want to give a blessing. Would you like to give a blessing?"

"Is it all right if I give a Buddhist one? I'm not that religion, but my yoga teacher taught it to me and I like it."

"Yes, we can all benefit from it I'm sure."

Morgan bowed her head and said something in a foreign language I didn't understand.

We all started eating. Morgan ate very slowly.

"How do you like working in the physics department?" Alyssa said to Morgan.

"I like woking with Professor Lieblich. She's nice."

"And the other people? Are they nice?"

Morgan looked unhappy. "I think most of them are."

"But not all of them?"

Morgan looked down at the table.

"I don't know," she said. "I'm not sure."

"Anything you want to talk about?" Alyssa said softly.

Morgan looked at Alyssa.

"I was thinking about what you said about your experience with that man," Morgan said softly.

"What was your reaction to it?"

"I feel like maybe I'm having a similar experience."

"That can happen to anyone."

"Alyssa, I feel like maybe I've made a mistake."

"Anyone can make a mistake."

Morgan looked at Lexi and then at me and then at Alyssa again.

"This has to be just between ourselves. You can't tell anybody else," Morgan said.

"I won't tell anybody," Alyssa said.

"We won't tell anyone else," I said.

"Nobody else," Lexi said.

"You swear?" Morgan said.

"Yes," Lexi and Alyssa and I said.

Lexi and I listened as Morgan talked with Alyssa.

"You know the chairman of the physics department?" Morgan said.

"Yes, I've met him," Alyssa said.

"Well, I just . . . I just . . . I don't know what to say. I just fell for him. I just couldn't help it. I just fell for him."

"And now you wonder if maybe it's not going in a good direction."

"Yes, that's right. I wonder if maybe it's not going in a good direction."

"It's easy to fall for someone, Morgan. It can happen to anyone."

"What can I do?"

"I know what I would do. But you have to make that decision for yourself. Nobody else can make it for you."

"But I fell for him. I was swept up by his attention to me. He captured me."

"Men will do that, Morgan. Men are just like vacuum cleaners. They'll sweep you up."

Morgan looked down at the table and didn't say anything.

Alyssa spoke to her very softly. "You don't want to be just a container for somebody. You don't want that," Alyssa said.

"No, I don't want that," Morgan said, just barely above a whisper.

We were all silent for a while. Then, tentatively, Alyssa and Lexi started to talk about other things, and I joined the conversation.

We talked about college sports. Lexi said the women's volleyball team might be good this year. We talked about how many games the volleyball team was going to win. Alyssa said at least sixteen. I said I didn't know they played that many games. Alyssa looked at me like I was a sports idiot. Which of course I am. I tried to remember what Alyssa said, so that if anybody asked me about sports later, I would be able to sound intelligent.

Then we talked about baseball, which seemed to be the big sport in this town. Was the baseball team going to find good replacements for the stars who were going to turn pro? Certainly, we agreed. I think if you're going to agree on something related to your favorite team, you should be optimistic. Apparently other people shared my view.

"The key is recruiting on the west coast," Alyssa said.

"The west coast? Why is that the key?" I said.

"Traditionally that's been a good source of players for us," Alyssa said.

Morgan listened and didn't say anything. We ate all the food and talked for a while. Lexi and Morgan said it was getting late and they thanked Alyssa for a great evening and they left. I said good night to Alyssa and Abraham, and went up to my storage closet.

I wanted to help Morgan. Unfortunately, wanting to do something and being able to do something are two entirely different things.

Chapter Thirteen

Lexi called me unexpectedly later that week.

"I'm going to call Britta and invite her to have some pizza with us at a popular place near the campus," Lexi said.

"Britta Shaeffer Richardson?" I said.

"Yes. Chairman Richardson's wife. Daughter of Captain Shaeffer."

"Great."

"I already told her you wanted to meet her."

"Thank you. What did she say?"

"She said that's fine. It doesn't surprise her when people want to meet her. Everybody wants to know someone in the Shaeffer family."

"Does she have time to meet everyone who wants to meet her?"

"No, but she'll make time for you. I told her you're going to do sex research."

I gave Lexi some times when I would be available. Lexi said she would talk to Britta and set up something and contact me with the plan.

A few days later I joined Lexi at A Slice Is Nice. They sell pizza by the slice, and have an indoor dining room and also a large screened porch with tables and chairs where people like to sit and eat their pizza when the weather is nice. It's across the street from the campus, so there are always some students there.

Britta had agreed to meet us there. We waited a few minutes near the entrance and then Britta arrived. Lexi introduced me to Britta and we bought some slices of hot pizza and we went out on the porch and found a table off in a corner, away from the crowd. We sat at our table and ate and talked. A Slice Is Nice has a license to sell beer, but we were just drinking water with our pizza.

Britta was thin and medium height. She had brown eyes and short light brown hair and a face that was pleasant but not beautiful. She was wearing a pale blue summer dress with a drop waist, and light grey shoes with soft white soles. She was wearing glasses with big square black frames. I'm not a style expert but I thought she looked fashionable.

Lexi listened while Britta and I talked.

"Am I what you expected?" Britta said to me.

"What do you mean?"

"Everybody knows my family is making sex dolls. Sometimes people think I must be some kind of siren, some kind of hypersexual person myself. But I'm not. I'm not even working in the family business. I'm a high school science teacher."

"I wasn't expecting a siren. But I agree with you. People can have unrealistic expectations. When you were growing up, did people have unrealistic expectations about your family?"

"When I was growing up, my classmates in school knew my dad was making sex dolls and they all wanted to meet him. They thought he was some kind of wild party person. But he's a businessman. Making sex dolls is a business. I'm not saying it's a delicate refined enterprise. It's not. It's a coarse business where the customers often have a harsh view of women. But my parents were normal parents. My childhood was normal."

"What was it like growing up in your family?"

"I remember we had dogs when I was growing up. My dad loves dogs. We had a dog that loved to chase tennis balls. He named her Penny. We would throw a tennis ball and Penny would sprint after it and bring it back to us. Unfortunately Penny didn't live very long. Penny died of cancer at a young age. I think my dad still misses that dog."

"Yes, people can become really attached to a dog."

"And growing up, my dad took us to baseball games. My dad loves baseball. He's a big sports fan. When you live in a college town, that means college sports. He loves the university baseball team. We saw lots of their games when I was growing up. Do you like baseball?"

"I'm not a big sports fan, but I know college sports are important in a college town," I said.

Britta didn't say anything. She munched on some pizza. I ate some also.

"Am I what you expected?" I said.

"I wasn't sure what to expect. I heard you were a sex researcher. Are you really a sex researcher?"

"I'm in academic medicine. I know how to do sex research. I don't have any money for it now, but I'm going to find some, and then I'm going to do sex research."

"Is he really a sex researcher?" Britta said to Lexi.

"He has an offer from the medical school saying he can run his own lab doing sex research. He's looking for money for it, as he said. He's a real researcher and he's also a real medical doctor. You seem doubtful. Why are you doubtful?" Lexi said.

"Because my relatives are in a type of sex business, and so my relatives and I meet all kinds of people, including lots of people who claim to be sex experts. Most of them are trying to make money from being a sex expert. They're trying to sell something. But when I get to know those people, I find out that being a sex expert is just a title they gave themselves. People can call themselves things that they really aren't."

"Jack is the real deal," Lexi said.

"Are you trying to sell something?" Britta said to me.

"I'm trying to get research money."

"How are you trying to get research money?"

"I'm trying to find people who will give it to me."

"You're not selling products and services?"

"I'm not selling products or services. Unless you think doing research is selling something."

"What will you do with the research money when somebody gives it to you?"

"I'll use it for research projects. I can use technology such as noninvasive imaging to look at people's brains."

"While people are having sex?"

"Not necessarily while they're having sex with a partner, but definitely during some form of stimulation. Maybe when they're watching an explicit movie, or maybe when they're using a vibrator, for example."

We ate some more pizza.

Lexi listened while Britta and I talked.

"Jack, I've never met a real academic sex researcher. So I want to hear your opinions about sex," Britta said.

"I'm happy to answer anything if I know the answer. It's true that I know how to do sex research, but that doesn't mean I know everything about sex."

"Lexi knows me pretty well. She knows I speak directly. I say what's on my mind," Britta said.

"That's how I talk also," I said.

"My relatives have been pretty successful in the sex doll business, if you measure success by how much money is coming in. But I sometimes wonder about that. Even though I love my dad, sometimes it bothers me that he's in the sex doll business."

"Why does it bother you?"

"In the sex doll business, someone can dress up a sex doll and try to make it unique if they want to, but fundamentally a sex doll is just offering a man an artificial object where he can rub the skin of his genitals. It's a machine made like the body of a woman."

"Yes."

"Really only like part of the body of a woman."

"Yes."

"And it doesn't have the brain of a woman or the personality of a woman. It just tries to replace the body. Part of the body."

"Yes."

"Is that really all that some men want? In this great big wide wonderful world where so many different pleasures exist, do some men really just want a place where they can rub themselves? You're a sex researcher. What's the answer to that?"

"I don't know, Britta."

"You don't know?"

"I don't know. Sorry."

"You don't sound like the experts I usually meet."

"Why not?"

"They have all the answers. If they don't know, they make something up."

"I don't have enough imagination to make something up."

"I think I'm going to like you," Britta said.

"You're asking me a general question about human nature. Sex research can't really study human nature in general. When I formulate a research question, I have to study a specific question that I can answer in an experiment."

"Maybe it's not a research question. But if you have any thoughts about it, I'm interested in your thoughts."

"Maybe some men just want a machine. Or maybe they want more than that, but that's all they can get," I said.

"What do they really want?"

"Maybe they really want human contact."

"You mean they really want love?"

"Not love. Just human contact."

"They want a living sex doll?"

"Maybe."

"Somehow that seems sad to me," Britta said.

She looked away. I thought maybe she wanted to talk about something personal.

"You don't have to talk about this, but if you've had a disappointing personal experience, if I can help you or if Lexi can help you, we're here to help you," I said.

Britta looked at me. "Do you have a magic wand that can make a problem go away?" she said very softly.

"I didn't bring my magic wand today."

"What kind of doctor are you? First I ask you a question and you say you don't know. Then you tell me you didn't bring your magic wand," Britta said, still speaking softly.

"I'm sorry," I said.

"Do you know how to be reassuring? I think they teach that in medical school."

"Yes, that's right. I remember I was in class that day," I said.

"My husband, the chairman of the physics department, is having some sort of inappropriate relationship with someone. It's obvious. He tells me he's working late and I don't question him. But sometimes I need to talk to him when he's working late and I call him and he doesn't answer. And sometimes he tells me he's at a conference and I don't question him about that either. But sometimes I need to talk to him when he's at a conference, and I leave a message at the conference for him to call me and the conference tells me he's not registered."

"I'm sorry to hear that."

"He acts strangely at home also. Instead of wanting to be with me and do things with me, he's developed an interest in sending and receiving text messages. He tells me it's work but this is something relatively new. I don't think it's work."

"I'm sorry you're having problems with him."

"You can't repeat this to anyone," Britta said.

"I won't repeat this to anyone," I said.

"You can't repeat this either, Lexi," Britta said.

"I won't repeat it to anyone," Lexi said.

"I suspect I know who it is," Britta said.

"You suspect you know who it is?" I said.

"It's pretty obvious, I think. You've met some of the people in the department. Lexi said she had introduced you to some people," Britta said.

"Yes," I said.

"Is there anyone in the department that you think is really sexy?" Britta said.

I didn't want to answer that. I wanted to know Britta's opinion. So I didn't say anything.

Britta paused, and then she said, "Did you meet Morgan?"

"Yes," I said.

"Morgan could be a model for a sex doll. She's top heavy," Britta said.

"Yes," I said.

"Big breasts. She's young and never had children, so she looks as sexy as anyone can look. She has a nice face, pretty eyes, nice legs," Britta said.

"So you think . . ." I said.

"I think my husband is using her as a human sex doll. He just wants a place where he can rub himself, and she's got a place like that and she lets him rub in there."

I had promised Morgan I wouldn't reveal what Morgan told me, so I couldn't tell Britta she was right. But I also couldn't tell her she was wrong. That would be untrue, and I wasn't going to lie to her. So I didn't say anything.

"We can't help you solve any mysteries. We're not in the detective business," Lexi said.

"Jack, why are men such pieces of scum?" Britta said. She wasn't angry. She seemed calm, and curious, like she really wanted to know the answer to her question.

"I don't know, Britta."

"Can you research that? Is that a research question?"

"I don't know how I would study that."

"Because if you could study that, I would give you some money to do the research."

"Thank you for the offer. I appreciate that."

"I think other women would also give you money if you could study that question."

"I'm sorry, Britta. I don't think I can do an experiment that will answer that question."

She looked unhappy. "What a mess," she said, with some irritation in voice.

"We understand how you feel, Britta," Lexi said.

"You're going through a difficult time now. But I'm sure things will get better for you. This problem will get resolved in one way or another and your life will get better," I said.

"Thank you. You're reassuring. You were in class when they taught that," Britta said.

"Yes."

"In some ways my husband is a really smart guy," she said, now not irritated. "He was able to become an expert in physics, and that's not easy to do. This just proves that intellectual ability and good judgment are not quite the same thing."

"They're completely unrelated," Lexi said.

"Are you going to do anything?" I said to Britta.

"I don't know. Maybe. I talked to a divorce lawyer. I don't know. We'll see."

Britta paused. Lexi and I didn't say anything.

"He's not all bad," Britta said. "I think about his good side, his good qualities. He's a good parent. He's good with our daughter. We had a pretty good life together before he started doing this."

Britta was giving us a carefully balanced analysis of her marriage. To me it seemed scientific, like you would expect from a science teacher.

"He could have had . . . we could have had . . . a really great life together. So much potential. He just wasted it. It's such a waste."

"No life is ever wasted, because everyone can always serve as a bad example," Lexi said.

Britta smiled. "You're right. My husband is serving as a bad example."

We ate some more pizza and talked about other things and tried to relax and be happy for a while, then we said goodbye and went our separate ways. I wondered how long Britta would remain married to Chairman Richardson.

Chapter Fourteen

Morgan called me.

"Doctor Rose, I'm going to talk to Chairman Richardson."

"Good."

"The next time I see him I'm going to ask him what he wants to do. About him and me. Do you know what I'm talking about?"

"Yes. I remember what you said at Alyssa's house."

"Do you think I'm doing the right thing?"

"Yes."

"Tell me, Mister Sex Expert, why is everything so complicated?"

"You want things to be simpler?"

"Yes."

"Talking to Chairman Richardson will help you."

"Will it make me happy?"

"It will help you make your life simpler."

"I'm going to do it. Wish me luck."

"Good luck, Morgan."

"Thanks, Doctor Rose."

Chapter Fifteen

Britta called me a few days later.

"Hello Jack, this is Britta. Have you got a minute? I don't want to interrupt you if you're busy saving lives."

"We have other people here that save all the lives. I don't know them very well. I pass them in the hall sometimes. I smile at them and say 'how's it going?' They don't stop and talk to me. I guess that's because they're busy saving lives. What's on your mind?"

"I told my daughter, Sophia, that I'd met you. I told her you were an interesting person to talk to."

"It's always a mistake to raise people's expectations. How old is your daughter?"

"She's twelve. She thinks she might want to become a doctor when she grows up. Either a doctor or a dancer."

"Two excellent careers."

"She wants to meet you."

"So she can give me advice about dancing? I'd love to talk with her."

"She wants to ask you about being a doctor."

"I don't have any dramatic stories I can tell her about saving lives here at the medical center. Medicine can be a satisfying career, but it's not always exciting."

"She needs to hear that."

"I would be happy to talk to Sophia."

"Can we meet at A Slice Is Nice?"

"Yes. That's perfect."

We agreed on a day and time, and said goodbye. I wondered what Sophia would be like.

Britta and Sophia were waiting for me near the entrance when I arrived at A Slice Is Nice.

"Sorry to keep you waiting," I said.

"We're early," Britta said. Britta was wearing a pale lavender sweater over a white blouse, with cream colored pants and light grey shoes with white soles. I'm not a style expert but I thought she looked good in pastels.

"Jack, this is my daughter, Sophia. Sophia, this is Doctor Rose," Britta said.

Sophia and I shook hands. Sophia was almost as tall as her mother. She was thin and had brown eyes and long straight brown hair, a little darker than her mother's. A thin light blue headband kept her hair off her face. She was wearing a white sweatshirt that said Toronto Dance Theatre in blue letters, with light grey pants and soft grey shoes with white soles.

"I'm happy to meet you, Sophia. I like your sweatshirt," I said.

"It's one of my favorites," she said.

"Let's get our pizza," Britta said.

We went to the counter and got some slices of hot pizza.

"Where would you like to sit?" Britta said to Sophia.

"Let's sit out on the porch," Sophia said.

We went out to the porch and found a table away from the crowd and sat down and made ourselves comfortable.

Sophia had some sort of a shopping bag with her.

"Have you been shopping, Sophia?" I said.

"Yes. We were at the discount store. Want to see what I got?"

"Yes. What did you get?"

"Look."

Sophia reached into her bag and brought out a plastic bottle of something.

"What is it?" I said.

"It's bubble bath. It has a little bit of a scent to it. Want to smell the scent?"

Sophia unscrewed the top and let me smell the scent. It wasn't very strong. It was like some sort of berries, maybe raspberries. I liked it.

"That's nice, Sophia. Do you like bubble bath?" I said.

"Bubble bath is the best form of soap. And everyone needs soap. When I take a bubble bath then I feel good. I know its going to be a good day. I think if you have soap everything will be fine."

"Sophia, your mother says you like to dance. Is that right?"

Sophia smiled. "I love dancing. Dancing is fun."

"What kind of dancing do you do? Are you a ballet dancer?"

"No, I don't like ballet dancing. Standing on your toes is too hard. I like modern dancing."

"What's your favorite thing to do when you dance?"

"I like the turns. I like to spin. Fast. I like doing fast spins."

"That seems like that would be hard to do. Is that hard to do?"

"You have to know the technique. And it takes practice. But it's fun. Want me to show you?"

There was nobody sitting near us, so she wasn't going to crash into anybody if she showed us a spin. But I wasn't sure Britta would approve. I looked at Britta.

"Let's ask your mother," I said.

Britta looked at Sophia.

"Just show us your technique slowly, Sophia. This isn't a good place to do full speed dancing," Britta said.

Sophia got up out of her chair and stood beside our table.

"It's pretty simple, really. You stand like this, and then you step and transfer your weight like this, and you keep your head still like this while you turn your body and step like this, and then you rotate your head all the way and turn your body to complete your spin," Sophia said, and showed us how to spin.

"I think that takes talent," I said.

"It's fun," Sophia said and sat down again.

"Does your mother ever make any videos of you dancing?"

"Yes. She makes good ones."

"I'll send you some," Britta said.

"I'd love to see them."

We ate some pizza, then Britta listened while Sophia and I talked.

"Do you think you want to be a dancer when you grow up?" I said.

"Maybe, but I'm thinking about being a doctor also. Do you like being a doctor?"

"I like it. But that doesn't mean everybody would like it. You need to think about the things doctors do, and ask yourself whether you would like doing those things."

"What are some of the things doctors do?"

"They do lots of things. One thing they do is check someone's pulse. Do you know how to check someone's pulse?"

"Show me how to do that."

I extended my left arm towards Sophia and rested the back of my hand and my elbow on the table.

"Hold your fingers like this, right here in this spot," I said to Sophia. She put her fingers on my wrist.

"Like this?"

"Can I move them a little bit?"

I moved her fingers to a slightly different place.

"Now press here. Can you feel my pulse?"

Sophia pressed on my wrist. "No. I don't think you have a pulse."

"Move your fingers slightly and try to find the spot where you can feel it."

Sophia moved her fingers slightly, looking for my pulse.

"There it is," she said excitedly, and smiled.

"Does it have a steady beat?"

"I think so."

"Then you can say it has a regular rhythm."

She held her fingers on my wrist. "Yes. It has a regular rhythm."

"That's good, Sophia. You're learning to do what doctors do."

"What else do doctors do? Can you show me anything else?"

"Have you ever heard of percussing?"

"No."

"That's tapping on someone's chest."

"Why would you want to tap on someone's chest?"

"If you tap on something that's full of air, you can tell it's full of air. And if you tap on something that's not full of air, maybe because it has fluid in it, you can tell it's not full of air. And that's useful information. And you can learn that just by tapping."

"I want to learn how to do that."

"I'll show you on myself. First I put the left hand where I want it. I put the palm and fingers flat against the chest like this."

I put my left hand flat against my chest.

"Now I take the right hand and use the finger tips to tap on a finger of my left hand on the chest, like this."

I showed her how to tap.

"You can try it on me if you want to. Stand behind me and try it on the back of my chest."

She got up out of her chair and stood behind me and practiced percussing.

"That's good, Sophia. I think you have talent."

She sat down again.

"Do you like doing doctor things?" I said.

"Doctor things are interesting. I don't know. I love dancing. I don't know what I want to do."

"You still have plenty of time to decide."

"I'm already twelve."

I asked Sophia about school, and she and Britta and I talked about school and ate our pizza. We finished eating and Britta and Sophia said they had to go, and we said goodbye. I hoped Britta would remember to send me some videos of Sophia dancing.

Chapter Sixteen

A few days later I got a call from Morgan in the morning at the start of the school day.

"Hello, Doctor Rose? It's me. Morgan."

"Hello Morgan."

"Am I interrupting an important meeting?"

"No, not at all. How's life?"

"I feel wounded today."

"Are you having symptoms?"

"I'm having my symptoms that we talked about. I'm at home. I can't go to work."

"I'm sorry you're not feeling well."

"But that's not why I'm calling. I'm calling because I talked with Chairman Richardson."

"What did you tell him?"

"I told him that this has gone on like this long enough and we need to get married if we're going to continue doing this."

"What did he say?"

"He said he can't marry me because he doesn't want to break up his home."

"I see."

"He's been just using me as a container."

"It looks that way."

"I feel wounded."

"I'm sorry you've been hurt."

"I don't want to work for him anymore, Doctor Rose. I've lost all respect for him. He's a piece of slime."

"I understand how you feel."

"Doctor Rose, why are men such pieces of scum?"

"That's a question that other people have also asked."

"Doctor Rose, you know how to do sex research. Can you do some research to answer that question?"

"I'm sorry, Morgan. I can do sex research but I don't know how I would study that exact question."

"I think women would give you money for your research if your research could answer that question."

"I agree with you, Morgan. I just don't know how I would study that question."

"I want to transfer to another job."

"That's a good idea."

"I think I'll be able to go to the office tomorrow."

"Good."

"I'll get started on the transfer process tomorrow."

"Let me know if I can help you."

"Thanks."

Chapter Seventeen

The next day I got another call from Morgan, early in the morning, a little before the start of the school day.

"I'm sorry to bother you again, Doctor Rose."

"I'm happy to talk to you."

"I'm at school today. Lexi's not available right now and I have a slight problem. Can we meet somewhere? I need to talk to you. Not just on the phone. And not in the physics department."

"Yes, we can meet. Do you want to meet at A Slice Is Nice?"

"Yes. That's good. How soon can we meet?"

"In a few minutes if you like."

"Yes. In a few minutes."

A Slice Is Nice starts serving their pizza at seven o'clock in the morning. I don't usually want to eat pizza in the morning, but sometimes when I'm trying to work out problems I feel like it's exactly what I need. The availability of good pizza when I need it is one of the (many) charms of this town.

I went over to A Slice Is Nice. Morgan was already over there, waiting for me near the entrance. We said hello, and I went up to the counter and got a slice of pizza.

Morgan said she didn't want anything.

"You're not having anything?" I said.

"I feel too sick to eat anything," Morgan said.

"Are you still having your symptoms?"

"No, those are better today."

We went out to the porch and found a table away from the crowd.

"Are you starting to look for another job?" I said.

"Yes. But to do that I want to find my employment records. I want a copy of the application I filled out when I was hired to work for the department. That has all my past history with addresses and phone numbers and everything. And I want to find my employment record for the time I've been with the department. I want my salary history, my evaluations, everything I need to transfer."

"Yes, I think you need that."

"But I can't find it anywhere."

"You don't have a copy?"

"Some things I saved but I apparently didn't keep a complete copy of everything, because when I look at what I have I see I'm missing a lot of things."

"That could be a problem."

"I'm thinking Chairman Richardson should have my file in his office, right? He's my supervisor, so he should have my employment records."

"Yes, I think so."

"But when I look in our office files I can't find anything like that."

"Can you ask him where the records are?"

"He's away at a conference today and tomorrow, so I can't easily ask him. And even if he were right here, I wouldn't want to ask him. I don't want to discuss my career plans with him. He's a piece of slime."

"I don't know what to tell you."

She looked down at the table and frowned. I hoped she could think of some other possibilities. She looked at me again.

"There's only one other place the records could be," she said.

"Where's that?"

"The chairman has a cabinet in the back of his office behind a plastic fig tree. He uses it like a private cabinet. He's the only person who has the key to it. I don't have the key."

"Can you look there?"

"I don't know how I would open it."

"Call maintenance."

"Can maintenance open a private cabinet?"

"If it's in his office, then it's university property, isn't it? And you work for him, so it seems appropriate for you to need to have it open."

"Will they have to drill out the lock?"

"They probably have some kind of master key or something."

"Can you stay with me in the office while they're opening it? I want someone in addition to myself who can say what happened if there are any questions."

"I'm happy to do it."

Morgan called maintenance. She told them her name and where she worked and what she needed. They said their workers were all busy at the moment but they thought somebody would be available to help us soon and they thought it would be no problem to open the cabinet. Morgan asked them to meet us at the Shaeffer building reception area.

We walked over to the Shaeffer building. Morgan took me back to the chairman's office and showed me the cabinet. It was a large metal cabinet, about five feet wide and about six feet tall and about two feet deep, with two doors. The color was dingy light grey. I'm not a decorator, but I thought the cabinet was ugly and the color clashed with the rest of the office. I liked the plastic fig tree in front of the cabinet, because it covered up some of the cabinet. The office needed about three more plastic fig trees.

I wondered what was inside the cabinet. We went to the reception area to wait for maintenance.

In a few minutes, Lucy came over from the maintenance department. She was the first female maintenance worker I had met at the university. I wondered how she got started working in maintenance.

Lucy was short and stocky and had long blonde hair which she wore in a pony tail. She looked young, probably still in her twenties. She walked quickly and seemed energetic. She was carrying a small metal tool box. She looked at Morgan and then she looked at me.

"Hey guys, how's your day going? I'm Lucy." She looked at Morgan again. "Are you Morgan? Are you the one having problems with a lock on your cabinet?"

"Yes. We want to open it and we don't have the key," Morgan said.

"You guys are in luck. Because I happen to know how to open cabinets. Show me what you got."

We guided Lucy to the cabinet.

"This is going to be easy," Lucy said. "About twenty years ago the university replaced all the old cabinets with a newer model. And when they did that, the people who made the purchase order knew that people who use cabinets tend to lose keys. That's been shown by experience going back years and years."

"So not having the key is an old problem?" Morgan said.

"You ever study American history? When George Washington was in the White House, he lost the key to his cabinet."

"I didn't know that."

"So when the university replaced all the old cabinets, the people who made the purchase order were aware of the problem. And they solved the problem in the easiest possible way."

"What's the easiest possible way?"

"They only bought cabinets with one of eight different locks. If you have the right set of eight different keys, you can open any cabinet lock on campus."

"That seems like that doesn't provide much security."

"You're not supposed to keep anything valuable in your cabinets. A cabinet is not a place to put your diamond necklace. You should only keep the typical boring official university stuff in your cabinet. And if you don't follow that rule, sooner or later you're going to have problems."

Lucy opened her tool box and brought out a ring of keys.

"We're going to find the key that opens your cabinet," she said.

She started putting each key into the lock and seeing whether the key opened the lock. After a few tries she found the key that worked, and she unlocked the cabinet and opened one of the doors a little bit.

She looked at us and smiled. "There you go," she said.

"That's a big help," Morgan said.

"Thanks very much," I said.

Lucy took the key off the ring of keys. "This is my only copy of this key but I'll make a duplicate back at the shop and I'll send it to you."

"Thanks," Morgan said.

Lucy put the ring of keys and the individual key back in her tool box.

"Wait. Before you go, I want to ask you something," I said.

"Sure," Lucy said.

"How did you get started doing maintenance?"

"I've always liked working with my hands. My parents run their own book binding business. They do a lot of thesis binding for students at school here. And they rebind some library books that need repairs. When I was growing up they taught me how to do book binding, and I helped them when they needed a little help, and that was fun. But they're not close to retiring and they don't need another person full time. So I found this job."

"How do you like being a maintenance worker?" Morgan said.

Lucy smiled. "I love it. It's a great job. For the right person, it's a great job. You work with your hands a lot. So if you don't like working with your hands, you wouldn't like it. But I love it."

I listened as Morgan and Lucy talked.

"When you're not working, when you're at home, do you like to do all your own maintenance work there too?"

Lucy laughed and shook her head. "I'm not *that* crazy. My husband does some of the work. He has a lot of talent. He can do a lot of things. And we don't try to do everything ourselves. We hire people. Which is nice because I need to relax sometimes."

"That is nice."

"You married?"

"No."

"Find yourself a guy who's going to help you."

I thought that was good advice. I hoped Morgan remembered that. But I didn't say anything.

"How did you apply to be a maintenance worker?" Morgan said.

"I applied on the regular university online job site. You think you might want to be a maintenance worker?"

"It's a possibility."

"Go ahead and apply for it."

"I might do that."

"Maybe we'll be working together."

Morgan smiled. "It could happen."

"Anything else I can do for you today?"

"No, I think that's it."

"I'll head back to the shop. Call me if you need anything."

"Thanks."

Lucy left us.

"I like her. She's a good recruiter for the maintenance department," Morgan said.

"Maybe we should both get jobs there," I said.

"We should have asked her about the salary."

"Might be a pay cut for you. But I think it would be a salary increase for me."

Morgan looked at the cabinet. "Let's see what's inside."

We opened the cabinet doors and looked inside the cabinet. There were no file drawers, just three shelves, with a box on each shelf, and a folder on the middle shelf and the bottom shelf. I pulled the box off the top shelf and put it on the floor. Morgan opened it up.

The box contained some file folders with papers in them. Morgan took out the folders and opened them and looked at the papers.

She smiled. "This looks like what I need."

"Good," I said.

"I'll put this at my desk."

"I'll wait here."

She put the folders back in the box and carried the box out of the chairman's office. In a minute she returned to the chairman's office.

"Should we close the cabinet?" she said.

"Wait. What are these other boxes and folders?" I said.

"Maybe more personnel records," she said.

"Should we look and see?"

"Sure. Why not?"

She reached into the cabinet and pulled out the box on the middle shelf and put it on the floor. Someone had written on it "for Tia."

"Remember Tia?" Morgan said. "She's the student who's working in the department office."

"Yes. I remember."

Morgan opened up the box. It had the top half of a Shaeffer sex doll inside.

"How strange," she said softly.

"Why does the box say 'for Tia?'" I said.

"I don't know. She has no reason to be using this."

"Were you and the chairman using this?"

She shook her head. "No."

"Is there anything that might tell us more about this?"

Morgan lifted the sex doll out of the box and looked in the box and looked at the doll.

"No. Nothing."

She put the doll back in the box. "This is odd," she said.

She reached into the cabinet again and pulled out the box on the bottom shelf and put it on the floor. Someone had written "for Tia" on it also. Morgan opened it up. It had the bottom half of a Shaeffer sex doll.

"Who was using this?" I said.

"I don't know."

There were still two folders in the cabinet. Morgan took out the folder on the middle shelf. It was labeled "Tia". She opened it up.

Inside the folder there were some color photographs of Tia standing next to some baseball players in the university uniform and a
man in street clothes.

"That's Chairman Richardson with Tia and some players. I wonder why she's in these pictures," Morgan said.

Morgan took out the folder on the bottom shelf and opened it
up. It had a list of names in it.

"Do you know those people?" I said.

Morgan looked at the names. She pointed to one of them. "This
one might be a baseball player. I don't know very many players'
names. But I think this one might be on the team." She pointed to
another name. "And this one."

"I don't see anything else in the cabinet. Do you see anything
else?" I said.

Morgan kneeled down and looked into every part of the cabinet. "That's all I see."

"This is odd."

"What are we going to do?"

"I don't know. But we can't just ignore this."

"Let's put the sex doll and the other things back in the cabinet
until we know more about this," Morgan said.

"Good idea," I said.

We put everything back and closed the cabinet.

"Let's have a little chat with Tia," Morgan said.

"All right," I said.

We went to Tia's office. She was there working on something.
The door was open. We stood in the doorway and asked her if she
had a minute to talk with us.

"Sure," she said. "Do you want to use the conference room?
I don't think anybody is in there now. We can all sit down. You
won't have to stand in the doorway."

That sounded like a good plan. We went to the conference room
and sat around a table there.

"Tia, we were looking for some records and we looked in Chairman Richardson's cabinet. The one in the back of his office. You know the cabinet I'm talking about?" Morgan said.

I listened as Morgan talked with Tia.

"The one behind the plastic fig tree?"

"Yes. That one. Tia, the chairman has some pictures in his file cabinet of you with him and some baseball players."

"He likes me. And he likes baseball players."

"And he has a sex doll in there also. In boxes that say 'for Tia.'"

"I was delivering sex dolls for him." Tia spoke casually, as if what she was saying was the most natural thing in the world.

"Who were you delivering sex dolls to?"

"To players on the school baseball team."

"Why were you delivering sex dolls to the players?"

"So they could test them out. The players had jobs testing sex dolls and reporting the results to the Shaeffer Sex Dolls Company."

"So the players were getting free sex dolls?"

"No, they didn't belong to the players. The players had to return them to the company. It was a regular job testing the dolls."

Morgan frowned. "You're making that up."

"No, I'm telling you what was going on."

"You were using the chairman's cabinet to store the dolls?"

"Yes."

"Who put the dolls in the cabinet?"

"Someone from the company brought them to the chairman's office."

"I never saw anyone bringing in boxes of sex dolls."

"They brought them in on Saturdays, when you weren't working."

"And I never saw you carrying boxes out."

"I did it on Saturdays also."

"Why did you do it on Saturdays?"

"I didn't want to have to answer a lot of questions like you're asking me now."

"Tia, were you and the chairman having some sort of deviate sexual relationship?"

"*¡De ninguna manera!*" Tia said forcefully.

"I think that means no," Morgan said to me.

"Did he tell you he would hurt your school record in any way if you refused him?" Morgan said to Tia.

"No," Tia said, still speaking forcefully.

"Did he promise you he would give you a good recommendation if you had sex with him?"

"No."

"Was everything you did with him completely voluntary?"

"Yes."

"This seems odd to me."

"It's not odd at all. It's all perfectly even."

"I don't like to see people exploiting you like this."

"Nobody is exploiting me. The sex doll company is paying me to deliver the dolls. *Es un buen trabajo.*" Tia smiled. "And the chairman tells me things that the university is considering. I know plans that are being discussed before they're announced. I have inside knowledge."

Morgan looked surprised. "What does he tell you?"

Tia spoke softly. "I don't know if I should be telling you this, but the university is considering building a new baseball stadium south of the campus. The money would come from the leader of the sex dolls company. They're still working on the details."

"I haven't heard anything about this."

"Very few people know about it."

"Does anybody else at the university know about your job delivering sex dolls?"

"The athletics compliance officer knows about it. The chairman discussed everything with the school's athletics compliance officer. The person who's a specialist in complying with the rules of amateur athletics. The compliance officer said it was all perfectly fine. You can ask him yourself."

"What's his name?"

"I don't remember his name. I don't have any reason to try to remember his name, because I don't have any questions I want to ask him."

At this point I got back into the conversation.

"Tia, I'm talking to you as a friend and not as a representative of the university," I said. "It's not a good idea to have sex with married men, and it's not a good idea to have sex with people who supervise your work."

"I'm not doing any of those things. I'm doing what I told you."

Morgan looked at me. "What do you think, Doctor Rose?"

"I want to talk to the compliance officer," I said.

"It was all perfectly harmless," Tia said.

"Tia, I just want to make sure everything is all right."

Morgan and I said goodbye to Tia and we went our separate ways. I didn't know what to make of all of this. I thought maybe everything Tia told us was absolutely true, but I'd feel more comfortable if I talked with the compliance officer.

Chapter Eighteen

Later that day, Britta called me.

"Morgan talked to me. She said she had been intimate with my husband. She said it was a mistake. She said you and Lexi helped her see it wasn't a good idea. I wanted to call you and say thank you."

"Lexi gets the credit for that," I said.

"Morgan said you helped also."

"What are you going to do?"

"I'm filing for divorce. I don't want to be married to somebody like this."

"Are you going to tell Captain Shaeffer?"

"I don't have much choice. My dad is going to ask me why I'm getting divorced. This is why I'm getting divorced. I probably won't mention Morgan's name. He doesn't know her. I'll just say my husband had an inappropriate relationship with a staffer."

"How do you think Captain Shaeffer will react?"

"He won't be happy. He has a lot of influence with your university's administration. He'll probably ask them to dismiss their department chairman. They might do that. We'll see."

"Thanks for calling. I'm sorry you got dragged into this."

"It's my husband's fault. He's smart in some ways but unfortunately he's foolish in other ways. He's smoolish."

"He's smoolish?"

"Smart and foolish," Britta said.

"Yes, he's that," I said.

"We can talk more some other time."

"Yes."
"Bye."

I like to follow the local news but I don't usually watch the news on television. I prefer to watch the local television news videos that the local television stations put on their websites.

The next day there was some news related to Chairman Richardson. The Channel Four "More On Four" Action News Team was reporting that the university had dismissed him and barred him from the campus. The university said he was dismissed for conduct which violated university policy, but it didn't go into details.

Channel Four said, "The chairman's wife released a statement today saying she plans to file for divorce. In her statement she also said, 'My husband should issue an apology or he will come to a bad end.' The chairman then released a statement in which he complained that his wife was threatening him. Our news team then reached her for comment, and she told us she is not issuing a threat but merely making a prediction. She told us she has no intention to harm her husband, but she knows a woman who might want to harm him. Our news team then contacted the chairman again and he said, 'Nothing that has happened was my fault and I apologize to anyone who has been hurt by anything I did, although it was not my fault.'"

Chapter Nineteen

A few days later Lexi called me.

"A friend of mine is now the acting chairman of the physics department," she said.

"Good. Is it anybody I know?"

"I don't think you met him. His name is Robert Roberts. Everybody calls him Deuce."

"Is Deuce going to help you?"

"I think he's going to agree to deaccession the neutrino detector."

"Great news."

"And when that happens, I'm going to put it in my house. I'll show it to all my visitors."

"I hope you find some visitors who give you some money."

After that, Morgan called me. She said she liked Deuce and was going to continue working for the depatment.

I asked Alyssa for the name of the university's athletics compliance officer. Alyssa said it was someone named Lance Walker. Alyssa said she knew him because they had served on a committee together. Alyssa said she liked him. I wasn't sure how much he knew about sex dolls, and I wasn't sure how much he would tell me about what he knew, but maybe I could learn something.

Lance had an office in the administration building. I called his secretary and said I was new at the school and a sports fan and wanted to ask him about rules for amateur athletics. She said he was always happy to talk with sports fans.

I made an appointment to see him. When I went to his office for my appointment I wore casual clothes, including a sweater with the university logo on it. His secretary greeted me outside his office and went in with me and introduced me and left us. Lance was a tall thin good looking Black man wearing business casual clothes. He stood up and smiled and we shook hands.

"I like your sweater," Lance said. He had a pleasant deep voice.

"Thanks. I'm new here. I'm a new fan. I'm showing my new allegiance."

"New fans are always welcome. Have a seat."

He sat in a big chair behind his desk and I sat in a smaller chair in front of it. He had a nice big office with walls made of dark wood panels, and lots of sports pictures on the walls. Some of the pictures were autographed. I was pretty certain that if he had a liquor license and a big screen television his office could be a popular sports bar.

Lance leaned back a little bit in his chair and asked me where I was working. I said I was working at the medical school and I asked him if he knew anybody there. He said no. I said I was renting a room from Alyssa Lincoln, the university's general counsel and vice president for community affairs. He said he knew her. He remembered serving with her on an advisory committee about promoting fitness and exercise for nonathletes in the university community.

He asked me whether I knew anybody else in the university administration. He said his wife Sasha was working in the president's office as an administrative assistant, part time in a job share. I said I hoped I would have an opportunity to meet her someday.

I looked around his office. He had a picture on his wall of some women volleyball players. I said the volleyball team might be good this year. He asked me how many games the volleyball team was going to win this year. I said at least sixteen. He said I was probably right.

I looked at some of the other sports pictures on his wall. He had some pictures of baseball players. I asked him whether he thought the baseball team was going to find good replacements for the stars who were going to turn pro. He said he thought they would. I agreed with him.

"The key is recruiting on the west coast," I said.

"Yes, I think you're right."

"Traditionally that's been a good source of players for us."

"That's right."

Lance looked like he might be a pretty good athlete himself. I was curious about his background.

"Did you play sports when you were in college?" I said.

"I played soccer. You ever go to any college soccer games?"

"No."

He smiled. "You should go to some games. It's a great sport."

"Did you play here?"

"No, I played at another college. I don't want to name them because their program may be different now than it was when I was there."

"What was it like when you were there?"

He looked serious. "They were exploiting the players."

"How were they exploiting the players?"

"The school offered degrees in fields that were not really serious academic disciplines. They were just there for athletes who wanted to play sports and didn't want to study. When you're playing sports, it's very tempting to take easy courses instead of doing the school work you would have to do in a serious major. I took easy courses myself when I was there."

"What did you study?"

"When I was at that school playing for them I was majoring in recreation program management."

"So do you have a degree in that field?"

"No. I got injured my junior year and I couldn't play. They didn't renew my athletic scholarship. I think they should have renewed it, but they didn't. They told me I should apply for a Pell grant, but that program wasn't fully funded. I left that school without a degree. That's the risk you take when you play sports. I'd given the school my time and my athletic ability and I didn't have anything to show for it."

"What did you do?"

"I transferred to here and I scraped up the money to pay my tuition here and I studied and didn't play sports. And I got a degree in business management. And when I graduated I got an entry level job in the university administration and then later was fortunate enough to get this job."

"I'm glad you've been able to have a good career after your soccer days."

"I've been lucky. But others who play are not as fortunate. Whenever I talk to athletes I tell them that they should work on getting an education along with working on their sports careers."

"Do they listen to you?"

"Some of them do."

I liked talking with Lance. He didn't dance around. He said what he believed.

"Compliance officer is a pretty important position," I said.

"It is, but that doesn't mean I'm running the athletic department. I'm working for the athletic department. And you understand that I don't make the rules."

"The rules are made by the NCAA?"

"Some rules are made by the NCAA. Some rules are made by state law. I keep track of all the rules and I make sure our school is in compliance with everything."

"I'm sure that keeps you busy."

He smiled. "I love doing it."

"Do the rules allow college athletes to make money?"

He looked serious again. "Yes, within limits. We're at the start of a new era in college sports. Some schools are starting to share revenue with athletes. That's a big change from the previous era."

"What are the rules for revenue sharing?"

"The rules are still being worked out. I'm sure the rules will change as we get more experience."

"Do you see any problems with revenue sharing?"

"I do see problems with it. But I realize that some college sports bring in a lot of money. I think college athletes deserve some of that money."

"Is revenue sharing the only way college athletes can make money?"

"No. Athletes can take a regular job if they want to do that. And athletes can be compensated for product endorsements. There are limitations and conditions on what's allowed, and I educate everyone about what's permitted and what's not permitted."

"Do you think eventually college athletes will be paid a salary for playing sports?"

"It's possible. College sports are a source of revenue for schools. Some people think a lot of that revenue should go to the athletes. That could happen in the future."

"That would be a big change."

"Yes it would be."

"I want to ask you about the baseball team."

Lance smiled. "They've done pretty well. Have you seen any of their games?"

I shook my head. "No."

"You should go to some games. We've had some great players here."

"That's what everybody tells me."

"What did you want to ask me?"

"I want to ask you what you know about sex dolls and the baseball team."

Lance looked surprised. "You heard about the sex dolls?"

"Yes. I know the person who was delivering the dolls."

Lance looked down at his desk. I hoped he felt comfortable talking with me about the sex dolls.

He frowned and looked at me. "I guess it's all right to talk about the sex dolls. It's a matter of public knowledge."

I nodded.

He said, "I mean, some people know about it."

"Yes."

Lance looked at some pictures on his wall. He seemed like he was still trying to decide whether he could talk about it. Then he stopped frowning and he looked at me.

"I know what Captain Shaeffer told me. He said he's hiring players to test sex dolls. He said he's providing dolls to the players for that job. He asked me whether that was all right."

"Did you approve it?" I said.

"I said everything was fine if it was a legitimate job. Every school has people in the community that are fans of sports at the school and want to help the school. Those people are called boosters. Under current rules, boosters cannot recruit athletes by giving them sex dolls if the athletes will agree to play for the college. Maybe in the future that will change. But under current rules, giving them sex dolls is not permitted. However, college athletes are always permitted to take a job. It just has to be a real job in the labor force. It cannot be an activity that was created just as an excuse to pay athletes. It must be something that a company would hire nonathletes as well as athletes to do."

I decided Lance was probably a pretty good compliance officer. He was good at explaining things. He was direct and he was concise.

"And you think testing sex dolls passes that test," I said.

"It depends on the facts of the case, Jack. If the baseball players were performing a job that was common in the industry and were being paid a wage that was common in the industry, then it's all perfectly legal. Captain Shaeffer told me that testing sex dolls is standard practice in the sex doll industry. He told me the baseball players were paid a wage that was common in the industry. So given those facts I said that was legal."

"It seems odd to me. Is there anything more you can do?"

"No," Lance said firmly. "Everything I do has to be based on evidence. I don't have any evidence of anything improper."

"You don't think it needs to be further investigated?" I said softly.

"No," he said, again speaking firmly. "I don't want to investigate one of our sports programs for no reason. If I make an allegation and I don't have any evidence to support it, then I'm not being fair to the sports program."

I wasn't going to be able to convince him to investigate anything. I said, "I understand."

"You said you know the person delivering the dolls."

"Yes."

"How do you happen to know that person?"

"I know some people in the physics department. They know Chairman Richardson. He's a friend of Captain Shaeffer."

"So you know the right people."

"I have good sources of information."

"What else are they talking about over there?"

"I heard about the plans for the new baseball stadium."

Lance looked surprised. He leaned forward in his chair.

"I'm not familiar with that. Are there actual plans, or is that just a rumor?"

"I heard from someone who I think is pretty reliable that the university is working on plans to build a new baseball stadium. I don't think it's just a rumor."

"Where would they build this stadium?"

"The plan is to build it south of the campus."

Lance frowned. "South of the campus is my neighborhood. Are you familiar with that neighborhood?"

"I haven't spent much time down there."

"It's a great place. You said you're living with Alyssa? The vice president and general counsel?"

"Yes."

"Where is her house?"

"It's on the west side."

"There's some big houses over on the west side. We don't have anything like that on the south side. But we have a nice neighborhood. They would have to tear down houses to put a stadium there. That would be a shame."

"Yes."

"What else did your source tell you about the plans?"

"Nothing specific. Just that the university is working on plans for a stadium there."

Lance looked worried. "That's not good."

"That's the plan."

"Thank you for alerting me to that. Let me know if you hear anything more."

"All right."

I didn't have anything else I wanted to talk about. I told Lance I didn't want to take too much of his time and I appreciated his willingness to take time out of his busy schedule to see me. He said he always likes talking to sports fans and would be happy to talk to me again sometime. He seemed genuine and I believed him. We both got up and we shook hands and I left his office.

I wondered whether the athletic department would regret making the compliance officer unhappy.

Chapter Twenty

A few days later, Britta called me. "Want to see a video of Sophia dancing?"

"I'd love to see a video of Sophia dancing."

"I'll send it to you."

She sent it to me and I watched it. Sophia was dancing to music from a Ginger Rogers and Fred Astaire movie. She was doing some fast spins. She looked good.

Chapter Twenty-One

A couple of weeks later, Morgan came to see me in my office.

"I wanted to tell you my news, Doctor Rose. The researchers finished the diagnostic study. They told everybody their results this week."

"That was fast."

"Yes. They didn't waste any time."

"What was your result?"

"They said I do have endo, according to the study criteria. I'm not happy to have it, but I'm happy that medical science can figure out what's wrong."

"Yes, I'm sorry that you have health problems, but it's good to have a diagnosis."

"I'm ready for the cure."

"Nobody has discovered the cure," I said. "People have tried lots of things, but they all have problems. Drugs have been tried, but we don't have good evidence that they will cure you. Surgery has been tried, but we don't have good evidence that it will cure you. You could try those things if you want to. Would they help you? I don't know. Or you can try an experimental treatment."

"What have you got?"

I looked in my drawer and took out some endo research documents.

"There's one treatment study currently recruiting."

"Will it cure me?"

"Maybe."

"Only maybe?"

"Endo is a challenge. It's still not well understood."

Morgan looked unhappy.

"I thought a lot of smart people were working on it," she said.

"A lot of smart people *are* working on it. But it's still not well understood."

"Does the study have a control group?"

"It does have a control group."

"So if I sign up for the study I might end up in the control group?"

"That's right. If you sign up for the study you will be randomly assigned to either the treatment group or the control group."

"Will I know which group I'm in?"

"No."

"And if I'm in the control group I'll only get placebos?"

"That's right," I said. "If the researchers thought there already was a proven treatment, the control group would get that treatment, and the study would test whether the experimental treatment is better than the proven treatment. But here, the researchers don't think any treatment is proven to be safe and effective. So the control group gets placebos."

"I want the cure."

"Sometimes placebos make people feel better. You may have heard of the placebo effect. The placebo effect can be powerful."

"So after a lot of research by a lot of smart people, we conclude that I can just take placebos and feel better?"

"Maybe."

"You're not sure what will help me?"

"The disease is not well understood. There's a lot of uncertainty."

"How long will the treatment study last?"

"It lasts two years."

"Two years? *Two years?* It lasts two whole years?"

"That's right."

"So I could be taking placebos for two whole years?"

"That's right."

Morgan didn't say anything. She stared at me for a few seconds and then she looked down at my desk.

"We use top quality placebos. Everybody in our trials says they like them," I said.

She looked at me again. A little smile flickered on Morgan's mouth for an instant and then it was gone. She seemed to relax. Her gaze wandered.

"You look good today," she said.

"Thank you."

"You don't look wrinkled. At least the part of your clothes that I can see doesn't look wrinkled."

"You want to see more?"

I stood up and walked out from behind my desk.

"Very nice. You ironed your clothes today," she said.

"I tried."

"It makes you look more professional."

"I appreciate your advice about how I can look better."

I walked back behind my desk and sat down again.

"What do you think I should do?" Morgan said.

"I can't tell you what to do. You should make your own decision. I like medical research. If I didn't like medical research I wouldn't be here. But that doesn't mean everybody should sign up for a clinical trial. As you know, experimental treatments have potential risks and potential benefits. You need to think carefully about those. We have a lot of information to help you think about those things. We want you to make an informed decision."

She nodded.

"Here's some printed material about the study," I said.

Morgan got out of her chair and took the printed material and sat down again.

"You should study that carefully and decide whether you think the potential benefits are greater than the potential risks."

"Thanks. I'll study this. Right now I'm thinking I probably want to be in the study. Even if there's a lot of uncertainty, I still need something. But I'll think carefully about it."

"Good. You know how the sign up process works. After you read the information, ask any questions that you may have. Make an appointment to see the endo research group and enroll if that's what you want to do."

We said goodbye and she left the office. I hoped she would sign up for the treatment study.

A few days later she called me and said she had signed up for the treatment study.

"I hope it helps you," I said.

"I'm sure it will."

"You're sure it will?"

"Yes, Doctor Rose, absolutely. Because the placebo effect can be powerful. You said that yourself. And you can't argue with yourself."

"You're right, Morgan. I can't argue with myself."

Chapter Twenty-Two

From time to time I thought about Lexi's coworker, Veronica. I wondered what she was doing. So I was happy when Veronica invited me to come to her house on a Friday night for dinner with her and her housemate Snow. Veronica said she and Snow wanted to get to know me better. I said I would be happy to see both of them, and I asked her if I could contribute something to the meal. "Just bring yourself," she said.

Veronica gave me directions. Veronica lived on First Street, which was the border between the campus and the town on the east side. The night of the dinner, I walked over to her house. The houses in her neighborhood were old and not quite as nice as the houses on the west side where Alyssa and Lexi lived, but the east side neighborhood was respectable and a good place to live.

Snow and Veronica greeted me, and then Snow talked with me about her work and asked me about my work. Then we had an excellent dinner. Veronica loved to cook. She had prepared a salad of artichoke hearts and sliced tomatoes and cashew nuts and red leaf lettuce, and for the main course she served coq au vin, and asparagus with cream sauce. For dessert we had fresh strawberries with whipped cream. It was all very good.

After dinner we sat in the living room. Veronica and Snow excused themselves and said they needed a little time to talk about something by themselves, and they gave me some magazines to look at. A few minutes later they came back into the living room and sat down near me.

Snow smiled at me. "Jack, I really like you. You seem bright and you have a nice personality."

"Thank you, Snow, but you don't know me very well. I have some very annoying character flaws."

"You have character flaws?" Veronica said.

"Yes," I said.

Snow and Veronica both looked worried.

"What are they?" Snow said.

I shifted my body a little in my chair. I was a little bit uncomfortable talking about my character flaws, but it was better for my friends to hear about them directly from me, instead of my friends discovering them independently and being surprised by them when I wasn't around to explain anything.

"I have too many to list for you now. We would be here all night if I listed all of them," I said.

"Then just tell us some of them. Tell us the really bad ones," Veronica said.

"Just the really bad ones?"

"Yes," Veronica said.

"All right. Here's one. I don't follow sports news closely. I don't pay attention to the school baseball team. The only way I know anything is when I listen to someone talking about the team. I meet someone else and I repeat what the first person said. The second person thinks I know a lot, but I'm just repeating what I was told."

Veronica looked surprised. "You don't follow sports news? I thought all men followed sports news."

"I don't follow it closely," I said.

"Why not?" Veronica said.

"I don't know," I said.

Snow looked at Veronica and then at me.

"Do you think your abnormality could indicate some kind of a medical problem?" Snow said.

"What did you have in mind?" I said.

"Maybe you have a deficiency of male hormones," Snow said.

"Do you think that's possible?" I said.

"Have you considered going to an endocrinologist?" Snow said.

Veronica frowned. She looked at Snow and then looked at me.

"I'm not sure going to an endocrinologist is the answer," Veronica said. "But you have to pay more attention to sports. If nothing else, you have to pay attention to the school baseball team. That's the heart of this town."

"I'll pay more attention to the school baseball team," I said.

Veronica smiled. "You're willing to work to improve yourself. I like that."

Snow smiled also. "Yes, that shows you're trying to overcome your flaws. That's good."

"Tell us another one of your character flaws," Veronica said.

"I'm not very good at ironing my clothes. Sometimes my clothes look wrinkled."

Veronica had an unhappy expression on her face. She looked at Snow.

"Did you hear that? He's not very good at ironing his clothes. What do you think?" Veronica said.

"That's not ideal," Snow said.

"When I first came here I ironed things sometimes but not all the time. Someone told me my clothes looked wrinkled. So I started doing more ironing. I'm trying to develop my skill. But I'm still not very good at it."

Snow looked at Veronica. "That's not ideal, but it's tolerable," Snow said.

"At least he's trying," Veronica said.

Snow looked at me again. "Tell us one more. Tell us one more really bad one."

"Sometimes I end a sentence with a preposition," I said. "If you spend time with me, it's something you have to put up with."

Veronica smiled. "That means you're one of us. We do the same thing. That just reinforces my belief that you're the kind of person we've been searching for."

"Yes, that's not something we worry about," Snow said.

"And if other people worry about it, then it's just something they need to get used to," Veronica said.

"Thank you for being so tolerant," I said.

"Jack, we really like you and we want to ask you something," Snow said.

"Sure. Ask me anything."

Snow looked at Veronica.

"Jack," Veronica said.

"Yes, Veronica?"

"Jack, we want to ask you whether you might be willing to do something for us," Veronica said.

"What did you have in mind?"

Veronica paused. She looked serious and maybe a little anxious.

"Jack, I'm not sure how to say this," Veronica said.

"What is it?"

"Snow and I, we were thinking we want to have a family. Would you be willing to help us? You would make an excellent father. I know you would. I want to have your baby," Veronica said.

"Now you've ended a sentence with a proposition," I said.

"I can't have sex with you, but you could donate sperm to me. I want to have your baby and I want to raise it here in my house with Snow. Snow and I will pay for all the cost of raising a child. And you can come and visit as much as you want," Veronica said.

"If you and Veronica had a child together your child would be a wonderful child," Snow said. "It would be smart and good looking and successful. You would be happy having a child. Please, Jack. Please consider this."

As soon as they said it, I felt like I wasn't able to do it. It was a nice idea, but I didn't have anywhere near the amount of money it would cost to raise a child, and I didn't have any commitment from the university that I would have a good job in the future. Veronica and Snow said they would pay the cost of raising a child, but Veronica was having trouble getting money for neutrino research. Snow appeared to be successful now but I didn't know how long that would last. And I didn't want to rely completely on other people to raise my child. I would feel responsible for raising my child even if Snow and Veronica said they would do it.

At the same time, I could see the advantages of having a child with Veronica. If Veronica had my child and the child inherited her brains it would be a very intelligent child. And if the child inherited Veronica's appearance it would be very good looking. So I had some regrets about declining her offer. I just felt that I would have more regrets if I became the father of Veronica's child.

I tried to explain all of this gracefully, but naturally they were not happy. Eventually we said goodnight and I went back to my storage closet in Alyssa's house.

Later I wondered whether I had made the right decision. Somehow it was easy for me to tell other people what to do. Now it seemed so much harder for me to decide for myself what I should do.

Chapter Twenty-Three

One day Morgan called me.

"The treatment study is helping me, Doctor Rose. I'm feeling better."

"I'm glad you're feeling better."

"I knew it would help me."

"Yes, I think you predicted that."

"Thanks for everything, Doctor Rose."

"Don't thank me. Thank the people who developed the experimental treatment."

"They're not doing anything to help me."

"They're not?"

"The people who are helping me are the people who make the placebos."

A few days later Morgan called me again. "Doctor Rose, have you got a minute?"

"Sure, what's up?"

"I got a bill in the mail, from the medical school health services billing company. I don't think it's correct. I think it's a mistake. I'm trying to get it corrected but I'm having trouble."

"What's it for?"

"It's for a series of ultrasounds. I haven't had any ultrasounds."

"Yes, that sounds like a mistake. What about your health insurance? Are they getting billed for this?"

"They might have gotten a bill, but they're not going to pay anything. I have a deductible on my insurance. I haven't reached my deductible. My insurance doesn't pay anything until I've paid my deductible."

"What have you done so far about the bill?"

"It has a phone number. I called them and talked to someone. They said they have no way of reviewing the accuracy of a bill over the phone, but if I write a letter to the billing review department, they'll look at it. So I wrote a letter, but they haven't replied. And I'm getting notes from the billing company telling me my payment is overdue."

"I'll see what I can do."

"Thanks."

"I'll look into it and call you when I know something."

"Thanks."

I made an appointment to talk to the medical school director of the business office. She was able to see me that same week, which was good. I explained the situation to her. She said all the billing was handled by an independent contractor billing company, which she said was Dickens, Deadwood, and Doorlicker, LLC. She said they were a politically well connected company that had been given a contract to do billing and consulting for the whole university. She couldn't help me. I would have to contact them. I wrote them a letter but they didn't reply.

Chapter Twenty-Four

One day I was sitting in the kitchen at Alyssa's house drinking some iced tea with her. Her dog Abraham was resting at Alyssa's feet. She was telling me her hopes and dreams.

"There's a state Supreme Court election coming up later this year," she said.

"I was not aware of that."

"It's in November. It's nonpartisan. There's no party primaries. Just one election in November."

"I see."

She looked unhappy. "The thing that really bothers me is that state Supreme Court judges are elected by voters. And most of the voters don't know anything about the candidates for the court."

"Why don't most of the voters know anything?" I said.

"Because knowing something is hard. Because in the elections when the judges are elected, lots of other races are on the ballot also. Voters are trying to learn about lots of other candidates for lots of other offices. And voters are busy people with other things to do besides trying to learn about candidates. We're asking too much from voters."

She paused. I didn't say anything.

"Some of the voters pay some attention to what the candidates say in their ads. But the candidates can't say anything intelligent about complex legal issues in a brief ad. So the ads tend to be misleading and not helpful."

"Yes, I agree," I said.

"Most voters decide who to vote for based on name recognition. They see names on the ballot and they vote for the name that they recognize."

"And what's your answer to this problem?"

"In an ideal world, the state Supreme Court judges would be chosen in a nonpartisan merit system. A nonpartisan panel would create a list of candidates based on experience and qualifications, and then the governor would select judges from the panel."

"Are you going to promote that plan?"

"I am. Yes."

"How are you going to do that?"

She smiled a little half smile. "Starting a few weeks from now, I'm going to take a leave of absence from my job at the university and I'm going to run for state Supreme Court judge. And my campaign is going to illustrate the problems with the current system."

"How are you going to illustrate the problems?"

"My campaign is going to feature Abraham."

Abraham recognized his name and looked at Alyssa.

"Abraham?"

"My campaign slogan is going to be: Vote for Abraham Lincoln for Supreme Court."

"But Abraham is a dog. He can't get on the ballot for a state Supreme Court judge election."

"True, but I can get on the ballot. I can get on with just the initial of my first name plus my full last name. I will be on the ballot as A. Lincoln."

"Won't that be deceptive?"

"No, because I will tell everyone that Abraham Lincoln is not me, Abraham Lincoln is my dog. I will promise that if I am elected I will consult Abraham Lincoln in all my deliberations."

"But you're mocking the state Supreme Court."

"No, no. I'm not mocking the state Supreme Court. I'm mocking the process by which the judges are chosen for the state Supreme Court. I'm going to prove that voters will vote for whatever name they recognize. Voters will vote for A. Lincoln for the court because they recognize the name Abraham Lincoln. The fact that I'm not Abraham Lincoln, the fact that Abraham Lincoln is my dog, illustrates the problem with how we select judges."

"I don't know what reaction you're going to get. I think you might get into trouble for doing this."

"Since you brought that up, let me give you my thoughts on the controversy this will create. My family happens to be a family of lawyers. My ex-husband is a lawyer, and my son Clark is also a lawyer. My ex-husband is still my friend. I know some people end their marriage and become antagonists. But my ex and I are not like that. He's a decent man, even though the marriage didn't last. He currently works as the chief of staff in the office of the attorney general for the state. My son is a young lawyer just starting out, and my son also works in the attorney general's office. My son is an entry level staff attorney."

"How is the attorney general's office going to react to your candidacy?"

"I expect that the attorney general will file some sort of a lawsuit against me."

"That might stop your candidacy."

"No, no. The effect will be the opposite of stopping me. The attorney general will file a lawsuit against me because he will want to appear to be promoting virtue at all times. That's good publicity for the attorney general. It helps the attorney general get reelected. But the attorney general will understand the purpose of my campaign. It will be a friendly suit. It will have no merit. I don't think there is any suit they could file that would have merit, under the circumstances. I'm raising an important issue of public policy. I'm raising it in an election campaign. Everything I say will be speech which has the highest level of protection that speech can have. And, of course, I'll get more publicity if they sue me."

"Sounds like you've thought about this carefully."

"What do you think? Did I convince you I'm right?"

"I can see the point you're making."

"Do you want to help me?"

"How would I help you?"

"You could be the treasurer of my campaign committee."

"I don't know how to do that."

"I'll show you. It's easy. It's just a little bit of paperwork. You don't have to raise any money. You just keep track of it."

"Don't you have lawyer friends that want to do that?"

"Lawyers usually want to support both sides equally in judicial elections. If they support only one candidate and another candidate wins, it could cause problems for the lawyer when they have a case in that judge's court. So a good lawyer isn't going to want to be a treasurer for one side."

"I'll be your treasurer if you show me how to do it."

"Thanks. I think we'll have fun with this."

Chapter Twenty-Five

Morgan called me again about her incorrect medical bill. I told her I had not been able to make any progress so far.

"The billing company is sending me notes saying their bill is overdue. Is there something else we can do?"

"I've always wanted to meet the president of the university. Have you ever met the president of the university?" I said.

"No," Morgan said.

"Do you want to meet the president of the university?"

"Can he help us?"

"We can try to be charming and maybe he'll like us and ask one of his staff assistants to look into the billing problem. And maybe Lexi will want to come with us and meet him also. And while we're there maybe he can tell us how to find research money."

"Does he have time to see us?"

"I don't know. We can talk to his administrative assistant and ask her."

"If we can get an appointment, I'd like to meet him."

"First I'm going to ask Lexi whether she wants to meet the president with us. I'll let you know."

"Thanks, Doctor Rose."

I asked Lexi if she wanted to join Morgan and me if we could get in to talk to the president of the university. She said she would like to meet him also.

Morgan and I went to the president's section in the administration building, to try to make an appointment. There was a suite of offices for the president and some administrative staff.

We were greeted by an administrative assistant who said her name was Juliette. I asked whether Sasha was there. I said I had met Sasha's husband, the athletics compliance officer. Juliette said Sasha was working a job share with Juliette and this was one of Juliette's days to work.

Juliette said it was a bad time to try to see the president.

"He's pretty busy," Juliette said. "Is what you want to talk to him about urgent, or can it wait?"

"I'm working in medical research and Morgan here is participating in a research study. And we have a friend, Professor Lieblich, who does research also, and would like to join us. The president has a reputation for being deeply committed to making the school a leader in research. We wanted to get his insights on research and how we can be successful finding research money and help enhance his reputation as someone committed to research. And we also had an administrative question for him," I said.

"Oh, research. I'm sorry, but he's pretty busy," Juliette said.

"We just need a few minutes," Morgan said.

"He's not even in town most of this month," Juliette said.

"Is he at a conference?" Morgan said.

"He's going to go to some of the top level summer league games for high school players," Juliette said.

"Summer league games?" Morgan said.

"The best high school baseball players have an opportunity to play in summer leagues not affiliated with any school. It's a chance to work on skills and also showcase their talent and try to get colleges interested," Juliette said.

"Are you a baseball fan yourself?" I said to Juliette.

"I love baseball. Don't tell anyone, but I think that's why the president hired me," Juliette said.

"We just need a few minutes," Morgan said.

"I'll see what I can do," Juliette said.

Morgan and I gave Juliette our contact information and thanked her and left her.

"Morgan, do you yourself have any connection to baseball?" I said after we left Juliette.

"I can't think of any. I don't play it and none of my relatives are famous players," she said.

"That's too bad."

Chapter Twenty-Six

From time to time I thought about Veronica and Snow. After that dinner with them I didn't have any contact with them for a while. I wondered how they were doing, so I sent Veronica a message. She replied that she would be testing electronics on Tuesday afternoon of next week, and invited me to come to her lab then and see her work. I thanked her for her invitation and said I would be there.

Veronica had been feeding me, starting with the cilantro bagel before I even met her, and then of course with the dinner with her and Snow. So I wanted to bring her something good to eat. I didn't know how she felt about pizza, but I thought maybe she would like some, so when it was Tuesday afternoon I went to A Slice Is Nice and got a simple cheese pizza. They put it in a box and put the box in a bag, because they think you can never have too much packaging. I took the bag of pizza with me to her lab.

The door was open. I stood at the doorway and looked in. Veronica was lying on a bench over near a side wall. She looked like she was holding something on her abdomen. She didn't look particularly comfortable. The large collection of machinery that had been silent on my last visit had now come to life and was humming and vibrating a little bit.

I knocked on the open door to attract her attention. She didn't hear me.

"Veronica," I said.

She didn't respond. I took a few steps into the lab.

"Veronica, it's Jack Rose."

She turned her head towards me.

"You said I could come visit you today in your lab. Remember?"

"Oh, hello Jack. How are you today?"

"I'm fine, but how are you? Are you feeling sick? Maybe I should come back another time."

"No, no. I was just resting."

She slowly got up off the bench and stood up to greet me. I could see that the object she was holding in her hand was a hot water bottle. She put it down on a table.

She took off her safety glasses and unclipped her hair and let it down.

"This is the perfect time," she said.

"Do you like pizza? I brought you a cheese pizza."

"Thank you, but I'm not hungry right now."

I put the bag of pizza on a table. We shook hands.

"Welcome to the lab," she said.

"Thank you."

"Do you want to see Coldilocks?"

"Coldilocks?"

"That's what we call the electronics that I'm testing today. It's built to operate in cold conditions. We took the name from a polar bear in the zoo."

"Yes, I want to see Coldilocks."

"Most of what the machines do they can do without me hovering over them. But I can't leave them alone completely. They're like children. I need to be here in case there's a problem. If you don't hear any alarms going off we're having a good day."

She started walking slowly over to a table with some electronic equipment on it. I followed her.

She pointed to some of the electronics. "This is an insulated cold box. Inside it I have some electronics that I'm testing." She pointed to another piece of equipment. "This is the refrigeration unit."

I pointed to a computer screen. "What's this measuring?"

She pointed to the same screen. "This is the monitor. You see this column? This is the temperature inside the cold box. You see that? That's really cold. That's what we want."

I studied the monitor.

She looked at me. "I have signals of known strength that I'm feeding into the electronics and I'm testing the sensitivity and the output."

"Very impressive."

"I need to sit down." She sat in a chair. "Have a seat," she said.

I sat in a chair near her.

"I feel really really tired but at the same time I can't sleep," she said.

"I should come back another time."

"No. Please stay. I don't want you to go."

"Are you feeling sick?"

"No, I'm healthy."

"Are you sure?"

"Sometimes things happen that are not medical problems."

"Do you feel like telling me about it?"

"Snow left me two days ago," Veronica said softly. "She said she didn't love me anymore. She moved out. I still love her."

"I'm sorry."

"I can't sleep. I can't eat. I'm a mess," Veronica said, still speaking softly.

"Is there anything I can do to help you?"

"You can stay here and talk to me."

"I wish I had the cure for being lovesick."

"You brought me a pizza. That's helpful. Sick people need nourishment."

"Yes, I think so."

"I'll try to eat some later." She looked at the table where she had put her hot water bottle. "Would you mind getting my hot water bottle and bringing it over here? Do you see it there on the table?"

"Yes, I can get it."

I got the hot water bottle and brought it to her. It was a soft flexible thin rectangular red rubber water bottle. The water in it was not quite hot, but it was warm. "Thank you," she said. She held the hot water bottle against her abdomen.

"Maybe you've heard the expression 'the tears of a disappointed womb,'" she said.

"Yes, I've heard that."

"Today my womb is disappointed and the rest of me is disappointed also."

"It's hard to go through a breakup with someone."

"Look at my eyes. Can you tell I've been crying?"

"Yes, I see."

"I'm leaking today."

"I admire your ability to work when you're not feeling well."

"I like my work," Veronica said. Her voice was a little stronger now. "That's the important thing. Do what you like and like what you do."

"Yes, I agree."

"Although what I really want to do most is work with Lexi on neutrino research. But if I can't do that, then I want to do this."

"I hope you and Lexi will get some research money for neutrinos."

"What do you think of Lexi?"

"I like her. She's nice."

"Lexi told me you might be looking for a place to live."

"Yes, that's true."

"Where are you living now?"

"I'm renting some space from Alyssa Lincoln in a house west of the campus."

"Is your place nice?"

"She has a wonderful house. But my space is a storage closet with a cot in it."

Veronica frowned. "A storage closet?"

"It's all right. It's a big storage closet."

"I don't know whether I can help you or not. You've seen my house."

"Yes, part of it," I said.

"You've seen the dining room and the living room of my house."

"You have a nice house."

"If you wanted some space in my house I'm not sure how it would work. I just haven't thought about it. But I definitely have some space that nobody is using now."

"I don't want to interfere with your social life. You'll meet somebody new and they might want to live with you."

"I'm not ready for that."

"If you want to show me your place sometime, I would like to look at it."

"I'd like to show it to you when I can. Right now it's kind of dirty. My partner didn't do a lot of cleaning and I haven't felt like cleaning after she left. Maybe in a few weeks I can find someone to clean it and then you can look at it."

"I can clean it up for you now. That's not a problem," I said.

Veronica looked surprised. "You can clean it up for me?"

"Yes, I can clean it up for you."

"You do housework?"

"Yes, I do housework."

"Are you gay?"

"No, I'm straight."

She looked at me skeptically. "You're male, and straight, and you do housework? How is that possible?"

"Certainly I do housework. Why are you asking me all these questions?"

Veronica smiled. "Wow. I'm starting to feel a little bit better now. You need to come over this evening after work. Can you come over?"

"I can come over this evening. I can walk over."

"I'll walk with you. I walked to work."

"All right."

"We can eat your pizza at my house tonight. Do you want to do that?"

"Sure."

"Can you meet me in front of this building at about six?"

"Yes, that's good. Do you have cleaning supplies?" I said.

"I have lots of cleanser products, and paper towels," Veronica said.

"What kind of floors do you have?"

"Lots of hardwood. Some laminate. A little stone."

"Do you have a Swiffer?"

"No."

"I'll get my Swiffer and bring it over. And some extra Swiffer pads."

"We'll meet at six. We'll meet in front of this building."

"Yes. Thank you."

"Thank you."

We stood up and shook hands and I left the lab.

Chapter Twenty-Seven

That evening Veronica and I walked over to her house. She wasn't feeling very energetic, so we walked slowly. Her house was next to the campus, so it wasn't a long walk. We warmed up the pizza and ate it and then we started cleaning her house. She worked downstairs and I worked upstairs. After a while she got tired and said she needed a rest break and went to up to her bedroom upstairs. I cleaned some more and I thought her house was starting to look pretty clean.

"I need a rest break," I said.

"Come into my bedroom and rest with me," Veronica said.

I went into her bedroom and sat in a chair. She was lying on the bed with all her clothes on and her shoes off.

"I don't want to be alone tonight. Can you stay with me tonight?" she said.

"I can stay if you want me to."

"Please."

I called Alyssa and told her I was going to spend the night at Veronica's house.

"My house has a bedroom next to this room. Snow used that room as an office. That room has a bed in it that you can sleep in tonight. And there's a bathroom you can have all for yourself."

"Thank you. You have a nice house."

"Do you want to listen to some music?"

"Sure."

"Do you like old music?"

"How old are you thinking about?"

"I'm thinking about Benny Goodman music. Do you like Benny Goodman?"

"I love Benny Goodman."

"We can hear some of his music from the speakers over there. If you bring me my laptop I can play the music through the speakers."

There was a laptop computer on a table. I brought her the laptop and sat down again. She sat up in bed and typed on the keyboard. Benny Goodman started playing softly. Veronica laid down in the bed again. She looked at me.

"Do you ever do any swing dancing?" Veronica said.

"No. Do you?"

"I haven't done any in a long time. Snow wasn't a dancer."

"Did you go dancing before you met Snow?"

"Yes. I used to teach swing dancing. That was fun."

"Where did you teach it?"

"At a club in the neighborhood on the south side of the campus. That place is still there. They have a nice dance floor. They play all kinds of music. They used to have swing music nights. I think maybe they still do. The manager at the time knew I loved it, so they hired me to teach it. That's how I met Natalie. She was my partner before Snow."

"Was Natalie a good dancer?"

"She was an excellent dancer. She could move with the beat. When I'm with somebody who can't keep time with the music it's not as much fun."

"Did Natalie work for the university?"

"Yes. Natalie was a secretary in the engineering department."

"What happened to Natalie?"

"She met a guy who was an assistant dean and she married him. I have no idea why she did that. He got a better job at another school and she went with him. I lost contact with them. I don't know where they are now."

"That's too bad that she left you."

"It's the story of my life."

We didn't say anything for a few minutes. We listened to Benny Goodman.

"I think there's something wrong with me," Veronica said.

"Why do you say that?"

"Women leave me."

"That doesn't mean there's something wrong with you."

"Do you think I should change my hair color?"

"Why would you want to change your hair color?"

"Maybe my hair color is what's wrong with me."

"There's nothing wrong with you."

"Do you think I should become a blonde?"

"No."

"Everybody loves blondes."

"You're amazingly pretty just exactly the way you are right now."

"If that's true, why are women leaving me?"

"Some people do foolish things. If a woman leaves you, that shows there's something wrong with *her*."

"My life is a mess."

"But your house is not a mess."

Veronica smiled. "You're sweet. Come up here and lie here beside me for a little while."

She had a large bed. I took my shoes off and got on the bed and rested next to her without touching her.

"Do you like my big bed?" Veronica said.

"Yes, it's very comfortable."

"Snow and I slept in it together."

"How does it feel to have me here in your bed?"

"It's different. I can't remember ever being in bed with a man. The closest I've come to doing this was when I was a child. We had a large dog, a mixed breed. He would get on the bed with me if I would let him. He would get right up against me."

"Perhaps that's my role in life. To be something like a dog for women."

Veronica laughed. "You're cheering me up."

We didn't say anything for a few minutes.

"You're a nice person," Veronica said. "It's too bad you're not a woman."

"I'm sorry. I'm not perfect. I have many flaws. I know that."

"It's not your fault."

She started to get out of the bed.

"I have an idea," she said. "Just keep resting. I'll be right back."

She got up and went to a closet and took out some dresses and came back to the bed.

"Do you mind if I put these over you?" she said.

"That's fine."

She carefully spread the dresses on top of my body, leaving just my head uncovered, and got back into the bed.

"Does that help?" I said.

"I still miss Snow. I miss her so much."

"I'm sorry you've been abandoned. But you'll meet somebody new. She'll fall in love with you. You'll fall in love with her."

"I'm not ready for that. I just want to focus on my research for a while. It's hard to do any work when you're in love and you want to be with your partner all the time. Maybe I'm fortunate I've been abandoned."

"Maybe you'll find another dance partner. Just a dance partner. Would you like that? Would you like to have another dance partner?"

"I don't know. Maybe. Maybe I would go dancing again. I can dance with someone even when I'm not in love."

"Have you ever met Sophia Richardson? She's the daughter of the former physics department chairman, Chairman Richardson, and Britta Shaeffer Richardson."

"No. I've never met her."

"Sophia is a dancer. She's twelve years old, but she's a really good dancer. If you want to dance with a twelve year old, she's really good."

"She's twelve?"

"Yes."

Veronica laughed. "You're making me laugh."

"It's just a thought."

Veronica was serious again. "I'm sorry. I shouldn't laugh. It's a good thought. Maybe that's what I need. Maybe I need a dance partner who's just a dance partner."

"She's a wonderful dancer."

"Would her mother approve of me dancing with her?"

"If you're teaching her dance steps, sure."

Veronica didn't say anything for a minute or two. We listened to Benny Goodman. Then she said, "I probably should just focus on my research for a while."

"I understand."

"Jack, why is life so complicated?"

"Does it seem complicated?"

"Yes."

"It's not as complicated as electrical engineering."

"It's much more complicated than electrical engineering."

We listened to Benny Goodman for a long time. When the music ended she fell asleep. I went into the other bedroom. I got ready for bed and I tested the bed there. It was very comfortable. I fell asleep and slept until morning.

When I woke up Veronica was already up and getting ready for work. We said good morning and I started getting ready for work. When we were both ready, Veronica sat at a table in the kitchen and drank some coffee and asked me to join her.

"Thank you for letting me stay with you last night," I said.

"Thank you for staying with me," Veronica said.

"You have a nice house."

"I'm not ready to have someone else in the house right now. But maybe later it would work."

"I'm all right where I am now, in Alyssa's house."

"Before you met your current landlady did you rent rooms from other women landladies?"

"Yes. Several times."

"When you were in medical school?"

"Yes. During all four years of medical school. And also during my intern and residency years. And my senior year as an undergraduate."

"Did you ever rent from a man?"

"No."

"Why do you only rent from women?"

"I just like renting from women."

Veronica got up and went to the refrigerator. I got up also.

"I'm going to have a little breakfast, and then I'm going to go to work. Do you want a little breakfast?" she said.

"No, thanks. I need to go back to Alyssa's house, and then I'm going to work."

"Do you need a ride back to Alyssa's?"

"No. I can walk. It's not that far."

"Are you going to be all right?" Veronica said.

"That's a question I should ask you," I said.

"I'm feeling a little bit better today. As long as I can work at the same time as I'm crying, I can get a lot done. But I'm worried about you."

"Why are you worried about me?"

"I think maybe you're not aware of the risk of what you're doing. You haven't seen what can happen sometimes."

"Everything will work out."

"You need to be careful renting from women. You don't realize what my species can do."

"I'm sorry you've had a bad experience."

"A woman can hurt you," she said.

"I will avoid anyone who might want to hurt me," I said.

"A woman can hurt you even when she doesn't want to."

"If you're going to be all right, I'm going to go back to Alyssa's house now."

"Go ahead." We walked to Veronica's front door. Before I left, she gave me a hug and said, "I'm going to try to think positively. It's true that my lover has abandoned me. But I'm not pregnant, and my house is clean. Not every abandoned woman can say that."

Chapter Twenty-Eight

Alyssa liked Lexi and Veronica and wanted to help them. Alyssa wanted Lexi and Veronica to have a chance to talk to Alyssa's foreign tenants, Irina and Dimitri. Alyssa thought maybe they could help Lexi and Veronica find some research money. So Alyssa invited Lexi and Veronica to an informal buffet dinner with Irina and Dimitri and me at Alyssa's house. Lexi and Veronica said they would be happy to prepare some of the food.

Alyssa included me because I was living in Alyssa's house, and because she knew Lexi and I wanted to work together. I was happy to have an opportunity to get to know Irina and Dimitri. I lived in the same house with them but we hadn't spent a lot of time together.

On the evening of the dinner, before Lexi and Veronica arrived, I was sitting in the living room with Irina and Dimitri and Alyssa and Alyssa's dog Abraham. Alyssa was talking about her plans to be a candidate for state Supreme Court judge. Irina and Dimitri had never studied American history and didn't know any American presidents, but they liked dogs and thought Abraham was charming and would attract lots of votes.

Lexi and Veronica arrived together. Lexi brought some meat loaf and tomato sauce that she had made, and Veronica brought some baked green peppers stuffed with corn pudding that she had made. They put it in the kitchen with the rest of the food. Abraham followed them into the kitchen, but it wasn't time for his supper. Then Lexi and Veronica joined everyone in the living room, and Abraham followed them out to the living room. Abraham was always ready for a social gathering.

Lexi had been introduced to Irina and Dimitri previously but had only spent a brief time with them and didn't know them very well. Veronica had never met them. Alyssa made introductions and reintroductions, and everyone talked about how the university brought so many different people together and they liked meeting new people and who else did they know here.

I was getting hungry, so I was happy when Alyssa said it was time to eat. We all helped carry the food from the kitchen to the dining room. Alyssa gave Abraham his supper in the kitchen and joined us in the dining room.

Alyssa had prepared green beans with sliced almonds, and a salad with red leaf lettuce and orange slices. I had helped her prepare the food, but I don't have a lot of cooking talent. Nobody had made any dessert. Alyssa didn't think a dessert was a necessary part of a meal.

We served ourselves and sat down at the dining room table. Irina and Dimitri sat next to each other. Alyssa asked Irina and Dimitri if they wanted to give a blessing. Irina said something in Russian, and we started eating. All the food was very good.

"Irina, where are you from originally?" Veronica said.

"We are from originally Saint Petersburg, in Russia. If you study the Russian history, you may see people call it Leningrad. That was its name back in the days of the Soviet Union. Do you know Saint Petersburg?"

"I've never been there."

"We earned our undergraduate degrees there. Then we left Saint Petersburg and moved to Oxford, in England. That's where we earned our graduate degrees. And after we earned our degrees we got jobs as postdocs there."

"Do you like Oxford?"

"Yes. It's a great place to do research. The only thing bad about it is the food. The food that the natives eat is execrable."

"The food is execrable?"

"Yes. I learned that word when I was studying English. It's the perfect word for the food in Oxford."

"How can you survive if the food is execrable?"

"We prepare our own meals. And we have friends who entertain us who are expert cooks."

"How long will you be at our university?"

"We are here visiting your university as visiting research faculty for the year. So we are here through spring of next year. Then we return to our home in Oxford."

"Welcome."

"Thank you."

"Irina, is this your first trip to America?" Lexi said.

"No. We were in America previously. The two of us, we were exchange students in this country when we were in the secondary school. You call it a high school. We met originally then. We came here as exchange students because we wanted to see America and learn some of the language. But we were not here at your school before."

"Dimitri, what do you think about our school so far?" Lexi said.

"You have a strong chemistry department here. And a very pretty campus. And we like the town. Everybody tells us you have a good baseball team here. So when it is a baseball season we want to watch them play."

Everyone was eating and talking and listening to the conversation. Dimitri and Irina managed to eat while answering questions.

"I like your meat loaf and tomato sauce. Very good," Irina said to Alyssa.

"Lexi made that. It's her special recipe," Alyssa said.

"Very good," Irina said to Lexi.

"I'm glad you like it," Lexi said.

"It has an interesting seasoning," Dimitri said.

"The meat loaf and the sauce have cilantro in them. And no salt," Lexi said.

"It's probably unhealthy," Alyssa said.

"Delicious," Dimitri said.

"What are you researching while you're here?" Veronica said to Irina.

"We work in the field of inorganic chemistry. Our research is related to batteries."

"Do both of you work in the same lab?" I said to Irina and Dimitri.

"No, no. We never work in the same lab. In all of our career, we never work in the same lab," Irina said.

"Would you like to work in the same lab?" I said.

"No, no. We tell everyone we will not work in the same lab. We must work in different labs. Always different," Irina said.

"Why don't you work together?" I said.

"Do you want to tell him?" Irina said to Dimitri.

"No, you can tell him," Dimitri said.

"If we work together we would kill each other," Irina said.

"Don't you love each other?" I said.

Irina smiled and looked at Dimitri. He looked at her.

"Jack does not understand," Irina said to Dimitri.

They looked at me.

"I love Irina very much," Dimitri said.

"And I love Dimitri," Irina said.

"When we are at home she sits in my lap sometimes. We watch something together on the streaming service," Dimitri said.

"That is a nice feeling, sitting in his lap. I like to be as close as possible," Irina said.

"Do you want to sit closer to me here?" Dimitri said.

Irina moved her chair next to Dimitri's chair. She put an arm around him.

She looked at me. "Jack, are you married?"

"No."

"Were you married?"

"No."

"When you are married, you are married twenty four hours each day, seven days each week. It is a commitment. But you don't want to feel like you are in a prison. You need to be apart sometimes."

"Yes. Apart sometimes," Dimitri said.

"When you are apart sometimes, then when you are together being together is special," Irina said.

"Yes," Dimitri said.

"If you are never apart, then . . ." Irina said.

"Then your pictures are in the news," Dimitri said.

"In the news?" I said.

"Yes. Wife and husband kill each other in double murder," Irina said.

"It is not pretty," Dimitri said.

"When you are married, you will understand," Irina said to me. She looked at Veronica. "What do you think? Do you agree?"

"I'm not married, so I don't know," Veronica said.

Everybody ate and didn't say anything for a while.

"Tell me more about your research," Veronica said.

"We research batteries. Batteries have two terminals. One is called the cathode and one is called the anode. We want to find the best composition of the cathode and the anode. Her research is with the cathode and mine is with the anode," Dimitri said.

"You're not both researching the same thing?" Lexi said.

"We never research the same thing," Irina said.

"You work in different labs and also different research questions?" Lexi said.

"Always. We don't want to compete with each other," Irina said.

"Why not?" I said.

Dimitri looked at me. "Because if we compete with each other, then we are in the news," Dimitri said.

Irina looked at me. "Wife and husband kill each other in double murder," she said.

"Not pretty," he said.

"When you are married you will understand," Irina said.

"How did you become interested in batteries?" Lexi said.

"People have much interest in that field in England. And in your country also. Many people think research will lead to a better battery technology. And much research money is in the field.

So we have no difficulty to find support for our research," Irina said.

"What is your field of research?" Dimitri said to Lexi.

"Veronica and I are doing research in development and use of neutrino detectors. Do you know anybody who works in that area?" Lexi said.

Dimitri frowned. "No, I do not." He looked at Irina. "Irishka, do you know anybody who works with neutrinos?"

Irina shook her head. "No, I regret, I do not."

"Why did you call her Irishka?" Lexi said.

"It is a diminutive. In the Russian culture sometimes a speaker will use a diminutive," Dimitri said.

"How does that work?" Lexi said.

"The Russian use of diminutives is complex and sometimes difficult to understand. Sometimes a speaker uses diminutives with a child, but sometimes a speaker uses diminutives as a form of intimacy with an adult. It all depends on the circumstances," Dimitri said.

"I'm sorry you don't know anyone who does neutrino research," Veronica said.

"Is that a popular area of research in your country?" Irina said.

"No. It's not popular at all. Nobody is interested and nobody wants to support it," Veronica said.

"Sorry you are having difficulty to find some support. Where do you look for the support?" Irina said.

"We've applied to all the government agencies in this country that typically support physics research. And we've asked for research money from some sources outside government," Lexi said.

"To find money for research in an unpopular field is very difficult," Irina said.

"Do you think it's possible someone in England might be interested in our neutrino research?" Lexi said.

"Certainly it is possible. Unfortunately I don't know anybody who is interested," Irina said

"I also don't know anybody in your field, but certainly it is possible people are interested," Dimitri said.

Nobody said anything. Dimitri ate one of the green peppers stuffed with corn pudding. He looked at Alyssa and smiled.

"Alyssa, the green pepper with corn pudding is delicious."

"Veronica made that," Alyssa said.

Dimitri looked at Veronica. "Delicious."

"The corn pudding has some heavy cream in it. That's the secret ingredient," Veronica said.

"What do you think?" Dimitri said to Irina.

"Delicious. Do you like to cook?" Irina said to Veronica.

"I love to cook," Veronica said.

"Thank you for helping to cook this feast," Dimitri said to Veronica.

"Thanks to all the cooks," Irina said to Alyssa.

Irina looked at Dimitri. "These nice people have prepared this feast for us. I wish we could do something for them."

Dimitri looked at Lexi and then Veronica. "I am sorry I don't know any research in England in your field, but there may be people who are interested in that area."

"Maybe some group or some agency can use our technology. Maybe they have some people and some resources. Maybe somebody would like to join our team. Maybe we could do research with them," Veronica said.

"I agree. You never know what you will find until you look," Irina said.

"What's the best way to look?" Lexi said.

"Try to find someone to help you look. You need to find someone who knows many more people than we know, and who is willing to help you," Dimitri said.

Irina looked at Dimitri. "Maybe Mikhail Godonov can help them."

Dimitri frowned and looked at Irina. "Misha?"

"Yes. Maybe Misha can help them. What do you think?"

Dimitri was silent, and I wondered whether he was going to answer. Finally he said to Irina, "That is a possibility, but it will not be easy." He looked at Veronica. "It will not be easy."

"Yes, not easy, but a possibility," Irina said.

"Who is Mikhail Godonov?" Veronica said.

"He is a friend of ours. He is from Russia originally and then he moved to Oxford like we did. He moved there several years before we did. He is one of the people who persuaded us to move there."

"What does he do in Oxford?"

"He is now the research director for a company that makes scientific instruments that are used in chemistry research. Misha knows many researchers," Irina said.

"You called him Misha," Lexi said.

"Yes. His name is Mikhail but everyone calls him Misha," Irina said.

"What is Misha like?" Lexi said.

"He is smart and he likes to help people. He introduced us to other researchers. We benefitted from his help," Irina said.

"Tell them about his reputation with women," Dimitri said.

Irina laughed. "He likes pretty women. If he sees a pretty woman he wants to talk to her. He wants to be her friend. He wants to attract every pretty woman he sees. But he is married. He has a wife."

"Does he have affairs?" Veronica said.

"I don't know what you mean," Irina said.

"Does he go to bed with the women he meets?"

"You mean sex? I know several women who have met him and they don't say he takes them to bed. I believe he loves his wife. Of course it is difficult to know things. There could be things that I don't know."

"How can we ask him to help us?" Lexi said.

"You can write to him. That is a first step. I can help you with that," Irina said.

"If we write to him, will he help us?" Lexi said.

"I think it is possible," Irina said.

Dimitri looked doubtful.

"He likes to help the people, but he knows the people he helps," Dimitri said. "He does not know you. You are some strangers. He helps people if they are not some strangers. You need to become friends."

"What can we do to become friends?"

"It is not easy," Dimitri said. "I think you need to meet him. If you can meet him, you can become friends. But to meet him will not be easy. I don't think you want to go to England, and even if you go to England, will it change things? He will not meet everyone who says they want to meet him. He needs a reason to meet people. I am sorry but this is not easy."

Everyone ate more food.

Irina was not as doubtful as Dimitri. "Veronica, I think meeting Misha is not easy but I think it is possible," Irina said.

"How do you think we can meet him?" Veronica said.

"It is possible he will come here and you can meet him here."

"Why would he come here?"

Irina smiled. "I think he would enjoy meeting you."

"What can we do?"

"We should explain to Misha the opportunity," Irina said. "I think he likes to travel. He travels sometimes. This is a good town. It is a good place. It has an interesting university. He may want to learn about research at the university. Everyone can invite him. If he wants to take a trip, he can come here," Irina said.

"I think he does not travel very much. I think his wife travels more," Dimitri said.

Irina looked at Dimitri. "Yes, I think you're correct. She travels more than he travels."

"Maybe *she* will help," Dimitri said.

"Yes, that is true. I think his wife can help also. Everyone can invite Gabriela also," Irina said.

"Have you met his wife?" Lexi said.

"Yes. We know Gabriela. Gabriela is also from Russia originally. Gabriela moved to England before we did. She met Misha in England and they married," Dimitri said.

"What does Gabriela do?" Lexi said.

"She is managing editor of a publishing company," Dimitri said. "Not the president but she has an important job. They publish books in all the fields and also they publish science journals."

"Does Gabriela know lots of researchers?" Lexi said.

"She knows many of the researchers wanting to publish something. And of course she has a team of editors and assistant publishers who help her. Editors and assistant publishers cover specific fields and they know everybody who is working in their fields. As a group, the editors and publishers know everybody in every field," Irina said.

"Gabriela and her team go around and look for the best people who are doing the best work and ask them to publish their best work with her company. She will try to become friends of the best people. If they publish their best work there, her journals will have a fine reputation," Dimitri said.

"Yes, and she looks for people who can write books also," Irina said.

"Do you think she can help us?" Lexi said.

"Yes, certainly. Gabriela or somebody who works for her will know anybody who is active in your field. Gabriela can give you that information," Irina said.

"I want to meet both of these people. How can we persuade them to come here?" Lexi said.

"I will contact them. I will ask them do they want to meet you," Irina said.

"Will they come all the way here to our little college town just to meet us?" Lexi said.

"I don't know. I don't know whether Gabriela will come here. Maybe she will not come here." Irina looked at Veronica. "But I think Misha will come here if you do something."

"If I do something?" Veronica said.

"We are all friends here. Friends speak honestly to friends. I am speaking honestly, Veronica. I think you can persuade Misha to come here," Irina said.

"How can I persuade Misha to come here?"

"First of all, you have a Russian name. So that will make him interested in you."

"That's true. I have some Russian ancestors."

"And second, speaking honestly, you are very pretty. You have a really very pretty face and a wide mouth with perfect teeth and a beautiful smile, and you are tall and thin. You have a very striking appearance."

"I don't see how that's related to what we're talking about."

"Will you let me send a picture of you to Misha?"

"Why does he need to see a picture of me?"

"Veronica, you and I, we are women. We are not little schoolgirls. We know how the world works. We have some experience with men. We know all men have some interest in pretty women. And Misha has a high interest in pretty women."

"I don't know what you're suggesting."

"If Misha sees your picture I am sure he will want to meet you."

"I don't want him to meet me because he likes my face and my body. I want him to meet me because he is interested in neutrino research."

"He will become interested in neutrino research if he sees your picture."

"Irina, if you send him my picture, he will only be able to think of my body. He will not be able to think of my mind."

"Not true. A man can think of a woman's body and her mind also."

"I don't believe you."

Irina looked at Dimitri. "Dimitri, we need your opinion of this," Irina said. "Can a man think of woman's body and a woman's mind also?"

"Well, now, I must tell you, that is difficult. That is really quite difficult. But I believe it can be done. There are some men who can do it. There are some men who can think of a woman's body and her mind also," Dimitri said.

Irina looked at Veronica but didn't say anything.

"Irina, if you send him my picture, he will think I am interested in having sex with him. I am not interested in that," Veronica said.

"I will tell him you are doing great work in a cute little college town. I will say nothing about sex."

"Even if you say nothing, if you send him my picture, you are putting sex appeal into neutrino research. We are only doing neutrino research. There is no sex appeal in neutrino research."

"Maybe there should be sex appeal in neutrino research. If that will help you get money."

"No, Irina. There can never be sex appeal in neutrino research. Neutrinos and sex are two separate things."

"Show me your reference that says there can never be sex appeal in neutrino research."

"And Misha is married. I don't want to break up his marriage."

"Veronica, all I say is send him your picture. I don't say have sex with him. I don't say become a partner in adultery. I don't say have his baby. All I say is send him your picture. If his marriage is so fragile that it ends when we send him your picture, then it is already broken."

"This whole idea seems like a mistake. I don't want neutrinos and sex to be connected. I don't want to interfere with Misha and Gabriela's marriage. I don't want Misha to be attracted to me because of my body. I don't want Misha to chase me around our lab. Sending him my picture is wrong for a lot of reasons," Veronica said.

Irina turned to Lexi. "What is your opinion, Lexi?" Irina said.

Lexi looked at Veronica. "I know exactly what you're saying. But I wonder if maybe Irina is right. We have a great machine and we have no money. All of our work is for nothing if we don't find money. Irina is not asking you to have sex for money. Irina is just saying use your appearance to help yourself. Everybody in America who is good looking uses their appearance to help themselves. Why do you think the beauty industry is a multibillion dollar industry? Who buys all those products? People using their appearance to help themselves."

Veronica looked at Irina. "Irina, I want to meet these people but I don't want Misha to have the wrong reasons for coming here. If you send him my picture he will come here because he wants my body. He will chase me around the lab."

"All right, Veronica. I understand how you feel. I will not send him your picture," Irina said softly.

"Thanks for understanding how I feel," Veronica said, also speaking softly.

Irina frowned. "But we still have a problem."

"Why do we still have problem?" Veronica said.

"What will happen if he comes here? You really are very pretty," Irina said, still speaking softly.

"I don't think I'm anything special."

"You don't but he will."

"I'll wear hideous makeup."

Irina didn't say anything. A smile slowly appeared on Irina's face.

"What are you thinking?" Veronica said.

"I have a better idea," Irina said.

"You'll dress me in ugly clothes?"

"If you want to protect yourself from Misha chasing you, we should send your picture to Gabriela. Only to Gabriela," Irina said.

"How will that protect me?"

"She will not let him come here alone. She will come here with him. She will watch him and stop him from doing anything bad."

Veronica didn't say anything. She looked at Dimitri.

"I agree with Irina," Dimitri said.

Veronica looked at Irina again. "Let me think about that idea," Veronica said.

"Or maybe they will both decide just to stay in England. They might not come here at all," Irina said.

"That's true," Veronica said.

"But there is nothing we can do that will guarantee that they will both come here," Irina said.

"Go ahead and think about the details of how we can invite both of them. Let me think a little more about sending my picture to Gabriela," Veronica said.

Irina looked at Alyssa.

"We need to think about all the things we want to say to them. All the things that will persuade them to come here. I will make a list. Do you have some paper and something to use to write?" Irina said.

"Yes, I'll get that for you," Alyssa said. She looked around the table. "Did everybody get enough to eat?"

"Yes," everyone said. We had eaten almost all of the food. There was a little bit of salad left. Alyssa, Lexi, and Veronica were all good cooks.

Alyssa got up from the table and left the room.

"Thank you for helping us," Veronica said to Irina and Dimitri.

"It is an opportunity for someone to work on an excellent research project. Thank you for trying to make a connection to other research workers," Irina said.

"Yes. It is definitely an opportunity for someone. We need to find the right person," Dimitri said.

Alyssa returned with some sheets of paper and a pen, and gave them to Irina and sat at the table again.

"Thank you, Alyssa. Now we will think of what we will say to them," Irina said.

"Yes, we need to think of how we're going to persuade them," Alyssa said.

"You are a high level university official. Maybe Misha and Gabriela will like to meet you," Irina said.

"I would like to meet them," Alyssa said.

"You have a nice house. Are you willing to entertain them here?"

"Certainly. We can invite them to have dinner at my house. Everyone can meet them for dinner," Alyssa said.

Irina started making notes.

"I will send a note to Misha and a separate note to Gabriela. I will promote your neutrino research in each note. I will invite them to meet the researchers and have an excellent dinner at the home of a high level university official."

"Good," Alyssa said.

"I want to send Misha a picture of the university. Something that will make it look interesting to them," Irina said.

"I'll send you a picture that you can use," Alyssa said.

"And they will want to meet other people at the university. We don't need to promote other research, but can you arrange any meetings with other people?"

"I'll tell the heads of our science departments that Misha and Gabriela will be here, and will provide contact information so they can arrange their own meetings," Alyssa said.

"Yes, that will be good. I will tell Misha and Gabriela they can schedule meetings with the department leaders."

"Good," Alyssa said.

"That will help. Can we offer them more? We all know there are things that attract people. We talked about some of them already. We talked about beauty, we talked about food, we talked about opportunities to meet people. One of the other important things is money. Can we offer them money?" Irina said.

"I think so," Alyssa said.

"That will be helpful," Irina said.

"The university has a modest budget for attracting speakers. I can offer some money for travel expenses and a payment for speaking if Misha comes here and gives a speech while he is here. Or if Gabriela gives a speech here I can offer her some money," Alyssa said.

"Alyssa, you're wonderful," Lexi said.

"Yes. Thank you," Veronica said.

"I'm not sure exactly how much I can offer. I need to talk to some people," Alyssa said.

"Very good," Irina said.

"And I can offer them information about hotels and motels and rental cars. Do I need to offer to make hotel reservations for them?" Alyssa said.

"No. They have administrative assistants that help them," Irina said.

"Do you think we're offering enough? Do you think we will persuade them to come here?" Alyssa said.

"That is very difficult to predict. Maybe," Irina said.

Irina looked at Veronica.

"What is your decision? Do you want me to send your picture to Gabriela?" Irina said.

"I don't know. Do you think it's a good idea?" Veronica said.

"Yes. I want to tell Gabriela you do not want to have something with Misha. What do you say in English you have with a man?" Irina said.

"A romance?" Veronica said.

"No. What is the informal word for something you have with a man?" Irina said.

"A fling?" Veronica said.

"Yes. A fling. I want to tell Gabriela you do not want to have a fling with Misha. And if Gabriela thinks there is too much probability Misha wants to have a fling, then Misha cannot come here alone. Gabriela must come with him," Irina said.

"Yes. I agree. You should say that and send Gabriela my picture," Veronica said.

"Do you have a pretty picture I can send to Gabriela?" Irina said.

"Yes. I'll send you one," Veronica said.

"I think we will have a good message to Misha and also a good message to Gabriela," Irina said.

Irina looked at her notes.

"I will send a message to Misha saying I discovered a couple of neutrino researchers doing great work in a cute little college town in America. I will say one of the researchers has Russian ancestors. I will say their work is important and is the best in the world in their specialty and might win a Nobel Prize someday. I will say the researchers want to meet Misha and Gabriela and learn about researchers in England and talk about working together. And I will say I know a high level university official with a beautiful home who wants to invite everyone to dinner and introduce everyone. And I will say Misha and Gabriela will also be able to meet science department leaders on the campus. And I will say if they agree to give a speech at the university then the school will give them some money for travel expenses and for speaking," Irina said.

Irina looked up from her notes.

"What do you think?" Irina said to Veronica.

"That's very good," Veronica said.

"What do you think, Lexi?" Irina said.

"I like it," Lexi said.

"Do you like it, Alyssa?" Irina said.

"Yes. It's good," Alyssa said.

Irina looked at her notes again.

"I will send a separate message to Gabriela. I will start by saying the same thing I said to Misha, and then I will attach a beautiful picture of Veronica and say she is even prettier in real life than she is in her picture. And I will say that Veronica is not married. I will tell Gabriela I am not sending Veronica's picture to Misha, because Veronica does not want to use her appearance to attract people, and does not want to interfere with their marriage. I will tell Gabriela that Veronica is a nice person and not interested in adultery, but Veronica is really very pretty and some men might be interested in her and I want to be fair to Gabriela, and so Gabriela may not want Misha to come here alone," Irina said.

Irina looked up from her notes.

"What do you think?" Irina said, and looked around to everyone.

"Irina, those are good messages," Veronica said.

"Yes," Lexi said.

"Those messages are perfect," Alyssa said.

"Irina, you have an excellent understanding of people," I said.

"No. I have an excellent understanding of inorganic chemistry. I can predict chemical reactions. I never know what people are going to do."

Chapter Twenty-Nine

Morgan and Lexi and I still wanted to see the president of the university. We had waited for the president's administrative assistant, Juliette, to contact us after we met her. But we never heard from her, and we thought maybe she had forgotten us. I thought we should go see her again. Lexi wanted to go with me, and Morgan wasn't available at the same time as Lexi, so Lexi and I went to see Juliette. But Juliette wasn't there on the day we went to see her.

Juliette was working a job share with Sasha Walker, and it was one of Sasha's days to work, so we met Sasha. She was a tall thin Black woman. She had short hair and was wearing a red sleeveless dress with small silver earrings and dark shoes. I thought she looked stylish. I told Sasha I had met her husband, Lance, the athletics department compliance officer.

I asked Sasha whether she was interested in baseball and she said she was interested in all sports and loved baseball, and thought her interest in baseball was probably the reason the president hired her. I introduced Lexi, who said her parents had given her the first and middle names Alexandria Cartwright because they loved the game. Lexi said on her mother's side of the family she was related to Rabbit Maranville.

"Have you ever heard of Rabbit Maranville? He was a professional baseball player in the early days of baseball," Lexi said.

"Rabbit Maranville? I've heard the name. I think he started in the dead ball era. Is that right? Was he from the dead ball era?" Sasha said.

"He started out in the dead ball era. But he played a long time. He ended up playing in the live ball era," Lexi said.

"I think Rabbit is in the Hall of Fame," Sasha said.

"That's right. He's in the Hall of Fame," Lexi said.

Sasha asked us whether we were interested in the old Negro League. She said some great players had played in the league before the sport was integrated. Lexi was familiar with it and she talked with Sasha about some of the players. Sasha said she liked Cool Papa Bell, who played for several different teams. He was in the Hall of Fame also.

We talked for a while and eventually Lexi mentioned that we wanted to get an appointment to see the president, and ask him about finding research money and also ask him about Morgan's billing problem. Lexi said she knew the president was very busy, but if we could get in to see him we wouldn't take very much of his time.

Sasha looked at the president's calendar. She said the president could only talk to us for a few minutes and she gave us an appointment for the next week.

Lexi asked Sasha whether she thought the president would be able to help us.

Sasha smiled. "Sure he can help you. He knows a lot of people and he can connect you to some of them."

"Good."

Sasha looked serious. "But you need to be realistic. There's a limit to what he can do for you. He doesn't have magic powers."

"That's too bad. I think maybe we need somebody with magic powers. You know anybody like that?" Lexi said.

"My husband says I have magic powers, because I can make a lemon sponge cake that's amazingly delicious. But it's really not magic. I just follow my grandmother's recipe."

"I feel hungry all of a sudden," Lexi said.

"Me too. Let's go get something to eat," I said.

"Thanks, Sasha," we said, and we left.

Lexi and Morgan and I were there on time and the president didn't keep us waiting. Sasha was working that day and she led us into the president's office and introduced us. Our university president's name was John Churchill. He had a nice large well lit office with walls that were a pale cream color. The floor was covered with a soft beige carpet. He had a big desk and a big chair for himself, and in front of his desk he had several chairs for visitors, plus a couch over against a wall. One side of his office had thin curtains covering big windows. When we first came in to his office he was sitting at his desk. He stood up to greet us.

"President Churchill, this is Professor Alexandria Lieblich from our physics department. She's the one I was telling you about earlier. She's related to the baseball player. And this is Doctor Jackson Rose from our medical school, and Morgan Young who works in the physics department. Professor Lieblich and Doctor Rose wanted to talk to you about research, and also Ms. Young wanted to talk to you about an administrative problem," Sasha said.

"I am delighted to meet all of you," he said.

We shook hands with him.

"Thank you, Sasha," he said, and Sasha left us. We all sat down.

The president was tall and thin, with short straight black hair that was starting to go grey. His skin was slightly tanned. He had a handsome face with even features. He was wearing a nice grey wool suit with a subtle herringbone weave, and a red and silver tie with a conservative pattern.

He was sitting behind his large polished dark wooden desk and we were in some padded comfortable old chairs. I looked around the room. He had some pictures on the wall showing him with various people. I didn't recognize any of the people who were with him in the pictures, but they all looked distinguished.

"You have a famous relative," the president said to Lexi. "My administrative assistant told me earlier that you're related to Rabbit Maranville, one of the Hall of Fame baseball players from the early days of baseball."

Lexi smiled at the president. "Yes, that's right."

Morgan and I listened while the president and Lexi talked.

"Rabbit Maranville played twenty three seasons in the major leagues. You have to be pretty good to play for twenty three seasons," the president said.

"Yes. He was pretty good."

"He played several seasons for the old Brooklyn Dodgers, before they were called the Dodgers. I think they were called the Robins back in that era."

"Yes. That was back in the early years of the game."

"I think being related to Rabbit is a great connection."

"Your name is Churchill. Are you related to Winston Churchill, the famous British leader?"

The president smiled. "He was a distant cousin."

"That's a great connection also."

The president looked serious again. "My administrative assistant said you wanted to talk about research. Are you doing research?"

"Yes."

"What's your area of research?"

"I'm doing neutrino research."

The president leaned back in his chair. "Is that anthropology?"

"It's physics. Neutrinos are tiny particles."

"How is that going for you?" The president sounded bored. I wondered what he would have said if Lexi had told him she was studying wizard dust.

"Good except I'm having trouble finding any money for it."

"Yes, money can be a problem."

"Do you have any recommendations?"

"The university offers lectures from experts on how to look for research money. Have you been to those?"

"I've been to several, and my colleague here has been to one recently with me. They're good lectures, but we were hoping you might have some additional thoughts."

"Is your colleague here doing research in the same field?" The president looked at me. Lexi and Morgan listened as the he talked with me.

"I'm hoping to do sex research, sir."

He leaned forward. "Sex research?" He frowned briefly. "Were you connected to Joan? I met her once. She created quite a scandal."

"I never knew anything about her illegal activities, but yes, I was going to be her assistant doing sex research."

"What did you think of Joan?"

"She was brilliant."

He smiled. "Do you wish she were still here?"

"Are you asking me whether I want to work with someone who's dishonest?"

He looked serious again. "If it had been up to me, Joan would have been given a second chance."

"A second chance?"

"Yes. Let her pay back the money she embezzled and let her keep doing her research here."

"You're very tolerant."

"Joan was a special person."

"She was certainly a brilliant researcher."

"I've been a university administrator for a long time, and I've known a lot of different people, but not very many like Joan. Let me tell you something. Brilliant researchers are a dime a dozen. The world is full of brilliant researchers. But Joan had something special. She had something you don't find every day."

"What was that?"

"She had the ability to bring money in to the university. That's the one thing we need more than anything else," the president said to me. Then he paused and looked away, toward the windows.

"What a woman," he said softly.

"We want to bring money in to the university also," I said gently.

The president looked at me again. "Yes, of course," he said. His voice was back to its normal strength.

He bent his body down a little bit and brought his arms up from resting at his side, and he rested his elbows on his desk and rested his head in his hands. It was the only time I saw him looking undignified.

"Let's think about what you can do," he said.

He half closed his eyes and didn't say anything for several seconds. I was happy he was trying to help us.

He opened his eyes and straightened his body and took his hands away from his face. He looked at me and then at Lexi.

"There's a couple of people you should go and talk with," he said.

"All right," Lexi said.

"I think you should talk to Captain Shaeffer. Do you know Captain Shaeffer? He's a businessman and also a loyal baseball fan."

"We know who he is but we've never met him," Lexi said.

"You should meet him. Tell him you're baseball fans. He knows me. Tell him I said you should contact him."

"We'll do that," Lexi said.

"And you should talk to Miss Valery also."

"Miss Valery?"

"Yes. Her last name is Caselli. Her late husband was a businessman and also a baseball fan. She knows me also. Tell her I said you should contact her. My administrative assistant, Sasha, can tell you how to contact everyone."

"We'll do that. Do you think they'll give us some research money?"

"I have no idea. But I know they're friends of the school."

"Thanks for your help," Lexi said.

"I'm happy to help," the president said.

"We have one other thing we wanted to mention and get your advice on," I said.

The president looked at his watch.

"Will this take long?" he said.

"No."

"I'm happy to help if I can."

"Morgan has received a university medical bill for some ultrasounds. But Morgan has never had an ultrasound. So the bill is wrong. But we're having trouble getting it corrected," I said.

The president looked at Morgan. "Is that from the billing company that the university is using?"

"Yes. I'm not familiar with this company. Maybe you know more about them," Morgan said.

"The billing company we use now is Dickens, Deadwood, and Doorlicker. That billing company has a contract with the entire university, not just for billing but also for consulting and information technology. It's a pretty big contract."

"Their service doesn't seem to be very good," Morgan said.

"We've done studies of their service. Studies of customer satisfaction with their billing service. We do studies because health care is such a big business for us. The amount of revenue generated by the university hospital and the university outpatient services would amaze you. We study every aspect of that business, including billing."

"Then you should know about the problems."

"In our studies, do you know what we find?" The president smiled. "Eighty eight percent of patients give our billing service the highest rating."

"It can't be one hundred percent?" Morgan said.

"Eighty eight percent is excellent. Eighty eight percent is better than the industry average," the president said.

"Do you study patient satisfaction with your medical care?"

"Patient satisfaction with our medical care is eighty four percent. Which is also higher than the industry average."

"What should we do about the incorrect bill?"

"You can write them a letter if you want to."

"We already tried that."

"You can write them again."

"Have you considered using a different billing service?"

The president's face showed an expression of maximum seriousness and concern. "I understand why you're unhappy. I completely understand how you feel about this. But let's be realistic here. No billing company is perfect. If we used a different billing company it would be making errors too. This company that we're using now is really not bad. I wouldn't worry too much about billing. Most of the medical bills that you get will be correct."

"I still think it's a problem."

The president looked at his watch.

"I hate to end our visit together. I've enjoyed meeting all of you. But I have another appointment. When you're president, it's just one thing after another."

"We understand," Lexi said.

We all stood. The president came out from behind his desk and came over to us.

"Thank you for seeing us," Morgan said.

"Yes, thank you for your time," I said.

"Thank you," Lexi said.

"I hope to see you again," the president said. I wondered whether his statement was true.

We left the president's office. We paused for a brief conversation in the hallway.

Lexi said she wasn't sure exactly how she wanted to solicit money from the friends of the university. She thought maybe her daughter could help us. She said she wanted to talk to her daughter.

Morgan said she wasn't satisfied with what the president said about billing and she wanted to do more about the incorrect bill. I said I would help her work on the problem and would talk to her later about it.

We went over to where Sasha was working. She was sitting at her desk working on something on her computer. When she saw us she looked up and asked us what we thought of the president. Lexi said he was just like Sasha had described him earlier. Lexi told Sasha what the president said about contacting the friends of the university and asked her how we could contact them. Sasha said she would find contact information and send it to us. "Thanks, Sasha," we said, and we left.

I thought about Cool Papa Bell. I decided Cool Papa was a better name than Rabbit.

Chapter Thirty

Britta called me.

"Want to see another video of Sophia dancing?"

"I'd love to see another video of Sophia dancing."

"I'll send it to you."

She sent it to me and I watched it. Sophia was dancing to Latin American music. She was doing some fast spins. She looked good.

Chapter Thirty-One

Irina got a reply from Gabriela Godonov. Gabriela wrote that she and Misha were happy to hear from her. They appreciated Alyssa's kind invitation and were so happy that Irina and Dimitri were doing research in a charming university town, and they deeply regretted that Misha was so terribly busy that he could not travel to America, but Gabriela would be delighted to travel to our town and see Irina and Dimitri again and meet their friends and speak at the university, and when was the best time for a visit.

We met at Alyssa's house to decide how to respond. We sat at the table in her dining room. Abraham came in to see what we were doing. We were not eating anything, so he wasn't very interested.

Lexi said we should tell Gabriela again that we're interested in who is doing neutrino research in England. Veronica said we should tell her again it's an area where people could work together and everyone would benefit, and if everyone on the project worked really hard maybe they could win a Nobel Prize together. Alyssa agreed that should be in our reply.

Alyssa committed to some days that we could offer for Gabriela to come for dinner and Gabriela could choose from those days. Alyssa said Gabriela could speak at the university a day or two after our dinner, and Alyssa had a specific amount of money she could offer Gabriela. Everybody agreed to everything and so we had a plan.

So Irina sent out our reply to Gabriela, including an invitation for dinner at Alyssa's house, listing some possible days. Everybody went back to work on all their different activities, and waited for Gabriela to reply.

In a few days Gabriela sent her response regretting that she couldn't visit on any of our possible days, and giving some days relatively soon when she could come to visit. Gabriela said she thought neutrino research was a wonderful field and she promised to find out who was working on it before her visit. The group agreed on the days for her visit and Irina sent her our reply. And so it wasn't long before we had a small, I would say intimate, dinner for Gabriela.

Chapter Thirty-Two

Veronica volunteered to cook some traditional Russian food for the dinner with Gabriela. Of course we didn't know whether Gabriela actually liked traditional Russian food. But Veronica was an excellent cook. If Gabriela didn't already like traditional Russian food, I was pretty sure she would start liking it after she sampled what Veronica could make.

On the day of the dinner, Alyssa turned her kitchen over to Veronica, who had everything ready that evening when Gabriela drove up in her rental car. Alyssa was watching out her living room window and she went to her front door and opened it as Gabriela walked up to Alyssa's house. Alyssa smiled at Gabriela.

"Welcome to my humble home. Come in," Alyssa said.

"Thank you. Good evening, I am Gabriela."

They shook hands.

"Gabriela, we're delighted to see you. I'm Alyssa."

Gabriela smiled. "Thank you for inviting me."

Alyssa and Gabriella came into the living room. Gabriela was carrying a box of something. She was tall and thin and had short black hair and pretty blue eyes. She was wearing a beautiful perfectly tailored beige dress with matching shoes. Her dress had a low scoop neckline and a hem below her knees. She had nice legs. Her dress looked like it might be made of silk. I've seen single women wearing dresses like that to parties when they were on the prowl for a mate, but Gabriela wasn't single and she was here without her husband. I wondered what was on her mind.

"You know Irina and Dimitri," Alyssa said.

"Wonderful to see you again," Gabriela said.

"And this is Lexi and this is Jack and this is Veronica," Alyssa said.

We all shook hands with Gabriela. She was about the same height as Veronica.

"Hello, Veronica. I recognize you from the picture. I am so happy to meet you," Gabriela said to Veronica.

"And this is Abraham," Alyssa said.

Abraham was standing next to Alyssa, watching all of us greet Gabriela. Gabriela went over to Abraham and bent down and said something in Russian to him. He wagged his tail.

"That means you are a handsome dog," Gabriela said.

"Please make yourself comfortable. What would you like to drink? Some wine, perhaps?" Alyssa said.

Gabriela sat on the sofa. We sat in chairs near her.

"Thank you, but I never drink while I am working."

"Working?" Alyssa said. "While you are working? Do you think this is work? Did you come here because you must do this for your job? I'm deeply offended. We're all friends here. We're here together because we want to relax and talk and have fun. Do you want to do that? Do you want to relax and talk and have fun?"

"Yes, I want to do that," Gabriela said.

"I promise you we will not do any work here," Alyssa said.

"Good," Gabriela said.

"If we decide we want to work we'll schedule a time when can go to the university and sit in a conference room. We'll work there. We won't do any work here at all, for any reason," Alyssa said.

"We will have fun," Gabriela said.

"Would you like some Pinot Noir?" Alyssa said.

"Yes, please," Gabriela said.

Alyssa got a bottle and poured a glass of wine for Gabriela.

Alyssa had already provided something to drink for everyone else. Veronica had a glass of grape juice. Lexi and I were just drinking water. Irina and Dimitri had glasses of wine in front of them but I didn't see them drinking. Alyssa had told Gabriela we were all there because we wanted to relax and have fun, but I think our top priority was to listen carefully to Gabriela.

"And I have something for you. I brought you some baklava. Do you like baklava?" Gabriela said.

"I haven't eaten baklava in years," Alyssa said.

"I hope you will try this," Gabriela said. She put down her wine glass on a small table and opened the top of the box she had brought with her and showed the baklava to Alyssa. "Some of them have a filling of chopped walnuts, and some of them have a filling of apricot jam."

"Yes, I'll try some. Which ones have the walnuts?"

"These here."

Alyssa took one of the pieces of baklava with walnuts. She started eating it. "That's very good. Let me get some plates for that." Alyssa went to the kitchen and got some small plates for the baklava and came back and handed them out. While she was doing that, Gabriela was offering it to everybody.

"Who else wants some?" Gabriela said.

"I'll try some," Lexi said. "Are these the ones with apricots?"

"Yes."

She took one of the pieces with apricots.

"Some for you?" Gabriela said to Veronica.

"Yes, please." Veronica took one of the pieces with walnuts and started eating it.

Gabriela also gave some baklava to Irina, Dimitri, and me. It was delicious.

"That's really good. Who made that?" Veronica said.

"I made it myself," Gabriela said.

Abraham was watching Gabriela. Gabriela looked at Abraham. Abraham raised one eyebrow. Gabriela said something in Russian to Abraham.

Gabriela looked at Veronica. "That means, 'I'm sorry Abraham. I don't have anything for you,'" Gabriela said.

Abraham lowered his eyebrow.

I was starting to like Gabriela. She could make good things to eat and she seemed to have a good rapport with dogs. She had a pretty good rapport with people also.

"How do you make those layers like that?" Veronica said.

"You start with a good filo dough. Then you wrap it around your filling."

"Can you give me the recipe? I want to learn how to make it."

"Do you like to cook?"

"I love to cook."

"Perhaps we can make some baklava together sometime."

"Let's do that."

"And I happen to know that when you eat baklava it blocks the absorption of alcohol, so it's like you're not drinking at all," Gabriela said.

"I'm not sure that's true," Lexi said.

We ate baklava and listened while Gabriela told us about herself.

"You've come a long way to see us," Alyssa said.

"I travel all the time. Part of my job in the publishing business. I like to go places and meet people," Gabriela said.

Gabriela talked about all the places she had seen as part of her work. She had been all over the world.

Gabriela steadily sipped her wine. When her glass was almost empty Alyssa said to her, "Would you like some more Pinot Noir?"

"Yes, please. Just a little bit."

Alyssa poured more wine for Gabriela. Veronica was still drinking grape juice. Gabriela looked at Veronica.

"Veronica, I must tell you, you look wonderful," Gabriela said.

"Thank you," Veronica said.

"I'm delighted to be here with you," Gabriela said.

"I'm happy you are here," Veronica said.

"I saw your picture and I knew immediately I needed to see you in person."

"Thank you for coming a long way to see us."

"Tell me about yourself. You have a Russian name. What is your family's connection to the country where I was born?"

"I believe my great grandfather was born in Russia. That was my father's father's father. That's where I get the name Chebychev. It's the name of a famous Russian mathematician. But I'm not related to the mathematician," Veronica said.

"I'm sure you have many interesting relatives," Gabriela said.

"My relatives are from different places, not all Russian," Veronica said.

"You and I are similar. My relatives are from different places also. My mother's family is from Latvia. Gabriela is a Latvian name. It was my grandmother's name in Latvia. My friends say maybe I am not a true Russian if my name is Latvian," Gabriela said.

Gabriela looked at Lexi.

"What about you?" Gabriela said to Lexi. "Do you have Russian relatives?"

"No. Sorry," Lexi said.

"And you?" Gabriela said to me. "Did your ancestors come from Russia?"

"No. My ancestors were from England, Scotland, Ireland, and France. None of them were from Russia. Sorry."

"That's all right. Not your fault. We are still all friends here," Gabriela said.

"I'm not Russian, but I like Russian culture," I said.

"What parts of Russian culture do you like?"

"I like Russian classical music. I like Russian ballet."

"What Russian composers do you like?"

"I like Tchaikovsky. He's my favorite."

"Yes. His music is very pretty," Gabriela said.

"Would you like to hear some music? We can listen to some Tchaikovsky if you like," Alyssa said.

"Do you have some we can listen to? I would like to hear some," Gabriela said.

"Yes, I'll turn on some music for us," Alyssa said, and went into another room.

Soon we heard Tchaikovsky softly in the background.

"That is beautiful," Gabriela said.

Alyssa came back into the room.

"Are you hungry? Are you ready for dinner? Let's go into the dining room. Jack, can you help serve?"

"Sure."

"Let me give Abraham his dinner and then I'll join you," Alyssa said.

Alyssa gave Abraham his supper in the kitchen and joined us in the dining room. Alyssa and I set the table and brought some food out from the kitchen and served the food while the others sat at the table, and then we sat at the table. For the main course Veronica had prepared small pies with a chicken and egg and potato filling. She also had prepared cabbage rolls stuffed with rice and peas, and a salad with chopped vegetables.

"Would you like to give a blessing?" Alyssa said to Gabriela.

Gabriela bowed her head and said something in Russian. She looked at Alyssa. "A traditional blessing."

We all started eating.

"Delicious," Gabriela said.

"Veronica prepared it," Alyssa said.

"You are a good cook," Gabriela said to Veronica.

"Thank you. I love to cook."

"What was it like growing up in Russia?" I said.

"My parents were translators," Gabriela said. "They met at work. They spent time at embassies in different countries. So we moved around as a family. It was interesting. When I was a child we lived in England for several years. I liked England and I decided that's where I wanted to live if I had a chance to live there as a grown up."

"What other careers did your relatives have?" I said.

"Several of my father's relatives went into civil engineering or industrial engineering. I think they were relatively prosperous. One of my ancestors was a professor."

"I'm glad they were successful," Lexi said. "I think it must have been a struggle for people in Russia going through the trauma of the First World War, and then the revolution, and then the hardships of the early communist years, and the Great Depression, and the Second World War, and then the Cold War, and now the years after that."

"Yes, my ancestors went through difficult times, but there were difficult times in other countries as well. And many people in Russia believed they were building a better society. They thought their future was going to be better than their past," Gabriela said.

"Would you like a little more Pinot Noir?" Alyssa said to Gabriela.

"Yes please. Just a little."

Alyssa poured more wine for Gabriela.

"And there was always the Russian cultural heritage. There was classical opera and classical ballet and classical symphony being performed. People took pride in it," Gabriela said.

Gabriela talked about Russian culture and the performers and performances she had seen. She had a detailed knowledge of Russian cultural history. She had seen the most famous ballets, including Swan Lake, Sleeping Beauty, The Nutcracker, Giselle, Romeo and Juliet, and Spartacus, and she told us about her memories of them. She told us about Russian operas she had seen, including Boris Godunov, A Life for the Tsar, The Tsar's Bride, and Eugene Onegin. She was a great representative for Russian culture. After listening to her I wanted go out and buy tickets to some performances.

We had a leisurely dinner, and then we adjourned to the living room, mainly because the chairs were more comfortable there. Gabriela sat next to Veronica.

"Gabriela, would you like some more Pinot Noir?" Alyssa said.

"Yes, please."

Lexi poured more wine for Gabriela. Veronica was still drinking grape juice.

"Gabriela, can we talk about science research?" Veronica said.

"Vera, we can talk about anything you want," Gabriela said.

Nobody interrupted Gabriela and Veronica. We just listened as they talked.

"I'm so happy you have come to visit us and talk about our work. You're very generous with your time," Veronica said.

"I'm happy to be here and talk to you. And may I say, Veronica, you have a beautiful smile," Gabriela said.

"Thank you. Gabriela, I just want you to tell me some things unofficially."

"Yes, of course."

"Nobody is going to quote you."

"I understand."

"What we say here does not leave this room."

"Nika, I will tell you whatever you want to know."

"We are all friends here."

"Yes, my friend."

"Gabriela, we all know that friends speak honestly to each other. Irina reminded me of that recently. I am going to be honest with you, and I want you to be honest with me."

"Nothing would make me happier, my dear friend."

"I want to talk with you about our neutrino detector, as a friend. Tell me honestly your conclusions without holding anything back."

"And I will do that, my friendly Vika. That is exactly what I will do."

"You know that Lexi and I, we have a little bit of a problem. We have this neutrino detector, and we need help. We want our neutrino detector to be used by many people, not just by Lexi and me."

"My friend with the beautiful smile, the entire world should use your neutrino detector. I believe that."

"We want to find a partner who can help us test it in new applications."

"My precious friend, you should have such a partner."

"We want to find a partner who can help us demonstrate the uses of our neutrino detector."

"Verochka, everything you tell me is wonderfully wise."

"I say it because it is true," Veronica said. "And friends speak the truth to each other."

"Yes, they do that."

"And we are friends."

"I am happy to say that you are correct."

"As a friend, tell me what England is doing in neutrino detector research. Can you help us find anyone who can work with us? Can you help us find anyone who will use our neutrino detector?"

"My beautiful friend Veronica, I am prepared to answer your question."

"I'm glad."

"Because before I came here tonight to visit you, I made inquiries."

"You made inquiries?"

"Yes, Verusha. I talked to everyone who might possibly know anything about neutrino detectors."

"Everyone who could possibly know?"

"Yes. I talked to publishers and editors and assistant editors and people who were just walking down the hall when I was talking."

"So you have been thorough," Veronica said.

"I have been thorough, my wonderful friend. I talked to scientists, and the heads of research departments, and the staff of research departments, and the janitors in research departments. I talked to friends and acquaintances and people who did not know me," Gabriela said.

"What did they tell you?"

"Veronica."

"Yes?"

"Vera."

"Yes?"

"My friendly Nika."

"Tell me, Gabriela."

"My brilliant new friend Nikochka."

"I want you to tell me, Gabriela."

"And I want to tell you, but it is difficult."

"Yes, Gabriela, tell me."

"I want to tell you, but I do not want to hurt a friend."

"Go ahead Gabriela. Whatever it is, you can tell me."

"My sweet Veronica, my dazzling scientist friend, it saddens me to tell you this."

"Tell me."

"Nobody is doing neutrino detector research. Governments will not provide any money for neutrino detector research. Industry will not provide any money for neutrino detector research. Nobody is interested in your field. It is lifeless. Inert. Barren. Desolate. Defunct."

"Really?"

"I am speaking the truth, my raven haired friend. This is not my decision. I believe many people should be working together with you. I believe there should be a great neutrino detector program. I feel sad that there is no interest."

"Really?"

"I'm sorry, my friendly Russian cousin. I hope you are not disappointed."

"Disappointed? You hope I am not disappointed? No, Gabriela, I'm not disappointed. I'm dismayed. I'm appalled. I'm amazed. I'm shattered. This goes way beyond disappointed."

"I'm sorry, my friendly queen of science."

"It's not your fault. I appreciate your coming here. I appreciate your telling me."

We all sat in silence for a while.

"What time is it? It must be getting late. It might be time to leave you. Thank you for your kindness to me," Gabriela said.

"Gabriela, you've had some alcohol. I don't want you to be out on the streets driving around now. It might not be safe," Alyssa said.

"What do you think I should do, Alyssa?"

"Rest here for a while. Call your hotel and tell them not to expect you tonight."

"Do you have a place for me to rest?"

"All of our beds are in use. But we have a very comfortable big couch in the recreation room. It's probably more comfortable than a bed. You'll like it," Alyssa said.

"I don't have any pajamas."

"I have some clean pajamas that you can use."

"I don't have a toothbrush."

"I have some new toothbrushes. I'll give you one."

"I don't want to trouble you."

"It's no trouble at all. You've come a long distance to be here. You must be tired. Rest here tonight. It will be good for you."

"Maybe I should do that. Can you show me the room?"

"Yes. I'll show it to you."

Alyssa led Gabriela to the couch and returned without her.

"Gabriela wants to help you very much. I'm sorry nobody is working in your field," Irina said to Lexi and Veronica.

"I agree. She wants to help you very much. Be patient. Who knows what will happen in the future," Dimitri said.

Veronica and Lexi offered to help clean up but Alyssa said that wasn't necessary, so they said goodbye. Alyssa and Irina and Dimitri and I cleaned up the kitchen and the dining room, and went to our rooms and got some sleep.

Gabriela stayed overnight. In the morning she came to the kitchen for a quick breakfast. Alyssa and Irina and Dimitri and I were already there. We all greeted her. Irina and Dimitri talked a little bit about their work. Irina and Dimitri said they had to go to the lab, and they left for work.

I listened while Alyssa and Gabriela talked. Alyssa asked Gabriela whether she enjoyed her visit here.

"I don't remember much about last night, Alyssa."

"We ate your baklava. It was delicious. Thank you. We had a nice dinner. You told us about Russian ballet, and Russian opera. You told us about ballets you had seen, and operas you had seen. And you talked a little about history. You have an interesting perspective on the country where you were born. I liked hearing it."

"I don't remember much."

"You seemed to like Veronica."

Gabriela smiled. "She's a wonderful person."

"Veronica was disappointed that there's no interest in neutrino research, but we appreciate your honesty."

"I'm sorry to disappoint her."

"Thank you for coming to visit us. We really appreciate it."

"Thank you for inviting me. I enjoyed meeting you and your friends. And I'm sure I will enjoy speaking at your university. This is a really nice town. I was planning to stay in your town for only a few days. Now I don't want to leave."

"Do you want to stay in town a little longer than you originally planned?"

"I don't know whether that's possible. I don't know whether my hotel has any rooms if I stay longer."

"Would you like to stay with us? You don't need to stay in a hotel. Did you leave your luggage there? You can get it and bring it here. We would love to have you stay here. You can sleep on the couch again. Was it comfortable? You can use the laundry machine to wash your clothes."

"Thank you. I would like that. Yes, your couch is comfortable like a bed. You're very generous. I'll call my husband and tell him I'm changing my travel plans. And I'll call my administrative assistant and ask him to rearrange my travel schedule."

"Thanks again for the baklava. Veronica said she wanted to learn how to make it. Do you remember when she told you that?"

"Did she say that? My memory of last night is not very good. Do you have her contact information? I'll call her."

Alyssa gave Gabriela Veronica's contact information.

"Perhaps Veronica and I can make some baklava together," Gabriela said.

"Do you want me to invite Veronica to come over tonight? So you can show her how to make baklava?"

"Yes, that would be wonderful."

"I'm not sure we have all the ingredients. You can look and see what we have."

"I can make a whole meal if you like. Would you like to try some Latvian food? I can make some fish stew for you. Would you like that? It has white fish, carrots, potatoes, tomatoes, and cilantro. I think it's delicious."

"Lexi loves cilantro. Do you want me to invite Lexi to come over tonight also?"

"Yes, that will be good."

"That's very nice of you to offer to make that for us."

"No trouble. I think you'll like it."

"I think you have my contact information. Make a list of the groceries you need and send it to me and I'll go to the store today and get them."

"That's kind of you. I will make a list."

"I need to go to work this morning. I'll see you again this evening."

"Wait. Alyssa, before you go, I just have one question."

"I hope I know the answer, Gabriela."

"Do you think there are any job opportunities for me here in your town?"

"Job opportunities? You mean for you and your husband?"

"No. Just for me."

Alyssa looked surprised. "You don't want to be with Misha?"

"He's happy where he is. I'm not so happy."

"Gabriela, I don't want to break up your marriage."

"You're fine. It's not your fault."

"Are you unhappy with your current job?"

"I like it here. I want to take a leave of absence from my current job."

"Why do you like it here?"

"I like the people here."

"You already have a great job in England."

"I work hard but the salary is not great. It may be time to find something new."

"Yes, that makes sense. But if you're going to come to this country to work, maybe you should look around at different cities to see which one you like best."

"I already know I like this one, Alyssa."

The expression on Alyssa's face changed. Earlier she was more relaxed. Now she seemed maybe a little bit worried, like she had just realized her life was becoming more complicated.

"Gabriela, is there something else on your mind also?" Alyssa said softly.

"What do you mean?"

"Do you want to stay in this town because of Veronica?" Alyssa said, still speaking softly.

"This may be difficult for you to understand," Gabriela said, also speaking softly.

"You can tell me."

"I'm in love with Veronica. When I first saw her picture I thought nobody could really look like that. And I thought if anybody really does look like that then they probably have flaws in other ways. I knew I had to meet her. And now I have met her and I know she is wonderful."

"Gabriela, I don't know that she feels the same way about you."

"That doesn't matter. I want to be here."

"If you stay here, do you think you can help Veronica find some research money?"

"If there is any money anywhere, I will find it. I just need a job here so I can live here."

"I don't know what jobs are open at the moment. I'll look around a little bit and see what I can find."

"Thank you. You're very helpful."

"I can't promise I will find anything."

"I appreciate your looking."

Alyssa said goodbye to us and left for work. Gabriela looked in the kitchen to see what ingredients were available and what she needed. After a while I left for work also.

That evening, Alyssa and Irina and Dimitri and Veronica and Lexi and Gabriela and I had an excellent dinner, prepared by Gabriela.

Alyssa said she had found a job opening for an instructor here at the university in the department of Russian language and culture. It was not tenure track and was just a one year appointment, with a possibility of being renewed at the end of the year. The job as posted required a PhD, which Gabriela didn't have. But as a personal favor to Alyssa, the chair of the Russian department said she would rewrite the posting so Gabriela would qualify.

Gabriela said she was interested.

"Gabriela, if the department offers you this job and you accept it, that's a serious commitment. You have to stay for the whole year. If you get tired of our little college town, you can't leave in the middle of the year and go back to England," Alyssa said.

"Yes, I understand. If I can work here, this is where I want to be. I believe I will be accepted here. I believe I will enjoy being here."

"You'll need to apply to the immigration authorities for permission to stay and work in this country. The university will help you. I'll introduce you to immigration lawyers who have had experience with similar cases."

"Thank you."

Gabriela spoke at a colloquium at the chemistry department the next day. That evening we asked her how it went and she said it was good. She liked the people she met.

A few days later the chair of the Russian department told Gabriela the department had completed the hiring process and she welcomed Gabriela to the department. Gabriela started working on lesson plans. The immigration lawyers found a way for Gabriela to stay in the country.

In her spare time Gabriela helped Veronica make more batches of baklava. I said maybe Lexi and Morgan would like some. Gabriela and I brought some baklava over to the Shaeffer Building and gave some to Lexi and Morgan. They thanked Gabriela and said they were happy she had come here. Gabriela said she was happier than they were.

Chapter Thirty-Three

Alyssa took a leave of absence from her job at the university. She announced her campaign, with Abraham, for the state Supreme Court. Her announcement didn't get much news coverage.

Alyssa went around making speeches, but she didn't attract any big crowds. She had a good web site and she put videos of her speeches on her site, but her site didn't attract a lot of viewers.

Chapter Thirty-Four

A few days after that, Morgan called me.

"Doctor Rose, it's Morgan."

"Good to hear from you."

"This baklava is delicious."

"Yes, it's quite tasty."

"Doctor Rose, I've been thinking about the incorrect medical bill."

"Yes."

"Do you think the university might be trying to bill me for ultrasounds for the gorilla at the zoo? The gorilla and I both have the name Morgan. And the gorilla does get ultrasounds."

"I suppose that's possible."

"I want to go to the zoo. Do you want to come with me?"

"Why do you want to go to the zoo?"

"Maybe someone there can fix the billing problem. And I want to meet the other Morgan."

"Sure. Let's go to the zoo together. Lexi might want to see the gorilla Morgan also. Can Lexi join us?"

"Yes, she should meet the gorilla Morgan also."

I talked with Lexi about going to the zoo. She wanted to see the zoo's Morgan with us. I said I would arrange a visit.

I called one of the doctors at the medical school who was on the research team doing the gorilla cardiology. He gave me the name of his contact person at the zoo. Her name was Ginger. I called Ginger and told her I worked at the medical school helping researchers. I said I heard about Morgan the gorilla and I wanted to see her. I asked whether I could come visit the zoo and bring some friends, and talk with Ginger about Morgan the gorilla and maybe also resolve an administrative problem we were having.

Ginger said unfortunately she had arthritis in her hips. She had been taking sick leave and was behind in her work and didn't have any time to meet us right now. I told her the medical school didn't just study gorillas. It also offered clinical trials for humans, and I said the trials for humans were just as good as the gorilla studies. I said she could meet me and talk about the possibilities if she was interested.

A few days later Ginger came to my office.

"How do you like working at the zoo?" I said.

"It's like having a big family with hundreds of children, who need hundreds of different things. It's challenging and also rewarding."

We talked about her medical condition. She was eligible for a paroxetine treatment clinical trial. I told her I was not one of the researchers conducting the trial. I was just helping recruit people who might be interested in enrolling in the trial. I described the trial process. I told her if she enters the trial she will either be assigned to the treatment group and be given the experimental treatment, or assigned to the control group and given a placebo. I told her she won't know which group she's assigned to.

I asked her if she had any questions.

"You're not one of the researchers doing the trial?" she said.

"That's right."

"Do you do some other variety of research?"

"I'm hoping to set up a lab to do sex research."

She laughed. "Do real researchers actually do that?"

"It's a legitimate field of study. But it's hard to get money to do it. I'm looking for research money."

"Yes, I know how hard it is to get money for research. At the zoo we're interested in conservation of different species. The people who study that are always struggling to get money."

"Yes, money is hard to find. Have you ever heard of neutrinos?"

"Neutrinos? What are they?"

"They're elementary particles. People in experimental physics study them. I have a friend who's trying to get money for neutrino research."

"Good luck to you and your friend."

"Thanks."

Ginger went home and thought about whether she wanted to be in the paroxetine study and came back and signed up. About two weeks after she enrolled in the trial she called me and said she felt better and she was so happy she was in the trial. She said whatever they were giving her seemed to be helping.

I told her there are no guarantees in experimental medicine but I hoped her good results would continue. I wondered whether she was getting the placebo or the experimental treatment.

After that, she got her job at the zoo under control and called me and said she would be happy to show the gorillas to me and Morgan and Lexi. I said we appreciated her help.

A few days later Morgan and Lexi and I were at the zoo. Ginger met us and I introduced everyone and Ginger gave us a tour. Visitors could walk on an asphalt walkway which went around to all the animal exhibits. We walked past the giraffe exhibit and the elephant exhibit and came to the gorilla home.

The gorillas lived in a large area, maybe eight or ten acres, with gently rolling terrain covered with grass and some small plants and some rock piles and a few big trees. In the distance we saw some structures that looked like gorilla houses. A double moat ran around most of the border and a tall fence ran along the rest of the border. Several wooden signs described how these gorillas were western lowland gorillas, which were endangered in the wild, and how a species conservation program at zoos was designed to preserve the species.

"I don't see Morgan the gorilla outside today. She must be in one of the gorilla houses," Ginger said.

"Too bad," Morgan said.

"But some of our other gorillas are out."

Ginger pointed to some gorillas in the distance.

"Over there you can see some gorillas playing in that big pile of leaves. Our gorillas like to play in leaf piles, so we make some leaf piles for them," Ginger said.

We looked at the gorillas playing in the leaf pile.

"That looks like fun," Lexi said.

We watched the gorillas for a while, then we asked Ginger if we could talk about the billing problem. She was interested in it and she listened to us and said she would investigate. She was curious about our work, so we talked with her a little bit about our research. She said sexual dysfunction among zoo animals was a problem sometimes, and if I ever got tired of studying humans she could find some work for me. We thanked her and returned to school.

Chapter Thirty-Five

Ginger called me about a week later. She said the zoo administration had conducted an investigation of the billing. The zoo administration checked the dates of doctors' visits to the zoo and dates on the human Morgan's bill and thought the bill that the human Morgan got was probably an attempt by the billing company to get paid for the ultrasounds of the gorilla Morgan.

Ginger said the cost of all the gorilla ultrasounds was supposed to be covered by the medical school's research grant and therefore shouldn't be billed separately to the zoo or to anyone else. She said the zoo admin people had three different theories about what was going on. One person in zoo admin thought the problem was caused by careless record keeping. They thought the school's medical records department created a chart to hold the results of the ultrasounds, but didn't note that Morgan was a gorilla in a research project. Someone in billing found the chart and decided to generate a bill, and made a guess that the bill should go to the human Morgan.

She said another person in zoo admin thought the billing company had an incentive to create extra bills because it was paid an administrative fee based on the total number of bills it sent out each month. This theory said that sending the bill was more than just careless record keeping. It was fraud by someone in the billing company who knew about the gorilla research but wanted to create a bill anyway. This theory said that the purpose of the bill was to increase the billing company's administrative fee.

She said several other people in zoo admin proposed a third theory. They also thought the bill involved fraud, but was not a scheme to increase the administrative fee. They thought someone in the billing company had a secret partner inside the medical school and together they generated fraudulent bills and diverted the proceeds to themselves. Insurance companies often paid the bills without realizing they were fraudulent.

She said because of the possibility of fraud we should contact someone in law enforcement and ask them to investigate. I thought about Alyssa's son, Clark, who was working as a staff lawyer in the attorney general's office. I said I would call him.

Ginger said gorillas spend their time playing in leaf piles, while humans spend their time struggling with billing companies. She asked me who was smarter, humans or gorillas. I didn't try to answer that. I thanked Ginger and bought an annual membership to the zoo.

I called the attorney general's office and spoke with Alyssa's son, Clark. I told him I was living in a storage closet in his mother's house. He knew exactly what storage closet I was talking about and he asked me how I liked living there. I said it was a nice storage closet and his mother had a great house and I felt fortunate to be there.

I told Clark about Morgan and the billing problem. He was interested and wanted to meet Morgan and me. I talked with Morgan and again with Clark and we eventually met for lunch at A Slice Is Nice.

Morgan and I arrived at the pizza place before Clark. We waited for him near the entrance and introduced ourselves when he arrived. We all got some pizza and we found a good table out on the porch away from the crowd. We sat at our table and talked.

Clark had very light brown hair, almost blonde. He had a handsome face with features which I thought looked strong and rugged. He seemed to take an immediate interest in Morgan and she seemed to take an immediate interest in him.

"Doctor Rose told me about the billing problem," he said to her.

"Thanks for meeting with us. What do you think is going on at the billing company?" she said.

"It's probably an innocent mistake. I never assume anything is fraudulent. But the attorney general's office needs to investigate this because of the possibility of fraud. One of my jobs is to look at things like this. So I'll be happy to look at it further."

"Thank you. I really appreciate your help," Morgan said.

"Clark, how is your mother's campaign going?" I said.

"She's having trouble generating publicity. She needs to do something to get more attention."

"I hope she can find a way to get more publicity," I said.

We ate pizza and Clark asked Morgan about her work and Morgan asked Clark about his work. As they talked, Morgan studied Clark's face and his body and Clark studied Morgan's face and her body, and they appeared to be in no hurry to finish their lunch. I thought Clark's interest in Morgan, and Morgan's interest in Clark, might extend beyond just the billing problem. I wasn't interested in watching them lusting after each other, if that's what they were doing, so I finished eating and I said I needed to get back to work and I left the two of them together.

After that, the billing company stopped sending Morgan bills for the ultrasounds. The attorney general's office never charged anybody with fraud in the case. Morgan said she thought the billing company got scared by the investigation. I wasn't sure exactly what was going on at Dickens, Deadwood, and Doorlicker, but I was happy that it stopped sending the bills to Morgan.

Chapter Thirty-Six

A few days later Lexi called me.

"My daughter Hadley wants to work with us. I think she can help us."

"Yes, I think so too."

"She's coming for lunch tomorrow. Would you like to come over then? We're having pasta and ground turkey and salad."

"I would love to come over then."

The next day I was at Lexi's house for lunch. Hadley was already there when I arrived. We stood and talked briefly in Lexi's living room. Hadley had colored her hair black.

"Is that hair color from Kool Aid?" I said to Hadley.

"No, this is Arctic Fox, semi-permanent," Hadley said.

"What does George think about that color?" I said.

She smiled. "You remembered George."

"You mentioned him the last time I saw you. I thought he might be important to you."

"He says it's not bad. I don't think he's wild about it."

She paused.

"What do you think about it?" she said.

"I think I agree with George."

Hadley was wearing a red shirt and grey pants and her soft blue shoes with white soles.

"That's a nice shirt for those pants," Lexi said.

"Thanks," Hadley said.

"But maybe it doesn't matter what I think. Maybe it's more important what your classmates think," Lexi said.

"It always matters what you think," Hadley said.

"Let's go in the kitchen," Lexi said.

We went in the kitchen and helped Lexi prepare the lunch. I helped prepare the pasta. I stirred the pasta in the boiling water. Lexi prepared the ground turkey and Hadley worked on the salad.

After a few minutes Lexi said, "That's probably done." She took a fork and picked up a piece of pasta from the water and sampled it. "Yum," she said.

She put her colander in the sink and I poured the boiling water and pasta into the colander. A cloud of steam rose out of the sink. We put the pasta in a large bowl and added the ground turkey and some homemade pepper sauce and some diced tomatoes.

We put the salad in another large bowl and carried the food over to the kitchen table and added some plates and some place settings and served ourselves and sat down. We all started eating. The food was excellent.

"The last time I talked with you, you were taking an English class, in summer school," I said to Hadley as we were eating.

"I'm taking the second part of the same class now. Our summer school ended. Now our fall semester is starting. The class is an introduction to different kinds of literature."

"What are you reading?"

"We're reading some great writing. *Macbeth*, by Shakespeare."

"That's a great classic."

"And we just finished reading Hemingway. *The Sun Also Rises*."

"Another classic."

"It's a great book. I read it, and I also went to the library and got it as an audio book and listened to a reader reading it."

"Is it good as an audio book?"

"It's excellent. When you listen to someone reading it out loud it transports you to the places he writes about."

Lexi said, "I remember reading that book. It's about Spain, right?"

"Yes. A lot of it is about Pamplona," Hadley said.

I listened as Hadley and Lexi talked.

"And they go to a fiesta, and there's bullfighting," Lexi said.

"That's right."

"Hemingway liked bullfighting."

"Want to hear some of it? I'll read it to you."

Lexi shook her head. "No. I don't like bullfighting."

"I don't like bullfighting either, but he's a great writer."

Lexi had a sour look on her face. "I'm not a big Hemingway fan."

"It's a classic."

"I liked that one you were reading before."

"Which one was that?"

"You know. That book about a guy pursuing his dream." Lexi smiled. "That was great writing."

"You mean that book by F. Scott Fitzgerald? Where that character talks about wanting something that's gone and is not coming back?"

"Yes. I love that book. He wrote beautifully. When you were reading it I loved listening to his beautiful writing."

Hadley smiled. "Do you want to hear it again?"

"Sure."

Hadley looked at me. "You want to hear it again?"

"I'm like Lexi. I love that book. I never get tired of it."

"Wait. I'll be right back."

Hadley got up from the table and left the kitchen and was gone a short time and came back with two books and sat down again. She opened one of the books and found a certain page in it and started reading it to Lexi and me.

"I thought of Gatsby's wonder when he first picked out the green light at the end of Daisy's dock. He had come a long way to this blue lawn and his dream must have seemed so close that he could hardly fail to grasp it. He did not know that it was already behind him, somewhere back in that vast obscurity beyond the city, where the dark fields of the republic rolled on under the night," Hadley said.

"The writing is enchanting," Lexi said.

Hadley continued reading to us. "Gatsby believed in the green light, the orgastic future that year by year recedes before us. It eluded us then, but that's no matter—tomorrow we will run faster, stretch out our arms farther. . . . And one fine morning—

So we beat on, boats against the current, borne back ceaselessly into the past."

"Yes, the writing is enchanting," I said to Hadley.

"He's a great writer and a great observer of human nature," Lexi said.

"He's wonderful," Hadley said.

Hadley closed the novel and put it on the table. The words she had read to us ran through my mind. Nobody said anything. We ate more of our lunch.

After a minute or two, Hadley looked at me and said, "And we're reading *Macbeth*."

"That's great also," I said.

"I love the scenes with the witches, and the prophecies," Hadley said.

"Yes. Those are good," I said.

"I brought the Shakespeare book also. Want to hear some of the scenes with the witches, and the prophecies?"

"Yes. I want to hear those."

Hadley looked at Lexi. "Want to hear the witches, and the prophecies?"

"Yes. I like those."

Hadley looked for a page in the book. She found what she wanted. "Here's a scene where the witches are adding things to a bubbling cauldron," she said.

She started reading.

"Fillet of a fenny snake,
In the cauldron boil and bake;
Eye of newt, and toe of frog,
Wool of bat, and tongue of dog,
Adder's fork, and blind-worm's sting,

Lizard's leg, and howlet's wing,
For a charm of powerful trouble,
Like a hell-broth boil and bubble.
Double, double toil and trouble
Fire burn and cauldron bubble."
She looked at me.
"I love that," she said.
"Our pasta seems bland now," I said.
"Do you want to hear the prophecies?" she said.
"Yes, I want to hear the prophecies."
She found another page in *Macbeth*.
"Here's a scene where the witches are making prophecies," she said.
She started reading.
" . . . laugh to scorn
the power of man for
none of woman born
shall harm Macbeth," Hadley said, reading from the book.
She looked at me. "Isn't that great?"
"Yes, that's wonderful writing," I said.
"I love that, and this is good too," she said.
She looked for another place in the book and found it.
"Macbeth shall never
vanquished be until
great Burnham wood to
high Dunsinane Hill
shall come against him," Hadley said, reading from the book.
She looked at me.
"I love the prophecies," she said.
"That's a great scene. I love the prophecies also," I said.
She closed the book and put it on the table.
"I wish I had the gift of prophecy," she said.
"Have you ever tried it?" I said.
"No."
"Then what makes you think you don't have the ability to do it?"
"You think I should try it?"

"Yes. Give us a prophecy."

"What do you want me to prophesize about?"

Lexi had been silently listening to all this. I looked over at her. "What do you think, Lexi?"

"Neutrino research. Give us a prophecy about the success of our quest for money for neutrino research."

"I'll see what I can do," Hadley said.

She thought for a long time.

"In Shakespeare, the witches who prophesized had a special potion. I need a special potion before I can make a prophecy. Where can I get a special potion?"

"We've got some homemade pepper sauce. Will that work?" I said.

"No, I want something that they might have used in Britain in the middle ages, like in *Macbeth*."

"See if there's anything in the refrigerator that would work," Lexi said.

Hadley went to the refrigerator and looked in it. She came back with something in her hand.

"I don't think we have a special potion. But I found some old parsley," she said.

"Old parsley is perfect for making prophecies," Lexi said.

Hadley sat at the table. She pressed the parsley against her forehead with her left hand.

"Let me hold your hand," Hadley said to Lexi.

Lexi extended her left hand and Hadley held it with her right hand. Hadley contracted her facial muscles and wrinkled her face, concentrating intensely. Her eyes were half closed. She looked at Lexi.

"You will get what you need," Hadley said.

"That's wonderful," Lexi said.

"Wait, there's more," Hadley said. She continued to concentrate intensely, wrinkling her face.

"You will get what you need when the sun rises in the west and sets in the east," Hadley said.

"Oh, no. That means it's impossible," I said.

"Wait, there's more," Hadley said. She continued to concentrate intensely while looking at Lexi.

"More?" Lexi said.

"You will get what you need when your hair is on fire and the sun rises in the west and sets in the east," Hadley said.

"When my hair is on fire?" Lexi said.

"Yes," Hadley said.

"Is there any more?" Lexi said.

"No," Hadley said.

Hadley relaxed her face and took her left hand away from her forehead. She relaxed her right hand and released Lexi's hand.

"Are you sure this prophecy is accurate?" I said.

Hadley looked at me quite seriously. "I have spoken," she said.

"There's probably a trick to it, just like in *Macbeth*. Some warrior that was untimely ripped from his mother's womb ended up defeating Macbeth. And an army cut down branches from the trees of Burnham Wood and used them to conceal themselves as they advanced to Dunsinane," Lexi said.

"I don't interpret them. I just make them," Hadley said.

"I agree with you," I said to Lexi.

Hadley took the parsley back to the refrigerator.

Hadley returned to the table. We ate the last of the pasta.

"What else are you interested in?" I said.

"I like everything. I like science," Hadley said.

"Are you interested in science research?" I said.

"I think what Mom does is interesting. She said maybe I could help look for research money."

"I thought maybe she could help us with Captain Shaeffer," Lexi said.

"What do you think is the best approach to Captain Shaeffer?" I said.

"I think maybe send him a letter," Lexi said. "It shouldn't be hard to write. Start by mentioning the university, and then mention the university president, the baseball team, sex research, neutrino research, and then end with baseball team. All the important things. Hadley can help write it."

"That might work," I said to Lexi. "Would you be interested in that?" I said to Hadley.

"Yes. I want to help," Hadley said.

"Give me your contact information and I'll contact you."

"All right."

Hadley gave me her contact information and I gave her mine. She said she had to go to the library and study, so we said goodbye and she left us. Lexi and I cleaned up the kitchen and played a few games of Yahtzee.

I thought about Hadley's prophecy. I thought about the way Hadley said, "I have spoken," so seriously, with such confidence. When someone speaks like that, what they say stays with you.

Chapter Thirty-Seven

The university had a planetarium. I wondered whether the prediction about the sun rising in the west and setting in the east might refer to a show at the planetarium. So I went to see the director of the planetarium. Her name was April Tomonaga. She said she had worked at the planetarium for thirty one years and had been the director for seventeen of those years. I asked April about shows at the planetarium.

"We don't have anything where the sun rises in the west and sets in the east. We just show things that you would see normally in the sky. We have all of the solar system, and all the stars, but just doing normal things."

"Would it be possible to show the sun rising in the west and setting in the east? Could you do that with your machine?"

"I don' t think that's possible. We run a sky simulation program, and there's nothing in the software that has the ability to do that."

"That's too bad."

"I'm sorry to disappoint you."

Chapter Thirty-Eight

Hadley and I drafted a nice letter to the Captain. We showed it to Lexi and she liked it, so we sent it out.

Lexi and I wanted to talk to the president again and make sure he approved of what we were doing. Sasha gave us an appointment and we went to his office when it was time for us. Sasha introduced us and left us with the president. The president remembered us.

"I'm delighted to see you again," he said.

We shook hands with him and we all sat down.

He certainly looked like a distinguished university president. Looking at him in our meeting, the thought crossed my mind that the reason he was hired was that he was nice looking and dressed well and he could tell people he was related to Winston Churchill.

"Sasha told me you're starting to solicit some money from friends of the university."

"Yes sir," Lexi said.

"Soliciting money is one of the most important things that we do here at this university."

"Yes sir."

"In fact, I think it probably is the most important thing we do here at this university."

"Yes sir."

"So you need to be extremely careful when you're doing it."

"Yes sir."

"Always support any previous plans that have been made."

"Yes sir."

"If you're talking with someone who has given money in the past for something like, for example, research about left handed canasta players, you must always tell them that it was a brilliant idea, a brilliant plan, it has made this university a recognized leader in the field of, for example, left handed canasta players."

"Yes sir."

"And if they have recently offered to give money for something new, you must praise them for their offer."

"Yes sir."

"And any money you ask them for must be an addition to anything they have already agreed to give, and not a substitution of one thing for another."

"Yes sir."

"Now I presume you are going to ask for money for scientific and medical research."

"Yes sir."

"I think that's a fine idea. We have great research programs here at this university and we have a great community that helps to support our programs."

"Yes sir."

"Were you concerned with any particular aspect of soliciting donations?"

"Sir, we just want to make sure we represent the university in a positive, ethical way. We welcome any ethical guidance you want to give us," Lexi said.

"Very good. I agree that it's important to follow the highest ethical standards."

"Yes sir."

"Keep in mind that the university has a code of ethics, and I think I have a copy of it somewhere."

"Yes sir."

"And if you ever encounter any situation where someone asks you to do something you think might be questionable, you need to call me and we can see if I can locate my copy of the code of ethics."

"Yes sir."

And with that advice, we departed from the president's office.

Chapter Thirty-Nine

We didn't hear anything from Captain Shaeffer for a while. We knew it was possible he might not respond to us at all, but we felt optimistic so we just waited.

And then one day I was looking at the mail and there was the reply from the Captain. I opened the letter and read some of it and didn't know quite what to make of it. Captain Shaeffer sent a handwritten letter on his company's letterhead, which was nice, but I had trouble reading his handwriting.

I called Hadley and told her I had a reply from Captain Shaeffer but I was having trouble reading it. Hadley said she would ask Lexi whether we could meet at Lexi's house and look at the letter. The next day Hadley called me and said I could come over and join her and Lexi for another pasta lunch later that week, and we agreed on a day and time. And so a few days later I was at Lexi's house again visiting Lexi and Hadley.

Lexi and Hadley greeted me. We went into the living room.

Hadley's hair was blonde now. Once again she had applied some eyeliner to accent her eyes. She had on a pale pink shirt and was wearing cream colored pants and soft blue shoes with white soles. That combination looked good on her.

Lexi listened while I talked with Hadley.

"How do you like being a blonde?" I said to Hadley.

She smiled. "It's fun. Do you like it?"

"It looks good. What brand is that?"

"This is my natural color."

"Does George like it?"

"He loves it."

"Do you get a little more attention from other men as a blonde?"

"Men stare at me when they think I'm not looking. But men were staring at me when my hair was black. So I can't say I'm getting more attention now."

I looked at Lexi. "What do you think?"

"I think her hair looks good. And I think I'm hungry. Are you hungry? Let's make some lunch," Lexi said.

We all went to the kitchen and helped prepare the food. We had a nice lunch of pasta and ground turkey and salad. After lunch we talked about the letter.

"Do you want to look at Captain Shaeffer's letter? I can read most of it but there's some parts where I have trouble," I said.

"I'll take a look," Hadley said.

I gave the letter to Hadley. She studied it.

"His handwriting is kind of odd. What do you think it says," Hadley said.

Hadley gave the letter back to me. I read it to her and Lexi.

"He says, 'Dear researchers, I have received your letter asking me to support your research at the university. It's a great school and I'm proud to say I'm a graduate of it. Certainly I want to support things that I believe are important. I notice you're asking for money to do sex research. I believe the sexual attraction between men and women has made the modern relationship between men and women into the greatest . . .'"

I couldn't read the next word.

"What does that look like to you?" I said to Hadley, and pointed to the word.

"I don't know. He has an unusual little loop in his handwriting that makes it hard to read," she said.

"Yes, I agree," I said.

"I think that word might be *force*. Read the whole sentence and see if that makes sense," she said.

I read the sentence to Hadley and Lexi. "I believe the sexual attraction between men and women has made the modern relationship between men and women into the greatest force in history."

"Can I look at that again?" Hadley said.

I gave her the letter.

"Sometimes his letters look halfway between one letter and a different letter. His letter *o* looks like his letter *a*," she said.

"Yes, it's hard to read," I said.

"What do you think, Mom?" Hadley said.

Hadley gave the letter to Lexi. Lexi studied the handwriting carefully.

"I think that letter might be the letter *a*. I think the word might be *farce*," Lexi said.

"Maybe," I said.

"Read the sentence with that word," Hadley said.

"I believe the sexual attraction between men and women has made the modern relationship between men and women into the greatest farce in history," Lexi read.

She studied the letter.

"I don't know. It could be either one," she said.

"Let's read some more of it," Hadley said.

Lexi gave the letter to me. I read more of it. "Looking at priorities for research, I certainly believe that this is . . ."

I couldn't read the next word.

"What do you think that word is?" I said.

I gave the letter to Hadley. Hadley studied it carefully.

"I think it might be *now*," she said.

"That's possible," I said.

"Then the sentence would be 'Looking at priorities for research, I certainly believe that this is now the time for doing sex research,'" she said.

Hadley looked closely at the handwriting.

"I'm not sure," she said.

She gave the letter to Lexi and pointed to the word.

"What do you think that word is?" Hadley said.

"That word might be *not*," Lexi said.

"Maybe," Hadley said.

"So the sentence would be 'Looking at priorities for research, I certainly believe that this is not the time for doing sex research,'" Lexi said.

"Read the rest of the letter and maybe that will clarify it," Hadley said.

"And finally, when we think about what we can do to help this great school, let us not forget helping the athletic programs remain competitive so that we will continue to have the satisfaction of crushing our rivals. Sincerely, Captain Shaeffer."

"I don't know. I think it's too hard to read," Hadley said.

"Yes. I agree," I said.

"And he doesn't say anything about neutrino research," Lexi said.

"He sort of drifted off topic," I said.

"Maybe you should go visit Captain Shaeffer and find out what he wants to do," Hadley said.

I looked at Lexi. "Shall we go visit him?"

"I think he would enjoy meeting you. But I think Hadley might be a better representative than I would be," Lexi said.

"You want her to go with me?" I said.

"I think so. I think Captain Shaeffer might like college students. It's just a feeling I have." Lexi looked at Hadley. "Do you want to meet Captain Shaeffer?" Lexi said to Hadley.

Hadley smiled. "Yes, I think that would be interesting."

We parted for the day and thought about our next steps. After hearing so much about Captain Shaeffer, I was glad we were finally going to meet him.

Chapter Forty

A few days later Hadley and I were on our way to the headquarters building of The Shaeffer Sex Dolls Company. Hadley was driving. Lexi let Hadley borrow her car.

Hadley's long blonde hair was parted on one side and held by a clip on the other side. Her eyes had a little bit of eyeliner and her lips were a pale lavender. She was wearing a black dress with a hemline a couple of inches below her knees and a slit on one side going up to her thigh, with black fishnet stockings and low black heels with ankle straps. I'm not a style expert but I thought she looked chic.

"Do you like my lipstick?" Hadley said.

"Very nice," I said.

"It's organic."

I wondered what impression she would make on Captain Shaeffer.

We arrived at the company offices, which were in a modernistic one story building with a wall of dark glass, surrounded by carefully maintained greenery. We parked and walked up to the front entrance. A large sign displayed the company slogan in large letters in a beautiful font. "Shaeffer sex dolls: They're better than call girls."

A security guard greeted us.

"We have an appointment to talk with Captain Shaeffer," I said.

"Captain Shaeffer is in the building over there," the guard said. The guard pointed to an unimpressive small building away from the main building.

"He doesn't work in the main building?" Hadley said.

"No. He's no longer active in the day to day management of the company. His son is running it now. Captain Shaeffer is chairman of the board and an advisor."

"Thanks," Hadley said.

We walked toward the small building.

"So his son runs the business now? And the Captain is an advisor? I wonder what advice the Captain gives his son," Hadley said.

"Make more money," I said.

The small building had a shaded wooden deck outside, and a door for people and a smaller door for dogs, with a flap that dogs could go through. A large black dog was napping on the deck. It looked like a black Labrador. It woke up and looked at us when we reached the deck.

We went in the door for people. The dog came through the dog door. There was a small reception area. A secretary greeted us.

"May I help you?" she said.

"We have an appointment to talk with Captain Shaeffer. I'm Jack and this is Hadley."

"I'll let him know you're here."

She picked up her landline phone and touched some buttons. "Captain, you have some visitors here to see you. Jack and Hadley." She paused, then said, "I'll tell them," and hung up the phone.

"He'll be with you shortly," she said to us.

"Whose dog is this?" Hadley said.

"That's Captain Shaeffer's dog. Her name is Kamala."

"Kamala?"

"Yes. She's named after the politician."

The Captain walked out to greet us. He looked handsome but a little rough and unrefined. He had a very short beard, which looked good on him. He was wearing jeans and casual dark shoes, and some sort of loosely fitting dark blue shirt. He was tall and lean and muscular.

He smiled. "I'm Captain Shaeffer."

"I'm Jack and this is Hadley."

He shook hands with me and then with Hadley.

"It's good to meet you, Jack. Welcome, Hadley."

Sometimes you meet someone and you immediately feel something is missing. With the Captain it was horses. He looked like he was ready to go out to the corral and saddle up his horse and head out on the trail. Too bad at headquarters there was no corral, no horse, no trail.

"It's great to meet you, Captain. I've been looking forward to this," I said. "Your daughter Britta may have mentioned to you that I met her, a few months ago. She said lots of nice things about you."

"What did you think of Britta?" the Captain said.

"She has a challenging job. She said she's a high school science teacher."

"That's right. It takes a special gift to be a good teacher. And science is a hard subject to teach. Britta can do that and lots of other things. That woman has got some smarts in her head."

The Captain looked at the secretary who had greeted us. "We'll be in the conference room." He looked at me. "Let's go back here."

We followed him into the conference room. Kamala followed us into the conference room and laid down on the floor. We sat at a table.

"I like your dog," Hadley said.

"She's a great companion. I've always had dogs. Years ago we had dogs when the kids were growing up. The kids always loved them."

"Yes, dogs can become part of the family," Hadley said.

"We had a dog that liked to chase tennis balls. Her name was Penny. Penny never got tired of chasing tennis balls," the Captain said.

"That's good exercise," I said.

"Unfortunately Penny didn't live very long. She got cancer and died at a young age. That was sad," the Captain said.

"I'm sorry to hear that," Hadley said.

"Nobody could explain that. I still miss her," the Captain said.

"That is sad," I said.

The Captan looked at Kamala. "Kamala doesn't chase tennis balls. That's not her personality. Kamala is a little more serious than that, but very good with people. She reminds me of a politician. That's why we named her after one."

"Yes, they all have their own individual personalities," I said.

"Just like people," Hadley said.

The Captain looked at Hadley. "You look wonderful. Are you a working girl?"

"I'm not sure I know what you mean, sir," Hadley said.

"You know, a professional."

"A professional what, sir?"

"You don't need to call me sir. Everybody calls me Captain."

"What would you like to know, Captain?"

"Hadley, are you here to have a good time with me later?"

"No."

"Captain, Hadley and I are here for a serious meeting," I said.

The Captain continued to look at Hadley. "Hadley, are you not a call girl?"

"Captain, Hadley is a student. She's not a call girl."

The Captain was still looking at Hadley. "I'm sorry, Hadley. I thought you were a call girl."

"Captain, why would you think she was a call girl?"

Now the Captain looked at me. "Because you're a guy, Jack, and you're here to meet with me and you want something from me and you brought a young woman with you. Years ago, when this company was smaller and not as well known in the market, sometimes we would struggle to get contracts or distribution deals. Sometimes if we were negotiating with a guy we would try to find out what he wanted, to close the deal. If we thought sex would help us close the deal, we would send over a call girl. And sometimes the offer would go the other way. Sometimes the other side would send over a professional to me. That's just how business was done."

"Captain, I'm from the university. People at the university don't make decisions based on sex," I said.

Captain Shaeffer laughed. "You're young and still naive. You'll learn."

"Do you still provide call girls sometimes?" I said.

"No, we don't." He stood up and walked over to a small refrigerator in the conference room. "Do either of you want a beer?" He opened the refrigerator and took out a can of beer.

"No, thanks," Hadley said.

"Not for me, thanks," I said.

He came back to the table and sat down. He opened the can and took a sip, then put the can near him on the table.

"You want some corn chips while we're talking? I think we have some," he said.

He went over to a cabinet and opened a cabinet door. He took out a large unopened package of corn chips and a large plastic bowl and some paper napkins. He opened the package of corn chips and emptied it into the bowl. He brought the napkins and the bowl of chips back to the table and put them where everyone could reach them, and he sat down again. He took some chips and started eating them.

"What were you asking me about?" he said.

"Call girls," Hadley said.

"Yes. Call girls. Our technology improved and we got to the point where we thought our product was better than call girls. So we stopped providing call girls and started sending out free product samples when we wanted to do a favor for someone. And we adopted our company slogan. Did you see the sign in front of the main building here? It has our company slogan."

"Yes. Your slogan says your sex dolls are better than call girls," I said.

"It's a fact," he said.

"Obviously you're proud of your technology," I said.

"Our technology has made us the industry leader. Our dolls are the most technologically advanced sex dolls you can buy. But our success is not just because of technology. It's because of something else also."

"What's that?"

"Jack, do you know the word zeitgeist?"

"I've heard the word."

"A lot of people misuse the word. So if you are going to use the word, be careful how you use it."

"I will."

"It means the spirit of the age. And the spirit of the age now is that machines can do everything. They can do everything, Jack. They can even be your partner in bed. Our company doesn't fight the zeitgeist. We embrace the zeitgeist. What we do is part of the zeitgeist."

He sipped his beer and ate some corn chips.

"Captain, as you know, we're from the university," Hadley said. "We sent you a letter about the research that people do at the university. We came to visit you because we want to follow up on that letter."

"Yes. Certainly."

"We appreciate your taking the time to respond to our letter and we appreciate your taking the time to meet with us today."

"I'm happy to meet with you, Hadley. I'm a friend of the university and I'm proud to call myself a graduate of it."

"Captain, we had a little bit of difficulty reading the letter you sent us. So maybe we should start by letting you tell us your reaction to our letter."

"My reaction to your letter. Let's see. It seems to me your letter said you wanted money for research."

"Yes. We want money for sex research. And we also want money for a physics research project, developing and using a neutrino detector."

"Hadley, maybe my letter wasn't the perfect phrasing of what I was trying to say. I just dashed it off."

"That's all right."

"But I must tell you I don't think this is the time to be doing sex research."

"I'm sorry to hear that, Captain."

"Hadley, we know enough about sex already to create a sex doll that's better than a call girl. How much further do we want to go?"

"There are important things still to be discovered, Captain. It might be very helpful to know them."

"Humans are very complicated. You cannot possibly understand everything that goes on in a real human."

"Maybe not everything, but we can learn a little more, and maybe that might help someone."

"Hadley, I just don't see that sort of thing as providing any benefit. At least that's my opinion right now. Maybe I'll change my mind later, but right now I'm going to decline."

"I'm sorry we haven't convinced you."

"Jack, what do you think of all this?"

"I agree with Hadley."

"You had something else in your letter, Jack. What was that?"

"Neutrinos, Captain. A team at the school has developed an advanced neutrino detector."

"What are neutrinos, Jack?"

"They're tiny particles. They're considered elementary particles. They're everywhere. They pass through everybody all the time and nobody notices."

"All the time? Day and night?"

"Day and night. Hundreds of billions go through every square inch of your body every second."

"And nobody notices?"

"Nobody notices."

"That's pretty amazing."

"Yes it is. And my colleague at school has made a detector, so now she can detect some of them."

"She can only detect some of them?"

"That's right. She can detect some of them. They're still pretty elusive."

The Captain looked at Kamala. "Do they pass through dogs too?"

"Yes. All the time," I said.

"The people at the university certainly study a tremendous variety of things. Neutrinos and sex and who knows what other things are being studied."

"Yes, Captain, it's a great research university. And we want to keep great research happening at the school."

"Jack, do you think neutrino research has any value?"

"Captain, all basic science research has value. Basic science research is the foundation for progress that helps everyone. Every practical advance in technology is built on an understanding of basic science. I'm sure you've heard of the Nobel Prizes."

"Yes, certainly."

"The Nobel Prizes provide international recognition of discoveries in basic science that often lead to technology that improves our lives."

"Can neutrino research win a Nobel Prize in physics?"

"I don't think it will win in physics, but I think outstanding neutrino research can win a Nobel Peace Prize."

"A Peace Prize? How would that happen?"

"A really advanced neutrino detector can be used to monitor compliance with nuclear weapons treaties."

"I see."

The Captain drank some of his beer and ate some chips.

"Jack, I like you and your friend Hadley, and I *am* interested in helping the university, but right now these particular projects we're talking about are just not priorities for me. I just can't give you any research money."

"I'm sorry to hear that, Captain."

"But you and your friend Hadley here seem like real bright people. I want you to stay in touch with me. I'm interested in what you're doing."

"We'll stay in touch."

"It seems to me that if you have a good idea in physics, you'll find somebody to support that idea. So keep looking and I think you'll be successful."

"I'm sorry we haven't persuaded you."

"As I mentioned, I want to support the university. I'll tell you one thing I believe helps the school. That's when it has outstanding athletic teams. Because I believe athletic teams are ambassadors for the school. A great team makes an excellent impression for the university. Not just locally, and not just in the state, but nationally."

"Yes, I agree."

The Captain sipped his beer.

"I'm working with the director of athletics on a plan for a new baseball stadium. I'm going to donate the money to build it. It's a very exciting project. The university is getting ready to announce it. I'm telling you now before there's been an official announcement. I think it will add a lot to the school."

"We'll be interested in the announcement."

"Jack, have you been paying attention to the baseball team in the last few seasons?"

"No. But people tell me they've been successful."

"They've been very successful. They've had a great record."

"I'm glad they're doing well. Why do you think they've been so successful?"

"Recruiting, Jack. Last year, and the year before, the coaching staff recruited some of the top graduating high school players in the country."

"That's impressive."

"That success helps the school, Jack."

He sipped his beer.

"You said you're a graduate of our university?" Hadley said.

"Yes I am and I'm proud of it."

"What are some of your memories of your time in school?"

"Let's see. I led a pretty quiet life. I remember I had three girlfriends total in all my years on campus. And only one of them got pregnant. She eventually became my wife. Those were good times."

"When you were a student at the university, what was your major?"

"Hadley, I majored in history. Does that surprise you?"

"A little bit. I thought you might have majored in engineering."

"Hadley, managers can hire as many engineers as they need. When I was young my father told me that the one essential skill that a leader must have is an understanding of people. I hope I picked up some of that when I studied history."

"What was your favorite part of history?"

"My favorite part of history was American history. You're going to school now?"

"Yes."

"Do kids these days study American history?"

"Yes, we study it."

"Do you think it's interesting?"

"Yes. I like it."

"Did you ever study the presidency of Warren Harding?"

"A little bit."

"Warren Harding was actually an underrated president. He promoted civil rights at a time when few people in government were interested in it."

"I didn't realize that."

"When you study history you can see how society changes over time."

"That's true."

"Hadley, did you know that Warren Harding had a daughter while he was married, but the mother of his daughter was not his wife?"

"Really?"

"Yes. That's a great love story. The mother of his daughter loved him so much that she had his baby even though she was not married to him."

"That's quite a love story."

The Captain looked at me. "Jack, can you imagine a woman having your baby when she's not married to you? I don't think a woman would be happy having a baby like that today."

"I think it would depend on the circumstances."

Captain Shaeffer finished his beer.

"Sir, we don't want to take too much of your time. We should head back to the campus," I said.

"All right."

"If you change your mind about giving money for research at the university, please call us," Hadley said.

"I'll keep your contact information."

"Thanks for your hospitality."

"Yes. Thanks, Captain," I said.

"Thanks for coming out to see me."

"Our pleasure," Hadley said.

"Hadley, Jack, I'm sorry I can't be more helpful to you."

We shook hands with the Captain and left him and walked back to Lexi's car.

I looked at Hadley. "He thought you were a call girl. Bringing you out here was a mistake. I'm sorry I brought you out here."

"No, no. I'm happy you brought me out here. I'm learning much more doing this than I would learn sitting in a classroom."

"That's what I'm afraid of."

"Please let me keep working with you. Please."

Chapter Forty-One

A few days after our meeting with Captain Shaeffer I got a call from his daughter.

"Hello Jack, this is Britta."

"Britta, good to hear from you. How's life?"

"Busy."

"Yours and mine."

"My dad said he met you. And you had a student with you."

"Yes. Her name is Hadley. She and I enjoyed meeting Captain Shaeffer."

"My dad said you asked him for research money. He said you wanted money for your research and for Lexi's neutrino detector research. He said he didn't give you any."

"His passion is baseball right now."

"I'm sorry he didn't give you any money."

"Don't worry about it."

"I'd give you some money myself, but I don't actually have any. I'm just a humble school teacher."

"Humble school teachers are exactly what America needs."

"I'm hoping to have lunch with you and Lexi. Would you like to join Lexi and me and my daughter Sophia for lunch sometime?"

"I would love to join you and the others for lunch sometime."

We found a time that worked for all of us, a few days later, and we converged on A Slice Is Nice. Britta and Sophia arrived first and were standing near the entrance waiting when I arrived. We were all wearing casual clothes. Sophia's sweatshirt said, "Let's Dance."

We said hello and we waited there a few minutes and Lexi joined us.

"Lexi, have you met my daughter, Sophia? Sophia, this is my friend Lexi."

"Hello Sophia. It's good to meet you. I like your sweatshirt."

"It's how I feel," Sophia said.

Lexi and Sophia shook hands.

We all got slices of hot pizza and we found a table on the porch in a corner away from the crowd. We ate our pizza and talked.

Sophia had some sort of shopping bag.

"Have you been shopping? What did you get?" Lexi said.

Sophia reached into her bag and pulled out a plastic bottle of something.

"We went to the discount store. I got some more bubble bath," Sophia said.

"Do you like bubble bath?" Lexi said.

Sophia smiled. "It's the best kind of soap. Everyone needs soap. When I take a bubble bath, I always feel better."

"Does it have a scent?" Lexi said.

"Yes, it's wonderful." Sophia opened the top of the bottle and handed it to Lexi. "Do you like it?" Sophia said.

Lexi inhaled some of the scent and smiled. "Oh, that's good. Yes, I see why you like that," Lexi said, and handed the bottle back to Sophia.

"Sophia, how much dancing are you doing now?" I said.

"I dance whenever I have time. Dancing is fun."

Britta looked at me. "Would you like to see another video of Sophia dancing?"

"I would love to see another video of Sophia dancing."

"I'll send you one."

"Sophia, do you still think you might like to be a dancer when you grow up?" I said.

"Yes. A dancer or a doctor."

"Two excellent careers."

"I haven't decided."

"Do you remember how to check my pulse?"

"Yes. Let me try that."

She moved her chair so she could sit close to me and she tried checking my pulse. She put her fingers on my wrist. After a few seconds she smiled. "There it is." She held her fingers on my wrist. "Your pulse has a regular rhythm today."

"Is it like dance music?"

"Yes. It's like dance music."

"That's good, Sophia. You would be a good doctor," I said.

Everyone ate some pizza.

Britta looked at Lexi. "How have you been, Lexi?"

"Busy. How have you been, Britta?"

"I've been busy too. The public schools have started back up after the summer holiday. I teach high school chemistry and also physics, so it's back to work for me."

"Do you like teaching?"

"I love it. It's a lot of work but it's something I enjoy. Most of the time."

"It's good to have a job that you enjoy."

"I've been thinking about your neutrino detector."

Lexi smiled. "It's the best in the world."

"Where is it now?"

"It's at my house. It's in a closet. It's small enough to fit in a closet. That's one of the many excellent things about it."

"Would it be possible to bring it to my school and show it to my class?"

Lexi looked surprised. "Show it to your class? Are they studying neutrinos?"

"In my physics class we talk a little bit about elementary particles. But it's hard to get kids excited about science by reading a textbook. They're much more interested if they can see something for themselves. Like Sophia feeling Jack's pulse."

Lexi looked doubtful. She paused, and then she said, "I don't know. I'm not sure how we could get the detector to your school."

"My father has a pickup truck that he lets me use if I need it. And he'll let me borrow a couple of employees to help load it into the truck. They'll wrap it up with packing material to protect it from damage. Can your detector be carried in a pickup truck?"

"Yes, that would work. How can you move it from the truck to your classroom?"

"The school maintenance people can move it. They move heavy furniture around. They have equipment for moving things."

"Will it be safe at your school? I don't want anything to happen to it."

"My physics class is a good group of kids. They'll be careful. It'll be safe."

"That sounds good. I think that would work."

Britta smiled. "Thank you. I really appreciate this."

"Thanks for your interest."

"Britta," I said, "is it all right to talk about your father's business when Sophia is with us?"

"It's all right to talk about it in a general way. She knows what he does." Britta looked at Sophia. "What do you think of my father's business, Sophia?"

"Boring," Sophia said.

"Boring?" I said.

"He makes machinery that weird people use. There's nothing more boring than machinery," Sophia said.

"Would you like to listen to some dance music on headphones?" Britta said to Sophia.

Sophia smiled. "Yes, I want to listen to some dance music."

Britta got some headphones out of her purse and some kind of electronic device. Sophia put on the headphones and started listening.

"How is the business these days?" I said to Britta.

"I'm not involved in the day to day management, so I don't know the latest sales figures. But I can tell you it's a very competitive business. The technology is advancing rapidly just as it is in a lot of other businesses. It requires constant research and development to continue having competitive products."

"What innovations will we see in the future?"

"There will be much more advanced automation. Dolls will have personalities and will be much more versatile."

"Dolls with personalities would be a big change," I said.

"Are there sex dolls marketed to women?" Lexi said to Britta.

"Lexi, there has never been a commercially successful sex doll marketed to women. That's a very tough market to make a product for."

"Why is that?"

"I think it's because consumer preferences are so different. But there's ongoing research and development. So I think we'll see products that will try to respond to market forces."

"What do you think we'll see?"

"Here's one possibility, Lexi. My family's company is testing a doll that has a male body and says, 'Darling, you look tired tonight. Let me fix dinner, and then I'll help the kids with their homework.'"

Lexi smiled. "That might be popular. What do you think, Jack?"

"Britta, you said you're not involved in the day to day management of your family's business. Would you like to be more involved?" I said.

"Yes. I feel like I have something useful to offer. I have a useful perspective. I think I could make a contribution to the continuing success of the business and I'd like to do that. Not as a full time manager, because I already have a full time job as a teacher, and I'm happy teaching. But maybe as a member of the board."

"How does your father feel about that?" Lexi said.

"He says it's not a good business for a woman to be in. He's kind of old school. And he still owns all of the shares, so whether I have a role is up to him. So far he hasn't wanted to bring me into management."

"I hope he changes his mind."

"He might. It's possible. We just have to wait and see."

We finished our pizza and ended our meeting and went our separate ways.

Britta and her helpers took the neutrino detector to her school to show her class. After a few days they brought it back to Lexi, and Britta reported that it was a big success.

Chapter Forty-Two

My birthday is in September. I don't normally do a lot to celebrate, but it's nice to do something. I called Lexi and asked her if she wanted to go somewhere and celebrate with me. She said no, she's in a phase of life where she spends enough time away from home when she's working. When she's not working, she likes to relax at home. She invited me to come over to her house.

"We'll have dinner in honor of your birthday," she said on the phone. "I'll put you to work. You can help prepare it."

"I'd like that."

"And we'll make you a birthday cake."

"I don't need a cake."

"It's not a birthday celebration without a cake."

"Let's make a different dessert."

"What would you like?"

"I don't know. I like berries. Do you like berries?"

"I have some frozen strawberries. Those are good. We can make something with them."

"Yes. We'll make something delicious."

I went over to her house on my birthday, after work. She led me to her kitchen, where she put on an apron and gave me an apron.

"We'll have a complete dinner. You can help prepare it. But you must put on an apron. All great cooks wear aprons," she said.

"Is that the secret of great cooking?"

"Yes. Wear an apron, and use a foreign language to describe anything you make."

I put on the apron.

"I do feel different with the apron on," I said.

"You look good wearing that. You look like a great cook."

"I just want my food to look like food."

"Our food is going to look nice. We'll have lots of pretty colors."

"Is that another secret of great cooking?"

"Yes. Food should look attractive. It should be as pretty as something you might see in an art museum."

"I've never eaten in an art museum."

"Let's think about what we want for the main course," Lexi said. She reached into one of her cabinets and brought out a cookbook. "Let's make something without a lot of salt. I don't like salt."

"What can we use to bring out the flavor if we don't use salt?"

"Spices." Lexi looked in the cookbook. "We can make spicy fried chicken. Would you like that? We won't put any salt in it."

"Will we put cilantro in it?"

"Just a little bit. We'll put in other spices with it."

"Yes, that would be good."

"We'll have a salad and our chicken and some vegetables and after we eat that we'll make our dessert."

"All right."

We both worked hard and prepared a nice dinner. For our salad course we had grapes and tomatoes and sliced carrots and red leaf lettuce, then for our main course we had the unsalted spicy fried chicken. And we had lima beans with diced tomatoes, and baked sweet potatoes with butter.

Everything was delicious, but we didn't eat very much of anything, because we wanted to save room for dessert. When it was time for dessert I asked Lexi what she wanted.

"I don't want to eat a lot of sugar. Let's do something with artificial sweetener," Lexi said.

"Yes. I don't want a lot of sugar."

"Let's make butterscotch bars, with artificial sweetener. Do you like those?"

"Yes. Those are good."

"And let's add strawberries to the recipe."

"Do strawberries go with butterscotch?"

Lexi smiled. "I don't know. Let's do the experiment."

"Yes. Let's do the experiment."

We found a recipe for butterscotch bars and made our batter. We got the strawberries out of the freezer and thawed them out. They were in a carton packed with some sort of syrup or juice. We added the berries and their liquid to our batter. We poured our batter in a baking pan and put our creation in the oven. As it was baking, the kitchen filled with the enticing scent of our dessert.

But our creation didn't solidify the way we were hoping it would. The strawberries added too much liquid. We took it out of the oven, tested it, put it back in the oven, cooked it some more, took it out, and tested it again. It was starting to burn on top but it still wasn't solid in the middle.

So we ate it in its unsolid state. The flavor was excellent. We had created a messy, gooey, strawberry, buttery, treat. There wasn't any left over when we finished eating.

"What do you think?" I said.

"I'm disappointed that we couldn't make it a little more solid. It was delicious, but we failed to get the ingredients right."

"I think it was a great success. The flavor was perfect."

"Yes, the flavor was a success. We created a failure and a success at the same time."

"Anybody who follows a recipe can create a success. But only people with imagination such as ourselves can create both a failure *and* a success."

Lexi smiled. "And nobody will believe us, because we ate all the evidence."

"Thank you for helping me celebrate my birthday."

"Thank you for having a birthday that I could help celebrate."

It was time for me to say goodnight and go back to my storage closet. And so I did say goodnight and go back to my storage closet. But I didn't want to leave Lexi. I had been with her many other times, for many other meetings, for many other reasons. At the end of each of those we had parted, and leaving her hadn't bothered me. Why was this time different?

Something had snuck up on me when I wasn't looking for it. I was now under the magical power of love, and maybe some wizard dust. I hoped some of the magical power had captured her also.

Chapter Forty-Three

Lexi and I continued our custom of playing Yahtzee on Saturday mornings. The next Saturday morning, before it was time for our game, I went to a florist and I got a dozen red roses. Then I went to Lexi's house, and I showed her the roses.

"I love you, Lexi," I said.

She smiled and gave me a big hug.

"I love you too," she said.

We didn't play Yahtzee that day.

We put the roses in a vase on a table. We sat on the couch in her living room and we held each other and we started kissing, a little awkwardly. We kissed for a few minutes.

"Let's go upstairs," Lexi said.

"All right," I said.

"Slowly."

Lexi held my hand and led me upstairs to her bedroom. She had a spacious bedroom with hardwood floors and a high ceiling, and in the middle of the room she had a large bed.

"Let's lie down," she said.

We both took our shoes off and got on the bed.

"What was it we were doing? Oh, I remember," she said.

We kissed for a few minutes.

She put a hand down inside my pants.

"May I touch you here?" she said.

"Yes, that feels good."

She rubbed me gently.

"Wait," she said.

She pulled her hand back from my pants. She started caressing my face.

"We need to have a conversation," she said.

"All right. What would you like to talk about?"

She stopped caressing my face. She stared at me silently for a few seconds.

"The influence of Schopenhauer on the later German philosophers," she said.

"I'm not following you."

"Sex, you silly boy. Sex. We need to have a conversation about sex." She started caressing my face again.

"That happens to be a subject that I'm interested in."

"We need to say what we want to happen here."

"Yes."

"And we need to listen."

"Yes."

"Can we do that?"

"Yes."

"I want you to touch me with your fingers. I want you to rub me with your fingers. I want you to penetrate me with your fingers. Only your fingers," she said.

"Only my fingers?"

"Yes. That works best for me. Are you disappointed?"

"No."

"If you touch me in the right places, it feels very good to me. Would you like me to show you how to do it?"

"Yes."

She got up off the bed. I stayed on the bed.

"Wait just a minute, and I'll show you." She went into her bathroom and came out with a small plastic bottle of something. "I think lubricant was the first great discovery of civilization," she said. She put the bottle on a table next to the bed.

"I'll be right back," she said, and she left the bedroom. She was gone briefly and returned. "I got a pen and paper and a clipboard to write on." She came back to bed.

"I'm going to draw a map of New York City and the surrounding area," she said.

"Why are you drawing a map of New York?"

"Because doctors have ruined sex."

"How have we ruined sex?"

"I shouldn't include you in this category, because I think you're wonderful. But your people have ruined sex."

"My people have ruined sex?"

"Yes. Doctor people."

"How have doctor people ruined sex?"

"They've made everything jargon. They don't use real English words. Everything is in Latin. Or it's worse than Latin. It's ancient Greek. Are you and I ancient Greeks?"

"No."

"Then we need to speak in a modern way. I'll show you."

"All right."

Lexi drew some lines on the paper. I looked at what she was drawing.

"Now, this is your view as you look at me," she said. "We'll start by drawing Manhattan. Think of Manhattan as slightly above the entrance to the reproductive parts inside me."

"All right."

"Over here on the right we'll draw Brooklyn and Queens." Lexi drew more lines on the paper. "Brooklyn and Queens are to the right of my entrance."

"All right."

"And over here is New Jersey." Lexi drew more lines on the paper. "New Jersey is to the left of my entrance."

"All right."

Lexi looked at me. "Are you familiar with New Jersey?"

"Not very much."

Lexi looked down at the paper. "Close to Manhattan, you have a town like Hoboken. Hoboken is right here." Lexi made a dot on the map. "When you go farther out into the northern New Jersey suburbs, you have towns like Montclair. Montclair is right about here." Lexi made a dot on the map.

"I'm not sure I can remember all the towns."

She looked at me. "I don't expect you to memorize a map of New York and New Jersey. This is just vocabulary. We need to understand the words we're using. I'll help you find the landmarks. When you see how easy this is, you'll like it."

"All right."

"And don't worry. As far as I know, sex has never ruined doctors."

Lexi got up off the bed. "Do you want to get ready? You can use the guest bathroom down the hall. I'll use the bathroom next to my bedroom."

I got up off the bed. We parted and got ready and returned to her bedroom. We got on the bed and started kissing. After a while she stopped kissing and she reached over to the table and got the plastic bottle. She handed it to me. "Just put a little bit on your fingers," she said. I covered my fingers with a few drops of the first great discovery of civilization.

I rubbed Lexi with my fingers and I penetrated her with my fingers. She grasped some of my fingers and she showed me what she wanted.

"Here. Yes. That's it. Move it like this. Yes. That's it. Now touch me here. Brooklyn," she said.

She moved my fingers to Brooklyn. She let go of my fingers and I pressed on Brooklyn and moved it a little bit with my fingers.

"Now Hoboken. Hoboken. Here."

She grasped some of my fingers and moved my touch to Hoboken.

"Push. Harder. Move your fingers like this."

She showed me how to move my fingers and then she let go of my fingers and I moved them like she had moved them. "Yes. That's it."

She closed her eyes.

"Oh. Right there. Oh. *Hoboken.* Now stop. Don't move your fingers."

She moved her legs and arched her back. She opened her eyes and grabbed a pillow and smacked me hard with it.

"I'm sorry. I should have warned you. I throw my pillow when I climax." She wrapped her arms around me and we both lay still for a while.

"Let me do you. Can I do you now? Can I touch you with my fingers?" she said.

"Yes."

She put a few drops from her plastic bottle on her fingers.

"Tell me what you like."

"I don't know what to say. I don't have a map."

"Is this good?"

"Harder than that."

"Like this?"

"A little faster."

"This?"

"Yes, that's nice."

She manipulated me with her hands and I reached a climax and made a mess.

"Sex is messy," I said.

"Jackson," Lexi said. She looked serious.

"Yes?"

"*Life* is messy."

Lexi got some paper towels and we cleaned up a little bit.

"Thank you. I never really understood the importance of Hoboken, New Jersey, until I met you," I said.

"You're lucky you met me."

"Yes, I am."

Chapter Forty-Four

I called Lexi the next day.

"I had a great time at your house yesterday," I said.

"Me too."

"You're a wonderful person."

"Who told you *that*?"

"I discovered it myself."

"Be careful what conclusions you reach when you're under the influence of sexual desire."

"I feel the same way about you no matter what's influencing me or not influencing me."

"Really? Would you like to come over today? Hadley isn't here and I have some time. Do you have some time? I can't repeat what we did yesterday. I'm taking a day to recover. If you're feeling sexy you need to satisfy yourself before you come over."

"I would love to come over."

"Come on over."

I took Lexi's advice and satisfied myself, and then I went over to her house. She greeted me with a hug.

"You want to play some Yahtzee today?" Lexi said.

"No. I want to hold you. Will you sit on my lap?"

"All right."

I sat down in one of her comfortable chairs in her living room and she sat in my lap.

"That was fun yesterday," I said.

"Yes, that was fun, wasn't it?"

"I'm supposed to be an expert but I think you know more about sex than I do."

"I don't have any special knowledge."

"You understand what works. You should write a sex manual."

She shook her head. "No. I only know what works for me."

"So you don't want to write a sex manual?"

"People don't need to read a book to understand sex. People need to listen to their partner. You should listen to your partner and your partner should listen to you. That's my sex manual."

"A lot of people find it hard to talk about sex. Hard to talk about what they want. Hard to listen to their partner talk about what their partner wants."

"I agree with that."

"You're good at helping people listen to their partner and talk to their partner. You could write a book about that."

"No. I don't want to be a sex expert. That's your job. I'm a neutrino researcher."

She stood up and looked at me.

"I'm afraid I'm crushing you. Do you want to go upstairs and lie in bed? Just lie down?" she said.

"Yes. Let's do that."

"I don't feel like running up the stairs today."

"All right."

We held hands and walked up the stairs and went to her bedroom and took our shoes off and laid on her bed on our backs next to each other.

"Do you like this?" she said.

"Yes. This is excellent."

"You were saying I should write a book."

"Yes."

"If I wrote a book, it wouldn't be a book about sex. I would write a book about something that's more mysterious than sex, and something that people spend more time searching for and have a harder time finding."

"What would you write about?"

"I would write about romance. People want to know how to find true love."

"Finding true love is hard to do."

"I don't have all the answers, but maybe I could help someone."

"What would you say in your book."

"I would say if you want to find true love, the first thing you must do is find a partner who you value as a unique individual, and who values you as a unique individual. And then you and your partner can look for it together."

"And do you take your own advice?"

"Yes I do."

"Have you found a partner that meets your description?"

"I have."

"What's his name?"

"His name is Jackson Rose."

"You mean somebody else is using my name?"

"I value him as a unique individual."

"You mean you're searching for true love with another guy who happens to have the same name as I have? Now you've really hurt me."

She smiled. "I'm sorry, Jack. I'm sorry our lives had to come to this point."

"At least you're honest about it."

"You're a silly boy. And I love you."

We rested in her bed for a minute without saying anything.

"When you're in bed with someone, do you ever wonder what it's like to be the other person?" I said.

"What do you mean?"

"Do you wonder what the other person is feeling? What's going through their mind?"

"Sometimes."

"I wonder about you sometimes. When we're in bed and you're lying on your back and we're kissing I wonder what you're thinking, what you're feeling."

"That's easy to answer. I'm trying to decide what color I should have the ceiling painted."

"You're a silly girl. And I love you."

"Do you want to know how I feel today?"

"Yes."

"Let me show you."

"All right."

"Do you have any sexual desire right now?"

"No. I took your advice before I came over."

"May I lie on top of you?"

"Yes."

She got on top of me, facing me, mostly covering me, but she slid her body down a little bit so she was a little closer to the foot of the bed than I was. She rested her head on my chest and held me with her arms."

"Do you like this?" she said.

"Yes."

"Do you like feeling our bodies pressed tightly against each other like this?"

"Yes."

"Do you want to do anything else right now?"

"No."

"Do you want to stay like this until the end of time?"

"Yes."

"That's how I feel. You know how it feels to be me now."

"Do you think other people feel like this when they're in bed?"

"I have no idea whatsoever."

We didn't say anything for a minute or two.

"Are you still comfortable?" I said.

"This feels wonderful. Are *you* comfortable?"

"Yes. This is nice."

"It's wonderful."

"I'm your mattress cover. I'm your lumpy mattress cover."

"No, no. Don't say that. You're much better than a mattress cover."

"What am I then? What would you call me?" I said.

"I don't know. Being here with you like this is wonderful. That's all I know," she said.

"I'm not your mattress cover?"

"You're my *je ne sais quoi*."

"I'm your *je ne sais quoi*?"

"Yes. I don't know what to call you. So that's what I'm going to call you."

We didn't say anything for a while.

"Did I answer all of your questions?" she said.

"I have one more."

"Tell me."

"What color should we have the ceiling painted?"

She pressed her arms tightly against me.

"Any color you want, darling."

We stayed in bed for a long time. Eventually she said, "I have some work I need to do."

"Me too."

We didn't move.

"I've forgotten how to move," she said.

"Me too."

She gradually got to a sitting position on the side of the bed. I gradually got to a position sitting beside her on the bed.

"Thank you for lying on top of me," I said.

She looked at me and smiled. "Thank you for your support."

"Am I a good support person?"

"You're much more than that. You're my *je ne sais quoi*."

"I'm happy to be your *je ne sais quoi*."

"Let's go to bed again next week, like yesterday."

"Good plan."

"Do you like blood?" she said.

"Blood is all right."

"I think next week we may see some blood."

Chapter Forty-Five

The next week I went over to visit Lexi and we had fun in bed. She was menstruating and we ended up getting blood all over.

"Look at all this blood. We look like we've been in battle. We look like we've been wounded in combat," I said.

"We *have* been in battle. It's an ongoing battle."

"What battle is that?"

"The battle of the sexes."

I laughed when she said it. I thought she was kidding. Then later I looked back on it and I realized she might have been serious.

Chapter Forty-Six

I spent more time with Lexi, but I was happy living in Alyssa's house. We had a good group there and we had a routine that felt comfortable. That was a time when I didn't feel that I needed to be with Lexi constantly.

Gabriela continued living in Alyssa's house and sleeping on the couch. Gabriela looked at a few apartments for rent, but the landlords didn't want to rent to her because she didn't have any credit history in America. Alyssa didn't worry about such things, which is why foreign people rented from Alyssa. Gabriela said the couch was as good as any bed, maybe better, so she didn't feel a great need to find another place.

Gabriela and Veronica enjoyed cooking together. Veronica came over about one evening a week and she and Gabriela prepared meals together. Everyone in the house contributed some money to buy the ingredients and everyone in the house ate the delicious food. I had some problems as a struggling researcher, but at least I was well nourished.

Chapter Forty-Seven

As we expected, the president of the university announced the school was going to build a baseball stadium south of University Avenue. I saw the announcement on a local television station's news report on the internet.

University Avenue was the southern border of the campus. South of University Avenue was a nice neighborhood. Building a new stadium in the neighborhood would require buying the houses and businesses there, evicting the owners, tearing down the buildings, and putting up the stadium. The stadium would only be used during the season, and not even every day then. When the stadium wasn't being used it would be just a lifeless structure. It would mean the end of a vibrant community.

The president said there was not enough room on the campus for the new stadium. The school could tear down the existing stadium, which was on the campus, but the new stadium would be bigger than the current one, and there would not be enough room on the existing site if they tried to build a big new stadium there. Of course they could make the new stadium no bigger than the old stadium, but they wanted something bigger. They had the money to build something bigger, and that's what they wanted to do.

I called Captain Shaeffer. I was going to violate the university president's rule about not criticizing the donations of friends of the university.

"Captain, I hear the school wants to build your stadium south of University Avenue."

"That's the best place for it."

"That's going to wreck the neighborhood. Tell them to build it further north."

"There's not enough room for a big stadium further north."

"Tell them to build a smaller stadium."

"I don't want a smaller stadium. This is going to have my name on it. I don't want my name on something small. I want my name on something big."

"You're making a big mistake."

"I have to go, Jack. I'll talk to you later."

Chapter Forty-Eight

Alyssa continued her campaign, with Abraham, for the state Supreme Court. Her campaign didn't get much news coverage. The news organizations seemed to think it was not very interesting.

When I saw Gabriela she always wanted to talk about the same thing. She loved Veronica and wanted to do something to show her love. I always told her if she wanted to help Veronica, she should try to get some money for neutrino research for Veronica and Lexi. And she always told me she was trying to find some money for them.

Chapter Forty-Nine

I think I mentioned earlier that there are two sex-related businesses in town. The university president had told us that the people running them were friends of the university. One was the sex doll business which the Shaeffer family was running. The other business was a condom company which had been started years ago by Leland Caselli. Leland's son Charles inherited the business from Leland, and then Charles' wife Valery Caselli inherited the business from Charles. Valery was now elderly and the two grandsons of Valery were handling the day to day management of the business.

The university president told us when we first met him that we should ask for research money from Valery Caselli. So we did a little background research and developed our approach.

Hadley helped me discover the Caselli family history, and also some of the business history of The Caselli Condom Company. Back in the early days of the company, researchers working for Caselli had discovered a reliable method of attaching flavor compounds to condoms, thus making condoms more attractive for oral sex. Caselli marketed condoms in flavors including raspberry, strawberry, chocolate, and rotisserie chicken. They advertised condoms with the slogan "Caselli condoms: you can lick them but you won't beat them." And they also used "Caselli condoms: the condoms for suckers."

We drafted a letter to Valery Caselli and sent it out. We asked for money for neutrino detector research and money for sex research. She wrote back promptly, on monogrammed stationery, telling us she couldn't commit to giving us money but if we wanted to talk with her she would be happy to see us, and perhaps we would like to come to her house for afternoon tea. We couldn't pass up an invitation to tea, so Lexi and Hadley and I went to see her.

We thought anyone who uses monogrammed stationery probably likes nice clothes, so we wanted to wear something relatively formal for her. Lexi wore a white blouse with a light grey jacket and skirt and dark low heels. Hadley wore a white blouse with a darker grey jacket and skirt and dark flats. I wore a light grey business suit with a white shirt and a red tie and dark shoes.

Her house was another of the nice old houses on the west side of the campus. Her house was about three blocks away from Alyssa's house. We were greeted at the door by her housekeeper and all purpose assistant, Maria. We introduced ourselves.

"We're here to see Ms. Caselli," Lexi said.

"Please come in. Everyone calls her Miss Valery," Maria said.

Maria guided us into the living room, which was beautifully decorated and maintained.

"I'll tell Miss Valery you're here," Maria said.

We stood around admiring the house. Miss Valery came in and we all introduced ourselves and told her what a wonderful house she had.

She was medium height and thin and had green eyes and short black hair with a wave in it. She was wearing a dark red pleated twill skirt with a matching jacket over a white blouse, with small gold earrings, and black flat shoes. I'm not a style expert but I thought she looked well dressed. I was glad we had all decided to wear something relatively formal to visit her.

"Welcome to Condom House," she said.

"Condom House?" Hadley said.

"Yes. I tell people I live in Condom House and sometimes they say to me, 'You mean you live in a condominium?' I say, 'No, it's Condom House.'"

"Who decided to call it that?" Hadley said.

"That's what my late husband called it."

"He named his house for his business?"

"He made important business decisions here. And he would entertain people here as part of the condom business. And he built the wall of condoms in our recreation room downstairs," Miss Valery said.

"The wall of condoms?"

"It's actually made from condom boxes. It's a nice design. Want to see it?"

"Yes," we all said.

Miss Valery led us all down to the recreation room. One entire wall was covered with parts of condom boxes. They were somehow blended and permanently attached to the wall in a seamless design like wallpaper. The color pattern and the arrangement looked oddly beautiful. It could have been modern art in an art museum.

"Wow. I've never seen anything like that," Hadley said.

"It's beautiful," I said.

"Yes. It's very nice," Lexi said.

We studied the wall and admired the design.

"You want to see a treasure from the early days?" Miss Valery said.

"Yes," Lexi and Hadley and I said enthusiastically.

"Look at this," Miss Valery said.

She was standing next to a framed magazine page on another wall. We went over to look at the magazine page.

"This is a magazine advertisement from many years ago. It was published a few years after the company was started," she said.

The page had a headline in large print that said, "Talk to your sweetheart about us." Below the headline it had pictures of Caselli condoms, and some advertising text in smaller print.

"If you want to sell condoms, you have to overcome a lot of problems," Miss Valery said. "One problem is getting two lovers to agree. The man has to want to use a condom and his partner has to want him to use a condom. Before two lovers run to the store and buy your condoms, they have to talk about it and they have to agree it's a good idea. How can you get them to talk about it? You can try advertising."

"That's a good ad. I like that," Lexi said.

"It's not a perfect answer to the problem," Miss Valery said. "Talking about anything related to sex is difficult. A lot of people are reluctant to do it. Our company does market research. We have a market research team that offers money to our customers if our customers will agree to be interviewed. And when our people interview them, one of the things we ask them is whether they have problems talking about sex. A lot of people tell us yes, they do have problems talking about sex."

"Yes, I think you're right," Lexi said.

"People don't feel comfortable talking about sex. Even when people want to talk about it, many people don't know how to talk about it. They can't communicate their needs to their partner."

Lexi nodded. "That's right."

"And talking is not the only thing that's important. People need to be able to listen. And that's difficult also."

"It's difficult, but it's not impossible. Talking and listening are skills. People can learn them, like they learn other skills," Lexi said.

"Sex is an ordinary part of life and people need to be able to talk about it. I believe that, but I'm realistic enough to know how difficult it is," Miss Valery said.

"That's a good ad," I said.

"Yes, I think that's very well done," Hadley said.

We all studied the ad.

"Let's go up to the dining room and have our tea," Miss Valery said.

We followed Miss Valery up to the dining room. It had beautiful wallpaper, and a dark wood chair rail running around it. I think the house was at least one hundred years old and the chair rail was original.

"Just sit anywhere," Miss Valery said.

We sat around the dining room table. Maria came into the room.

"Would you like tea now?" she said to Miss Valery.

"Yes, please," Miss Valery said.

Maria went out.

"I'm sorry that my two grandsons could not be here to meet you. But they're busy running the business. There's no rest when you're in the condom business. People are always using your product, so you always have to make more," Miss Valery said.

"Are you still active in the business?" Hadley said.

"I'm chair of the board of directors. I own all of the stock, and I believe that with ownership comes responsibility. But I'm fortunate because both of my grandsons are talented business managers, and they manage the business day to day."

"Is the condom industry prospering now?"

"It's growing slowly. It's going through a lot of changes. Technology changes in many businesses, and that includes our industry. And consumer preferences change also. It's not easy to remain competitive in the industry."

Maria came in with a cart with china and silver and a teapot and a tray of cucumber sandwiches. She took from the cart the china and silver needed for tea and sandwiches and put it at each of our places. She poured hot tea for us and served the cucumber sandwiches. She left on the table a small pitcher of cream and a sugar bowl, which we passed around.

Maria went back to the kitchen and we all sipped our tea and ate the sandwiches. The bread was white bread sliced thin with the crusts cut off and each slice cut into quarters. The filling in the sandwiches was cucumbers sliced very thin and slathered with cream cheese. They were delicious. Everything was excellent. I felt like I had gone from A Slice Is Nice to another universe.

"Thank you for the tea and the cucumber sandwiches. Everything is wonderful," Hadley said.

"I'm happy you're visiting me and I'm happy you like my humble tea service," Miss Valery said to Hadley.

"Yes, it's perfect," Lexi said.

"Yes," I said.

Miss Valery looked at Lexi. "Now, Professor Lieblich, let's talk about you and your work."

"Everybody calls me Lexi."

"You teach and you also do research?"

"Yes."

"How do you like teaching?"

Lexi smiled. "I love it. It's very satisfying when I can help people learn something new."

"I like your enthusiasm. I think all good teachers have that. I suspect you're good at your profession."

"I do like teaching."

"Let's talk about your letter. In your letter to me, you said you needed money for your research. Therefore we should talk about money, although I'm really not entirely comfortable talking about money," Miss Valery said.

"All right."

"Professor Lieblich, talking about money can be just as difficult as talking about sex. Money is such a personal thing. Money is hard to talk about."

"Yes, that's true."

"As I indicated in my reply to your letter, I'm sorry to have to report that I cannot offer you any research money. I don't think any of you knew my dear late husband. He was a kind and generous man, and in his estate plan he provided for our children with some money and he left all of his stock to me. He did not restrict in any way my legal ability to dispose of what he left me. But during his lifetime everyone knew what was important to him, and I feel an obligation to support things that he would have supported."

"Yes, that's certainly understandable," Lexi said.

"My husband loved baseball. He was not good enough to be a professional athlete, but he loved the game and he played on the university team many years ago when he was a student. I'm quite certain that was before any of you were born."

"Yes," Lexi said.

"And when he got older, he gave money to the university to pay for various improvements to the baseball facilities. And other people shared his interest. This town that we live in is a college town and it's also what I call a baseball town. The university baseball team has always been good, although in some years it's been better than in other years. It has always had a lot of fans in the town. I think you know there's another sex business in this town, a sex doll company, and the family who runs that business has also supported baseball at the university."

"Hadley and I met Captain Shaeffer," I said.

Miss Valery looked at me.

"My husband knew Captain Shaeffer. And my husband had friends in the athletic department for many years, and in the years that I've been alone I too have developed friends in the athletic department. We have a connection because of my husband, you see."

"Yes," I said.

Miss Valery looked at Lexi.

"In the past few years I've been in contact with my friends in the athletic department about donating money to the school. They've talked to me about donating money for a new baseball stadium, but unfortunately we were never able to agree on exactly what we wanted or where we wanted to build it."

"I understand," Lexi said.

"Now, we all know the Shaeffer family is also interested in giving money for a new baseball stadium, and I think their interest in donating to the school is good. As you know, recently your school announced a plan to build a new stadium south of University Avenue using money donated by Captain Shaeffer. To me that seems like the wrong location. The neighborhood south of University Avenue is a great neighborhood. I don't think the university should do anything to disrupt that area. And I believe there are other people who share my views. So I question whether your school will go forward with that plan."

"Yes, we agree with you that south of University Avenue is the wrong location," Lexi said.

"But at the same time I do see the need for a new baseball stadium. I've watched games at the current stadium, and it's adequate but nothing special. A new stadium could provide better locker rooms for the players. It could provide a field with better drainage, so the field could dry faster after rain storms. It could provide better seating for the spectators. It could provide better eating areas for everyone watching the game. There are many ways the stadium could be better," Miss Valery said.

"Yes, I think you're right," Lexi said.

Miss Valery looked at me.

"I think a baseball team is a little bit like a young woman," Miss Valery said.

"Why is that?" I said.

"If a young woman is wearing old dirty clothes, no makeup, her hair is a mess, then nobody wants her. But if she puts on something new and pretty and maybe reveals a little of her body, and wears nice makeup and fixes her hair to look nice, then when a young man walks by her, he starts to get an erection," Miss Valery said.

I smiled. I looked at Lexi and Hadley. They weren't smiling.

"Please forgive me for bringing sex into this, but as I told you, I think sex is a normal part of life and people need to be able to talk about it. The same thing that's true about a woman is true in a very general way about a baseball team. If you put the team in better surroundings, even though it's the same team, it will be more attractive. People will be excited by the team, not in a sexual way but I think it might be a similar passion," Miss Valery said.

"I see what you're saying," I said.

Miss Valery looked at Lexi.

"If your school decides not to go forward with the plan south of University Avenue using the Shaeffer money, and if the Shaeffer family doesn't want to pursue other options, then I want to get back in contact with the athletic department and see whether I can reach an agreement with them on a different plan for a stadium."

"I understand," Lexi said.

"Now at the same time, I think what you're doing is important work, Professor Lieblich."

"Please call me Lexi."

"Lexi sounds so much less dignified than Professor Lieblich," Miss Valery said.

"I'm not a very dignified person. Sorry."

"No, that's fine, Lexi, as you call yourself. It may take me a while to get used to saying Lexi."

"I understand. Do whatever you're comfortable with."

"As I was saying, Professor Lexi, I think what you're doing is important work. You're detecting these little particles, and you have this detector that actually could be used in some important applications."

"Yes. That's right," Lexi said.

"I've never heard of these little particles that you're detecting."

"Nobody has heard of them, except researchers. That's one reason why people don't give me research money. When I first met Jack he said I should rename them."

"Rename them?"

"He said I should call them something else."

"What did he say you should call them?"

"He said I should tell people I was detecting wizard dust."

Miss Valery smiled. "Wizard dust. I like that." Miss Valery looked at me. "Doctor Rose, what made you think of wizard dust?"

"A lot of people are interested in wizards."

"So if you say you're doing research on detecting wizard dust, a lot of people will think it's important research."

"Yes, I think so," I said.

"Doctor Rose, suppose somebody wanted to know how scientists detect wizard dust. What would you tell them?"

"I would say detecting wizard dust is not easy. We need a very good detector to detect wizard dust."

"And suppose somebody wanted to know about wizard dust research. What would you tell them?"

"We need to do research to make the detector the best possible detector. And we need to work with other people who can use the detector to do important things. And all of that requires research money."

"Doctor Rose, I like your approach. I think you have a real talent for explaining research."

"Thank you. Please call me Jack."

"Well, if you insist, I'll call you Jack. You're an informal group."

"Yes. We're not very formal."

Miss Valery shifted in her chair and looked at Hadley.

"Are you a student at the university?"

"Yes."

"What do you think of all this?"

"I'm learning from it."

"Hadley, your colleagues are proposing some research which really is far beyond anything I thought would be possible."

"Modern technology opens up a lot of new research possibilities."

"What do you think about the idea of sex research?"

"I think there's a need for it."

"Maybe that will help people of your generation. Maybe research will bring people more answers to problems."

"Yes, I think so."

Miss Valery looked at Lexi. "Professor Lexi, I said earlier that many people feel uncomfortable talking about sex."

"Yes."

"And I believe many people are not able to communicate their needs to their partner. I think that can be a serious problem."

"Yes, that's a serious problem."

"Do you think maybe sex research could somehow help people communicate their needs to their partner?"

"Yes, I think so."

"Do you think it's possible to teach people how to communicate their needs?"

"It should be possible."

Miss Valery looked at me. "What do you think, Doctor Jack?"

"I agree. It should be possible."

Miss Valery didn't have any more questions about research. I was glad she was interested in it.

She looked over at the wallpaper. Then she looked at each of us. "Professor Lexi and Doctor Jack and Hadley, I'm very happy we met and I'm impressed by your research proposals. I'm sorry I can't help you in my current circumstances, but I'll keep you in mind. If things change, I'll reconsider."

"Thank you. We appreciate your interest," I said.

"Would you like a little more tea?" Miss Valery said.

"Yes, please," we all said.

"Do you like classical music?" Miss Valery said to Lexi.

"Certainly."

"Who's your favorite composer?"

"We were listening to some Tchaikovsky recently. It was very nice."

Miss Valery looked at me. "Would you like to listen to some Tchaikovsky now?"

"Yes, we love Tchaikovsky."

Miss Valery looked at Hadley. "Do you like his music?"

"Yes."

"Let's listen to a little Tchaikovsky and have a little more tea. Please excuse me for just a moment."

Miss Valery got up and left the room. Soon we heard his music playing softly. She came back into the room and sat down. Maria came back with her cart and served another round of hot tea and cucumber sandwiches. I wanted to never ever leave.

But we finished our tea and sandwiches and music and said our goodbyes and reluctantly left Maria and Miss Valery.

Chapter Fifty

A few days later I was watching local news videos and I saw a report of the first major developments in Alyssa's campaign for judge of the state Supreme Court.

The video started with the typical anchor in the news room. "The Channel Four 'More On Four' Action News Team is covering breaking news at this hour in the race for state Supreme Court judge. With more on the story, let's go live to the office of the state attorney general."

Then the video switched to a reporter doing a standup report from the attorney general's office. "The attorney general today is announcing a big, sweeping lawsuit against Alyssa Lincoln, a candidate in this year's election for a judge of the state Supreme Court. Candidate Lincoln has made her dog, Abraham Lincoln, a central focus of her campaign. Candidate Lincoln has said voters decide whom to vote for based entirely on name recognition, and voters would be willing to vote for a canine judge if it had a familiar name, such as Abraham Lincoln. In the suit filed today the attorney general accuses the Lincoln campaign of slandering and libeling the state Supreme Court, and the suit asks that she be disqualified. Our news team has not yet been able to reach the candidate and her dog for comment."

After that, the local television news reported two or three times a week on the attorney general's suit against Alyssa. A lot of what they reported seemed repetitious to me. But they seemed to like covering the story. Every piece of paper filed by anybody in the case got on the news. The television stations each had their own expert who was interviewed repeatedly about developments. Anybody who watched the news became familiar with Alyssa's campaign.

Chapter Fifty-One

One day Miss Valery called me.

"Professor Jack, I'm not calling to donate money today. I'm not giving money for the reasons we discussed. But I do want to help the university. It's a great school and it deserves the support of the people in the community."

"Thank you."

"Caselli Condoms can give you a donation out of our inventory of condoms. We can send it to your school's student health services. Does your school want them?"

"Yes. Student health can use them."

"We can give you fifty cases of coffee flavored condoms. That includes twenty five cases of regular coffee and twenty five cases of decaf. There are four condoms in a box and fifty boxes in a case, so if my math is correct that's a total of ten thousand condoms."

"Thank you. That's much appreciated. That should last all the way through homecoming weekend."

Chapter Fifty-Two

One day I went to Lexi's house and she said she had received a letter from someone at the university, on their official department stationery.

"Dear Professor Lieblich," Lexi said, reading the letter to me, "My name is Anna Cortez and I'm the head of the university department of art and design. My daughter is in high school and takes a physics class taught by Britta Shaeffer Richardson. My daughter tells me that her physics teacher brought to school a machine which you and your associates created. I believe it is called a new something detector. A new tree or something like that. I'm not sure how you spell that word. My daughter reports that the sleek minimalist design of your machine captures the essence of the modern industrial design movement."

Lexi smiled and continued to read the letter. "I am pleased to report that our department has received national recognition as a center for excellence in the study of contemporary commercial and industrial design. This year we are hosting the national conference of the American Contemporary Design Association. Designers from all over the country will be displaying their work. We would love to display your work as an example of modern design produced at our university. Please contact me if you would like to have your work displayed at our conference. Sincerely, Anna Cortez."

Lexi looked at me. "I am now a great contemporary designer."

I smiled. "Are you gong to contact Anna?"

"I don't think so. Anna doesn't know anything about physics."

"I think it would be fun to have your machine displayed at a conference."

"You can contact her if you want to."

"Can I tell her you're willing to let them display it?"

"Yes, if they do all the work."

I contacted Anna and we arranged for the neutrino detector to be displayed at the national conference. Anna had some people helping her, and they scheduled a visit to Lexi's house and picked up the neutrino detector and carefully transported it to the conference.

I went to the conference because I wanted to see what people were designing. Most of the things on display were more practical than a neutrino detector. They had some heating and air conditioning machinery, and some agricultural machinery, and some things that I didn't recognize. Everything looked professional but unexciting, except for Lexi's neutrino detector. Lexi had designed something which, in my opinion, looked like it could be the start of a new standard in industrial design. Of course, I'm not an expert in design. I wasn't sure how design professionals reacted to Lexi's design.

So I decided to go to the awards banquet at the end of the conference. Everyone had a good meal, and then a woman named Mimi Chen got up and went to the podium and introduced herself. She said she was executive director of the American Contemporary Design Association. She made a short speech, praising everybody who had shown products at the exhibit. Then she announced the award for best new design.

I'm not saying I predicted Lexi would win it. I'm saying I knew she had a chance. So when Mimi Chen announced Lexi was the winner, it wasn't a complete surprise to me. The award was a nice honor, but it didn't carry with it any money for research.

I was sorry Lexi wasn't there to receive her award. At the end of the awards banquet I introduced myself to Mimi, and I said I was a friend of Lexi and I thanked Mimi for giving Lexi the award. Mimi said she was happy I had come to the conference and she liked meeting new people who were interested in design. She asked me for my contact information and I gave it to her. She said she hoped to see me at another conference.

When the conference was over, Anna's workers carefully brought the neutrino detector back to Lexi. Lexi was not impressed by winning the award.

"I need money," she said.

Chapter Fifty-Three

One day I got a call from Lexi. She sounded excited.

"Jack, this is it. This is it. This is it."

"This is what?"

"I got a message from a research grant administrator. Somebody I've never met. Somebody I don't know. He's come out here all the way from Washington. Our nation's capital, Jack."

"Yes, I'm familiar with the place."

"He's out here for a conference. But he heard I was doing neutrino research and he wants to meet me."

"Good."

"I'm so excited."

"You sound excited."

"He's going to meet me in front of the student center at four. Are you available then? Do you want to meet him?"

"Yes. I can be there."

"Good. I'm so excited."

"See you then."

I met Lexi in front of the student center at four. Lexi said look for a guy wearing a name tag from a meeting. Not long after that, someone came walking up who was wearing a name tag. We introduced ourselves and he said he was the Washington man we were hoping to meet. We stood there and he talked with Lexi.

"I'm delighted to meet someone who's doing neutrino research. We're very interested in neutrino research. We're starting a major effort to support it," he said.

Lexi smiled. "I'm so happy to meet someone who's interested in supporting neutrino research. What agency do you work for? Are you with the National Science Foundation?"

"No, although I have great respect for their support of basic research."

"The Energy Department?"

"No, no, I'm not with the Energy Department."

"What, then?"

"I'm with the Department of Agriculture."

"The Department of Agriculture? Why are they interested in neutrino research?"

"Because we're seeing very exciting developments in neutrino research."

"You are?"

"Yes. We're starting to get the data this year. So far, we see that the neutrino has better heat tolerance than Cabernet Sauvignon, which is important in this changing climate. And the tannin levels are exactly where we want them. The neutrino is an excellent new variety."

Lexi frowned. "Are you talking about wine grapes?"

"Yes. Aren't you talking about wine grapes?"

"I'm talking about particles."

"You mean the particles that remain in the vat after you process the grapes?"

"No. Elementary particles. In physics."

"How is that related to wine making?"

"It's not related to wine making."

"Oh, I'm sorry. I thought you were interested in grapes for wine."

"I like grapes, but they're not what I'm researching. I'm sorry."

The man smiled. "That's all right. I enjoyed meeting you anyway. I'm sure your research is important. I hope you have a lot of success with what you're doing."

Lexi smiled. "Thank you."

"If you know anybody that does agricultural research, tell them you talked with me and I'm looking for neutrino researchers. Agricultural neutrino researchers."

"I'll pass that along."

Lexi took a step back. She looked like she was ready to depart.

"Do you know anybody who does sex research? That's the other thing we're interested in," the grape research man said.

"Jack here does sex research."

"You do sex research?" he said to me.

"That's right."

"Sex research in plants?"

"No, sorry," I said.

"If you ever get tired of what you're doing now, and you want to work in a great field with lots of resources, try sex research in plants."

"Thank you for that career advice. I'm always interested in hearing what fields are getting money for research," I said.

"I'm happy to meet both of you. I wish the two of you a lot of success."

"Thank you."

The man from Washington left us.

"I'm starting to think I might never get any money for neutrino research," Lexi said.

"You'll get research money," I said.

"When will I get research money?"

"When your hair is on fire and the sun rises in the west and sets in the east. Just like Hadley said."

Chapter Fifty-Four

Alyssa mentioned to me one day that John Smith wanted to come over to her house and talk with her. John Smith was the only other candidate on the ballot for the election for state Supreme Court judge. She wanted me to meet him, and I was curious about Alyssa's competition. We found a time that worked for everybody and she invited John to come over then. And so on the agreed day and time he arrived at her house and Alyssa and Abraham and I met him at the door.

"Hello John, come on in," Alyssa said.

"Hello Alyssa," John said.

"John, do you know Jack?"

"Hello John. It's good to meet you," I said.

Abraham was standing next to Alyssa.

"Abraham, this is John. John, meet Abraham," Alyssa said.

Abraham looked at John and wagged his tail. I thought that was a gracious way to treat a rival.

John was well dressed. Alyssa was well dressed also. If the voters voted for whoever wore the best clothes, it would be a close election.

We walked in to the living room. John looked at me.

"Alyssa, I thought we were going to meet alone," John said.

"I want Jack to join us."

"Why does he have to be here?"

"Jack is my campaign committee treasurer. He's my most important campaign worker."

"What I want to say is just between you and me," John said.

"If you have anything to say, you need to say it to Jack and me together."

John paused. He had a sour look on his face, like he had just bitten into a lemon.

"I don't like this," John said.

"Why are you so disagreeable? Come on now, let's all sit down and make ourselves comfortable," Alyssa said.

"Would anyone like some iced tea?" I said. "We have some already made in the refrigerator. I think I'll have some myself."

"Would you like some tea, John?" Alyssa said.

"No, I don't think I'll have any."

"What about you Alyssa? Are you having some?" I said.

"Yes, thank you."

"Any for you Abraham?" I said.

Abraham looked at me and raised one eyebrow. John still had a sour look on his face. Alyssa walked over to one of the chairs and sat down. Abraham went over next to Alyssa's chair and stretched out on the floor. John went to a chair opposite Alyssa and sat down. I went out to the kitchen briefly and poured some tea into glasses and came back and served it and sat near Alyssa. I could hear them talking while I was busy with the tea.

"Now, how can we help you?" Alyssa said cheerfully.

"Don't think I don't know what you're doing," John said.

"That's a double negative, John. Try not to use a double negative."

"Don't tell me don't use a double negative. I can use a triple negative if I want. I can say negative negative negative."

"Come on now, John. Let's not argue about syntax."

"Grammar. It's grammar, Alyssa. We're arguing about grammar."

"Why are you so disagreeable today?"

"Because I don't agree with you. How can I be agreeable if I don't agree with you?"

"Look on the bright side, John. Look on the bright side. What about your campaign? Isn't that what you want to talk about? Let's talk about your campaign. Isn't that going well? I heard your campaign was going very well."

"Where did you hear that?"

"It's true, isn't it? Your campaign is going well."

"My campaign *was* going well. My campaign was going *very* well."

"See, John? That's the bright side."

"My campaign was going very well until you started doing what you're doing."

"What is it that I'm doing, John?"

"Don't play dumb with me. You know exactly what you're doing."

John stared at Alyssa. Abraham stared at John. Alyssa sipped her tea.

"I asked you a question, John."

"You've gotten in bed with your ex-husband," John said in a very soft voice.

Alyssa laughed. "That's ridiculous, John. I'm not sleeping with my ex-husband. Jack, am I sleeping with my ex-husband?"

"She's not sleeping with her ex-husband. As far as I know," I said.

"I'm speaking metaphorically. Metaphorically, you're in bed with your ex-husband."

"Come on John, don't speak metaphorically. Speak English," Alyssa said.

"You and your ex-husband are working together against me. The two of you are a team. The two of you are a pair of conspirators conspiring to defeat me."

"John, I'm not a doctor. Jack here is a doctor. I'm not a doctor. But I have read a little about paranoia. Paranoia can be a very powerful force. Paranoia can take over a person's mind. Paranoia can completely change a person's personality. But there is hope. There is hope, John. There is hope, through treatment."

"Don't play dumb with me, Alyssa. You know what's going on."

"I can ask Jack to get you a referral to a mental health professional if you wish."

"Alyssa, I want you to drop the suit against you."

"You want me to drop the suit against me? That doesn't make sense, John. Why are you talking like that? Are you feeling ill? Do you need to lie down?"

"Alyssa, listen to me."

"I've been listening to you during this entire conversation. That's why I'm concerned about your mental health."

"Alyssa, your ex-husband is chief of staff of the attorney general."

"Everybody knows that, John. That's never been a secret."

"And your son is a staff attorney in the attorney general's office."

"That's also well known."

"Your ex-husband and your son are helping the attorney general."

"That's their job."

"The attorney general is suing your campaign."

"Everybody knows that. What are you trying to say, John?"

"He's helping you. He's helping your campaign. It's not ethical. It's not fair. He's giving you an unfair advantage."

"John, do you know anything at all about the law? If the attorney general wins his suit against me, I'm off the ballot. If I'm off the ballot, I have no chance to win the election. My campaign is over. Finished. Done. That's the opposite of helping me."

"Alyssa, do you know anything at all about the law? The suit that the attorney general filed against you has no chance of success. None at all. It's completely frivolous. You have the right to say what you're saying in your campaign. You know that. I know that. The attorney general knows that."

"So what, John? Who cares? If, as you say, the attorney general has filed a frivolous suit against me, who cares?"

"Alyssa, my campaign has confidential in-house polls. I won't release them publicly."

"If you won't release them publicly, why are you telling me about them?"

"They bother me, Alyssa. They bother me a lot."

"Why do they bother you?"

"Before the attorney general filed his suit against you, nobody knew you were in the race. Now, after the attorney general sued you, it's been this steady drip of free publicity for you, constantly in the news. Drip, drip, drip. Something in the news about it almost every day. The attorney general says this. The attorney general says that. Just an endless stream of free publicity for you and Abraham Lincoln. According to my private polls, your name recognition is now higher than mine. You have a chance to win the election."

"John, you and I just need to trust the voters. We need to respect whatever choice the voters make. That's how democracy works."

"You could stop this suit against you right now if you wanted to. This is a conspiracy against me by you and your ex-husband and your son and the attorney general."

"If you like, Jack can send you some medical articles about paranoia."

"Alyssa, I have other appointments today. I have places I need to be today. I've taken enough of your time." John stood up.

"You're leaving us?" Alyssa stood up and held out her right hand as an offer to shake hands, but John wouldn't shake it. "Thanks for coming over, John."

John started walking toward the door, then stopped. "Alyssa, I'm going to win the election."

"Maybe you will."

"I will do whatever it takes to win the election."

"Are you going to get a dog of your own? How about a Dalmatian? Those are good dogs."

John smiled.

"You're smiling, John. Are you starting to look on the bright side?"

"Don't mess with me, Alyssa."

John left. We watched John go.

"Bye John," I said, and turned to Alyssa. "What do you think?"

"I wonder if a Dalmatian could beat a golden retriever in an election for the Supreme Court."

Chapter Fifty-Five

I was watching news videos and I saw something disturbing. The Channel Four "More On Four" Action News Team was reporting that Terrie Smith, wife of Supreme Court candidate John Smith, had gone missing. Nobody had seen her for several days, according to anonymous news sources. The campaign itself was vague about what was going on. John Smith had released a statement that didn't say much. "I thank everyone for their kind thoughts and offers to help in this difficult time. Terrie would have wanted me to continue my campaign, and so I will continue to ask you to vote for John Smith for Supreme Court judge in the election on November 3 of this year."

Chapter Fifty-Six

Morgan called me. I wan't expecting to hear from her.

"Doctor Rose, remember when we met Alyssa's son?"

"Yes, I remember."

"What did you think of him?"

"He seemed nice. He seemed bright. He seemed interested in helping people. What do you think of him?"

"I agree with you, Doctor Rose."

"I think he's like his mother. She's like that."

"I don't know her very well."

"Have you been going out with him?"

"How did you know that?"

"Just a guess. Is he married?"

"No. I'm staying away from married guys."

"You're very wise."

"His real name is Kent. But everybody calls him Clark. He likes that."

"That's cute."

"He's asked me to go with him to a student production at the university theater. We're going this weekend."

"What are they performing?"

"They're doing *Ladies Prefer Blondes*. It's a musical. It's based on *Gentlemen Prefer Blondes*, but all the leading characters are lesbians."

"That sounds entertaining."

"Clark and I are going to relax and do some fun things together in this town. Lots of things happening here."

"I'm sure of that, Morgan."

"Doctor Rose, do you remember when Alyssa said men are like vacuum cleaners? She said they sweep you up."

"Yes, I remember when she said that."

"Do you think men are like vacuum cleaners?"

"Sometimes they are, Morgan."

"I think I might be getting swept up."

"I think Alyssa was talking about falling for someone."

"I think I'm falling for Clark."

"I hope you and Clark have a great time together."

"Doctor Rose?"

"Yes, Morgan?"

"You're a sex researcher."

"If I can find some money."

"Can I ask you a question?"

"Certainly. I hope I know the answer."

"You promise not to tell anyone about this?"

"Yes. I promise."

"Has there been any research done about rape fantasies?"

"Rape fantasies?"

"Yes."

"People have some theories about them."

"I'm having rape fantasies."

"Do they disturb you?"

"No. They're not like nightmares. They're fantasies. But I wonder whether I'm losing my mind."

"Rape fantasies are actually pretty common. They're normal."

"I'm having fantasies in which Clark forces me to have sex."

"That's normal."

"But I don't want to be raped."

"Nobody wants to be raped."

"Why am I having rape fantasies?"

"Because you want to be intensely desired. And you want to have control."

"I don't have control when I'm being raped."

"In a fantasy you have control. In a fantasy your mind is controlling everything that happens. When you have a fantasy you're not imagining a real event. It's a fantasy."

"Why don't I have fantasies about consensual sex?"

"Because your mind wants to imagine something more intense than that. But your fantasy is not really about rape, which would be horrific. Calling it a rape fantasy is probably misleading. You're having a fantasy that's not an exact description of anything that happens in the real world. Call it a sex fantasy."

"Doctor Rose, I feel like I'm losing my mind."

"You're not losing your mind. You're falling in love."

"Maybe it's the same thing."

"You'll be fine."

"Do you think I should see a psychiatrist?"

"No. Psychiatrists help abnormal people. You're not abnormal."

"I'm not abnormal?"

"That's right. You're normal."

"Do you think taking something like Prozac would help me?"

"There's no scientific evidence that taking Prozac helps normal people."

"I was reading an article online where someone said taking Prozac can help anyone feel better."

"Taking placebos can help anyone feel better. Normal people who take psych meds and say they feel better are experiencing the placebo effect."

"I think I'm already taking placebos. In your medical school's endo treatment trial."

"I don't know whether you're in the control group or not. They don't tell me those things."

"Doctor Rose, I still feel like I need help. Who helps normal people?"

"Friends help normal people."

"I don't do enough to help *you*. I'm always calling you with my problems but I don't help you with yours."

"Not true. You've helped me a lot."

"When did I ever help you?"

"The first time I met you. You told me to iron my clothes. That was good advice."

"Did that advice help you?"

"Yes. It helped me look better."

"Did it help you get research money?"

"No. Not yet. But it's going to help me get research money. Someone is going to like the way I look and they're going to give me research money."

"I hope so."

"Morgan, I think you and Clark will have a great time together."

"Do you have any advice for me now? Is there anything you think I should do?"

"I can only think of one thing, Morgan."

"What's that?"

"You should ask Lexi whether she might be willing to give you some ideas on how to communicate your needs in bed to Clark."

"Is Lexi good at that?"

"She's the best. I don't know if she would be willing to discuss that with you. I didn't ask her whether she wants to talk with you. But she's an expert. If she wants to talk with you, she's somebody you should listen to."

"Thanks for your help, Doctor Rose. You're very wise."

"I'm not. But I do listen to people who are. Sometimes I learn something from them."

"Thanks for listening to them."

Chapter Fifty-Seven

One day I was watching news videos and I saw another disturbing news report about Terrie Smith, wife of Supreme Court candidate John Smith.

"The Channel Four 'More On Four' Action News Team has spoken with sources close to the John Smith campaign who have asked to remain anonymous. Our sources tell us that it is now believed that Terrie Smith, wife of John Smith, may have been abducted by space aliens. We contacted the John Smith campaign headquarters and they released this statement from the candidate. 'I thank everyone for their kind thoughts and offers to help in this difficult time. Terrie would have wanted me to continue my campaign, and so I will continue to ask you to vote for John Smith for Supreme Court judge in the election on November third of this year.'"

Chapter Fifty-Eight

Lexi invited me to come over to her house on a Tuesday morning. I came over and she greeted me at the door. She was wearing casual clothes, as was I.

"Thank you for coming over. I have to go to work this morning, but I wanted to see you and I have a little time now," she said.

"I have to go to work later also, but I have time now, and it's always good to see you."

"Let's go upstairs and lie in bed. And just talk. Can we do that?"

"Sure."

"I don't feel like racing today."

"That's fine."

She held my hand and we went upstairs to her bedroom.

"I want to lie on top of you. Do you want me to lie on top of you?" she said.

"Yes, I want you on top of me."

We took off our shoes and I laid on her bed on my back and she got on top of me facing me. Lexi had a comfortable mattress.

"Am I crushing you?" she said.

Lexi weighed maybe half my weight.

"No, you're as light as a feather."

"Jackson, what's going to happen to us? What are we going to do?"

"You're going to go to work. I'm going to go to work."

"Have you ever been married?"

"No."

"I've been married. It didn't last. I didn't want to stay married."

"I'm sorry it didn't work for you."

"I didn't want to stay married, and I don't want to get married again."

"You should do what you want to do."

"But it's not that simple, Jack. There is a part of being married that's very satisfying."

"What part is that?"

"Having a serious connection to someone is very satisfying. Life can be crazy sometimes for everybody, single or married. Going through all the craziness of life is much more satisfying with somebody close to you than going through it alone."

"You should do what you want to do."

"But I don't *know* what I want to do. Because having a serious connection with somebody has its own problems. When I was married, I was married twenty-four hours a day, seven days a week. I always had to think about my partner, and of course he always had to think about me. When you have a serious connection to someone, you can't just do whatever you feel like doing at any moment."

"Yes, that's true."

"Jack, will you do me a favor? Will you lie on the floor? I want to lie down next to you."

"On the floor?"

"Yes. I want to show you something."

"Sure."

We both got up out of the bed.

I laid down on on my back on the floor of her bedroom. She had hardwood floors throughout her house. The floor felt hard. Lexi laid down on her back on the floor beside me. She snuggled up next to me as much as she could while still lying on the floor.

"How do you feel?" she said.

"The floor is pretty hard. But being next to you feels good."

"When you have a serious connection to someone, this is what it's like."

"It's like lying on the floor?"

"It's hard, Jack. Having a serious connection to someone is hard."

"How could it be hard? Women and men are made to be together. A woman and a man being together is the most natural thing in the world."

She started laughing. "Jack, have you had any experience at all living in this world?"

I thought about her question. "No, I suppose not. I've never been married. I've never lived with someone I was in love with. I haven't even spent much time lying on the floor."

She became serious. "Do you like gardens?"

"Yes, gardens are good. I like your flower garden."

"When I was married, my husband and I had a garden."

"What did you grow?"

"I planted some day lilies, like I have now."

"Your day lilies are pretty."

"My husband wanted to grow vegetables. He wanted to grow corn and peas."

"So did you have a vegetable garden?"

"We did. He had half the garden for his vegetables and I had half for my flowers."

"Did you like your garden?"

"I wanted to have a lot more flowers, Jack. Maybe I'm selfish but I wanted a lot more flowers."

"You're not selfish."

"You're sweet to listen to me and not criticize me."

"I love you."

"What you and I have now is nice. It's nice. Seeing you is nice when I see you. When we're in bed together, that's nice too. Being held in your arms is nice. Holding you in my arms is nice. Sex is nice. That's a nice feeling. I like that. But how long does that last? And then what else do we have? I don't think we have a serious connection."

"Yes, I understand."

"Do you want to have a serious connection with me?"

"Yes, I want that."

"Are you sure? Having a serious connection is hard."

"I want that."

"Live with me."

"Yes. I want to live with you."

"Will you be happy living with me and my flowers?"

"I like flowers. And I love you."

We got up off the floor and got ready for work and walked to the campus. After work I moved to Lexi's house. I was happy to be able to live with her and her flowers.

Chapter Fifty-Nine

Lexi and I tried to establish a routine for our lives in the same house. We ate meals together when we could. The first evening after I moved into her house we were sitting in her kitchen eating spicy fried chicken and salad.

"I like to keep the house pretty warm in the daytime, if I'm home. Are you comfortable? Is the house too warm for you?" she said.

"No, this is good."

"At night I turn the thermostat down. I can't sleep if it's too warm at night."

"I'm the same way."

"When I was married we got a dog. We named her Ambassador because she was great at making new friends. Everybody loved her. She was a mixed breed, medium size. We got a dog bed for her and put the dog bed right on our bed. We got a blanket for her so she could stay warm when I turned the thermostat down."

"What happened to her?"

"After I got divorced I got custody of her. She lived a long life. She was a great dog. When you're in bed with me at night, you'll be the first warm body with me at night since she was there."

"Sometimes I think my role in life is to be something like a dog for women."

Lexi laughed. "That's not your role in *my* life."

"What am I then?"

"You're my *je ne sais quoi*."

"I'll try to be a good *je ne sais quoi*. But that will be hard to do, because I don't know what it is."

Chapter Sixty

I was watching news videos and I saw another disturbing news report about Terrie Smith, wife of Supreme Court candidate John Smith.

"The Channel Four 'More On Four' Action News Team has spoken with people close to the John Smith campaign who have asked to remain anonymous. Our confidential informants tell us that it is now believed that Terrie Smith, wife of John Smith, might have voluntarily gone away with space aliens. Our news team is working at this moment to try to confirm this new information. We contacted the John Smith campaign headquarters and they released this statement from the candidate. 'I thank everyone for their kind thoughts and offers to help in this difficult time. Terrie would have wanted me to continue my campaign, and so I will continue to ask you to vote for John Smith for Supreme Court judge in the election on November third of this year.'"

Now there were daily news videos about Terrie Smith, wife of Supreme Court candidate John Smith. Every day someone was speculating about her. Had she gone away with space aliens? Had she perhaps fallen in love with a space alien? Was she having secret sexual encounters with space aliens?

John Smith was releasing statements every day now. All of them concluded by asking everyone to vote for him.

One day Captain Shaeffer called me.

"The news is reporting that Terrie Smith, wife of Supreme Court candidate John Smith, is having secret sexual encounters with space aliens," he said.

"Yes, I saw those reports."

"What do you think about that?"

"I'm a little bit skeptical. Sometimes people want to get their name in the news. Starting a rumor about space aliens would do that."

"Is it possible that people could have secret sexual encounters with space aliens?"

"I'm not aware of any cases where that's been proven."

"Could you study that?"

"That would be hard to study."

"I would give you money to study that. That would be a fascinating topic to study."

"Thank you, but I've not had any training with space aliens. I'm not sure I'm qualified to study them, and I don't know anybody else who's qualified either."

"All right, but if you find out anything about sexual encounters with space aliens, can you give me a call?"

"Yes, I will."

"Thanks, Jack."

The day before the election I was watching news videos and I saw some news about the Supreme Court campaign.

"Terrie Smith, wife of Supreme Court candidate John Smith, has reportedly been found alive and well. There is no word on exactly where she has been while she was missing. John Smith has released the following statement. 'I thank everyone for their support throughout this difficult time. We are delighted to have Terrie back with us. She asks only that you vote for me, John Smith, for Supreme Court judge on election day, which is tomorrow.'"

On election night, I got a call from Alyssa.

"I'm conceding to John. It looks like he's going to end up with about ninety percent of the vote," she said.

"I'm sorry you didn't get more votes. You worked hard. You ran a good race."

"Thank you for your help, Jack. I really appreciate everything you did. We just couldn't overcome the space aliens."

"Whichever candidate has the space aliens is just unbeatable."

"But still, we made history. This is the first time a dog has gotten ten percent of the vote."

"We've given hope to golden retrievers everywhere."

Chapter Sixty-One

Veronica continued to come over to Alyssa's house about once a week and cook dinner with Gabriela. I was still invited to come to their dinners, along with everyone in the house, although I was no longer a resident there. Lexi was also invited to the dinners, which was nice.

One day when I was there for dinner, Gabriela brought a guest. Before we sat down at the dinner table, Gabriela introduced her.

"This is Christine Olivier."

Christine was medium height and had blue eyes and short dark brown hair and wore glasses with wire frames. She was thin and well dressed. She looked like a successful business executive. Alyssa and Irina and Dimitri and Veronica and Lexi and I all said hello to Christine and shook hands with her and introduced ourselves.

"Christine is a managing editor at a Swiss publisher called Noch, Loch, und Schleffenhousen," Gabriela said. "I've known Christine for years, and she's published foreign editions of several books that my company published in England. This is her first visit to this town."

"Welcome to our town, Christine," Alyssa said.

Christine smiled. "I'm delighted to be here."

We all served ourselves and sat at the table and ate our dinner and talked with Christine.

"Veronica, when Gabriela showed me your picture and told me you like to cook, I wanted to meet you," Christine said. "You're even prettier in person than you are in your picture."

"I don't think I'm anything special."

"In the past few years my company has published several cookbooks, and we've found that when everything is right they can be very successful. Veronica, I want you to consider publishing a cookbook with our company."

"A cookbook? You want to publish a cookbook with me?"

"That's a great idea, Veronica. You should do that," Alyssa said softly.

"Yes, Veronica. I want to publish it in America and also in Europe," Christine said. "My company will translate it into European languages. You have the potential to be a very successful author of a cookbook. We'll publish your cookbook in a nine by twelve inch hardcover and we'll put a big picture of your face, smiling, on the front of the jacket. You have a wide mouth with perfect teeth and a beautiful smile. People will see your picture and they'll buy the book without even looking to see what's inside."

"What *will* be inside the book?"

"International cuisine is popular right now. Your name is Russian, so you should do Russian food. But not the usual Russian food. People want something new. So you need to think of something that's new and fresh and create some recipes."

"I'm not a food expert. I'm a neutrino researcher."

"Gabriela tells me you're a good cook. After we've published your book, we'll sponsor you on a promotion tour. You'll go places and demonstrate your recipes and promote your book. You'll be very popular."

"Christine, I'm a neutrino researcher."

"And that's fine, Veronica. You don't have to choose between what you're doing and writing a cookbook. You can do both."

Christine had a soothing way of speaking. Persuading reluctant authors to write for her was not an easy job, but she was good at it.

Veronica looked at Alyssa. "You think I should do that?"

"I think it's a great opportunity, Veronica," Alyssa said softly. "And maybe your book can have a little bit of a biography of you and say you're a brilliant neutrino researcher when you're not in the kitchen," Alyssa said.

"Certainly we can do that," Christine said.

Veronica looked at Christine. "I should be spending my time looking for research money."

"Veronica, I think you can be very successful as a cookbook author. I like you as an author so much that I'll make a special offer to you that I have never made to anyone else."

"What's that?"

"Veronica, if you publish your cookbook with us, we'll give ten percent of your sales to a fund that you can use for neutrino research. Ten percent of our wholesale revenue from sales of your book will go to your research fund. That's in addition to our standard royalty contract."

Veronica didn't say yes, but she didn't say no either. I was starting to believe she was going to write it.

"That's a great deal, Veronica," Gabriela said.

"But I've never written a cookbook."

"You're a good cook. And you'll look great on the cover. Your book will easily sell out its first printing," Christine said.

"What do you think, Lexi?" Veronica said.

"You should do it."

"What do you think, Jack?" Veronica said.

"You should do it."

"I don't know," Veronica said.

"You don't have to decide today. You can think about it," Christine said.

"I'll think about it," Veronica said.

"I brought over two cookbooks that our company published recently. I'm going to leave those here. You can look at them to see what kind of work we do."

"Thanks, Christine. I'll look at them."

We talked about other things and had a good dinner. I hoped Veronica would accept Christine's offer.

Chapter Sixty-Two

When I moved over to Lexi's house, I didn't realize how living with Lexi was going to affect me. I thought it would be fun to be with her, and when she wasn't around I would find things to do that would keep me happy. But being with her made me want to be with her more. When she wasn't around, anything I was doing seemed unsatisfying, because she wasn't there.

I wanted to be with Lexi every minute of every day, but of course that wasn't possible. Lexi included me in her life as much as she could. Our jobs often took us in different directions, but she always told me where she was going and I told her where I was going. At the end of the day we would sit in her kitchen and eat supper and talk about our day. And at night she would lie on top of me in bed and call me her *je ne sais quoi*.

Chapter Sixty-Three

The university board of trustees created a design review committee to study the design of the proposed baseball stadium. The design review committee studied it and wrote a report saying everything was appropriate. People who lived in the neighborhood south of University Avenue were starting to organize the opposition.

One of the librarians at the medical school called me. She said she lived down there in a house that she owned. She said she and all of her neighbors thought the stadium plan would wreck everything. They were circulating a petition against the plan and collecting money for a lawsuit. I signed her petition and gave her some money.

I called Lance Walker, the university athletics compliance officer. I hadn't talked with him since our meeting about Tia distributing sex dolls to baseball players. I knew he lived in the neighborhood that would be affected by the stadium. I asked him how much influence he had in the athletic department. I thought maybe they would listen to his objections. But he said they were ignoring his complaints.

Lexi and I talked to one of the university president's administrative assistants and got a few minutes on the president's calendar. When we met with the president, Lexi told him we were concerned about the ethics of destroying a great neighborhood. I listened while Lexi and the president talked.

"Yes, certainly we're all concerned about ethics," the president said. "You're concerned about ethics, I'm concerned about ethics, the entire university community is concerned about ethics."

"Yes sir," Lexi said.

"I think about ethics every day. Literally every day. Well, I mean, not literally every day. I mean, I don't think about ethics on weekends or university holidays, or anything like that, but you know what I mean."

"Yes sir."

"Ethics are at the very core of this university. The very heart of this university. I think you know that."

"Yes sir."

"But here's what I'm saying. Here's the point I want to make. I like ethics as much as anyone else, but let's not get so carried away with ethics that we forget why we're here."

"And why is that, sir?"

"We're here to run a great university. We're here to make a great university go forward."

"Yes sir."

"And so we have to ask the question, 'what is good for this great university?'"

"Yes sir."

"And every great university needs great sports teams."

"Sir, we like sports also but that's not our top priority."

"After this new baseball stadium is built you'll be working in a university with great research programs and a great baseball team."

"Sir, if your administration goes ahead with your plan to build the stadium, we're going to leave this school."

"Really? Why?"

"Because you're wrecking a part of a community that we love. Our sense of ethics tells us that's wrong."

"I don't know why you would feel that way. My entire focus is on only one thing. Ethics and what will make this a great university."

"Yes sir."

"I guess that's two things."

"Yes sir."

"Now, if you'll excuse me, I need to prepare for another meeting."

Chapter Sixty-Four

One day Veronica called me. "Jack, I have an idea that I might be able to use for a cookbook. I want to get your reaction."

"What's your idea?"

"Pine cones."

"Pine cones?"

"Yes. Here's my title. *Russian Pine Cone Recipes: How To Make Delicious Russian Cuisine From Ingredients That Are Almost Inedible.*"

"Can people eat pine cones?"

"Yes, Jack. But you have to be careful. Not every conifer tree is a pine tree. You can't eat cones from nonpine conifers. Those can be poisonous."

"Where are you going to get pine cone recipes?"

"Some very old out of print books talk about cooking with pine cones. And I can update old recipes by doing some experimentation. What do you think?"

"It's different. It hasn't been overdone already."

"Should I do it?"

"Sure. Why not? Have you talked with Christine about this idea?"

"No. I wanted to get your reaction first."

"I like it. If you write it, I'll read it."

Chapter Sixty-Five

Miss Valery wanted to see us again. She invited Lexi and Hadley and me to her house again for tea. So once again we found ourselves on her doorstep admiring her beautiful old house, and being welcomed by Miss Valery's all purpose assistant Maria, and then being welcomed by Miss Valery herself. Once again we sat in her beautiful dining room and Maria served tea and cucumber sandwiches.

Miss Valery was worried about the university's desire to build a large baseball stadium south of University Avenue, south of the campus. When we first met Miss Valery, she had said that she agreed with us that the plan wasn't a good idea. Now she wanted to know whether we thought it would go forward.

"We talked with the university president," Lexi said. "He thinks it's a great plan. He's doing everything he can to promote it. We told him it was a bad idea, but he didn't want to hear that."

Miss Valery looked at me. "How much opposition is there?"

"There's quite a bit," I said. "People are organizing against it."

Lexi and Hadley listened while Miss Valery and I talked.

"I think if there's a lot of opposition the university may decide to reconsider," Miss Valery said.

"That would make sense, but I don't see any signs the university is reconsidering. Do you know Lance Walker, the athletics compliance officer?"

"I met him once."

"I talked with him. He's in the area where the stadium would be built. He's opposed to it. He's part of the opposition to it. But he said the university is ignoring his objections."

Miss Valery looked worried. "If you're running an athletic department and you have any sense at all, you never want to make the compliance officer unhappy."

"I agree. But the university administration is doing everything it can do to go forward with the plan."

"I think the high level people in the administration will realize eventually that it's a bad idea."

"I don't know."

"I just hope they realize it before it's too late to stop it."

We drank the tea and ate the sandwiches. Everything was excellent.

Lexi and Miss Valery talked about something they had talked about previously. Hadley and I just listened.

"Miss Valery, after we left you last time, I was thinking about what you said about sex," Lexi said.

"What did I say that you were thinking about?"

"You and I were talking about how some people have problems related to sex. We were talking about how people have difficulty communicating their needs."

"That's true."

"Since you're in the condom business you've studied that problem carefully. Have you ever thought about maybe writing something that would put all your ideas together? I think you have a lot to offer."

"You're very kind to say that. But I'm not an expert on how to solve that problem. I've struggled with it as much as anyone else."

"Really?"

"Yes. I think back to when my husband and I were first married. Neither one of us really knew how to talk about sex."

"That's a difficult time for anyone," Lexi said.

"Professor Lexi, when my husband and I were first married, we didn't know how to talk to each other about our own needs. We didn't even know how to talk about basic anatomy. Finally a friend of ours advised us we needed an easy common vocabulary that both of us could use. Our friend said think of the anatomy of the sexual parts of a woman's body as places on a map."

"Yes, that's a great idea. When I was married I learned how to do that. It helps a lot."

"We tried it but it was still unsatisfying."

"What map were you using?"

"We were using a map of Philadelphia."

"Philadelphia? You were using a map of Philadelphia?"

"Yes, that's right."

"A woman's body doesn't look anything like Philadelphia."

"I was thinking if you got on the train at Lancaster and took the train all the way into the center of the city and got off at Thirtieth Street Station . . ."

"*Stop.* That's enough. Don't talk about Philadelphia. It's the wrong map. You'll never really understand a woman's body by looking at a map of Philadelphia."

"Maybe that's why my husband and I were having problems."

"Yes, I think so."

"What map should people use?"

"New York City. People need to use a map of New York City. A woman's body looks like New York City. And northern New Jersey."

At this point I got into the conversation.

"Northern New Jersey is the key," I said.

"You seem to have a lot of practical knowledge, Professor Lexi. I'm glad you're doing sex research," Miss Valery said.

"I'm not doing sex research. Jack is doing sex research."

Miss Valery looked surprised.

"I thought Doctor Jack was doing wizard dust research," she said.

"Jack thought of the name wizard dust. But he's not doing wizard dust research. I'm doing wizard dust research."

"You're doing wizard dust research?"

"Yes. That means neutrino research."

"Tell me again what neutrinos are."

"Tiny particles."

"But Professor Lexi, you seem to have so much practical knowledge about sex. You should be writing about it. I think you can help people."

Lexi shook her head. "No."

Miss Valery looked at me. She spoke softly. "Do you think Lexi can help people?"

"I think so."

"Can she help people learn how to communicate their needs?"

"Yes."

Miss Valery looked at Lexi and smiled.

"The two of you make such a cute pair. I would like to help both of you if I can, but I need to think about what my dear husband who is no longer with us would want."

"Yes, we understand," Lexi said.

We finished our tea and reluctantly said goodbye and headed back to campus.

Chapter Sixty-Six

Veronica called me about a week later.

"I talked with Christine about my cookbook," Veronica said.

"What did Christine say?"

"She likes the pine cone idea. I'm going to do it. I signed a publishing contract."

"Great. This could be big, Veronica."

"Christine said I need people to be excited about pine cones. We need some other source of interest in pine cones, beyond just my book. She said she's working on some ideas."

"I hope you're very successful."

Chapter Sixty-Seven

Juliette from the president's office called me.

"The president wants to meet with you and your friends Morgan and Lexi."

"Did he mention what he wants to talk about at the meeting?"

"Billing. He said he remembers you were interested in billing and he wants to discuss it with you."

"I'm always happy to meet with him. And I think Lexi and Morgan feel the same way."

Juliette set up a meeting for the next day and we were all there.

The president shook hands with us and smiled. "Morgan, Lexi, Jack, I'm so glad you could come to see me on short notice." We all sat down.

"We're always happy to see you. What can we help you with?" Morgan said.

"Morgan, you were here a while ago and you were talking about an incorrect bill you received from the billing company that the university medical center uses."

"Yes."

"I'm now having a problem with the billing company myself."

"I'm sorry to hear that, sir," Morgan said.

Lexi and I listened as the president talked with Morgan.

"I won't bore you with all the details, but my daughter is on my insurance, and she had some symptoms and she went to our university medical center. They thought she might have appendicitis and they did some tests. They ruled it out and she's fine now, I'm happy to say. So that's good."

"Yes sir, I glad she's feeling better."

"The medical center billed my insurance. One of the items on the bill was for an anesthesia consult. My insurance company said an anesthesia consult was not medically necessary, and the company is not going to pay the bill. So now the billing company is billing me."

"Yes, that's a problem."

"What do those clowns in the billing company think they're doing?"

"Are you sure this is totally the fault of the billing company? If the medical center does things that are not medically necessary, that's the fault of medical center."

"The billing company should stop the medical center from doing this."

"I'm sorry you're having this problem."

"Morgan, it's outrageous. The billing company is completely incompetent."

"Sir, you told us that eighty eight percent of patients like the billing company. So most of the time they do a good job."

"What about the twelve percent that are unsatisfied? Doesn't anyone care about those? That's inexcusable."

"What are you going to do about it?"

"I'm going to ask the board of trustees for permission to terminate the university's contract with the company that handles billing. Dickens, Deadwood, and Doorlicker."

"Good luck to you with that project."

"Whatever happened with that bill you were talking with me about?"

"We talked to someone at the zoo about it. The attorney general's office investigated it. We haven't heard anything more about it."

"The zoo? Do you mean the internal medicine department? I think that place is a zoo."

"No. I mean the real zoo. The zoo that has zoo animals."

"Really? I don't know why they would be interested in a medical bill. I don't think they'll want to help me with my daughter's bill."

"You're right, sir. I don't think they'll be interested in your daughter's bill."

"Now if you will excuse me, I have another meeting. There's no rest in this job."

The next day I called Alyssa and asked her if she thought the university would terminate its contract with Dickens, Deadwood, and Doorlicker. She said she thought the company had spent a lot of money helping the governor get elected, and she thought it was unlikely the governor and his friends on the board of trustees would allow the university to terminate the contract.

Chapter Sixty-Eight

I received a call from someone on the Channel Four "More On Four" Action News Team.

"Doctor Rose, Channel Four is working on a news story, and we want to ask you some questions."

"Ask me anything."

"Doctor Rose, do you know someone named Christine Olivier?"

"Yes. I've met her."

"She tells us that you're a professional sex researcher. Is that true?"

"I'm looking for research money in that field."

"She tells us that eating foods made from pine cones can improve sexual function. Can you confirm that?"

"I don't have any information on that. I'm sorry."

"She tells us that there's a conspiracy in medical science to suppress information about the beneficial effects of pine cones. In your opinion, why is medical science trying to suppress this information?"

"I'm not aware of a conspiracy on the subject."

"She tells us that it's because doctors have been paid off by pharmaceutical companies that are trying to sell expensive prescription drugs for sexual dysfunction. Can you confirm that you've been paid off by pharmaceutical companies?"

"I'm not aware of any payments to any doctors."

"How much are they paying you to tell lies?"

"I have some things I need to work on now."

"Why are you afraid of the truth?"

"I need to get back to work now."

"Is it true that you secretly eat pine cones yourself?"

"I have to go now."

Chapter Sixty-Nine

The university had a two and a half week break for the holidays in the last part of December and early January. The school was pretty quiet then, but people in the town were celebrating the December holidays.

Hadley stayed with Lexi and me in Lexi's house over the holidays. Hadley was still a blonde. We ate well during the holidays. Lexi and Hadley invited Hadley's friend George to come over for some of the dinners. Hadley's friend said he wanted not just to eat meals with us but also to help prepare some of the food. He was talented. Everybody liked him.

He and Hadley cooked a turkey, and made some stuffing, and baked some sweet potatoes. The turkey lasted for a couple of dinners, and when it was down to scraps and bones Hadley and George made turkey soup with the leftover turkey. And we had plum pudding with hard sauce. The plum pudding was from the grocery store, but Hadley and George made the hard sauce, using butter and sugar and rum. It was delicious. George also helped clean up the kitchen.

I asked Hadley how serious she was about him. Hadley said she had known him for a long time, and he had always been a good friend. But now she felt like he was more than that, she said. She said she wanted him to feel like she was more than that, also. She asked me if I had any advice.

"Don't change your hair color," I said.

Hadley gave us a present. She said she had found some research money for Lexi and me. She made a big batch of fake money and gave it to us. She did a good job making it. She covered a piece of paper with a repeated design of fake money, then she ran a lot of copies and used a paper cutter to cut up everything into single fake bills. It was a nice present. I wondered whether it was as close as we were going to get to what we wanted.

Everybody went back to school in January and tried to focus once again on what they needed to be doing. The people who couldn't focus completely on what they needed to be doing talked about the baseball season which was going to start in the not too distant future.

Chapter Seventy

January was cold and the days were too short, so I was happy when February arrived. The university recognizes something called President's Day as a holiday in February, but to me the important holiday is Valentine's Day.

Lexi and I thought we should celebrate Valentine's Day by making some sort of a special dish of our own, not necessarily a dessert, but something suitable for the day. In the evening we worked on it.

"Let's start with a pie crust," she said.

"Good plan," I said.

We mixed flour and shortening and rolled it out on a board.

"Now what?" I said.

"Let's make it into heart shaped pie crust bowls," she said.

We cut the crust material and bent it into five heart shaped bowls.

"Cute," I said.

"Let's bake it while we figure out what we want to put in it," she said.

We heated up the oven and put the crust material in the oven on a baking sheet. Lexi looked in her refrigerator.

"Now what?" I said.

"I'm not sure," she said.

She got some things out of her refrigerator.

"We have sour cream, plain yogurt, fresh ricotta, frozen strawberries, frozen peaches, and cherry tomatoes," she said.

"Let's use all of those. Not all together."

"Yes, let's do that."

We let the pie crusts finish baking, then we took them out of the oven and put one or two of the ingredients in each pie crust. We put them back in the oven to heat them up. When they were hot, we took them out of the oven and we started eating our creations.

"I remember when I was a child, I used to visit my grandmother. She would always have something delicious for me that she had made herself," Lexi said.

"There's nothing better than home made treats," I said.

"I like making things in the kitchen, but I'm so busy with other things I usually don't have time. Maybe I need to re-examine my priorities."

"I think so."

Lexi smiled. "Instead of designing a portable neutrino detector, I should have designed an edible neutrino detector."

"If you did that you would be deluged with money."

"Yes, I think so."

"Stockholm would create a special prize for you. They would give it to you every year as long as you supplied them with your edible research."

"Why didn't I think of that when I was starting my neutrino research? I took the wrong path."

"It's not your fault."

"Whose fault is it?"

"Your advisors. You had bad advisors."

Lexi laughed. "I see you've learned one of the most important rules of research."

"What's that?"

"It's all right to fail, as long as you can blame somebody else."

We sat in the kitchen and devoured the food until we couldn't eat any more of it.

"I need to rest after all that," she said.

"Yes, definitely."

"Do you want to walk upstairs with me and lie down?"

"Good plan."

We walked upstairs and we took our shoes off and we both laid down on our backs on her bed next to each other.

"Happy Valentine's Day," she said.

"Happy Valentine's Day to you also."

"That was fun improvising in the kitchen."

"Yes, that was fun."

"Sometimes I think everything we do together is improvised."

"What do you mean?"

"I don't really know how to live with someone. I don't have an instruction book. I just make it up as we go along."

"At least you're not listening to bad advisors."

"I love you, Jack."

"I love you, Lexi.

Chapter Seventy-One

Time passed quickly, and soon it was the end of winter according to the calendar, and we were starting to have some warmer days. Lexi, on the other hand, seemed cool. She seemed less happy to be with me, and less interested in doing things with me.

One day after work, when we both had some free time, she said, "Let's go over to the outdoor track and walk around."

We went over to the track. It was a beautiful spring late afternoon at sunset, with a cool soft breeze. The sun was low on the horizon, behind some low clouds, and the fading sunlight made pale red streaks in the clouds.

"Let me hold your hand," Lexi said.

We held hands.

There were two other people walking on the track. We waited until the other people were on the other side of the oval, and we started walking at a moderate pace. She looked at me.

"Jack, this is hard for me to talk about."

"You can tell me whatever you want to tell me."

"I can't do this anymore. I can't live with you. You can't live with me. I'm sorry," Lexi said softly.

"Did you lose your affection for me?"

She let go of my hand and stopped walking. I stopped with her.

"How could you say that?" she said.

Her voice broke a little as she spoke, and I thought she was going to start crying, but she composed herself. She put her arm around my waist.

"Let's keep walking," she said.

We started walking again. Our pace was a little slower now.

"I love you very much. I wish we could keep doing this but it doesn't work for me," she said, looking at me and speaking softly.

"I'm sorry this isn't working for you."

She looked down at the ground. "I'm sorry also." She looked at me again. "I want you to be a part of my life. But I need to be free. I need to be separate. I need to have my own life."

She took her arm off my waist.

"Let's hold hands," she said, and she held my hand. We walked a little faster.

"Does that make sense?" she said with a stronger voice, and then without waiting for me to answer she said, "It's complicated, Jack. I like being with you but I need to have my own independent life. When you're in my house I don't have my own life. I have *our* life. I don't have my plans. I have *our* plans. I think about what *we* will be doing. Where *we* will be going."

I didn't say anything.

"I can't do anything without considering how it affects you," she said. "I feel responsible for you."

"I understand."

"I don't want to feel responsible for you. I don't want to feel responsible for anyone else. Not even my daughter. I want to feel responsible for myself and nobody else."

I didn't want to be a problem for her. "I'm sorry you feel responsible for me," I said.

We walked in silence for a minute.

"Do you think I'm selfish?" she said.

I thought she was wonderful and I wanted to be with her constantly. Being with her made me feel happy. Maybe *I* was selfish. "No," I said.

"I'm afraid of what will happen if I let you stay in my house any longer. Do you remember when we had dinner at Alyssa's house with Irina and Dimitri?"

"Yes."

"Do you remember what they said?"

"Yes."

"If we are together too much, then . . . It will not be pretty."

I wanted to be with her every minute of every day. But sometimes people want something that they just can't have.

"I still want to do things with you. But I need to be free. I need to be separate," she said.

"I'm not your *je ne sais quoi* anymore?"

"You're still my my *je ne sais quoi*. You're my *je ne sais quoi* now more than ever. But you can't live with me. I'm sorry."

"All right," I said softly.

We walked in silence. I looked at the sunset. Slowly the streaks in the clouds became a brighter red.

"That's a pretty sunset," I said.

"Yes. What do you notice about it?"

"I notice the red streaks in the clouds."

"You notice anything else?"

"No. What do you notice?"

"It's in the west."

"You're right."

"It's not in the east."

"You're right."

"When I look at the sunset I think about what Hadley said."

"You believe what your daughter said?"

"No. I think she reads too much. But when I look at the sunset I think about her and I think about research money. We have to face the facts."

"What do you mean?"

"Nobody wants to give us any research money. We'll never get any research money," she said. Her voice broke a little as she spoke and once again I thought she was going to start crying. But once again she composed herself.

"We'll get research money," I said.

"When will we get research money?"

"One day the sun will set in the east and your hair will be on fire and then we'll get research money."

"Be serious."

"I am serious."

"The sun never does that. We'll never get research money."

"Lexi, listen to me. You're a very smart person with a great research project. And when people meet you, they like you. You can charm people. People fall in love with you. People want to help you. People are going to give you money."

"Damn you," she said sharply.

"What's the matter?"

"You're making me feel better. Don't try to make me feel better when I'm trying to separate myself from you. This is already hard enough and now you're making me feel better. How can I separate myself if being with you makes me feel better?"

"I'm sorry."

We walked in silence. It was starting to get dark.

"I'll find another place to live," I said.

"Can you go back to Alyssa's house?"

"I think so."

"Alyssa has a nice house. It's a nice place to live."

I stopped walking, and she stopped. I let go of her hand.

"I'll find a place," I said. "I'll call Alyssa. I'll let you know what I find."

I started to walk away from her and leave the track.

"Wait. Before you go, I want to hold you," she said.

I stopped. She walked up to me. She spoke so quietly I could just barely hear her. "I know this is hard for you. This is hard for me also."

She wrapped her arms around me.

"Think about all my annoying character flaws," I said. "That will help you separate yourself."

"Yes. I'll try to do that. And you can think about *my* character flaws. That will help you separate yourself from me."

"You don't have character flaws."

"Damn you," she said sharply. She took her arms off me.

"I'll let you know what I find," I said, and I left her.

Alyssa said I could live with her again, so I moved back to her house. I could see Lexi's house from Alyssa's house, and all I could think about was how much I wanted to be with Lexi.

For three days I lived in Alyssa's house and tried to forget Lexi. But living that close to her reminded me of Lexi constantly, and I forgot everyone except Lexi.

I was failing, and I needed to be somewhere else. I called Veronica and told her what happened. She said I could live in her house, so I moved there, to live with her.

Chapter Seventy-Two

Are there any men reading this? I have something I want to say to you. Guys, listen to me on this.

You know those women you think are so hot? You know the ones you think have so much power over you because you want them so much? You know the sexy women you think you would do anything for, just so you can be with them?

They have nothing.

Do you know what I'm saying? Here's what I'm saying. You're single. Maybe you're young, or maybe not. Maybe you're ready to get married, or maybe you're not ready for that. You want to meet women. So you ask your friends and neighbors to introduce you to some women. You join groups where you can meet women. The same groups that women join so they can meet men.

And so you meet women. You meet lots of women. All kinds of women. And some of these women have sex appeal. They have pretty faces and big breasts and long legs and wear sexy dresses and soft bras without much support, so you can see their boobs shake a little bit as they walk over to greet you. Or maybe they don't wear a bra at all. They wear something with buttons up the front and they unbutton the top button. And you go somewhere with one of these women and you just sit there and talk and you're getting an erection just chatting with her. And you're thinking, "Wow, this woman has a lot of power over me. I want her so much. I would do anything for her, just to be with her."

Here's what I'm telling you: No. You're wrong. She has no power over you. You don't believe me, but I'm right.

Maybe she likes you enough to want to spend time with you, while she's hoping to eventually meet someone who's better looking and has more money than you. Maybe she's able to enjoy sex with people she doesn't know very well, and you're convenient. Maybe she goes to bed with you and you have a great time and you want to do it again and you think this proves how much power she has over you because you want her so much.

But here's the thing.

When she leaves you, when she breaks up with you, when she says, "I don't want to see you anymore," you will put some lubricant on your hand and you will jerk yourself off to relieve your sexual tension. And the feeling you get from your hand will be the same as the feeling you got from her. And then a week later you will have difficulty even remembering her name.

And then later maybe you meet some other women. They're not very tall, and they're sort of flat chested, and their faces are nothing special, and they don't try to be sexy all the time, and you think they're just random women. But maybe you go out with one of them, and maybe you find out that she's bright and funny and sweet and kind, and she's interested in you. And maybe the two of you are together for a while. Maybe she goes to bed with you, and when she goes to bed with you it's because she wants you and not just because she wants sex.

Guys, pay attention to me here.

A woman like that, a woman who is bright and funny and sweet and kind, and interested in you, a woman like that can get into your mind. She can get into your heart. She can make you ache for her, and you can't make the ache go away without her.

You will not have any difficulty remembering her name.

Chapter Seventy-Three

Are any women reading this? This chapter is for you.

Would you like to find true love?

Are you familiar with the history of the American manned space flight program? President Kennedy was the president who proposed sending a man to the moon and returning him safely to earth. Kennedy gave a famous speech at Rice University where he talked about why Americans should send astronauts to explore the moon. He said something like, "We choose to have a moon exploration program not because it is easy, but because it is hard." That's not an exact quote, but it's the essence of what he said. It was an excellent speech. Very inspiring.

A straight woman looking for true love is in the same category as the moon exploration. You should choose to do it not because it's easy, but because it's hard.

If you've had any experience with men, you know there are three types of men. There are guys who just want you for your body and are willing to attack you. There are guys who just want you for your body but will not attack you. And there are gay guys. Guys in the first category are dangerous, and guys in the second category are useless.

Guys in the third category often become close friends. Go to lunch with a gay friend and talk about how much trouble you're having meeting new men. Then listen to your friend talk about how much trouble he's having meeting new men.

Unfortunately, ruling out the first two categories doesn't prove that the third category is what you're looking for. Sometimes real life can be like high school. The correct answer to the test can be "none of the above."

The great Sigmund Freud, pioneer of modern psychiatry and psychoanalysis, asked the question: "What do women want?" I can answer that question.

What you want, what you're looking for, what you need, what you must find, is a *mutant*. He's a person with a mutation. He's an abnormal life form.

The best analogy I can think of is that his brain is like a television with a news channel and a movie channel. When you want to talk about something serious, he listens to you like he listens to the news. When you're ready for a party, he can change the channel and go into entertainment mode and have fun with you.

He has that ability because something happened to the DNA in one of his ancestors. Maybe a cosmic ray struck it. It mutated. It was DNA that controls the development of the brain, and it was in a cell that reproduced and became part of the genetic heritage of future generations.

So the mutant guy inherited abnormal DNA which caused his brain to develop this abnormal ability to see you as a complex individual person who has interesting thoughts and feelings apart from sex. And of course he also has this parallel sexual attraction to you which he can switch on at appropriate times. And you'll need that sexual attraction when you want to commit parenthood with him and raise mutant children.

How common do you think these mutant people are? One in a million? You think they're more common than that? Maybe one in a hundred thousand? I don't know the exact number, but they're rare.

And you like the challenge of finding one of these rare people. I hope.

Chapter Seventy-Four

Are any women still reading this? Here's one more chapter for you.

Do you know the difference between a fairy tale and real life? In a fairy tale, when the princess finds true love, that's the end of the story. In real life, when you find true love, it's not the end of the challenges you face.

Sometimes people find true love and it doesn't last. Maybe you still love your mutant guy, the father of your mutant children, but his love for you fades away. Maybe he abandons you for somebody else. That can lead to some very sad days. You cry a lot, and you hope you don't become dehydrated.

I don't want to disregard your unhappiness. But I'm an optimist (yes, really, I am) and I say you will eventually recover from his leaving you. You will eventually feel better, and meet somebody else, and life will be good again.

But suppose, instead of him losing his love for you, suppose he still loves you and you still love him, but your lives just don't fit together. Having him in your life all the time doesn't work for you, because it conflicts with your independent life that you want and need, but having him *not* in your life all the time doesn't work either, because you still love him and want and need to be with him. It's the classic love triangle. A woman, a man, and the woman's independent life.

When I describe this problem, if it has never happened to you, you probably think it's nothing. These people that are caught in this situation all have choices. Can't they just choose what they want?

You might even see it happen to somebody else and you still think it's not a problem. And you're right. It's not a problem, when it happens to somebody else. When it happens to you, it's a problem. When it happens to you, you will see how agonizing it can be to make choices you don't want to make.

Will you recover from your agony? Yes, of course. I'm an optimist, so I believe of course you will recover. How will you recover? I have no idea. I cannot imagine how anyone could escape from this tangle. I'm an optimist with no imagination.

Chapter Seventy-Five

Veronica lived on First Street, which was the eastern boundary of the campus. Since Lexi's house was on the west side of the campus, the campus now separated me from Lexi's house.

When I first moved in to Veronica's house, all I wanted to do was lie on her couch.

"I just feel like I don't have any energy. I can't even push a Swiffer," I said to Veronica.

"If my friend Lexi has taken away your ability to do housework, then she's going to put a strain on my friendship with her," Veronica said.

Veronica looked at me lying on the couch and tried to think of ways to help me.

"Would you like to try my hot water bottle?"

She filled it up with warm water and gave it to me and I rested it on my abdomen. It felt good.

During my first three days in Veronica's house I had the same routine. When I had to be at the medical school I went to the medical school. When I didn't have to be there I spent my time lying on Veronica's couch.

On the fourth day I was lying on the couch when Veronica walked over.

"Mind if I sit with you?" she said.

"Go ahead."

She sat in a chair near me.

"Jack, when you were growing up, did you have an older sister?"

"No."

"How about a younger sister? Did you have a younger sister?"

"No."

"Did you maybe have a half sister?"

"No."

"Maybe a tall sister? Or a short sister? A loud sister? A quiet sister?"

"No."

"Did you have a sister of any kind?"

"No."

"Not even for a week? Not even for a day?"

"Not even for an hour. Not even for a minute. I have been completely sisterless for my entire life."

"Jack, you've been going through life at a disadvantage."

"You think so?"

"I'm not saying you need to have a sister with you constantly. I'm not saying that. You may go for years without needing a sister at all. But here's what I'm saying. Sometimes in life, sometimes, a guy needs to have the kind of advice that a sister gives to that guy."

"And you think maybe I need that now?"

"You need a sister's advice now. I know that."

"Can you be my sister? Just for today?"

"I can do that, Jack."

"What would you tell me, as my sister?"

"You need to rebalance your life. Your life is out of balance. You need to adjust your life so that you're able to do things you want to do. Things that will make you happy."

"How would I do that?"

"Get up off the couch. Think of things that you want to do without Lexi. Do those things."

"Without Lexi?"

"Jack, I know how you feel about Lexi. I'm in love with Lexi myself. Being with Lexi is great fun. But there are other things in life. If you think only about Lexi you'll miss those other things."

"How can I find the other things?"

"Just look around you. Wherever you happen to be at any moment, maybe something is going on there that might be interesting."

"I'll do that. Because you're my sister and you are wise to the ways of the world."

"Good."

"What's going on around me now that might be interesting?"

"I'm writing a first draft of my cookbook with my pine cone recipes. Do you want to look at that? I'd be interested in your comments."

"I don't know anything about cooking with pine cones. I wouldn't know what to tell you."

"It's not written for pine cone specialists. You can learn something new."

"I'll take a look at it."

She got a copy of her first draft and brought it to me.

"Thank you," I said.

I started reading her first draft. It was interesting.

Chapter Seventy-Six

After I moved over to Veronica's house, one of the first people I heard from was one of the last people I thought would call me there. It was Captain Shaeffer, and he was actually interested in helping me, in his own way.

"Jack, my man, my guide to all things academic, I heard some bad news about you," he said on the phone.

"What did you hear, Captain Shaeffer?"

"I heard you were evicted by your main squeeze."

"Lexi and I are no longer living together, that's true. Who told you?"

"I can't reveal all my sources, Jack, but word gets around. How are you feeling?"

"It only hurts when I'm awake."

"I'm sorry you're having problems."

"Thank you for your kind words, Captain."

"And I want to try to make you feel better. Can I come visit you?"

"I'd love to see you, but I have to ask Veronica if it's all right with her. Veronica is my landlady now. Have you met Veronica?"

"No, I don't think so. Is she good?"

"She's wonderful. Let me see what she says. Hold on."

I put the phone down. I got up and went to talk with Veronica.

"I got a call from Captain Shaeffer. He's still on the line. Do you remember Lexi and me telling you about the Captain?"

"Your possible money man? Yes, I remember."

"He wants to come over and try to cheer me up."

"That's a worthy cause."

"Can I tell him he can come?"

"Sure. Potential donors are always welcome."

"Thanks."

I went back to my phone.

"Veronica and I would love to see you, Captain. Are you coming over today?"

"This afternoon, Jack, after lunch."

"I just have one word of advice for you, Captain."

"What's your advice?"

"When you meet Veronica, you're going to want to tell her how pretty she is. But don't do it."

"Is she nice looking?"

"She's beautiful. But don't tell her that. She's already heard it a thousand times."

"What can I say to her?"

"Say something about her mind."

"What should I say about her mind?"

"I don't know. She's doing research in a difficult field. Think of something."

"All right."

"Thanks for thinking of me, Captain."

"See you soon, Jack."

The Captain came over that afternoon. Veronica and I greeted him at the door. He was wearing jeans and a soft knit dark blue shirt and brown leather casual shoes. He was carrying a box with him. He introduced himself to Veronica.

"You have the mind of a goddess," he said to Veronica.

"Is that good?" Veronica said.

"Yes. And you're doing research in a difficult field."

"That I am. Come in and make yourself comfortable."

Captain Shaeffer and Veronica and I went into the living room and sat in Veronica's comfortable chairs. She listened while Captain Shaeffer talked with me.

"I brought something with me that will help you," he said to me.
"Thank you."

He opened up the box. "Look at this." He got up and walked over to me and gave me the box. "This box has plastic samples of all the breast sizes that are available with our best sex dolls. Look through all of them and see which one you like the best. I can have a doll with your choice ready for you in two days. As a test model. You can try it out. Free. No charge for you while you decide whether you like it." He went back to his chair and sat down.

"Thanks, Captain. I appreciate your efforts to help me. Really I do. But I'm just not interested in breast sizes right now."

"You're not? What are you interested in? The pelvic region? You want me to bring over some samples of different pelvic regions? We have samples available that I can bring over to show you."

"Thanks, Captain, but I'm just not interested in the pelvic region either."

"Are you ill? Do you need to go to the emergency room?"

"Captain, men don't always want sex all the time. Sometimes they want something else."

"I know that, Jack. But I didn't bring over any beer with me, because I thought you had that here with you already."

"Sometimes a man just wants to hold a woman in his arms, and to be held in her arms."

"Are you not listening to me? I can have a doll ready for you in two days. You can hold it in your arms. It can hold you in its arms. I just need to know what breast size you want. Just look at the samples and tell me and I'll start working on it."

"Captain, a machine can't do everything that a person can do."

"Are you not aware of the zeitgeist? Machines can do everything people can do. And machines are going to replace people in many ways that our parents' generation never thought could ever be possible. My company proves that every day. We're developing a doll now that can make a grocery list and give it to you and ask you to pick up a few things on your way home from work."

"Captain, I'm happy your company is innovative. I admire innovative companies. But I think you misunderstand the zeitgeist."

"No, there's no misunderstanding about the zeitgeist."

"Machines cannot do everything. Women can do everything. That's the zeitgeist. Women are doing everything. Not machines, women. Real women."

"You haven't spent any time with our dolls, but you've already decided they can't help you. You should at least try one."

"And can I say one other thing about your business?"

"If it's nice, yes."

"Why don't you bring your daughter Britta into the business? She would give your company a new perspective. She could help you see possible new directions for your company."

"Britta is a smart girl, but she's busy with her family and she's happy with her career as a high school teacher."

"You don't have to make her a full time employee, but you could put her on your board of directors. And you could ask her for her opinions and listen to what she tells you."

"The sex doll industry is a male industry. It's a rough business. You meet a lot of rough guys in it. Do you think I'm rough?"

"Sometimes."

"I'm nothing compared to some of the other guys in the business. It's not a refined ladylike business. It would be too coarse for Britta."

"She might surprise you."

"Jack, I need to get back to work. I just came over here to try to help you after what happened."

"Thanks for thinking of me."

"Are you sure you don't want the sample breasts?"

"I'm sure."

We all stood up and I gave Captain Shaeffer his box and we all walked to the door. We said goodbye and Captain Shaeffer left. I wondered whether anybody else had ever told Veronica that she had the mind of a goddess.

Chapter Seventy-Seven

A few days later Britta called me.

"Jack, I talked with my dad. He said he went over to visit you and Veronica. I'm sorry you're having problems."

"That's right. He was here."

"He said he offered to make a sex doll for you."

"That's right. I told him I didn't want one."

"He likes you, Jack."

"He's a good man."

"I can't offer you a sex doll, but maybe Sophia and I can cheer you up a little bit."

"You want to come over? I'd love to see you. And your daughter, Sophia. I have to check with Veronica and see if she approves."

"Check with Veronica. Sophia and I are thinking about you."

"I'll call you back. Thanks for wanting to cheer me up."

We said goodbye. I asked Veronica whether she wanted to see Britta and Sophia. She said she did, so I called Britta back and asked them to come to visit us.

Veronica and I greeted Britta and Sophia at the door. Britta was wearing a pale blue sweater over a white blouse with cream colored pants and soft blue shoes with white soles. Sophia was wearing a light grey sweatshirt that said "Don't just sit there. Dance." She was wearing a blue shirt under it, and she was wearing light grey pants and some shoes that looked similar to her mother's. I'm not a style expert but I thought they looked good together.

Sophia was carrying a small shopping bag.

"Welcome. Come in," Veronica said.

They came in. Britta shook hands with us. "It's good to see you, Jack, Veronica."

"Thanks for coming over," I said.

"Have you met Sophia?" Britta said to Veronica. Britta turned to Sophia. "This is Veronica."

Veronica shook hands with Sophia.

"Hello, Sophia. I like your sweatshirt," Veronica said.

Sophia smiled at Veronica. "My sweatshirt says how I feel," Sophia said.

"I like dancing too. I used to teach dancing," Veronica said.

"Hi Sophia. How have you been?" I said.

Sophia smiled at me. "We brought you a present," she said and gave me the shopping bag.

"Yes, Sophia thought you needed this," Britta said.

I looked in the bag. There was a plastic bottle of something. I took it out of the bag. It was bubble bath.

"Thank you, Sophia," I said.

"It's bubble bath. You need that," Sophia said.

"Will it make me feel good?"

"Better than good."

"Then I definitely need this."

"Make yourselves comfortable, everybody," Veronica said.

We all sat down in Veronica's comfortable chairs.

"I didn't realize you taught dancing, Veronica," Britta said.

"Yes, I was a dance teacher, but I haven't done that in a while," Veronica said.

"I think Sophia has a lot of talent," Britta said.

"What kind of dancing do you like?" Veronica said to Sophia.

"I like different kinds of dancing. My favorite is doing spins," Sophia said.

"Yes, spins are fun," Veronica said.

"I like trying to see how fast I can spin," Sophia said.

"Do you want to show us some spins?" Veronica said.

"We don't want to damage anything in your house," Britta said.

"Oh, that's not a problem. We can move some things and she'll have plenty of room right here. Let's move our chairs back, and move these things here," Veronica said.

We rearranged some furniture.

"Do you want to show us your dancing?" Veronica said to Sophia.

Sophia stood on one side of the room and quickly stepped and spun over to the other side of the room.

"That's how I spin," she said.

"That's good, Sophia," Veronica said.

"Veronica, do you like to do spins? Maybe Sophia would let you do some spins with her," Britta said.

"I haven't done any spins in a long time."

"I'm sure you can still do them," Britta said.

"Maybe," Veronica said.

"Can Veronica dance with you?" Britta said to Sophia.

Sophia smiled. "Are you a dancer too?" she said to Veronica.

"I dance a little bit. Can I dance with you?" Veronica said.

"Sure. We can dance together."

Veronica stood up and walked over to Sophia.

"Have you ever tried spinning with a partner?" Veronica said.

Sophia frowned. "I don't know how to do that."

"Would you like to try? I think you'd be good at it."

"How does it work?"

Veronica showed Sophia how to stand and how to hold her and how to move. They moved slowly through the steps, without any music. I could hear the dancers' feet hitting the floor and Veronica softly giving instructions.

"Like this?" Sophia said.

"That's good," Veronica said.

They continued slowly through the steps.

"That's good. I think you have talent," Veronica said.

They practiced the steps over and over. They started doing the steps a little bit faster. Veronica was quite a bit taller than Sophia, but they both danced well and I thought they looked good together.

Britta and I started talking about her work as a high school sci-ence teacher. She said she had a good group of kids this year and she was enjoying her job. She talked about trying to make science interesting and accessible to everyone in her class, when her stu-dents started with different levels of interest. She had a challeng-ing job and I admired her ability to do it.

Veronica and Sophia got tired of dancing. Veronica sat down, and Sophia came over to me.

"You looked good, Sophia," I said.

"Can I check your pulse?" Sophia said.

"Yes, see if I have a pulse today," I said.

I extended my left arm. Sophia bent over me. She put her fingers on my wrist and looked for my pulse. She found it and smiled. "I can feel it."

"You're multitalented, Sophia," I said.

"Is that good?" she said.

"I think so," I said.

"Are you multitalented?" she said.

I laughed. "No."

"We should be going. I know you have things to do, and we do also," Britta said.

Everyone stood up.

"I enjoyed seeing you, Britta. I enjoyed seeing you, Sophia," I said.

"Yes, thanks for coming over," Veronica said.

We all walked to the door.

"Can we dance again?" Sophia said to Veronica.

"Yes, I think we should dance again, Sophia. We can talk to your mother about when would be the best time to do that," Veronica said.

"All right. Don't forget," Sophia said.

"I won't forget," Veronica said.

Sophia and Britta said goodbye and left us. I wanted to watch Veronica dance with Sophia again.

Chapter Seventy-Eight

One day Morgan came to visit me and Veronica. She was dressed conservatively, as if she were dressed for the office. We welcomed her and we sat with her in Veronica's living room. Morgan was carrying a cardboard box.

"Doctor Rose, I heard about what happened with you and Lexi. I'm sorry you're having problems."

"Thanks for thinking of me."

"How are you feeling?"

"It's hard to adjust to it, but I'm trying."

"I brought you something that will help you."

"Thank you. I appreciate that. What did you bring me?"

Morgan gave me the box she was carrying.

"Placebos."

"Placebos?"

"Yes. Placebos can cure anything. If you're lovesick, you need placebos."

"What kind of placebos are they?"

"Look inside."

I opened the top of the box.

"I made them myself. I made tiny little pills from flour and water and I baked them."

I looked at her homemade pills. "You could go into the placebo business."

"I only do this for you, Doctor Rose. Try one."

I ate one of the pills. "That's good. That's a good placebo."

Morgan looked at Veronica. "I'm worried about him. Is he going to get better?"

"I think so. It's a slow process but I think he's going to get better."

"Morgan, what are you and Clark doing these days?" I said.

"We're having fun. We went to a pops concert at the university. They had some very good student performers. They sang standards from Dorothy Fields and Jimmy McHugh. The students have a lot of talent."

"I'm glad you're having fun."

"Clark and I were sorry that Alyssa lost the election for judge of the state Supreme Court."

"Alyssa ran a good race."

"Clark says he wants to run for election to the state Supreme Court someday. His campaign slogan is going to be 'The Supreme Court needs a phone booth and Clark Kent.'"

"Great slogan. I hope he wins."

Morgan frowned. "Doctor Rose, when I see you like this it makes me worry about Clark and me."

"Why?"

"What if our love doesn't last? What if we break up?"

"I think you're going to stay together."

"But what would happen if we do break up? I could be just like you."

"Then I would bring you some placebos. You have nothing to worry about."

Morgan smiled. "Would you do that for me?"

"Certainly I would do that for you."

"Morgan, can I offer you something to drink? What would you like?" Veronica said.

"No thanks, Veronica. I can't stay. But I wanted to deliver the placebos to Doctor Rose because I know he needs them."

"I'm starting to feel better."

"The placebo effect can be powerful," Morgan said.

"Thanks for your help, Morgan. You're very wise," I said.

"I'm not. But I do listen to people who are. Sometimes I learn something from them."

"Thanks for listening to them."

"I don't want to take too much of your time," Morgan said. She stood up. "I leaving you under Veronica's care."

We all stood up and walked to the door. Morgan said goodbye and left us.

"Would you like a placebo?" I said.

Veronica tried one. "That's good. I like that. I think Morgan has a good understanding of medicine."

Chapter Seventy-Nine

Sophia and Britta and Veronica agreed on a schedule for Sophia and Britta coming over to Veronica's house so that Sophia and Veronica could dance together. I was there the next time they came over. Sophia brought me some more bubble bath as a present. It had a wonderful flowery scent.

Sophia and Veronica danced for a while. Britta sat at a table and worked on some school work she brought with her. I sat at the table with Britta and watched the dancers. When Sophia and Veronica had done enough dancing for the day, they sat down at the table with me and Britta, and we all talked.

"You're a good dancer, Sophia," I said.

"Yes, Sophia, that was good," Britta said.

"Dancing is fun."

"And you're good also," Britta said to Veronica.

"Sophia is a good partner," Veronica said.

Britta looked at me. "Jack, how is everything going for you?" Britta said.

"Not very well," I said.

"We're happy to help you in any way we can."

"I miss Lexi. I miss living in her house. I think about Lexi every day. Being with Veronica is nice, but I still want to live with Lexi."

"It takes time to adjust to anything different."

"We had something together that was wonderful, while we were together. Now it's gone and I don't think it's coming back. I need your advice."

"Don't ask me about having a close connection to someone. I wasn't successful at that," Britta said.

"I wasn't successful either," Veronica said.

"But you've had a lot of experience. I'm sure you know something," I said.

"I'm still learning," Britta said.

"Britta, did you ever read anything by F. Scott Fitzgerald?" I said.

"Yes. He's a great writer. I love to read him," Britta said.

Veronica and Sophia sat quietly, listening to Britta and me.

"I keep thinking about the ending to one of his books, where the narrator talks about a character wanting something that was in the past," I said.

"Yes, he was famous for that," Britta said.

"The narrator says the character arrived at a blue lawn and saw a green light, and he thought he had found what he was seeking. But he wanted something that was gone and wasn't coming back."

"Yes. I love reading that. He wrote beautifully."

"The narrator says it eludes us now, but we keep running after it, reaching out, and so we beat on like boats against the current, borne back ceaselessly into the past."

"It's wonderful writing. He's a great writer."

"I think that's what I'm doing. I'm wanting something that's gone and isn't coming back."

"You don't know that."

"I feel sad." I looked at Sophia. "Sophia, someday you'll read F. Scott Fitzgerald. You'll get a lot of insight from him."

Sophia looked at me but didn't say anything.

"Jack, I want to tell you something, and when I say this I want to feel that I'm connected to you, and you to me. I want to put my hand on your arm while I tell you this," Britta said softly.

"Yes, I want that," I said.

Britta reached across the table and put her hand on my arm. Britta stroked my arm and spoke to me softly and slowly. Sophia watched her mother.

"The best advice is something you won't find in the brilliant prose of F. Scott Fitzgerald. His gentle lambent voice will fill your head with longing and regret, but he's misleading you about life.

He's misleading you about people. Real life is more complicated than the story in his book. People are more complicated than the people in his book. It's true that people don't always get back together, but they don't always stay apart either. It's not wrong to want to be with someone again. It's not wrong to hope to be with someone again."

Listening to Britta, and feeling Britta stroking my arm, was comforting.

"Don't believe everything the great writer says about the green lawn and the blue light," Britta said.

"The lawn was blue and the light was green," I said.

She stopped stroking my arm.

"I can't remember the damn colors, Jack."

"That's all right, Britta. I feel a little better, listening to you."

She started stroking my arm again.

"I say as you go through life you should always have hope. If you always have hope, you'll be fine," Britta said.

Sophia looked surprised.

"No, Mom, that's wrong. That's *wrong*. Don't say that," Sophia said.

Britta stopped stroking my arm, and looked at Sophia.

"Why is that wrong?" Britta said softly.

"You should always have *soap*. If you always have *soap*, you'll be fine," Sophia said.

"Can he have both? Can he have soap and hope also?" Britta said gently to Sophia.

Sophia looked at me and then at Britta. "I suppose so," Sophia said.

I thought about what Sophia said, and what Britta said. Maybe great writers know things that twelve-year-olds, and mothers of twelve-year-olds, don't know. But also maybe twelve-year-olds, and mothers of twelve-year-olds, know things that great writers don't know.

"Sophia, you might not need to read F. Scott Fitzgerald. You might have a pretty good understanding of life already, without reading him," I said.

Britta stroked my arm again.

"As you go through life, you should always have soap, and you should always have hope. If you always have soap, and you always have hope, you'll be fine," Britta said.

Sophia reached out and touched me.

"She's right," Sophia said.

Veronica reached out and touched me also.

"Yes, she's right," Veronica said.

"Thank you. All of you are helpful," I said.

"We try," Britta said.

We sat there in silence briefly with their hands on me. Then they pulled their hands away.

"I do feel a little bit better after talking with you. All of you are good therapists," I said.

"We'll send you our bill," Britta said.

"Don't use Dickens, Deadwood, and Doorlicker as your billing service," I said.

"Call us anytime," Britta said.

Britta and Sophia said goodbye and they left us. I was glad they had come to visit me. I had soap and I was starting to have some hope.

Chapter Eighty

The next day Veronica and I were in the kitchen in her house. I was sitting at a table and she was standing next to the stove testing ideas for recipes. While she was working on her cookbook, I was looking at one of her rough drafts.

She stopped her work and looked at me. "Can I interrupt you?"

"Sure."

She sat at the table with me.

"I was thinking about you and Lexi. Have you seen Lexi at all since you came over here?"

"No," I said.

"Have you talked to her?"

"Only when I first came over here. I told her I was here."

"You know what we should do?"

"What should we do?"

"We should invite Lexi to come over. For dinner."

"Are you sure that's a good idea?"

"It's an excellent idea. When you first came over here you had no energy. Now, you're back to your normal energetic self."

"I don't feel especially energetic."

"You're not lifeless like you were when you first came over here. She'll want to see you. Do you want to see her?"

"How do you know she'll want to see me?"

"When she asked you to move out of her house, did she tell you she didn't want to see you again?"

"No. She said she still wants to do things with me sometimes."

"So she wants to see you."

"She hasn't called me."

"I think she wants to be pursued. You need to call *her*."

"How do you know when somebody wants to be pursued?"

"You don't always know when somebody wants to be pursued. One hundred years ago, a woman could send a perfumed letter to a man. That was a clear signal that she wanted to be pursued. Today we have email, so women don't send perfumed letters anymore. So in general it's more difficult to know what people want now. But in Lexi's case it's pretty clear."

"I'm never certain of what's the best thing to do. I'm glad I have you to help me. You're an expert."

"Jackson, nobody who thinks carefully is certain of anything. If you're absolutely certain about something, then you probably don't understand it fully."

"Is that what you learned from your experience doing research?"

"That's what I learned from my experience with people."

"You're better than an expert, because you know the limits of your knowledge."

"Do you want to invite Lexi?"

"Yes. We'll invite her to come over."

"For dinner. We should invite her to come over for dinner. We can serve something that she likes. I think she likes what she made for that dinner at Alyssa's house when Alyssa was entertaining Irina and Dimitri and Lexi and us. I think she likes that meat loaf and tomato sauce made with cilantro and no salt. Do you remember that?"

"I remember Alyssa entertaining the Russians. I don't remember the food."

"Lexi made meat loaf and tomato sauce, with cilantro and no salt, when we were with the Russians at Alyssa's house."

"You have a good memory."

"I remember good food. It's a survival skill."

"I need to stay close to you, then."

"Yes, you do. Do you want to help with the cooking when we entertain Lexi?"

"Yes, I want to help."

"You can be the chef. I'll assist you."

"Good plan."

I called Lexi.

"Lexi, this is your *je ne sais quoi*. How's life on the beautiful west side of town?"

"Hello, Jack. It's good to hear your voice. Are you doing all right?"

"Let's have dinner and talk about life, Lexi. Veronica and I want you to come over and have dinner with us. We're making something with cilantro in it."

"Thank you, Jack. I'd love to come over for dinner. I never turn down an offer to eat something with cilantro in it."

We agreed on a day and a time. A few days later Lexi came over for dinner.

"Lexi, welcome to my humble abode. Have you met my friend Jack?" Veronica said when Lexi arrived.

I smiled at Lexi. Lexi looked at Veronica.

"He looks familiar. I feel like I know him from somewhere," Lexi said.

Lexi looked at me and smiled. "I know we've met before, but I can't remember where. Was it Trouville?"

"I think it was Biarritz," I said.

Lexi walked up to me and wrapped her arms around me and hugged me. "Hello, Jack."

"How you been, Lexi?" I said.

She took her arms off me and stepped back. She looked a little bit sad. "I'm all right."

"Just all right?"

"Just all right. How about you, Jack?"

"I'm all right also. Just all right. How are the neutrinos these days?" I said.

"They come and go. I can never keep one around. You know how it is."

"Yes, I know how it is."

"Played any Yahtzee recently?" Lexi said. She seemed a little bit happier when she was talking about Yahtzee.

"No. Don't have anybody to play with."

Lexi looked at Veronica. "Are you familiar with Yahtzee?"

"I've heard of it. I think you mentioned it. But I've never played it."

"Want to learn? It's a great game. And I brought my dice with me."

"You want to do that before we eat?"

"If you're interested."

"Sure. Why not?"

We all sat down at a table in Veronica's living room. Lexi taught Veronica how to play Yahtzee, and we played for a long time. Then we had a nice dinner featuring meat loaf and tomato sauce with cilantro and no salt. After dinner Lexi went back to her house. As she was departing, Veronica asked her to come back and play more Yahtzee whenever she had some free time.

Gradually Lexi became more comfortable playing at Veronica's house, and Veronica got more comfortable having Lexi there with me. We got to the point where Lexi would come over sometimes when Veronica wasn't there, and Lexi and I would play Yahtzee without Veronica.

Sometimes, after we had played Yahtzee for a while, Lexi would want to lie on top of me. Veronica had a comfortable couch where we would do that. At the end of her visit, Lexi would get up off me and go back to her house, and I would wonder whether I would ever adjust to being away from her.

Sophia visited Veronica every week, and they practiced dancing and they found they liked working together. When I watched them I could see Britta's daughter had an intense desire to become an expert dancer. You don't often see that in a child but she had it. Veronica maybe had a little less intensity but she had a lot of natural ability and she loved dancing. When they first started dancing together I thought they were mismatched, because of the age difference and the height difference. Then after I watched them for a while I only saw two really good dancers doing something difficult and making it look effortless.

Britta made some videos of the two dancing together. The videos were watched by various people and eventually went to Christine Olivier. Christine thought a twelve year old girl dancing with Veronica was cute and marketable. Christine contacted Sophia and Britta and Veronica and said she wanted to make and sell a series of dance instruction videos by Veronica and Sophia. They all reached a financial agreement, and so in addition to everything else they were doing, Veronica and Sophia became professional dancers.

Chapter Eighty-One

One day Lexi and I were playing Yahtzee at Veronica's house, and Veronica wasn't home, and we were talking about research. The long hard money chase had crushed Lexi's research hopes. I knew it was difficult, but we needed to keep looking for money.

In the middle of a game, she stopped playing. She shifted her body in her chair and spoke to me quietly, with an anxious look on her face.

"Do you remember when Hadley was talking about what she was reading in English class last summer? When you were at my house?" Lexi said.

"Yes. I think she talked about literature a couple of times."

"Yes. And one of the things she was talking about was the work of F. Scott Fitzgerald. She was reading to us from the ending of that novel."

"I remember that. It's beautiful writing."

"I think that novel describes us looking for research money, Jack. I think we're trying to get something that it's not possible to have."

"Try not to get discouraged."

"Our dream seems so close that we can hardly fail to grasp it. But we don't know that it's already behind us, in the obscurity, where the fields are rolling."

"You mean the vast obscurity beyond the city?"

"Yes."

"Where the dark fields of the republic roll on under the night?"

"Yes. We're hoping that this is the start of a golden age of neutrino research, and a golden age of sex research, but the golden age of research was in the past and it's not coming back. We're trying to reach out for something that will always elude us no matter how fast we run, as Fitzgerald said in the story."

"Lexi, F. Scott Fitzgerald wrote beautifully. Some of the prettiest sentences ever written in the English language were written by F. Scott Fitzgerald. But don't take all that stuff too seriously."

"We're just like that character in the novel, Jack. The character in the novel had come a long way, and found a green lawn, and looked across the water and saw a blue light, and the character in the novel thought he was certain to get what he wanted. But in reality the character was trying to get something that was impossible to have, because it was in the past and was not coming back."

"The lawn was blue, Lexi. And the light was green."

"I can't remember the damn colors, Jack."

"Don't worry about your research quite so much."

"I'm just afraid we're going to fail."

"Failure is part of success. I've failed many times. All successful people have failed at times."

"Sometimes I meet successful people and they say their career has been just one long continuing success and nothing else."

"There's a word for people like that."

"What's the word?"

"Liars."

"I'm afraid we're going to fail, Jack. My own daughter said we're going to fail."

"Hadley never said that."

"She said we would be successful when my hair is on fire and the sun rises in the west and sets in the east. My hair is never on fire and the sun never does that, Jack."

"Prophecies don't always mean what you think they mean."

"What does it mean to prophesize about my hair being on fire?"

"It doesn't mean your hair is really on fire."

She didn't say anything.

"Lexi, you were there when she was quoting Shakespeare. Nobody could harm Macbeth until Burnham Wood came to Dunsinane. Remember that?"

"Yes."

"Did Burnham Wood come to Dunsinane?"

"Yes, but that was a special case."

"And no man of woman born could harm Macbeth. Remember that?"

"Yes."

"And did a man harm Macbeth?"

"Yes, but that was a special case also."

I didn't say anything. Lexi looked down at the table.

"Maybe Hadley's prophecy refers to my hair color," she said softly.

"That's possible."

Lexi looked at me. "But that doesn't reassure me. I'm still afraid we're going to fail."

"Lexi, When I was growing up, a wise person gave me some advice that I've tried to remember, and you should try to remember it also."

"What was the advice?"

"I'll try to say it to you the way it was told to me. Ain't no sense worryin' about somethin' you got control over, 'cause if you got control over it, ain't no sense worryin' about it. And ain't no sense worryin' about somethin' you got no control over, 'cause if you got no control over it, ain't no sense worryin' about it."

"That doesn't reassure me, Jack. We have all these problems and I don't know what we can do."

"You want to know what we can do?"

"Yes. I want to know what we can do."

"I'm going to tell you exactly what we can do."

"Tell me."

"We can play some more Yahtzee, Lexi. That's what we can do."

We played some more Yahtzee.

Chapter Eighty-Two

Lexi's birthday is in the spring. I didn't know when it was, but Veronica knew and she told me and wanted to do something to celebrate it. Lexi said she didn't want to do anything special. Veronica said everybody has to eat, whether it's their birthday or not, so Lexi at least should come over for dinner, and have a birthday cake, and Lexi said that would be fine.

Veronica thought about making a cake with cilantro in it, because Lexi liked cilantro. Veronica wasn't convinced a cake with cilantro would be edible, so she decided to test the concept first, as an experiment, before making anything she would actually serve to anyone. Her career was in experimental science, so she had the personality of an experimenter. Veronica made some small test cakes with different levels of cilantro. I helped her a little bit when she was making them, and I helped her quite a bit when we were eating them. Veronica thought they were all pretty terrible. I thought they were edible, but a cake was the wrong place for cilantro. It was like a woman wearing a bathing suit to a college graduation.

So Veronica made a more traditional birthday cake, with flour and sugar and canola oil and vanilla and ginger and molasses and baking soda. And since she still wanted to make something with cilantro, she made a dinner with diced tomatoes and ground chicken cooked together with canola oil and cilantro, and a salad of sliced tomatoes and cucumbers on lettuce with vinegar and cilantro dressing.

Veronica found a picture of Alfred Nobel online. She printed it and put it in a cheap frame, and she wrote on it, "To the future researcher, whoever you are, who can create a portable neutrino detector, no prize can be adequate to honor your achievement. With much love, Alfred."

Lexi came over to Veronica's house. Lexi had colored her hair red.

"Do you like my new hair color?" Lexi said.

"I love it," I said.

"It's great," Veronica said.

"Does it look like my hair is on fire?"

"Yes, definitely," I said.

"I can't believe this is really going to make a difference. But if I didn't do this, then I would always be wondering what would happen if I did this. Do you remember when we first met, at Alyssa's house?"

"Yes."

"You said I shouldn't change my hair color unless I had a really good reason."

"Yes."

"You said when a really good reason came into my life I would know it."

"Yes."

"Do you think I have a really good reason?"

"Yes."

We had a nice dinner. We gave Lexi the picture. Lexi liked it.

"If you show this to people, they'll appreciate your achievement," Veronica said.

"Appreciation is nice, but it's not enough. I want money," Lexi said.

Veronica served the cake and told Lexi about our experiments with cilantro as a possible cake ingredient.

"That's good research," Lexi said to Veronica. "You have talent."

"Having talent is nice, but it's not enough. I want money," Veronica said.

"Jack, what do you think of all of this?" Lexi said.

"I think you're hard to please," I said.

"What can we do?" Lexi said to me.

"I'm going to let Veronica answer that," I said.

"We can play some Yahtzee, Lexi. That's what we can do," Veronica said.

"Yes, that's a good idea. Let's play Yahtzee," Lexi said.

We played some Yahtzee.

Chapter Eighty-Three

I was looking at news videos and I saw something about the university. "University planetarium director April Tomonaga has retired after thirty one years at the planetarium, seventeen of them as director. 'It's been stimulating and challenging and I have enjoyed working with many wonderful people,' she said. The university has hired a new director, William Wells, who will start work Monday. 'I look forward to finding new and innovative ways to bring the excitement of the planetarium experience to an even larger segment of the community,' he said."

On Monday I went to the planetarium to talk with William Wells. He was a well dressed Black man. He looked like he was maybe thirty-five or forty years old. He was busy with trying to learn all the details of his new job, but he gave me a few minutes of his time.

"I really want to see the sun rise in the west and set in the east," I said.

"I'm not sure that's possible to do with the machine we have and the program we have," he said.

"I can make a donation to the planetarium if you can buy some software that can show this."

"This must be really important to you."

"It is."

"That's refreshing to see that you care so much about the planetarium. We want to be an important part of people's lives, but we don't always achieve that. I'll see what I can do."

"Thank you."

A few days later there was another news report about the planetarium. "The university planetarium announced today that it will present a new program called *What If?*. The program will ask the question, 'What if things ran backwards in our sky?' In the program, the sun will rise in the west and set in the east. The moon and the planets and the stars will also move in the opposite direction compared to their normal motion. The planetarium director said, 'We want to stimulate interest in the sky above us by presenting a program that has never been seen here.'"

Chapter Eighty-Four

Lance Walker, the university athletics compliance officer, called me.

"Jack, you asked me a long time ago about the players on the baseball team having jobs testing sex dolls."

"Yes, that was a concern of mine."

"I told you at the time that it was perfectly fine."

"Yes, I remember."

"I told you it was perfectly fine because I had talked to Captain Shaeffer and he told me it was done within the rules. I assumed he was telling me the truth. But I didn't have any evidence beyond that. I wasn't actually certain that it was done within the rules."

"Yes."

"When you told me that you were concerned about it, I said I wasn't going to do anything more about it."

"That's right."

"But after you left my office, I changed my mind and I launched an investigation to find out what actually happened."

"Did you launch an investigation only because I was concerned about it?" I said.

"Do you think there was another reason?" Lance said.

"I thought maybe the school made you unhappy because you didn't like the plan to tear up your neighborhood and build a new stadium."

"I'm going to leave that speculation to other people, Jack."

"All right."

"I couldn't reveal the investigation to you or anyone else outside the department, because during the investigation process all our investigations are confidential. Does that make sense?"

"Yes, I understand."

"When we complete an investigation, we announce the results. In a few minutes I'm going to be releasing a statement to the press about the results of our investigation. I'm going to be reporting that we found serious violations of the rules, by the baseball staff and others connected to the university. Our investigation found that the players were given sex dolls and were not required to perform any work in return. The sex dolls were provided by Captain Shaeffer of the Shaeffer Sex Dolls Company, and distributed through Chairman Richardson of the physics department. The baseball coaches and the president of the university were aware of the sex doll gifts to the players."

"Wow."

"I'm calling you now to thank you for bringing this to my attention."

"Thanks for investigating. And thanks for letting me know the results."

Chapter Eighty-Five

A few days later I was looking at news videos and I saw more university news. "The state university board of trustees today dismissed the president of the university, because of what the board called failure to provide adequate supervision of the athletic department. The board promoted the current university general counsel and vice president for community affairs, Alyssa Lincoln, to become acting university president until a permanent replacement is found. The new acting university president, together with her dog Abraham, was a recent unsuccessful candidate for judge on the state Supreme Court."

After that, there was another news report. "Following the recent action by the state university board of trustees, acting university president Alyssa Lincoln issued this statement. 'I am grateful for this opportunity to lead this great university. Under my leadership, we will affirm the principle that integrity is more important than victory on the athletic field.'"

Then following that news report I noticed there was another news report. "Today, Alyssa Lincoln became acting president of the state university. In her first statement on the job, she said she will affirm the principle that integrity is more important than victory on the athletic field. Our news team is conducting a public opinion survey about her remarks. We are asking the question: In your opinion, which is more important? Integrity, or victory on the athletic field?

To respond to our survey, go to our website, go to the page that says survey, and complete the form. We will have the results this evening on our ten o'clock news program."

A few hours later it was time for the station to release the results of the survey. I went online and looked at the latest video from the news team. It was their top story. "The results of our survey today are: integrity 38%, victory on the athletic field 54%, un-decided 8%."

The next day there was more news about the school. A news video reported, "Acting university president Lincoln today announced that the university was canceling plans to construct a new base-ball stadium south of University Avenue. She said she believed the proposed site was inappropriate, because it would disrupt an area which is an important and valued part of the university com-munity. She said the school was going to reopen discussions about alternative plans and would consider ideas from other possible donors."

Chapter Eighty-Six

The day after after the news about the stadium, I got a call from Captain Shaeffer.

"Jack, how you been? I haven't talked with you in a while."

"I'm all right. What about you? Are you disappointed about the stadium?"

"I was at first, Jack. When I first heard the news, I thought it was a sad ending to a project I worked hard for. But then a strange thing happened."

"What happened?"

"My daughter Britta called me. And she said this is actually better for me and my family than if the stadium had been built where I wanted it. She said building it where people didn't want it would have damaged the family name. It would have hurt my reputation. I would look like an out of touch rich guy. And do you want to know something, Jack?"

"What's that?"

"I think Britta is right. She convinced me, Jack."

"So are you going to give the money to build the stadium somewhere else?"

"No, Jack. I still don't like the alternatives. I'm just going to hold on to my money for a while. I'm not in any hurry to give it away. I'll talk to Britta about what she likes. We'll see what develops. And another thing, Jack."

"What's that?"

"When the baseball players were given the free sex dolls from my company, that was my idea. Britta didn't know anything about it. She found out about it when the compliance officer released his report. And when Britta found out about it, she told me that giving sex dolls to the baseball players was a mistake. And she convinced me she's right about that also."

"Why were you giving sex dolls to the players?"

"I wanted to help with the recruiting. I wanted our school to be able to attract the best players. I was hearing rumors that other schools were offering call girls to players they were recruiting. So I thought our school should give sex dolls to our players. Shaeffer sex dolls are better than call girls, Jack."

"How did Britta convince you giving sex dolls to the players was a mistake?"

"She said baseball brings in plenty of money for the university. If the baseball program wants to give more benefits to the players, the baseball program can afford to pay for any benefits they want to give to the players. They don't need my help. She said I should think about women's sports. She said women's volleyball is a great sport and it doesn't have a lot of money. She said if I want to increase my support for school athletics, I should support women's volleyball. Of course, if I'm going to help the women's volleyball program I'm not going to give the players sex dolls."

"That woman has got some smarts in her head."

"And as I was talking to Britta, I started thinking about what you said about the zeitgeist. You said I couldn't see the real zeitgeist. You said the zeitgeist is not machines are doing everything. You said the zeitgeist is women are doing everything that men are doing."

"That's right, Captain."

"And on the subject of women, your university just made one acting university president."

"They certainly did."

"Your acting president is a woman."

"Yes."

"She's female, Jack."

"Most women are, Captain."

"So I decided to put Britta on the board of directors of Shaeffer Sex Dolls."

"I'm very happy to hear that."

"That woman has got some smarts in her head. You said that yourself, Jack."

"I was quoting you. You told me that a long time ago when I first met you."

"Thank you, Jack."

"For what?"

"For connecting me to the zeitgeist."

"I can't take credit for that. You connected yourself to the zeitgeist."

"I'll let you go, Jack. I know you have things to do. Just remember one thing."

"What's that?"

"If you ever want to go to bed with a body that has the greatest tits you ever saw, all you need to do is give me a call."

"I'll remember that, Captain."

Chapter Eighty-Seven

A letter arrived at Veronica's house addressed to Ms. Rose Jackson. Veronica showed it to me and said it was obviously for me. She said somebody got my name backwards and thinks I'm a woman.

I opened the letter. I read it to Veronica.

"Dear Ms. Jackson, You and I have never met, but I have heard about your interest in sex research. I'm the president of the Western Sex Association. Our members are professionals in the field of sexual sociology. Our group is holding its annual convention this fall at the Bronze Mountain Resort and Conference Center. We would like you to be our keynote speaker. We're interested in your perspective as a woman when you view the current developments in sex research. We will pay all your travel and hotel expenses at the conference and will give you an honorarium. Please let me know whether you will be able to accept this invitation. Sincerely, Barbara Washington Monroe."

I looked at Veronica.

"What do you think?" I said.

"That's a nice letter," she said.

Chapter Eighty-Eight

The next day I got a call from Miss Valery.

"Jack, I want you and Professor Lexi to come over to my house. I want to talk with you about all the developments at the university. I have other things going on, so there won't be time for tea together, but I do want to see you."

"I would love to see you again, and I'm sure Lexi feels the same way."

We found a time that worked for everyone and we visited Miss Valery. We sat in her living room.

"Professor Lexi, I love your red hair," Miss Valery said.

"Thank you," Lexi said.

"Professor Lexi and Jack, this may be on the news later. I'm telling you now because I want you to be the first to know."

"The first to know what?" I said.

"I've been talking with the president of your university."

"About what?" I said.

"Several things. She said the university is considering other stadium plans in other locations. She said did I want to give any money for another stadium plan?"

"What did you tell her?"

"I said no, Jack. I said I've been following the news about the athletic department. The news isn't good. The athletic department is caught in a scandal. I don't want to be associated with a scandal. I need to protect my good name. My dear departed husband would say the same thing."

"Yes, Miss Valery, I believe he would."

"I told your university president that I want to give my money for research in a field that has been neglected for too long."

"What field is that?"

"Jack, I'm giving money for sex research."

"Thank you, Miss Valery. You're wonderful."

"Wait. Don't thank me yet. Wait till you hear who I'm giving the research money to."

"Who are you giving it to?"

Miss Valery looked at Lexi. "I'm giving it to Professor Lexi."

Lexi looked surprised. "Really? You're giving it to me?"

"Yes, Professor Lexi. When we were talking the last time you were here, I realized you can help a lot of people who have problems with sex."

"Thank you for thinking of me, but I'm doing neutrino research. I'm not doing sex research."

"I know that. But people need sex more than people need neutrinos. You can help a lot of people. You know how to communicate sexual needs. People need to learn what you know. I want you to do research on how married people can be taught how to communicate their needs."

"I just know the difference between New York and Philadelphia. That's not sex, that's geography."

"I think you know a lot more than that. You're a good teacher. You know how to teach skills. We need research on teaching people to talk to their partner. People need to learn that. As I said, you can help a lot of people."

"But I'm a neutrino researcher."

"And now I hate to rush you out the door, but I have an appointment with my lawyer about the paperwork."

Miss Valery walked with us to the door. We said goodbye and we left her.

Chapter Eighty-Nine

The next day I was at the university and I got a call from Mimi Chen. She was executive director of the American Contemporary Design Association. I had met her at their recent conference and she remembered me. She said she was looking for Professor Lieblich. Ms. Chen said she called the physics department and someone in the department office said Professor Lieblich was not in her office, and they were not sure where the professor was.

Mimi knew I was a friend of the professor and she had my contact information and she thought maybe I would be able to locate the professor. I told Ms. Chen that I was planning to meet the professor for lunch and I would ask the professor to call Ms. Chen.

Lexi met me for lunch at A Slice Is Nice. She was curious, so Lexi called Mimi during our lunch. Lexi didn't want to disturb the other diners, so she used her earphones and spoke softly.

"Hello, is this Mimi Chen?" I heard Lexi say to her phone. "This is Professor Lieblich. Everyone calls me Lexi. What can I do for you?" Lexi said.

There was a pause and then Lexi said, "Yes, Mimi." There was another pause and then Lexi said, "Design students? People studying design?"

There was another pause and then I heard Lexi say, "Thank you, I appreciate that. I'm not able to give you an answer right now. I need to think about that. Can I think about that and call you later this week? Yes. Thank you. Goodbye."

After Lexi ended the call, I said, "What did she say?"

"The American Contemporary Design Association has been given money by a nonprofit foundation. The money is for setting up programs for education and training of students in design. Mimi says they will give me a three year grant, which could be renewed at the end, if I will add design students to my research team and help them get practical experience in modern design."

"You should do it."

"I don't know anything about design."

"You can learn about design. If you have design students on your team, they can teach you about design."

"I'm a neutrino researcher."

"That's fine. You're a neutrino researcher with a design class on the side."

Lexi didn't say anything for a while. Then softly she said, "Remember when we were playing Yahtzee and we were talking about that writer that Hadley likes?"

"F. Scott Fitzgerald?"

"We're just like that character in the novel. We're trying to reach out for something that will always elude us no matter how fast we run."

Lexi closed her eyes and rested her head in her hands and didn't say anything. I told her things would get better, but she didn't respond. After a long time she opened her eyes and we finished our lunch and parted.

Chapter Ninety

When things don't go your way, you need someone to talk to who knows you well but not so well that they lose their objectivity. I read that in an advice book somewhere and I was never sure that would help, but this seemed like a good time to test out that concept. I mentioned it to Lexi and Veronica, and they said we should meet with Alyssa.

Alyssa was now using the office that had been President Churchill's office when he was president of the university. The president's office was part of a group of offices in the administration building. I went over there and I looked for one of the administrative assistants, so I could ask for some time on Alyssa's calendar. But Juliette and Sasha, who had been working there when President Churchill was there, were not there anymore. I met someone who said his name was Ron.

"Are you the new administrative assistant?" I said.

"I'm a student assistant. A student with a part time job as an assistant to the president."

"What happened to Juliette and Sasha? They were working here in a job share as administrative assistants."

"They're over at the athletic department now. They got a job share working for the sports information director."

"Is that a good job?"

"Oh, yes, it's a great job. Much better than working here. When you work over there, you have a chance to meet some of the great athletes who play for the university. Jobs like that are very hard to get. They only got it because of the recent shakeup in the athletic department. Maybe you heard about that."

"Yes, that was in the news."

"Can I help you with something?"

"I work at the medical school. Some of my friends and I want to make an appointment to talk with the acting president."

"Certainly. I can set that up for you. I'll find a time for you on her electronic calendar."

We made an appointment on her calendar.

"Are you interested in sports yourself?" I said.

"I'm interested in the business side of sports. I'm studying business. I'm interested in how teams can increase their revenue."

"Have you ever thought about a career in university administration?"

"No, I've never considered that. Do you think that would interest me?"

"Maybe."

I thanked Ron for his help and wished him well in his studies.

When it was almost time for our appointment, I met Lexi and Veronica at the Shaeffer Building and we walked over to Alyssa's office together. We took a few steps into her office. She saw us and smiled a big smile and said hello. We said hello to her and she walked over to us and shook our hands and welcomed us. We all sat down.

"How do you like your new office?" Lexi said.

"It's nice. But I don't quite feel at home in it."

"I guess that takes time," Lexi said.

I looked around the office. The pictures of the former president that had been on the wall were gone now. Alyssa had put up some of her own pictures, showing her with various distinguished looking people I didn't recognize. Apparently if you're going to lead a major university, you need pictures of yourself with distinguished looking people. If nobody recognizes the distinguished looking people, that's fine. Their job is just to look distinguished.

"Looks like our former president didn't leave anything here," I said.

"He left some things in his desk. I guess he doesn't want them anymore," Alyssa said.

"What did he leave in his desk?" Lexi said.

Alyssa opened a drawer in her desk and looked in it and took out a ball. "Here's a softball that somebody wrote an inscription on. 'Best wishes to the one at the top from the home run queen.'"

"I wonder why he didn't take it with him."

"I don't know. Maybe he doesn't like softball players as much as he likes baseball players."

"What else did he leave?"

Alyssa took a shirt out of the drawer.

"Here's an old t-shirt. It's not in very good condition but it's still wearable. It says 'conference champions.'"

Alyssa looked in the drawer again. "Not much else in here. A couple of rubber bands and a paper clip."

"Did you do anything special to celebrate getting your new job?" Lexi said.

"No."

"No parties?" Lexi said.

"No parties. Nothing special. But my son Clark gave me a present."

"What did he give you?" Lexi said.

Alyssa went over to a closet in a corner of the room. She took out a shirt. "You like this?" She had a bright red long sleeve t-shirt that said Wonder Woman in big blue letters across the front.

"You should wear it," Lexi said.

"No, I don't want to wear it. People would think I don't take my job seriously."

"That's a great shirt," Lexi said.

Alyssa put the shirt back in the closet and returned to her chair behind her desk and sat down.

"My student assistant said you wanted to get some advice from me," Alyssa said.

"Yes, we want your expert advice," Lexi said.

"I don't know how expert it is, but if I can help you I'm happy to help."

Alyssa listened to us while we told her our problems. Lexi told her about Mimi's offer of money for training design students. Alyssa already knew about Miss Valery's offer of money for sex research. Veronica told Alyssa about the deal for Veronica and Sophia to make dance instruction videos. Alyssa already knew Veronica had gotten an offer from Christine to publish a cookbook. Veronica told Alyssa she had agreed to do it. I told Alyssa about the Western Sex Association's belief that my name is Rose Jackson, and their offer to give money to me under that name to speak to them.

"I've looked for money everywhere and all I've gotten is offers for things that I don't want to do," Lexi said.

"I've looked for money everywhere and all I've found is people who want me to go in a different direction," Veronica said.

"I've looked for money everywhere and I haven't found what I want," I said.

"I'm a failure," Lexi said.

"And I'm a failure," Veronica said.

"And I'm also a failure," I said.

Alyssa leaned forward in her chair. She looked at Lexi.

"Do you still believe you and Veronica have created something special?"

"Yes, I believe that," Lexi said softly.

Alyssa looked at Veronica.

"Veronica?" Alyssa said. "Do you believe that?"

"Yes," Veronica said softly.

Alyssa looked at Lexi. "Other people are going to see that."

Lexi shook her head.

"Jack told me a famous quotation that I really like," Alyssa said. "Maybe he told you also."

"What is it?"

"Failure is a success that hasn't happened yet."

"He told me that."

"Failure and success are different because they happen at different times," Alyssa said. "Failure is earlier. Success is later. Success comes after failure. You have to wait a little longer for it. Don't stop too soon. Your search is a success that hasn't happened yet."

Lexi shook her head. "No. I looked everywhere. I failed." She looked at the floor.

"You've only had a few experiences," Alyssa said. "There are many more experiences you haven't had yet. Every day is a new day with new possibilities. Every day you might be contacted by someone who might offer you money. Someone might call you tomorrow and offer you money. You need to keep looking, and see what happens."

Lexi looked at Alyssa. "No, Alyssa. I've looked everywhere for research money. I even changed my hair color. Nothing has been successful," Lexi said.

"I like your red hair," Alyssa said.

"I thought red hair might help me find research money. But it didn't help me."

"It looks good."

"I've come to the end of the road," Lexi said.

"No, no, don't talk that way. You've barely even left your driveway. You have a long road in front of you," Alyssa said.

"We're like characters in a novel that my daughter was reading for a literature class," Lexi said.

"What novel was your daughter reading for a literature class?" Alyssa said.

"She was reading a novel by F. Scott Fitzgerald. One of the characters in the novel had come a long way, and found a green lawn, and looked across the water and saw a blue light, and the character in the novel thought he was going to get what he wanted. But in reality the character wanted something that was impossible to have. He wanted something that was in the past and was not coming back. I'm like that character in the novel, Alyssa. I want support for neutrino research, but the popularity of neutrino research is gone and it's not coming back. Jack is like that character also."

Alyssa frowned and looked at me.

"Is that right, Jack?" Alyssa said.

"No. The lawn was blue and the light was green."

"I can't remember the damn colors, Jack," Lexi said.

Alyssa looked at Lexi. "Lexi, people should read great literature, but they should read great literature critically," Alyssa said.

"It's all in the novel. My life is just like the novel."

"Lexi."

"I'm a failure."

"Lexi, listen to me."

"F. Scott Fitzgerald was right."

"Lexi, you can't believe everything you read in a novel. Somebody who writes a novel is telling a story. They're trying to entertain you. You can't take everything completely seriously."

"Yes, I know they're telling a story. But stories in novels show fundamental truths about human nature. F. Scott Fitzgerald was showing a fundamental truth about human nature."

"Lexi, he was a great writer, but you can't take everything he said completely seriously."

"Do you believe stories in novels show fundamental truths about human nature?"

"Sometimes they do, Lexi. Sometimes they do. But that still doesn't mean you have to take the green light and the blue lawn seriously."

"I'm a failure."

"Lexi, F. Scott Fitzgerald never met you. He never knew anything at all about neutrino detectors. He never knew anything at all about research money. He never knew anything at all about women in science. You can't assume that his novel has any relevance to your life. You have to carefully decide for yourself whether anything he wrote is at all relevant to what you're trying to do."

"But he's such a great writer."

Lexi looked down at the floor. Nobody said anything. I thought about F. Scott Fitzgerald. His beautiful words ran through my mind.

Lexi slumped in her chair and closed her eyes. "I feel sick."

"What's wrong?" Alyssa said.

"I don't know. I just feel sick."

"Do you want to lie down? You can lie down on the couch if you want."

"Yes, I want to lie down on the couch."

Lexi opened her eyes and got up and walked over to the couch on the side of Alyssa's office and laid down on it and closed her eyes again.

"Lexi, I want you to have the Wonder Woman shirt."

"I don't feel like Wonder Woman."

"You *are* like Wonder Woman. The shirt will help you feel like her."

"But your son wants you to have it."

"I'll tell him you need it more than I do. He'll understand."

Alyssa got up and went to the closet and took out the shirt. She took it over to Lexi and draped it over her chest.

"I'm giving you the shirt," Alyssa said.

"Thank you," Lexi said.

Alyssa went back to her chair behind her desk. She looked at me.

"What do you think about the design students? If Lexi works with the design students, can she help them?" Alyssa said.

"I think so. Lexi has wonderful artistic ability."

I looked over at Lexi on the couch. She didn't say anything.

"Can I ask you about the sex research?" Alyssa said softly.

I looked at Alyssa. "If you want to."

"If Lexi takes on the work Miss Valery wants her to do, do you think she can help people?"

"Yes. I know she can help people."

Alyssa looked at Veronica.

"Do you feel neglected?" Alyssa said.

"No."

"We've been focusing on Lexi."

"That's all right."

"You're going to be successful too."

"I'm like Lexi. I can't get a research grant for neutrino research."

"You can get money to write the cookbook, and your publisher is giving a percentage for research. If the cookbook is successful, that's a start. And you'll get money for the dance instruction videos, and that's a start also."

"Did I make the right decision when I agreed to that?"

"Yes. Doing those things will help you," Alyssa said. "It will bring in money, which is good, and it will help you meet people and make friends who might help you later, which is also good."

"I feel like a failure."

"Remember the famous quotation that Jack told me. Failure is a success that hasn't happened yet."

"That's a nice sentiment."

"It summarizes what I was trying to tell Lexi. It applies to you also. It's not clear who said that originally. It may have been Benjamin Franklin."

"I'll try to remember that."

"I'm sorry I don't have a Wonder Woman shirt for you too, Veronica. But I have the softball inscribed by the home run queen. I want you to have it. Think of it as recognition of your work."

Alyssa tossed the softball to Veronica.

"Thank you. I'll try to justify your confidence in me."

Alyssa turned to look at me. "Jack, you're going to be successful also."

"I can't get any money for sex research."

"But you can get money for speaking, and that's a first step."

"Do you think I should give the speech to the Western Sex Association?"

"Yes, Jack. You should give the speech."

"But they think I'm a woman. What if they don't want a man to give the speech?"

"Tell them you can do anything a woman can do except have a baby."

"What if they don't believe me?"

"Tell them they don't understand the zeitgeist."

"What if they still don't believe me?"

"Put on a dress and give the speech."

"Will they listen to me?"

"They'll be fascinated by everything you say. They'll want you to come back again."

I wondered whether I could find a dress that would fit me.

"I want you to have the t-shirt that says conference champions." Alyssa tossed the t-shirt to me.

"Thank you. You've always tried to help me. I appreciate that," I said.

Alyssa got up out of her chair and walked over to Lexi on the couch and stood next to her.

"Mind if I sit with you?" Alyssa said.

Lexi opened her eyes. "Go ahead."

Alyssa sat on the edge of the couch near Lexi's feet and looked at Lexi.

"You ever watch classic movies from the golden age of Hollywood?" Alyssa said softly.

"Sometimes," Lexi said, also speaking softly.

"You think maybe we can learn things from classic movies?"

"Aren't movies just movies?"

"The best ones are written by great writers that understand life."

"Are the movie writers better than F. Scott Fitzgerald?"

"Sometimes they are."

Lexi didn't say anything for a few seconds. Then she said, "I feel sick."

"I think you remember that movie about refugees trying to get to Lisbon during World War Two. You were quoting a line from it at my house when I introduced you to Jack."

"Do you remember everything I say?"

"No, only the important things."

"I remember that movie. At the end there's a scene at the airport where Rick sends Ilsa off on the plane to Lisbon. Rick and Captain Renault are left at the airport and plan their future together. It's a great ending."

"What do you think makes it a great ending?"

"Rick does the right thing. Early in the movie he claims he's only interested in himself, but in the end he helps other people. That's the right thing to do. It's a great ending."

"That's your guide."

"How is that my guide?"

"You should do the right thing."

"What's the right thing?"

"Helping other people."

Lexi closed her eyes. "I feel sick."

"These people need you," Alyssa said. "You can help them. When you help them, you'll feel better."

Nobody said anything for maybe half a minute.

Lexi opened her eyes and looked at Alyssa. "You're right," Lexi said. "I should do the right thing. It's the right thing to do."

Alyssa smiled.

"I'll take the money," Lexi said. "I'll help the design students. And I'll do what Miss Valery wants."

As Lexi was talking with Alyssa I felt a gnawing hunger deep inside me. I wondered whether this is how it feels to be unsuccessful. Then I realized I actually *was* hungry. For food. When they finished talking, I got up out of my chair and went over to Lexi and Alyssa.

"Are you hungry, Lexi?" I said. "Let's go get some pizza."

"Yes, I need pizza," she said. Alyssa stood up and Lexi sat up on the couch and then stood up next to Alyssa. Lexi was holding the Wonder Woman shirt.

"Veronica, you want to go get some pizza?" Lexi said.

"Sure," Veronica said. She stood up and came over to Lexi and Alyssa and me.

"We've taken enough of your time. Thank you for everything," Lexi said to Alyssa.

"Thank you," Veronica said.

"We have things to do. And I'm sure you have things to do also. Thank you for your help," I said to Alyssa.

"Don't give up. Be patient. Someone might call you tomorrow and offer you money," Alyssa said to me.

"Thank you for your encouragement," I said and smiled at Alyssa and shook her hand.

"Yes. Thank you," Veronica said. She also smiled at Alyssa and shook her hand.

"Thanks. You've been wonderful," Lexi said and smiled at Alyssa. Alyssa held out her arms and Lexi embraced her.

We said goodbye to Alyssa and left her office. She was smart and knew a lot about how the world works. And when she said everyone was going to be successful, that was a nice thing to hear. I liked hearing her say that. But I still wanted research money.

We went to A Slice Is Nice and ate some pizza.

Chapter Ninety-One

Captain Shaeffer called me the next day, when I was arriving at work. I wasn't expecting to hear from him.

"Jack, my friend, how are you?"

"I'm doing all right, Captain. How are you?"

"Jack, I've been thinking."

"I'm in favor of thinking, Captain. What have you been thinking about?"

"I've been thinking about all the things you told me. About research and everything. You told me how important research is, and how it can advance human knowledge and help society. You told me how research that makes an important discovery can win a prize for the researchers. Maybe the Nobel Prize."

"That's right. It can do those things, Captain."

"When you first told me that, I didn't really accept what you were telling me. But I've been thinking about it, and it makes more sense to me now."

"I'm glad to hear that, Captain."

"And I've been thinking about what you said about neutrinos. You said they were everywhere."

"That's true, Captain. They are everywhere."

"And you said they're going through us all the time."

"That's right Captain, Hundreds of billions go through every square inch of your body every second."

"And Jack, I've been thinking about my dear sweet dog, Penny, who died when she was so young. She had cancer, and it took her away from me. Did I ever mention her to you?"

"Yes. The first time I met you, you mentioned her. I can understand how you feel. People can become very attached to dogs, and when you lose one at a young age, it's a great loss."

"Jack, I know research can't bring her back, but maybe research can find out something that would help others."

"I'm sure you're right, Captain."

"Jack, you're a smart guy. I knew that the moment I looked at you."

"Thanks, Captain, but looks can be deceiving."

"Jack, I'm donating money to start a research institute to do research on the effects of neutrinos on the health of dogs. My lawyer is drawing up the papers right now. I want you to be in charge of it. Will you do that for me, Jack?"

"Captain, thank you for thinking of me, but I don't think neutrinos have any effect on the health of dogs. There's nothing to study."

"Has there ever been a research institute dedicated to studying this?"

"No, not that I'm aware of."

"Well then it's a new field. It needs to be studied. Jack, do me a favor. Don't make a decision right away. Take some time and think about it. Will you do that for me, Jack?"

"Captain, I respect your interest in research. Let me think about it, and we can talk more about it later."

"Thanks Jack. You're a great friend."

"Thanks, Captain."

"Jack, I need to get back to work. I'm helping some engineers in my company with a very important new product."

"What is it?"

"Jack, we're developing a sex doll that can watch sports on television. This doll has a robot arm that works just like a human arm. This doll can sit on the couch and pass the nachos to the guy next to her."

"I'm sure that will be popular, Captain."

"Jack, this is going to be the first sex doll that women will buy and give to their husbands. Women can say 'Darling, I'm going to work in the garden now, but you have your doll that can pass the nachos to you while you watch the game.'"

"I'm not sure women are going to buy a sex doll to give to their husbands, but your company is certainly innovative."

"Jack, our sex dolls are the most technologically advanced sex dolls you can buy."

"Yes, I believe that."

"Jack, has anyone ever won the Nobel Prize for developing advanced sex dolls?"

"No, Captain. Maybe you'll be the first."

"Should I give sex dolls to the members of the committee that votes on who wins? I want them to be familiar with my work."

"Maybe they're already familiar with your work."

"Britta has some ideas for some new sex dolls also. She's a smart girl, Jack."

"I've always liked her."

"I have to go now. I'll talk to you later, Jack."

"Goodbye, Captain. Thanks for your confidence in me."

I wondered whether I should have chosen a different career years ago.

Obviously things were not going well for me. I knew I needed help. In other words, I needed to talk to therapists and I needed to eat pizza. I called Veronica and Britta and told them about my most recent conversation with Captain Shaeffer, and said I needed an emergency meeting for lunch at A Slice Is Nice. They both wanted to meet right away. Britta asked whether she could bring Sophia. I said yes. Sometimes a twelve-year-old can see things that adults can miss. So we met at my favorite pizza place, on a beautiful sunny spring day.

We went up to the counter to order our slices of hot pizza.

"Do you have anything special today?" Britta said to the young man at the counter.

"Today you can order any of our regular toppings, or you can have our special asparagus tips, cranberries, and Neufchatel cheese topping."

"I don't know. What do you think?" Britta said to me.

"I've had that before," I said.

"Is it good?"

"I like it a lot."

"I'll try it. I'd like a big slice with your special topping," Britta said to the person at the counter.

"What would you like, Sophia?" Britta said.

"I'll try that also," Sophia said to the person at the counter.

"Do you have anything with pine cones?" Veronica said to person at the counter.

"No. Sorry," he said.

"Then I'll have the same thing the others are having."

"I'd like that also," I said.

Veronica turned to me. "Wait till I make pine cone food famous."

We all got our food and sat at a table out on the porch and ate our pizza slices.

"All of you were great therapists for me when I first moved away from Lexi, when I moved to Veronica's house and I needed your perspective, I needed your insight. I need that again, not about Lexi but about research," I said.

"We're happy to help you," Britta said.

"Yes, certainly," Veronica said.

I told everyone about my conversation with Captain Shaeffer.

"I feel uncomfortable telling him he's wrong. But he needs to understand reality. I wish the quest for research money were more straight forward. This whole process has been a mess. Distractions and complications and problems," I said.

"I think my father likes you," Britta said. "He respects you. You just have to be patient. He doesn't have a medical background, so he doesn't look at things the same way you do. But he's interested in your work. Don't give up. Be patient."

"Everything you've been through is normal. Looking for research money is a messy process," Veronica said.

"You say everything is normal, but I don't like it when my life is messy and uncomfortable."

"Listen. Sometimes your life is going to be messy and uncomfortable. If that's your only problem, you have a great life," Britta said.

We ate some of our pizza.

"Do you like that?" I said to Sophia.

"Yes, it's good," she said.

"What should I tell Captain Shaeffer?" I said to Britta.

"Don't tell him he's crazy. Listen to him respectfully. Some of what you know about human medicine applies to dogs. Explain what you can in a language he can understand. Find out about veterinary medical research that he might be interested in. Talk to him about that."

"I agree with Britta," Veronica said.

"I was thinking he would eventually support research we want to do. But I'm starting to wonder if that's ever going to happen," I said.

"You've only known the guy for less than a year. These things take time. He likes you. Be patient," Britta said.

"I agree with Britta. Be patient. Be nice to the Captain. Educate him about reality. After he satisfies his curiosity about canine medical problems, he's going to throw us some money for what we want to do," Veronica said.

"You think so?"

"Remember what Ben Franklin said. Failure is a success that hasn't happened yet," Veronica said.

"That's a familiar quote. I've heard that before. I'm not sure Ben Franklin said that," Britta said.

"You think somebody else said that? Who do you think said it?" Veronica said.

"I don't know. Maybe it was Abraham Lincoln," Britta said.

"Why would a dog say something like that?" Veronica said.

"Are you trying to make me laugh?" I said to Veronica.

"I'm just trying to convince you that you can be successful."

"Veronica is right. Every rational person believes you can succeed. Every person who has more than a squirrel brain believes you can do great things," Britta said.

"But that's not enough. I need the grant administrators to believe it also," I said.

"Jack, you can't spend your time worrying about success," Veronica said. "You just can't do that. You have to appreciate what you have right now. Look how far you've come in this town already. When you first came to this town, you didn't know anybody. You didn't even know where to get good pizza."

Veronica looked at Sophia. "Do you like eating pizza with us?"

Sophia smiled. "Yes."

Veronica looked at me. "Now you have loyal friends like Sophia and Britta and me who are happy to eat pizza with you whenever you want."

"With cranberries and asparagus tips and Neufchatel cheese," Sophia said.

"That's success, Jack," Britta said.

"I'm happy I met you. That's a success. But I don't feel like my career is a success."

"You need to be patient and persistent and have some hope that everything will go well," Britta said.

We ate some more pizza. I looked at Sophia.

"What do you think?" I said.

"I wish it had more asparagus tips," Sophia said.

"Yes, they're delicious," Britta said.

I looked at Britta. "You're telling me to have hope. But I can't be happy just hoping all the time. I need to see something positive happen. Some famous person said hope makes a good breakfast but a bad supper. Don't ask me who said that," I said.

"This isn't supper. This is lunch," Sophia said.

"Is hope still good for lunch, Sophia?" I said.

She smiled. "Yes."

"In that case, I'll keep hoping."

"Sophia, I think you have good insight," Britta said.

"Britta, your father talked a little about his business. Can I mention what he said?" I said.

Britta looked at Sophia. "Can Doctor Rose talk about my father's business?"

Sophia frowned. "Boring," she said.

"Sophia, did you get enough to eat?" Britta said.

"Could I please have another piece of pizza?" she said.

"Sure. I've got some money." Britta gave Sophia some money. "You can get what you want."

Sophia smiled. "Thank you." She went to the counter to order more pizza.

"Britta, your father said you had some good ideas for some new sex dolls," I said.

"I told him we need to update our products for the modern era. I'm working on some ideas."

"What are you working on?"

"One idea I have is to put facial recognition technology in a sex doll. So the doll would recognize its partner. Then it could say its partner's name. It could even want to be with only one specific person."

"So a sex doll could become emotionally attached to one specific person?" I said.

"I think we're at the point where we have the technology," Britta said.

"Would that be a female doll or a male doll?" Veronica said.

"It could be either one. The technology would work for both."

"You could you make a doll with a male body that only wants one specific woman?" I said.

"I think we can do that," Britta said.

"That would be a major advance," I said.

"Yes. Finally, a man who's faithful to one woman. Of course, the man wouldn't be a human, just a doll," Britta said.

"Could you make a doll with a female body that wants one specific woman?" I said.

"Yes. I think we can do that. We have the technology now," Britta said.

"I love the concept," Veronica said.

"And we're working on a sex doll that wants romance and not just sex," Britta said.

"How would that work?" Veronica said.

"If you play romantic music and you have soft lighting, the doll asks for a kiss," Britta said.

"I like your innovations," Veronica said.

"Developing new products is always a challenge. It's never easy. But we're trying," Britta said.

"You're making sex dolls more human. That's a big improvement," I said.

"I think there's a market for sex dolls that are more human. But it's not all good. Sometimes I have some doubts about it," Britta said.

"Why do you have doubts?" I said.

"If Shaeffer sex dolls become more like real people, then maybe we're going to cause more married people to cheat on their partner. We're giving people the opportunity to have a more satisfying relationship with a sex doll instead of their spouse," Britta said.

"You've always been doing that. All sex dolls do that," I said.

"Not really. With the older sex dolls, nobody was getting emotionally involved with their sex doll. Now we're making more realistic dolls with personalities. I see a danger of people becoming emotionally attached to their sex doll, more than to the person they're married to," Britta said.

"I suppose that's possible," I said.

Sophia returned with more pizza.

"What did you get?" I said.

"I got more of the same thing we had. It's good," she said.

"You were talking about the business," I said to Britta.

"I think its a problem of ethics. What are the ethical boundaries for sex doll makers. All new technologies can present ethical problems. Sex doll technology is just like any other new technology," Britta said.

"What you can do about that?" Veronica said.

"I told my father I thought there were ethical questions we should consider," Britta said.

"What did he say?" Veronica said.

"He said he thinks ethics are important," Britta said.

"So is he gong to do something about ethics?" I said.

"He said he wants to hire someone to be our ethics consultant. I agreed with him," Britta said.

"Did he say who he wants to hire as an ethics consultant?" I said.

"He wants to hire John Churchill, the former president of the university. My father knows him and likes him. My father says John shares my father's view of how important ethics are," Britta said.

"John Churchill thinks making money is always the top priority," I said.

"As I said, John shares my father's view of how important ethics are. My father says he loves ethics, but he says we need to remember that we're running a business, and we can't let ethics interfere too much with the business," Britta said.

"At least he thinks about ethics sometimes," I said.

"He does think about ethics. He's not unethical. He's just ethical in moderation," Britta said.

We all ate the rest of our pizza.

"Did we cover everything you wanted to talk about?" Britta said.

"Yes. You're very helpful. I'm sorry I'm not able to help *you*. I wish I could give you some advice that would help you," I said.

"You help us all the time," Britta said.

"Today you advised us about pizza with the asparagus tips and cranberries and Neufchatel cheese," Veronica said.

"Was it good?" I said.

"It was excellent," Veronica said.

"Yes," Britta said.

"What did you think, Sophia?" I said.

"It was good, but it needed more asparagus tips," she said.

"I wouldn't have gotten it without your recommendation," Veronica said.

"So you see we work well together," Britta said.

"I'm glad we were able to meet and eat pizza together," I said.

"Yes. Problems are just a pizza lunch that hasn't happened yet," Veronica said.

"Did Benjamin Franklin say that also?" Britta said.

"Yes. To Abraham Lincoln," Veronica said.

"Let's meet again soon," Britta said.

"You've solved my problems. Who's going to bring the problems next time?" I said.

"I'll try to find some for next time," Veronica said.

"Thanks, Veronica. We appreciate it," I said.

"I'm always happy to help," Veronica said.

We said goodbye and went our separate ways. I wondered what pine cones would taste like on pizza.

Chapter Ninety-Two

Lexi called me. I was happy to hear from her. She invited me to come to her house for supper. She invited Hadley also. I came over and we all helped prepare the food. Lexi made a salad. I helped prepare some ground turkey. Hadley cooked some linguini. We got some mild red pepper sauce and some diced tomatoes out of the refrigerator. We ate at the kitchen table. We had a good meal together.

As we ate together, Hadley talked about her prophecy. She looked at Lexi. "I figured sooner or later you would try coloring your hair."

Hadley looked at me. "And sooner or later you and the planetarium people would get together and find a way to change the sun rising and setting."

Hadley looked at Lexi again. "And after you did that I knew you would make the prophecy come true, because you wanted it to come true," she said.

"But the prophecy didn't really come true," Lexi said.

"Yes it did, Mom."

"You said when my hair was on fire and the sun rose in the west and set in the east we would get what we wanted. But we didn't get what we wanted. I got money, but it's not money for what I wanted to do," Lexi said.

"Mom, I never said you would get what you wanted."

"Yes you did. That was your prophecy."

"No it wasn't. Apparently you didn't listen carefully to my prophecy. I said you would get what you *need*."

"But what we wanted is what we need."

"Come on now, Mom, you know that's not right. Do you want to drive a new Mercedes?"

"Yes," Lexi said enthusiastically.

"Do you need to drive a new Mercedes?"

"No," she said softly.

"You need money and you got money."

"How did you know we were going to be successful finding money?"

"You're persistent, and you make a good impression on people, and you had Jack helping you, and he makes a good impression on people. And I was helping you also," Hadley said to Lexi.

"You have a special talent. You have a gift for prophesy, a magic power," I said.

Hadley looked at me.

"No, I don't think so," Hadley said.

"You don't?" I said.

"Do you remember what I was holding when I made my prophecy?"

"I think you were holding a piece of parsley."

"Yes, I was holding a little bit of parsley. What else was I holding?"

"I don't remember."

"I was holding Mom's hand in mine."

"That's right. You were holding Lexi's hand."

"If anyone has a gift, it's Mom. I was just drawing her power into me."

Lexi looked at me and said, "Do you think I have special powers?"

I said, "Maybe you and Hadley both have special powers."

"Both of us?"

"Yes."

"Why would we have special powers?"

"I don't know. Maybe it's from all the diced tomatoes you eat. Every time you and Hadley are together you're eating something with diced tomatoes."

Lexi looked at me skeptically. "Can people get special powers just from eating diced tomatoes?"

I put a serious expression on my face. I said, "I have spoken."

Lexi and Hadley smiled. Hadley said, "I like the way you say that."

I looked at Hadley. "I don't say it as well as you do."

Hadley looked at Lexi. "Mom, do we have any more diced tomatoes? I feel like eating more diced tomatoes."

"I think we have more in the refrigerator."

Hadley went to the refrigerator and got another container of diced tomatoes and brought it to the table. We all ate more diced tomatoes. They were good.

Chapter Ninety-Three

Lexi called me on a Saturday morning.

"Jack, can you come over to my house now?"

"I can in about an hour. Will that work?"

"Yes, that's good."

"What's up?"

"I'll tell you when you get here."

About an hour later I was at the door of her house. Everything in her yard was green and growing. Her day lilies were a profusion of green leaves, but without any flowers yet. Her apple tree looked like it was thriving, and was growing some apples which were still small.

Lexi came to the door.

"Good to see you," I said. "Your yard looks nice."

"Thank you. Welcome to my humble cottage. My humbler cottage. Come in," she said, and I went in.

"Your hair looks nice also."

"You like the red?"

"The red is a pretty color for you."

"Do you like the red better than blonde?"

"I thought the blonde was a pretty color also."

"You're easy to please."

"Sometimes I am." I didn't see or hear Hadley. "Hadley not around today?"

"Hadley's not here today. She's with some friends at school."

"So it's just you and me today? What would you like to do? Play some Yahtzee?"

"Let's go up to my bedroom. Just to talk."

"All right."

We went over to the stairs. She looked at me and smiled. "I'll race you up the stairs."

"All right."

She ran up the stairs, with me close behind. At the top of the stairs she said, "I won," and started laughing.

"You're too fast for me."

"Do I always elude you, no matter how fast you run?"

I smiled. "Yes, you do."

She became serious. She walked up to me and wrapped her arms around me. "That's only when we're running up the stairs."

"Yes."

She took her arms off me. "Is your heart pounding?"

"A little bit."

"Do you feel like resting on the bed?"

"Yes. Let's rest on the bed."

We went to her bedroom. It was a sunny day and her bedroom had a lot of natural light. The room was warm and the air seemed fresh. I was happy to be in her bedroom in her humble cottage.

We took off our shoes and got on the bed without taking off the bed covers. We laid on our backs, next to each other. She held my hand.

"You're too far away," she said.

"I'm right here next to you. I can't get much closer."

"When you're living with Veronica, you're too far away."

"You said you wanted to have your own independent life."

"I do want to have my own independent life. But I want you to be a part of my life also."

"How does that work exactly?"

"I want you to move back to Alyssa's house."

"Alyssa still has the Russians living with her. Irina and Dimitri. And Gabriela is living there also."

"Irina and Dimitri will be gone after the spring semester. And Alyssa doesn't have anybody new signed up yet to live there after they go. Alyssa would just have you and Gabriela."

"What if I move back to Alyssa's house and being that close to your house makes me miss you all the time?"

"You'll be all right."

"What if I sit in Alyssa's house and look out the window and see your house and wish I were with you? Won't that be just like that character in the novel that your daughter was reading?"

Lexi sat up in the bed and looked at me. "Jack, listen to me."

I sat up in the bed also, and looked at her.

"Do I have a blue lawn?" she said.

"No."

"I hate blue lawns, Jack. I've never had a blue lawn. And I never will have a blue lawn. I wouldn't live in a house with a blue lawn."

"You're trying to reassure me. I appreciate that."

"And do I have a green light at the end of a dock?"

"No. You don't have a dock and you don't have a green light."

"I hate green lights. Putting a green light at the end of a dock is an awful, terrible thing to do. Someone who puts a green light at the end of a dock is just asking for trouble. I would never do that."

"I appreciate your telling me that."

"I have never put a green light anywhere on my house or in my yard. And I never will. Even my Christmas lights don't have any green lights. So you have nothing to worry about."

"I think the novel was using the green light as a metaphor."

"You need to forget every metaphor in the whole damn novel, Jack. We have to make our own metaphors. Who lives their lives using other people's metaphors? The only people who do that are English literature majors."

"I appreciate your efforts to reassure me. You're trying to make me feel better. That's a nice thing to do."

"Am I succeeding?"

"I feel a little better, but I still feel uneasy about moving closer to you."

"I want to lie on top of you. May I lie on top of you?"

"Yes, I want you to lie on top of me."

I rested on my back lying in the bed. Lexi got on top of me, facing me. She was a little closer to the foot of the bed than I was. She rested her head on my chest.

"If you move back to Alyssa's house you'll discover you can be part of my life and also have a life of your own. I think you'll like that."

I didn't respond immediately. I thought about what she was telling me.

Maybe she was right, but I wasn't sure. I wondered whether I was strong enough to follow her plan without falling apart. "I don't know," I said.

"We need to find out. We're experimental scientists. We need to do the experiment."

I didn't say anything. Lexi started caressing me with her right hand.

"I need to lie on top of you sometimes, just like this," Lexi said softly. "And I need to be away from you sometimes. And you need a life of your own also. When you're living in Alyssa's house, I think we'll both be happy."

"I want to believe you. But I'm not sure. What if I move back to Alyssa's house and I have an intense desire to be with you and you're away from me?"

Lexi rolled off me and stood up and walked over to a closet.

"I'll give you one of my dresses. When you miss me you can hold it and pretend it's me." She took a pretty dress out of the closet. "Do you like this one?"

"Yes, that's pretty."

She put it on a chair and came back to the bed and got on top of me again. "Let's do the experiment. Try living in Alyssa's house," she said.

I was still uneasy, but I do have the personality of an experimental scientist. "Yes, let's do the experiment. I want to live in Alyssa's house."

Lexi unbuttoned the top buttons of my shirt and started kissing my neck and my chest.

"Lexi?"

"Yes Jack?"

"Do you feel like having a conversation?"

"You want to have a conversation?"

"Yes, Lexi."

"Right now?"

"Yes. Do you want to have a conversation?"

Lexi shifted her body and rolled off me. She sat next to me in the bed and looked at me.

"Do you want to talk about the influence of Schopenhauer on the later German philosophers?" she said softly.

"Yes."

"It's been a long time since we talked about that," she said.

"It's been too long."

"I hope I can still remember all the towns."

"I'm sure you can remember all the towns."

"Some of the towns in New Jersey are hard to remember."

"I'll help you. I can help you remember the towns in New Jersey."

"You can help me?"

"Yes, I can help you."

She smiled. "What are you, Mister Geography now?"

"Yes, that's me. Mister Geography."

She was serious again. "Did I ever show you Englewood Cliffs?"

"No. Is that a good place?"

"Sometimes. Let's try to find Englewood Cliffs today."

"All right."

"We need to get ready. I'll use my bathroom. You can use the guest bathroom down the hall."

"Good plan." I got up off the bed. I started to walk to the guest bathroom. She stayed sitting on the edge of the bed.

"Jack?"

I stopped and turned toward her and looked at her. "Yes my darling?"

"Can I ask you something?"

"You can ask me anything you want."

"Do you think I'm a troublesome woman?"

I walked back to the bed and sat next to her. "Why would I think that?"

"Because I won't let you live with me."

"That doesn't make you a troublesome woman."

"It doesn't?"

"We've done a lot of things together. Met a lot of people. In everything we've done together you've never been troublesome. You've been a wonderful partner."

"I've tried to be a good partner."

"There are only two things that make a woman a troublesome woman."

"What are they?"

"A blue lawn and a green light. And you don't have those. You told me that yourself."

She smiled. "Jack?"

"Yes my darling?"

"I love you."

She stood up and started to walk toward her bathroom. I stayed on the bed.

"Lexi?"

She stopped and turned toward me. "Yes Jack?"

"Do you think I'm a troublesome man?"

She walked back to the bed and sat next to me.

"Why would I think that?"

"Because I came into your life and disrupted it."

"I always feel like you want to help me."

"I do want to help you."

"All the people you and I met disrupted my life a little bit," she said. "But that wasn't bad. The person who really disrupted my life was that writer. The one who wrote about the damn colors."

"Yes, I understand."

"I think it should be illegal to teach English literature to college students."

"Yes, I agree."

"After all that we've been through, I now understand that his novel is not describing my life."

"That's right."

"Except for one part of it."

"One part of it? Really?"

"Yes."

"Which part is that?"

"The character in the novel believed in the orgastic future. That's the phrase the novel uses. The orgastic future."

"And you believe in the orgastic future?"

"I do believe in the orgastic future." She smiled. "I believe we're going to have one this morning."

"I hope you're right."

"We need to get ready."

We got ready. We found Englewood Cliffs and it was very nice. We tried New Rochelle, New York, and it was very nice also. We were together for a while and then we parted, and I knew what Shakespeare meant when he compared his lover to a summer's day.

Chapter Ninety-Four

Irina and Dimitri finished their year at the university and left town. I moved out of Veronica's house and went back to Alyssa's house. Alyssa said she was happy to have me back. Abraham seemed happy to have me in the house again.

The university liked Gabriela's work. They renewed Gabriela's job for another year and told her in the next budget cycle they would probably have enough money to create a permanent tenure track position for her.

Veronica asked Gabriela to live with her, and Gabriela accepted. Alyssa's house seemed almost empty with just Alyssa and Abraham and me living there. After all the changes, I was back in the house where I started. But I wasn't still sleeping in the storage closet. I guess that's progress.

Alyssa had a nice big bed in her guest bedroom. I encouraged Abraham to sleep in it with me, and he liked it. I took the dress Lexi had given me and at night I spread it over Abraham next to me, leaving just his head uncovered. Most of the time he liked having it on him. Sometimes he got too hot and he would shake it off.

Veronica called me. She wanted to talk about Gabriela.

"I want to try having a partner again. When I come home I just want to be held in a woman's arms," Veronica said

"Yes. Being held in a woman's arms can feel wonderful."

"When I'm holding someone and we're in love, there's something that happens in my mind that makes the world seem like a different place."

"Yes. It's some sort of magic thing."

"I believe we'll have a good future," Veronica said. "I hope I'm not just being fooled by the green light and the green lawn. Or maybe it was the blue light and the blue lawn."

"Veronica, I want you to promise me one thing."

"What's that?"

"Promise me that you'll stop reading great literature."

"Why?"

"When people read great literature, that's when all the problems start."

"You might be right, Jack. What are you going to read?"

"When I feel like reading something, I'm going to read a cookbook."

"Do you want to read a cookbook about pine cone recipes?"

"Yes, that would be excellent."

"I need to get to work."

Chapter Ninety-Five

I was with Lexi one day when she got a call from someone neither one of us knew. Lexi put them on speaker so I could hear them talking.

"Hello, is this Professor Lieblich?" the caller said.

"Yes, this is she. Can I help you?" Lexi said.

"Professor Lieblich, my name is Felicia Sandoval. I'm a research professor of design and visual studies at the Atlantic Institute of Technical Design. I wanted to talk with you about your work. Do you have a minute now, or should I call later?"

"I have time to talk now. Please call me Lexi."

"Lexi, at our institution we have researchers who depend on research grants to continue their research. You know what I'm talking about."

"Yes, certainly."

"Here at our institution we look upon you as a very successful scholar."

"Really?"

"Yes, absolutely. You're well known here because you've received a multiyear grant from the American Contemporary Design Association. The competition for grants like that is intense. And you've won a grant. So as I said we look upon you as a very successful scholar."

"I don't feel very successful."

"We have a series of lectures at our institution on the topic of how to successfully find research money. Based on your success, you're the kind of person we want to hear speak. We want to invite you to be a speaker at our lecture series. We'll pay your transportation expenses and your meals and lodging and give you an honorarium."

"Thank you, but I'm not sure you understand my background. First of all, I'm a neutrino researcher."

"Your specialty doesn't matter, as long as you're not doing something completely crazy and idiotic, like sex research or something like that. You're a researcher. That's the important thing."

"Thank you for not being narrow minded, but second of all, I've looked for research money constantly and in every conceivable place and I've failed to find any. I've failed many times."

"I'm sure your struggles will be interesting to our researchers. We can learn a lot from them. Sometimes we learn more from failure than we do from success."

"If that's true, then I've learned a vast amount."

"And you can share it with us. We need you."

"I don't think I'm anything special."

"You're humble. I like that. The more we talk, the more I think you're the perfect person to speak to us. You don't need to decide right now. You can think about it and call me later."

"Yes, I need to think about it."

"That's fine. Think about it and we'll talk later."

"Thank you for calling."

"I enjoyed talking with you."

"Goodbye."

Lexi looked at me.

"What do you think?" Lexi said.

"You should go and give the speech. Just don't tell them about the sex research."

She smiled. "I think I will go and give the speech. I think it might be an interesting group. And I'll wear my Wonder Woman shirt."

"Yes. They'll like that."

Chapter Ninety-Six

About a week later, Lexi invited me to join her and Hadley at her house for dinner. We ate and we talked about school and work and people and life in general.

We didn't want to spend a lot of time talking about neutrinos and sex. We had been focused on the money chase for those two things for a year, and the money chase had worn us down. Lexi was certainly tired of it, I was tired of it, and even Hadley, who had not been quite as intensely involved, was tired of it.

At the end of the evening, after we had cleaned up the kitchen and I was ready to leave, Lexi mentioned her desire to do something that would be a nice break from the long hard money chase.

"Let's go to the zoo this weekend and look at the new zoo babies. Those are always adorable," Lexi said.

Hadley looked at the zoo's web site to see what zoo babies were on display. "Oh, wow, lots of zoo babies."

"Are they adorable?"

"Do you like shrews? Here's three northern short-tailed shrews."

"What's the zoo naming them?" Lexi said.

"Dickens, Deadwood, and Doorlicker," Hadley said.

"Are they cute?"

"They look a little bit like mice."

"That doesn't sound very exciting. What else do you see?" Lexi said.

Hadley studied the website. "They have two little newborn baby lemurs. They look ultra cute. We need to go see these," Hadley said.

"What names did the zoo give them?" Lexi said.

Hadley said, "Jack and Lexi."

Notes

Chapter One
"I thought we couldn't possibly fail to grasp our research dreams," is an alteration of a phrase from F. Scott Fitzgerald. For the full reference to his work, see the notes to Chapter Seven.

Chapter Three
" . . . you'll regret it. Maybe not today. Maybe not tomorrow. But soon, and for the rest of your life," is from the movie *Casablanca*, in the scene where Ilsa Lund (Ingrid Bergman) leaves Richard Blaine (Humphrey Bogart), screenplay by Julius J. and Philip G. Epstein and Howard Koch, produced and distributed by Warner Bros. Pictures Inc., 1942.

Chapter Six
"A rose by any other name would smell as sweet," is a paraphrase of a line from *Romeo and Juliet*, act 2, scene 2, by William Shakespeare. In some editions of the play, the line is from act 2, scene 1. See the *Oxford Dictionary of Quotations*, Eighth Edition, edited by Elizabeth Knowles, Oxford University Press, Oxford, 2014, page 713, number 3.

Chapter Seven
"Shall I compare thee to a summer's day?" is from Sonnet 18 by William Shakespeare.

The quotations from F. Scott Fitzgerald here and other places are from the ending to *The Great Gatsby*, published by Scribner's, New York, 1925.

Flopsy, Mopsy, and Cottontail are characters created by Beatrix Potter, an author of children's books.

Chapter Ten
Muñecas sexuales de Shaeffer — las mas avanzadas del mundo is Spanish and means "Shaeffer sex dolls—the most advanced in the world."

"Hola, soy Tia. Mucho gusto," is Spanish and means "Hi. I'm Tia. Great pleasure (to meet you)."

"De nada," is Spanish and means "It's nothing."

Chapter Seventeen
¡De ninguna manera! is Spanish and means "Certainly not!"

Es un buen trabajo is Spanish and means "It is a good job."

Chapter Thirty-Six
The quotations from *Macbeth* are from act four, scene one, by William Shakespeare.

Chapter Forty-Four
je ne sais quoi is a French phrase that means "I don't know what."

Chapter Seventy-Nine
An excellent one paragraph analysis of the work of F. Scott Fitzgerald is in *Cary Grant: A Brilliant Disguise*, by Scott Eyman, Simon and Schuster, New York, 2020, page 363. Scott Eyman says Fitzgerald has a lambent voice.

Chapter Eighty-One
The quotation beginning "Ain't no sense . . ." is often attributed to baseball player Mickey Rivers. When and where this was first said is not known. "When it comes to erudition, these guys are way off base," by Gene Wojciechowski, Los Angeles Times, June 23, 1993.

Chapter Ninety-One

The quotation about hope is a paraphrase of a quotation from Frances Bacon. *Oxford Dictionary of Quotations*, Eighth Edition, edited by Elizabeth Knowles, Oxford University Press, Oxford, 2014, page 51, number 14.

Acknowledgements

Publishing a book is a group effort. I gratefully acknowledge the work of the people who made this book possible. Several people helped me create the book.

Karen Martin gave me lots of good advice, and was a joy to work with.

Alison Kolesar has wonderful talent and imagination. She created the illustrations; designed the dust jacket; designed the case; and provided helpful opinions on many topics.

Lindsay Lake, who is one of the best in the business, and who works with Bookmobile Design & Digital Publisher Services, designed the interior and typeset it, and she gave me expert recommendations.

Katie Keating is with a company called Fancy. She made helpful comments about my writing.

Edna Helmers, CPA, at Cartlidge Belnap Helmers, was a great problem solver for the business of publishing.

Mike and Janet Moore, in Reno, assisted me with activities of daily living when I had health problems. I am deeply grateful for their aid, which helped me to return to my work on the book.

Thank you to all of you.

About the Author

After an undergraduate degree in economics, the author earned a law degree and practiced law. He then returned to school and earned a medical degree and a master of science degree, and practiced medicine. This is the first of his novels. He has also written a sequel, titled *A Success That Still Hasn't Happened Yet*.

The typeface used for the text is Palatino, a typeface which was designed in 1948 by Herman Zapf, a famous and influential typographer. Palatino is named after an Italian Renaissance calligrapher and is inspired by Renaissance calligraphy. It is known for its excellent readability, and is one of the most beautiful typefaces of the Renaissance revival.